GHOSTS & THE ANCIENT STONES

(Penumbra Papers #5)

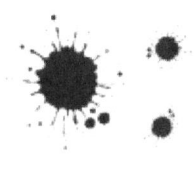

Silver James

Contact: silverjames@swbell.net

Cover design © by *Clary Carey*, clarycarey@gmail.com

Image: Beautiful foggy wet view of the Royal Mile in Edinburgh © dennisvdwater

www.depositphotos.com

ISBN: 978-0-9969995-5-7

Dedication

To Tim Hiddleston,
not that he'll ever know this book
is dedicated to him much less actually read it,
but whatever. I can dream.
That said, he and the real Loki,
aka my demon cat overlord of magic,
mischief, and mayhem,
have a lot in common.
And this book is also dedicated to *my* Loki
for the 4 a.m. zoomies and his insistence
that the insomnia they induced made this book better.
I leave it to you, the reader, to decide.

SILVER JAMES

Acknowledgments

Writing is mostly a solitary business, but lucky authors have a support group of family, friends, and readers who drag them out of the ol' writing cave and force them back into reality on a regular basis. I'd like to take this opportunity to thank those who contribute, cheer, cajole, bribe me with coffee and occasionally drag me kicking and screaming into and out of my cave.

I appreciate all the help I get from everyone involved in producing a book. Of course, the important ones are the readers. A big wave to all who enjoy my books. Y'all rock my world! A heartfelt "thank you" to Patti W. for her patience and absolute surety that I'd get this book written, to Karrie L. and her sweet cards of encouragement, and Dawn M. for cats. Many thanks to all who hang out on my FB page too. Y'all make me smile even when I'm grumpy.

I couldn't do this without the help and support of my wonderful husband, known to my readers as Lawyer Guy aka LG. And last but definitely not least, I want to recognize my cover artist, Clary, for taking my blurred visions and producing wonderful covers for me, and last but definitely not least, my beta reader and sister from another mister, Beth S.

One last caveat: Any and all mistakes are my own.

In the Beginning...

Maybe it started with the millennium or perhaps the series of dramatic celestial events that followed in the first decade—like the stray star named The Flyer aligning with Mars in conjunction with a solar eclipse. Maybe it was a hole in the ozone. Whatever caused the Veil between the Human plane and the Magick Realms to tear, all hell broke loose. Literally. It turns out there really are monsters under the bed and the things that go bump in the night are bigger and scarier than anyone ever imagined.

The world's best and brightest from every discipline—physics, theology, anthropology, and chemistry, to name only a few—tried to explain the rip in the cosmic curtain. The monsters have been here all along, flying just under the radar of normal perception. They've been masquerading as Mundanes—their term for Humans.

Vampires. Faeries. Gargoyles. Dragons. Werewolves. Witches. Creatures of legend and nightmare. Overnight, reality took on a whole new meaning. Since the Big Rip, preternatural folks of all kinds intermingle with Humans in ways mysterious and magical...or criminal. The FBI's answer? The Magical Activity, Grievances, and Inhuman Crimes Unit is in charge of any investigation involving the Magicks. The FBI director handpicked Special Agent Sade Marquis to lead the unit. An agent with an X-Files mentality, it's Sade's job to deal with all the bad nasties. And she's gathered a group of dedicated agents and consultants to help.

Given the code name The Penumbra Papers, the files are buried deep within some anonymous warehouse outside of Washington, DC, inside a wooden box with a mystical marking branded into its sides...

Oh, wait. Sorry. That's the Ark of the Covenant. The Penumbra Papers are actually buried in a bottom file drawer in the office of the Director of the FBI. Within those files resides the records of the forces of light and dark fighting in the shadows which Humans had only glimpsed before the dawn of this new age.

Of course, Sade knows the truth of the matter. She was raised by a master vampire, her foster brother is a werewolf, and she has a certain immunity to magic. That's Sade's secret, and she is very, very good at keeping secrets. Which makes her very, very good at her job. In turn, that makes the Magicks very, very afraid of her...and the MAGIC Unit. As they should be—

GHOSTS & THE ANCIENT STONES

Chapter One
Perfectly Confused

Supervisory Agent Sade Marquis stood hands on hips, lips pursed, head tilted. "That what I think it is?"

Her FBI partner, Caleb Jones, crinkled his nose. "Yup."

"Zombies?"

"Nope."

"Magic?"

"Nope."

"Then why are we here? If Magicks aren't involved..."

"I didn't say that."

She cut her eyes to Caleb as he knelt next to the minivan's bumper. She looked closer at the back window. "Okay, that's fucking weird."

The werewolf snorted. "Uh, d'uh. What was your first clue, Sherlock? I mean, a bloody handprint smeared only on the back window of a mom-mobile is totally weird. And watch your language."

Her turn to snort. "You're a male werewolf. My dropping the occasional f-bomb is not going to damage your fragile psyche." She leaned closer and peered through the window. "What's that?"

Caleb raised his chin, sniffing the air. He rose enough to peer through the back window to see what she was looking at. "Cake. And you drop f-bombs like they're balloons at the end of the Super Bowl."

She pulled on purple Nitrile gloves and moved to open the rear driver's side door. She leaned over the bench seat and studied what appeared to be a child's birthday cake contained in a plastic box.

Icing roses and frou-frou piping lined the edges. Confetti sprinkles covered the flat surface of the icing. Spelled out in fancy blood-red curlicues were three words: *It's the endgame.*

"What the fuck does that even mean?" she asked no one in particular. Crawling out of the van, she glared at Caleb. "What aren't you telling me?"

"Have you talked to Nikos Constantine lately?"

"Why would I talk to the bloody dragon?"

"Because that's *his* bloody handprint."

"Well...fuck." A coup in the Dragon Realm was a very bad thing. But if the violence stayed there, it was out of her jurisdiction. The FBI's MAGIC Unit only got involved if it was Magick-on-Human crime.

"You can say that again."

"Well, fuck."

Caleb gave her the Werewolf equivalent of the fisheye, complete with a lip curl and flash of a canine. "When was the last time you saw him?"

She had to think about it. At a loss, she stared at the man who'd been by her side for almost as long as she could remember. He'd come into her life as a wolf puppy and stayed—part foster brother, part best friend, part watch dog, and the only partner she'd had since graduating from the FBI Academy at Quantico.

"I'm not sure." Her face crinkled in deep contemplation. "Have I tripped over him since that deal in New Orleans?"

Caleb fought the urge to roll his eyes. That *deal* in New Orleans involved a Gargoyle war and they'd been lucky to survive it. "I don't know, Sade. You tell me. I went home to Adele so we could pack for the move back here to DC."

She glanced at him, concern now showing in her expression. "She okay with that? With leaving the mountains?"

"Considering Director Bailey set her up in the Forensics Lab, my mate is now in hog heaven." He grinned, flashing a hint of canines.

Adele McCoy had been a forensics investigator with the Colorado Bureau of Investigation when she met Caleb during an undercover assignment. They'd gone up against a manitou, with a little help from some friends. A human, Adele was still navigating her way through the sticky web that was life in the Magick world.

"Well, speaking of, call the lab rats and have them come pick up the van. And the cake." She glanced around the empty street. This was not a place that would normally attract Magicks of any sort, much less an urbane dragon shifter like Nikolas Constantine, the Drakon of Clan Kholikikos. "Are there any other scents?"

Caleb shook his head. "None. No hint of magic, except on the handprint, and it reeks of Dragon in general and Nikos in particular."

"Curiouser and curiouser."

"So?"

"So what?"

"When *was* the last Nikos popped up?"

Sade lifted one shoulder in a negligent shrug as she stripped off the protective gloves. "Honestly? I don't remember. And yes, that's weird too because he was popping up all the damn time which drove Sinjen fucking crazy."

Caleb studied her, alerted by a slight quaver in her voice. "When's the last time you saw Sinjen?"

Her other shoulder lifted as she turned away from him. He didn't need a sniff test to tell she was dodging the question and what the feelings welling up inside her meant. "A week. Or so." She added the last two words in a mumble.

"Your schedule or his?"

She shot him a look that all but begged for him to drop the subject but he wasn't about to do so. Caleb loved her and seeing her

9

wounded in any way just pissed him the hell off. Not that he'd admit that to her. If the vampire was messing with her head, he'd go hunting with a wooden stake for ammunition.

"Mostly mine," Sade said. "He was supposed to fly here for a few days since I went to see him in Chicago last, but..."

"Ah. The California troll incident."

"Yeah. And then Lake Champlain."

"Locals should rename the place Lake *Complain*."

"No fucking kidding. The troll in San Francisco was real at least. President Wynne finally sent in a team of negotiators from the motherfucking Department of Transportation. The gawddamned idiots in New York and Vermont are on my shit list. I can't prove Champ exists or doesn't. Prehistoric critters don't fall under my jurisdiction. It's not a magical creature, if it does exist, and I'm not authorized to fucking drain the gawddamned lake to find out for sure."

"Tell me how you really feel, Sade."

"Shut the fuck up, Caleb, or I'll tie your gawddamned tail in a knot." She glanced around the area again and had to smooth down the hair on the back of her neck. She dropped her voice to a whisper to ask, "You feel that?"

Caleb didn't look around. He let his other senses do the searching for him. Something was out there. Something with magic. Just what it was? He didn't know. Too elusive. Too...faint. Not close then. "We need to stick around until the van is towed."

"Put a rush on it." They were in fucking Alexandria, Virginia. A sanctioned tow truck should be here quick. "And have the rats meet it at the lab. I don't want any Humans out here."

"You're Human," Caleb reminded her.

"But I'm not alone and I'm not *just* Human."

Caleb had heard that before. Didn't believe it then and didn't believe it now. She might be immune from most magic but bullets, knives, and flamethrowers still worked on her mortal body.

Her cell phone buzzed in her pocket and Sade pretended like she didn't jump. Pulling it out, she glanced at the caller ID. "Speaking of the devil," she muttered. She swiped the face of her smart phone to accept the call and demanded, "Where the fuck are you?"

"A pleasure to speak to you as well, darling Sade."

"Don't call me that. Where are you?"

"Where are you?"

"Standing in what passes for the hood in Alexandria staring at a mom-mobile with your bloody handprint left behind as evidence."

"Staring at what?"

"Your bloody—"

"No," Nikos interrupted. "What is a...what did you call it?"

"A mom-mobile. A minivan. What a soccer mom drives."

"Ah. I see." But he didn't sound like he did.

"It's a vehicle, Nikos, driven by moms all over the world as a convenient way to transport their offspring. I want to know how your handprint ended up on the inside of the back hatch window."

"What else is there in this...mom-mobile?" His voice held amusement now.

"A birthday cake."

"It is not your birthday."

"Nor is it yours."

"We do not celebrate birthdays, *khriso mou*."

"I am *not* your treasure, Nikos. I am going to kick your silver dragon ass if you don't answer my questions."

"Since it is not your birthday and it is not my birthday, who's birthday is it?"

"Nikos..." Sade growled his name and noticed Caleb's smirk. She *was* sounding a bit wolfish at the moment.

"Is there a name on the cake?"

"No. Just a message."

"Ask your bloodhound if it is magic." She was not about to say anything of the sort to Caleb. He and the dragon barely tolerated each other, despite having worked as a team several times.

"It's not. In fact, the only magical thing about this whole scene is your print."

"Tell me what it says." He sounded imperious now.

"It's the endgame."

"What is?"

"You tell me, Nikos. That's the fucking message on the gawddamned cake."

"Language, darling Sade."

"Fuck you, you pain-in-my-ass dragon."

A sound came through the speaker. Was he...purring?

"There are many things I would do with your very sweet ass, *khriso mou*, and none of them would cause you pain unless you desired it."

"Oh my fucking gods, Nikos. You are such a—"

She didn't finish the sentence as Caleb lunged at her and took her to the ground, then rolled over and over with her until they were in the recessed entrance of a derelict building. Before she could demand a reason, her Human ears picked up the hissing whistle.

"Incoming!" Caleb yelled as he covered her body with his. The minivan exploded and shrapnel rained down around them. Caleb was up and kicking in the door. He hauled Sade to her feet and they darted inside.

She had to depend on his Werewolf vision to steer them through the dark interior. He found the back exit and paused, listening and sniffing. Sade always expected him to partially shift—to grow long wolfy ears and a muzzle when he did this. Part of her was always a little disappointed when he remained Human.

"Clear," he whispered and then kicked the door open.

"Why are you whispering?" she panted as they raced across an overgrown lot toward the alley.

"Seemed like a good idea at the time."

Sade heard another voice calling her name and she looked around suspiciously. That's when she remembered the phone still clutched in her hand and the infuriated dragon on the other end. "Hold you motherfucking horses, Nikos," she barked into the phone. Glancing over at Caleb, she added, "Guess we can call and cancel the tow truck and lab geeks. Any idea on how we're getting back to our car?"

Secondary explosions sounded, one followed by a whooshing fireball, the other by creaks and groans as the front of the building they'd just exited collapsed.

"Damn." She didn't try to hide the awe in her voice. "I don't know who the fuck is out there but they're shitting-bricks serious."

"You can say that again," Caleb muttered and he immediately clapped his palm over her mouth the moment she opened it. "I'll call for a clean-up in Aisle nine."

Chapter Two

In Control

Sade and Caleb sat in identical chairs in the reception area outside of FBI Director George Bailey's office. His administrative assistant, a tiny woman with knowing eyes, ignored them. Caleb slumped in the uncomfortable chair, eyes closed. Sade stared at the nameplate on the front of the desk. ALICE COOPER. She tried making different words out of the letters, without success.

The intercom on Alice's desk buzzed and the director's voice boomed, "Send them in."

The two agents pushed out of their chairs and trudged toward the door that led into the inner sanctum. It opened with a whisper. Someday, Sade would figure out just what sort of magic the director's right hand wielded. She made sure Alice didn't see the side-eye glance flashed her way.

The door swung shut behind them and the two sank into only slightly more comfortable chairs arranged in front of Bailey's desk. The dark surface always reminded Sade of an aircraft carrier. The director tapped an index finger on the one piece of paper on that massive desktop.

"Not much of a report, Supervisory Agent Marquis, yet you state you are in control of the situation."

Sade sat up straight, balanced on the front edge of the chair. The Director addressing her by her full rank was a bad thing. "Not everything is black and white, sir."

He arched an eyebrow. "Next you'll talk about plus or minus and other shit."

Yeah, the Old Man was not happy. "On the positive side, Agent Jones and I are still breathing and we have photographs of the evidence."

"And the negative?"

"The perpetrator or perpetrators blew up the evidence, along with our official vehicle."

"Your suspect?"

"Don't have one."

"It is my understanding that the handprint in the minivan belonged to Clan Kholikikos's Drakon."

Sade glanced at Caleb. He offered her a look that spoke volumes—like "*what was I supposed to do*," "*I had to tell him*," and "*the dude did call and distract you right before the mortar attack*." She returned her gaze to her boss and said, "According to Agent Jones, it did."

"You have an alternative explanation, Agent Marquis?"

She wondered if she looked as shifty-eyed as she felt. "Maybe."

Both men stared at her and rather than feeling like prey, Sade raised her chin. She stared at her partner, ignoring her boss for the moment. "The *only* scent you picked up in the minivan belonged to Nikos. Yes or no?"

Caleb narrowed his focus wondering here Sade was headed. "Yes."

"What about the cake?"

"What about the cake?"

"You didn't pick up any scents on it?"

"No. There was no magic to it. At least in the sense of normal situations."

"Any other scents?"

Still confused, Caleb shook his head. "None."

"How is that possible?" Sade persisted.

Caleb flicked his eyes toward the Director, wondering if the Old Man had any clue as to what Sade was up to. Bailey continued to stare at Sade. "How is what possible?"

"Who made the cake, Caleb?" Sade sounded like their second-grade teacher on the verge of losing her patience.

"Nikos?"

Laughter burst out of her. "Nikos baking *and* decorating a cake? Seriously?" Neither man laughed and Sade sighed out her disappointment in their inability to get it. "Nikos is a prime male dragon, the Drakon of his Clan. Which is the ruling clan of Dragonkin. Do you really think he knows enough about a kitchen that he could make and decorate that cake?"

"So he bought the cake from a bakery," the Director said.

Sade stared at Caleb. "But there were no. Other. Scents."

He tilted his head, a wolfish action on his part but he didn't care. Then the light bulb clicked on. "There were no other scents," he growled. "There would have been Human scents, and...baking scents." He blinked several times. "The cake had no odor."

"And the only scent you were able to pick up was from the bloody handprint." She turned her attention back to her boss to make sure he got the connection. "We were meant to find that vehicle, the cake, and the palm print."

Bailey didn't blink as he studied her. "Why?"

"I don't know yet, except maybe it's as simple as someone wanted Caleb and I there so they could lob mortars at us to kill us."

The Director leaned back in his chair. It didn't creak. He steepled his fingers, stared at them through a moment of silence before he mused, "There have been no rumblings of any problems in the Dragon Realm. At least none that would spill over here."

"That doesn't mean that Nikos is beloved by all his Clan. He's the Drakon." Which meant he was the Clan's enforcer. Not only did he protect the royal family, but he guarded the whole kit and caboodle from outside interference and dealt—swiftly and quite likely bloodily—with all inside situations. She could think of a few dragons who wouldn't mind taking Nikos down. Then there were those outside the Dragon Realm, including a certain vampire. Except Sinjen wouldn't play games. He'd just go for the jugular. Literally.

She stared out the window, eyes focused on one of the Smithsonian buildings barely visible several blocks away. "This whole thing feels...off."

"So figure out why."

Cutting her eyes to the Old Man, she resisted sticking her tongue out at him. It took a lot of self-control. "Why target Nikos to get at me?" she wondered.

"It's obvious why they'd target you to get at Nikos."

"That's ridiculous, Caleb."

"Is it?"

"Yes."

"We all know he's...well, let's say *infatuated* with you."

"That's bullshit." Sade snapped off the rest of what she'd intended to say when the Old Man cleared his throat. "Sorry, sir."

"No you aren't, but I happen to agree with your partner. The truth isn't bullshit."

"But it's *not* true."

Both men gave her identical "oh really?" expressions. She didn't appreciate the fact her partner *and* her boss appeared so incredulous.

"Okay, fine," she groused then muttered, "whatever," under her breath.

"Do you have any leads?"

She just managed to hold back an aggrieved sigh and was saved when Caleb answered, "No, sir."

"We have some strings to tug," Sade interjected and received a sharp kick to her ankle from Caleb.

"Then get out of here and go tug them."

Relieved, she and Caleb quickly stood and exited before the Old Man called them back. They passed Alice's desk, giving her a nod.

Just before they stepped out into the hallway, the little woman called, "Do be careful out there, you two."

Opting for the stairs, Sade glanced back over her shoulder at Caleb. "Did that sound a little ominous to you?"

"What the Director said?"

"No. Alice. And what *is* she?" Sade had been convinced that Director Bailey's admin had more than a touch of magic running in her veins from the moment she first laid eyes on the woman.

"Don't go there, Sade." Now Caleb sounded a little ominous.

She made big eyes at him. "Go where?"

"Places where you shouldn't stick your nose."

"My nose got pressed to the glass the moment Oberon kidnapped me when I was a baby."

She had a point, but she was still Human and that meant she was mortal. Granted, while the chess game played by Oberon and Mathias using Sade as a baby pawn had left her with some unusual...talents, she still wasn't a Magick. Werewolves could live for a couple hundred years and while they weren't immortal, they were damn hard to kill. Sade, for all her bravado, could die between one heartbeat and the next.

"Alice is what she is. We have tougher hides to skin."

A picture of Elmer Fudd, wearing his cap and carrying a big shotgun, holding his fingers to lips and whispering, 'Be vewy, vewy qwiet. I'm hunting dwagons" popped into her head and made her giggle.

"Do I want to know?" Caleb muttered as he reached around her to pop open the door to their floor.

"Probably not."

They split up, Sade headed to her office on the far side of the small bullpen. The MAGIC Unit wasn't huge. A few agents moved in and out, mainly for training, though Sade supervised a few agents in addition to Caleb. She found a message on her desk.

Agent Marquis—some guy named
Chris Saint John called. He's flying
into Reagan via private jet tonight.
Says he'll meet you here sometime
after 8.

Sade stared at the message, choking on the slightly hysterical
bubble of laughter welling in her throat. Chris? Saint John? Dear
lord. She'd have to burn the evidence of her incompetent agent.
Kristian St. John had never been called "Chris" in his life. But why
was Sinjen coming here? Okay. She knew why he was coming. To
see her. Because she'd canceled his trip a few weeks ago. It had been
almost a month—okay, *over* a month since they'd last been together.

Wanting to bang her head against the desk, she wadded up the
message instead. Then she smoothed it out and fed it through the
small shredder next to her desk. Scrunching her fingers through her
hair, she pretended she wasn't getting a headache. She *missed* Sinjen.
Way more than she wanted to. Which spelled trouble. Which she
didn't need any more of, given her current case. But at the same time,
being apart from him was almost a physical ache and that scared the
bejeebus out of her. She'd made some discreet inquiries but had come
up blank. Yes, Werewolves tended to mate for life if they found their
true mate. And yes, they could feel the pull if they were apart for too
long. Dragons also mated, and there was some sort of mystical bond
formed, but not one of her informants would elucidate.

Gargoyles bonded. Sort of. It was a conscious act and the bond
could be broken by either party. Elves and the Fae? She let out a
groan. They *married* for power, prestige, and progeny. Witches and
warlocks were basically Human and wizards were just...a pain in her
ass, but basically souped-up-on-magical-steroids Human. Then there
were Vampires. They didn't mate. They didn't marry. They didn't *do*
Humans except for sex and blood. Vampires didn't love. All she had

to do was consider the master vampire who'd raised her. She'd been a pawn and she'd heard him admit that he would see her dead rather than lose his game with Oberon. If it became necessary.

She'd been three.

No. Vampires didn't do love. Obsession? Maybe, but not love. Which didn't explain Sinjen. Or did it?

Chapter Three

Patience is a Virtue

Sade stared at the notes she'd made on this case. She'd made phone calls. She'd even emailed a few people. No one knew where Nikos was currently. Oddly, she was able to confirm that Stavros and Xan, the Drakon's second and third, *were* at the royal residence outside of Athens. That was a puzzle. Other than the time Stavros had been banished, those two were always glued to Nikos's side. But no one could—or *would*—account for Nikos's whereabouts.

Her phone buzzed and she picked it up. "Marquis."

"You got a visitor down at security, Agent Marquis."

"Thanks. Tell him I'll be down in a few."

She stretched and glanced at the time on her phone. 9:00 pm. Sinjen had made good time. The flight from Chicago usually took close to two hours and he wouldn't have been able to leave until sundown. Nervous, she shut down her office. This time, she took the elevator.

When the doors opened down in the lobby, the security guards pretended they weren't a little intimidated by Mr. Tall, Dark and Fangy. The two males, anyway. The female? She was doing her level best to throw herself at Sinjen, all but forcing her neck to his mouth.

Sinjen, as usual, ignored the woman. His eyes were fixed on the elevator doors as they opened and Sade walked out. She always took his breath away, seeing her like this, striding with such confidence across a floor, coming to him. He remembered, as he invariably did, the first moment he'd seen her in the subbasement of the Cook County Detention Facility in Chicago. That magnificent hair. Those bottle-green eyes. The beauty mark near her mouth that punctuated every movement of her lips.

She stopped in front of him. Tall enough her eyes were almost level with his. He breathed her in and watched her eyes soften as they searched his face. He never knew what she was looking for but always knew the moment she'd found it. Her mouth softened, her eyes took on a subtle emerald glow.

He didn't touch. Didn't kiss her. No matter how much he wanted to. Instead, he whispered, "Hello, Lady Sade."

Sinjen turned slightly and offered her his arm. She hesitated, her eyes darting toward the security station then she gave a mental shrug and hooked her hand through it. He led her to the doors, which opened automatically after she scanned her ID. A sleek, black limo idled at the curb. The vampire opened the back door and handed her inside. Sade slid across the seat to make room for him. He settled beside her after closing the car door. Without a word, the driver smoothly merged with the late evening traffic and made all the correct turns to take them toward her house.

After a few minutes of silence, Sinjen asked, "Have you eaten?"

"I'm fine," she replied automatically.

He favored her with a knowing look. "When is the last time you ate?"

Okay, she had to think about that. She'd had a pizza delivered last night after she and Caleb made their reports. A danish and coffee for breakfast on the way to the office before meeting with the Director and department heads. Lunch? Since she couldn't remember, she figured probably not. And she'd obviously worked through dinner waiting for his arrival.

"That is what I thought." He leaned forward and tapped on the glass separating the passenger section from the driver. He said one word when the window whispered down just far enough to be heard. "Tortino."

The glass slithered back up, sealing them in. Sade hated feeling defensive and wondered why she was. It wasn't like she and Sinjen barely knew each other. They'd been to hell and back—quite literally, and more than once.

"I'm sorry," she murmured.

He arched one brow above his beautiful, sapphire blue eyes. "For what?"

"You hate DC."

He almost smiled. "And yet here I am." He reached over and took her hand, twining his fingers with hers. "Chicago is not your favorite place and it is not fair that you do all the traveling."

What could she say to that? He spoke the truth, as she saw it. Still. This silence felt uncomfortable, at least to her. Sinjen appeared perfectly content, leaning back against the soft leather, their shoulders touching, their hands together resting on the very soft and very expensive material of his dress slacks.

The limo circled the block so they could exit onto the sidewalk in front of the restaurant. Tortino was mostly a neighborhood spot, though this was a pretty upscale neighborhood. Sinjen exited without releasing Sade's hand. The limo was already out of sight by the time he held the restaurant's door open for her. The hostess recognized them both immediately. She grabbed two menus and led them to a corner table away from the main part of the dining room. It was Sade's favorite. They sat catty-corner from each other, so they both had a wall at their backs.

He'd taken her to an Italian restaurant in Chicago, back when they'd first met. She supposed it could have been considered their first date. Sinjen certainly regarded it as such. He'd been...courting her back then. Was he courting her now?

The waiter appeared with one glass of ice water. This was no slight to Sinjen. They knew what he was, took his presence in stride. Sinjen ordered wine without looking at the menu. Sade ordered her meal and handed the menu to the waiter, unopened.

"You look tired." He finally broke the silence.

She supposed she did. She hadn't slept well—who would after surviving a mortar attack and filling out reams of bureaucratic paperwork because her car got blown up and a building destroyed. It wasn't like either of those things was her fault. She was tired and worried and tense. And he saw it all, etched there on her face.

Sade shrugged. "Long day."

"And I complicated it by coming to your office instead of your home." What he meant was that he'd complicated her life by arriving with very little notice.

"No. I would have been working late anyway."

"A case?"

How did she explain without explaining? If she mentioned the dragon, there'd be a fight. If she mentioned the mortar attack, there'd be a fight. If she just shrugged it off, there'd be a fight. Maybe that's what they needed to clear the air. But not here in Tortino. She liked the chef and the owner and the wait staff. She enjoyed the food and would be sorry if she could no longer eat here.

"Sort of." She looked around, though the tables immediately surrounding them were empty. "Not something I can discuss here."

He nodded, pretending he understood. Sade did not want to tell him what had wound her up so tightly. He should be angry but that was Sade. She didn't trust easily. Still. Good thing he was a patient man. Also, she worried over those she cared about. And she anticipated what his reaction would be when she mentioned the infernal lizard, the attack on her and Caleb, and all the rest. Yes, patience was a virtue when dealing with Sade Marquis.

He leaned back in his chair as the waiter appeared with the wine.

"I'm sorry," she said again once the waiter poured her wine and retreated.

"Why are you sorry now?"

"The job, I guess. We make plans, I get called in, have to cancel on you."

After a long moment, Sinjen responded with a single word. "Yes."

She fidgeted. Sade had no problems with silence. As a rule. But she didn't know what do with the tension she felt stretching between them. Sinjen's expression looked...mild. She was tense. He was...she didn't know. Not relaxed but not angry. Amused? Confused? Slightly irritated, she decided.

Her food arrived. She pushed the pasta around on her plate. She cut a bite off the beef but didn't move the fork after. Her hunger had fled.

"Eat, Sade," Sinjen commanded quietly.

She forked the bite into her mouth and chewed deliberately. The meat tasted wonderful—perfectly cooked and seasoned, but her stomach rebelled slightly as she swallowed. She ignored the tinge of nausea and took another bite. If she didn't eat, Sinjen would simply sit and stare his disapproval. Damn vampire. He'd learned that cajoling didn't work, that threats didn't work, that arguing didn't work. But sitting so still she couldn't see him breathe and staring at her in mute reproach? Yeah. She could handle about five minutes of that before she'd boil over.

Another bite and swallow. A sip of wine. A bit of pasta twirled on her fork before stabbing another piece of the veal. Wash. Rinse. Repeat. She kept her focus on her plate, ignoring the darkly sensual man sitting within touching distance. She'd just swallowed her final bite when the waiter appeared.

"Dessert?"

"No," Sinjen spoke before she could.

"Of course, sir. Anything else?"

"No."

The waiter gave a little half bow. "I will bring your check."

Five minutes later, they were outside on the sidewalk watching the black limo slide to a stop in front of them. Sinjen opened the door, they got in and settled. The driver eased the elegant vehicle back into traffic and within minutes, the limo stopped in front of her townhouse.

She lived about two blocks from Logan Circle, on a street that remained fairly busy no matter the time of day. Sade didn't mind the noise. She'd gotten used to it having once lived in the French Quarter of New Orleans. That's why she'd invested in this red-brick three-story townhouse. It had a small balcony overlooking the street with a postage-stamp sized yard in the front and a slightly larger private courtyard in the back.

Sinjen waited while the driver retrieved his bag from the trunk. Sade unlocked the door and stepped inside. She should be relieved now that she was home on her own turf. But she wasn't. The man with her took up all the air in a room when he entered it. She'd never grown used to the effect he had.

Stepping inside, Sinjen set his small roller bag down near the entrance, turned and locked the door. Sade strode away from him and he admired her retreat. She wouldn't admit that's what it was but he knew. He wondered what she would think if he admitted that he loved watching her walk—coming *or* going because it always reminded him of that first time.

Sade paused in her crossing of the room to switch on lamps. Their soft glow chased shadows back into the corners. She disappeared into the kitchen. Sinjen hid his smile in case she suddenly returned and caught him. Instead, he picked up his bag and climbed the stairs to her room on the second floor. He shed his jacket and hung it in her closet. Stripping the tie, he left it on the top of her dresser. He popped the top three buttons of his white dress shirt. He could hear her moving around downstairs. Still avoiding him then. Well enough. He enjoyed the hunt.

Chapter Four

Heartbeats

Sinjen set his trap well. He unpacked the clothes he'd brought then stripped out of the rest of the suit he'd worn on the plane. Naked, he padded into the large master bath. This block of townhouses was made up of narrow homes. The previous owners had purchased the adjoining house and combined the living space. The renovations located all the public spaces on the first floor. The second floor consisted of a large master bedroom and bath with a walk-in closet and access to the balcony. The third floor contained another full bath with two bedrooms, one of which served as Sade's home office.

Availing himself of the massive shower stall, he washed away the grime of travel. He stepped out long minutes later and listened. Sade had turned on the television down in the living area. He smiled. Snatching one of the luxurious cotton towels hanging next to the shower, he dried off. He brushed his teeth. He considered shaving then decided against it. He enjoyed the feel of Sade's fingertips rasping across the night's growth of stubble.

Pulling on a pair of cotton sleep pants, he stretched out on Sade's bed and waited. He was patient, though he didn't have to wait long. He heard her stirring downstairs, caught the silence after she switched off the television. He felt her coming closer, smiled when a step creaked. He waited as she neared the door, eyes closed, remembering. Remembering so much about this woman. His body stirred, as it always did, with thoughts of her.

He eased off the bed, approached the closed bedroom door. Knew the moment she reached for the knob. Opened it before she could turn it. She paused on the other side of the threshold, her eyes searching his before she took in his face, his bare chest, the rest of his body. And then she relented and simply stepped into him, relaxing as his arms circled across her back, her own embracing his waist. Her cheek rested against the hollow of his shoulder.

"Honey, I'm home," he murmured. It was an old joke between them but she didn't smile.

Sade raised her head to look at him. "Are you?" she whispered.

He cupped her cheek in his palm. "Yes," he murmured. "I am."

Sinjen felt her breath catch at the admission. He backed into the room drawing her with him. She didn't fight the move. Stopping next to the bed, he inhaled. Her hair still held the fragrance of gardenias but Sade? Her natural scent was rich and earthy. She smelled of Irish moss in the rain and a spicy musk that hinted at cloves.

He traced her lips with his thumb before he bent to kiss the beauty mark at the corner of her mouth. He moved just enough to capture her lips. She shivered and her fingers clinched against his skin. Her eyes remained closed as she leaned toward him, an open invitation.

Sinjen noted the dark circles beneath her eyes and wondered what troubled her. She'd been stiff and distant until this moment. Sade had something on her mind but only God knew when she would reveal what had her upset. *Patience,* he reminded himself.

Sade broke the kiss and tried to pull away. He tightened his arms as he brushed her lips with his again. He teased her, gently. Nudging her with his nose, his tongue. A light skirmish in the battles that so often flared between them.

Sade's brain, as it always did when he kissed her, turned to mush. Her knees went wobbly as shivers skittered through her. She clung to him, partially pissed that he could have this effect on her and partially charmed because he did.

"Fuck me."

Sinjen laughed. "I intend to."

For once, he hadn't chided her language but she hadn't meant to voice that thought out loud either. The question in her head was what she'd meant. Or been asking for. Was she fucked? Or did she, indeed, want him to fuck her?

"Still, fuck remains such a vulgar word for what I intend for tonight, Lady Sade." His words tickled her skin as his mouth trailed across her cheek to her ear. He paused on the wildly beating pulse under the soft skin of her throat. Her pulse quickened in anticipation. "Not yet," he promised.

Again, Sade had to lock her knees to remain upright. The part of her brain that never shut up laughed at her. *He should write the manual for romance authors.*

"Shut up."

He paused in his explorations and tilted his head away so he could look at her. "Beg pardon?"

"Wasn't talking to you." Her voice came out low, the tone snarly. Then she grabbed his face in her hands and kissed him. Hard. Her tongue tangled with his and her fingers shifted into his hair. Now it was time to battle.

Her clothes seemed to magically disappear. Long, clever fingers had divested her of weapons, holster, and optional clothing. She stood now in bra and panties. She leaned into him. Hard. Overbalancing them both until they hit the bed, her on top. That didn't last long. He twisted and suddenly, she was flat on her back and he was fitting his hips between her thighs. Right where she wanted him.

"You are no longer the virgin," he murmured between laving her nipples. "But you are still a treasure."

She stiffened at his words and he lifted his head to stare down at her. And knew. The infernal dragon somehow had a role in whatever put those dark circles under her eyes.

Sade shook thoughts of Nikos out of her head, knowing from the look on Sinjen's face that he'd realized what his words had triggered. She didn't have room for the dragon in her life. Nor for his complications. Life was convoluted enough with just one sexy vampire in it. And a fae. A werewolf. A gargoyle. And a silver-eyed dragon rearing his ugly head.

Watching the wheels turn in her head. Sinjen growled. Enough. She was his. Always. And he would prove that to her. Again. And again. And as many times as it took. He knew what to do. Kisses. Slow, inescapable, claiming. He covered her soft skin with them, added small nips and bites. Her skin heated, the scent of cloves becoming stronger.

He focused on her breasts, licking and sucking while his fingers stroked down her side and across her belly. They teased through silky curls meeting with creamy heat. He stroked through the lips of her sex and he pressed the pad of his index finger against her clit. She inhaled sharply and he smiled. He knew her body. Knew how to elicit such a response.

From the moment he'd first laid eyes on Sade, Sinjen had wanted all of her. That hunger had not decreased in the intervening time. He was greedy. Always would be when it came to her.

Sade panted, arched her hips against his hand and growled a little when he stilled. Hiding his smile, his fingers slid in and out of her sex, his thumb continuing to tease her clit. She clamped her thighs around him.

"Ambergris," she murmured, causing him to quirk a brow. "You smell like ambergris when you make love to me."

Interesting. He had never considered his own scent, concentrating as he always did on hers—on the rain and moss and cloves until he buried his nose in her hair to inhale the sweet gardenia scent of her shampoo.

"More," she demanded.

"More," he agreed, his cock swollen and dripping with need for her. Her groping hand found his erection and wrapped around it. He loved the feel of her fingers, of her mouth, surrounding him. Later. They would play later. Now, she wanted more, as did he. It had been too long.

Sade worked his cock with slow pumps and squeezes. She tried to angle the tip toward her entrance, but he raised his hips, pulling her hand and arm up. She moaned. Why was he delaying things? He knew she wanted him. Surely, he knew. "Please," she all but whimpered. "I want you inside me."

"Yes," he finally agreed, pulling her hand away from him. He braced above her for only seconds before he plunged into her, deeply, with a satisfied groan. He lay still.

"More," she demanded again, squeezing her inner muscles around his cock..

"Yes, Lady Sade," he murmured against her throat.

She inhaled deeply. "Do it." This was no plea, nor a helpless demand. This was a command.

Sinjen's fangs scraped across the soft skin of her throat. Her pulse beat wildly beneath his lips. Slow and easy, he withdrew his cock, leaving it barely touching the swollen lips of her entrance. She growled, her displeasure evident. Holding his body away from hers he pressed his hips down and watched her body swallow his cock, inch by slow inch until his tip pressed against her cervix.

"I hate you," she groaned.

He lowered himself to lay against her. "Of course you do." He pulled out and thrust again, smiling as she groaned. "More?" he asked, his smile devilish.

She pinched his ass and he laughed aloud. "Then more it is, m'lady."

Sinjen sped the tempo, matching the wild pounding of her heart. He drove into her harder and her body responded as it always did—opening wider, taking him fully. She whimpered as her hips curled and pushed, her hands seeking a grip on his shoulders.

He lifted his head to watch her, saw her expression as she tightened around his cock. As the first spasms hit her, he struck. His fangs gleamed a brief moment before sinking in the pulse throbbing along her neck. Her climax erupted around him and he emptied into her as he drank deeply, if sparingly. He never took his fill of her. To do so would be to drain her life away. Her blood was still the sweet nectar he remembered from their first time together. Finished but not sated, he swirled his tongue over the two pinpricks in her skin. There would be no sign of his bite by morning.

Rolling off her and the bed, he strode into the bath. After cleaning himself, he wet a cloth with warm water and returned to clean her. Sade lay sprawled where he'd left her, loose-limbed and sated. After gently seeing to her, he winged the cloth back into the bath, closed and shuttered the windows, and climbed in beside her.

Settling Sade into his arms, Sinjen pulled the covers over them both and lay still. He listened as her breathing and heartbeat synchronized with his. He held her, there in the dark, marking her heartbeat and each breath she took. Cherishing each one. He'd been damned for most of his life but laying here with her? Small glimmers of hope sparkled like the first stars in the sky at night.

Sade was his. No matter how hard she tried to pull away or to hold him at arm's length, he knew. And she knew. That's why she fought him. She was a challenge, one that both invigorated and infuriated him. He smiled against her hair as she nuzzled his skin in her sleep. He would lay here, watching her, holding her, loving her until the sun forced him into the death-like trance that was Vampire sleep—*la morte d'aube*, the death that comes at dawn.

The hours of the night ticked away second by second. Sade slept. Sinjen held her. He knew things weren't right between them, except for this time, this respite from their lives when they focused only on each other. She was a day dweller and needed her sleep when he was at his peak. He could give her this, could share her with the sun. They weren't quite broken. Not yet. Still, he didn't know how to fix them.

She cared for him. He could taste it when he drank from her. She probably loved him, though that term's definition still eluded him. She was his. He would never let her go. Obsessed with her? Yes. Yet he didn't care. No woman had ever affected him this way. As a Knight Templar, he'd been mostly immune to the wiles of women. Oh, he'd bedded a few in his youth, and far more after being turned by Mathias but not one of them evoked the deep emotions he carried for Sade.

His skin itched and he could feel the sun peeking over the eastern horizon. Sunrise was here. He could fight the sleep but there was no point. Settling in beside Sade, he held her close. The last sounds he heard were her heartbeat and soft exhalation of her breath. The last scent filling his nose was the odd combination of sweet and spice that was her. The last thing he saw as his eyelids lowered was the slight upturn of her mouth.

Between one human heartbeat and the next, he was gone.

Chapter Five

About A Dragon

Sade opened her eyes to mere slits. Her room was dark and the only sound was that of her own breathing. Opening her eyes fully, she eased away from the arms wrapped around her. Sinjen's body held very little warmth currently. She fumbled on the bedside table for her phone to check the time. It wasn't there. Her brain short-circuited a little. It had to be early still, though after dawn.

Easing away from Sinjen's lifeless body, Sade crawled out of bed. She paused to arrange him into a more comfortable position and settled the covers around him. She double-checked the shutters and curtains. All was fine. She grabbed her robe off the back of the bathroom door, did minimal morning libations, and tiptoed downstairs. Which was ridiculous. For all intents and purposes, the man upstairs in her bed was dead to the world. Literally.

She wanted coffee. No, she *needed* coffee. And wanted it. Coffee, as far as she was concerned, was its own food group. She set the coffee maker to dripping and rummaged in the fridge. Then the pantry. Nothing edible. There were times when she envied Sinjen not needing food. Impatient, she pulled out the coffee pot and stuck a cup in its place. When the cup was full, she switched them back without spilling a drop or getting burned. That meant it would be a good day, right?

Then she remembered that her phone was down here. Somewhere. She still needed to figure out the time. She found her phone on the table next to the couch. The screen flared and flashed the number 6:55 at her. Still early but she'd also missed a call from Caleb. Dammit. He knew Sinjen was in town so the call had to be important. He'd called at 5 am.

She hit the return call button without listening to voice mail. "What?" she barked as soon as he answered.

"You didn't listen to my message."

"No. Easier to talk directly to you." Sade made a d'uh face even though he couldn't see it.

"You need to pack."

"For what?"

"The Old Man is sending us to Paris."

"Would that be a Paris in one of eighteen US states?" She could all but see Caleb rolling his eyes.

"How do you even know that?"

Her smirked was evident in her voice. "How many games of Trivial Pursuit did you lose to me growing up?"

"Never mind. We're going to France. Meet me at the Air France counter at Dulles by ten am. Our flight leaves at noon. I have all the paperwork."

"Whoa there, champ. *Why* are we going to Paris?"

"Because Interpol and the DGSI have invited us to come."

Sade pondered that bit of information. "And why would they do that?"

"Seems there's a little Dragon trouble brewing."

"Fuck me."

"Sade..."

"Shut up, Caleb. I get to cuss whenever there's a dragon in the room."

"You cuss no matter who's in the room."

He had a point. "Fine," she groused. "How long am I packing for?"

"At least a couple of days."

"Carry-on bag then. That simplifies things."

"Don't forget your passport."

"Roger that." Something else occurred to her. "Can we get extra ammo at the Embassy?"

"Let's hope we don't need it."

"Ah, but we're dealing with Dragons. I'll see you by ten, Caleb."

She gulped down her coffee, turned off the coffee maker, and hustled upstairs. Halfway through her hurried shower, she remembered the vampire asleep in her bed. That set off another flurry of cussing. There was no help for it. Duty called and all that bullshit. At least they'd had a night together and this was probably for the best. She never knew what to do with Sinjen when he was here and she had regular office hours. Forget being on an investigation. Those hours were insane. And she was, technically, in the middle of an investigation.

Dressing in casual slacks, boots, and a pull-over shirt, she expertly selected and folded clothes into the largest size carry-on bag she could get away with. She added a pair of running shoes and another pair of sturdy boots. She grabbed a backpack that would fit under the seat and filled it with electronic cords, converters, and a few personal items, including the leather pouch with her passport and other IDs. She added a tailored blazer that went with every pair of slacks and jeans she'd packed, and a slouchy jacket that was both warm and waterproof.

She looked around her closet, the bath, and her bedroom. She had everything. Except Sinjen. She should write him a note. And then she should call him when she reached Paris. Maybe write him a longer note and not call him when she reached Paris. That's what she'd do.

She found paper and a pen and scribbled out her message:

> Duty calls. Flying to Paris this morning
> at Interpol's request. Be gone a few days.
> You might as well go back to Chicago.

I'll call you when I get home.

She paused in her writing and chewed her bottom lip. She never knew how to sign off. Should she be sappy and sign it "Love you" or businesslike and just sign her name. She settled for the ubiquitous "XO Sade." Setting the note on the nightstand on his side of the bed, she bent over and dropped a kiss on his lips. They were cold to the touch, which still occasionally freaked her out a little. She brushed a wisp of hair off his forehead and resolutely stood. They wouldn't be working out their problems any time in the near future. She added her holster and her badge to her belt, grabbed the bags and her phone and headed out. Between the second floor and front door, she decided to take the Metro rather than wait on a ride share. The Silver Line would have her to Dulles almost as fast. She snagged a light-weight leather jacket off its peg near the front door and put it on to cover her weapon. Slinging the backpack and grabbing the handle of the carry-on, she slipped out the door and locked it.

Sade hated going to Dulles. There was no easy way to get there. Walking at a brisk pace, she'd made it to the Metro station at McPherson Square in just over ten minutes. She didn't mind the walk, not this time of the morning. At McPherson, she used her FBI ID and pass to get through security with her weapon and boarded the Silver Line headed to Dulles with minimal fuss.

Settling in for a ride of about 45 minutes, she did what she did best—she people watched. She had to change trains at Wiehle-Reston East and wasn't surprised to find Caleb waiting for her at the Reston station where they boarded the airport train.

Getting through the formalities of carrying weapons not only on-board an aircraft but one headed to a foreign country took a bit of time. Luckily, they had it. They even got a lift from Customs and Border Patrol to the Air France departure gates. Sade was shocked to discover they had first class tickets, courtesy of Air France.

Seven and a half hours later, they deplaned at Charles de Gaulle Airport and were met by two large men wearing suits and looking serious. Stiff and bleary-eyed, Sade sighed. "DGSI or Interpol?" she muttered under her breath.

Caleb shrugged. "One each?"

"I guess they could be brothers from other mothers."

"Mademoiselle Marquis?" The one in the black suit asked.

"That would be me."

"Your weapon, *s'il vous plaît*." The man stuck out his hand, expecting her to surrender her Beretta without a word.

She stared at his hand then slowly trailed her eyes up his arm and chest to fix on his face. In the process, she discovered he was a bit shorter than she so it was easy to look down her nose at him.

"Your identification, *s'il vous plaît*." The "please" came out with a hint of sarcasm.

Both men blustered and postured. Sade and Caleb simply stared. When Sade saw a uniformed customs officer, she raised her hand and gestured him over. He approached warily, eying the two men. In perfect French, Sade introduced herself, explained the situation and offered to accompany the uniformed officer to a secure area for further discussion. While this conversation took place, the men fidgeted for a few moments and then they edged away.

Caleb knew the moment they began to turn to run. He grabbed each man by the collar of his jacket and hauled them back with such force, he deposited them on floor, ass first. Within moments, more security personnel swarmed the area. The men were handcuffed and hauled away.

"Well, that was interesting," she muttered for Caleb's ears only.

"Indeed, Agent Marquis."

She swiveled to face the newcomer with the excellent hearing. He was tall and as handsome as a movie star. Well-built, dressed impeccably, and a vampire.

"I am Lieutenant Jean-Louis Durand currently assigned as a liaison to Interpol." He held out his ID wallet before his gaze shifted to Caleb. "And you must be Agent Jones." Durand held out a hand. Caleb shook it. "Do you have other baggage?"

Caleb answered for them both. "No, sir."

"Please, call me Jean-Louis and I may call you Sade and Caleb?"

"Since we're being friendly, sure." Sade gave him a smile that didn't quite reach her eyes.

"Please, this way. I have a car. We will slip through the security area and be on our way."

Sade stopped. "We don't need to go through passport control?"

"No. You are expected and here at our request."

He led them on a fairly direct path, waving at various officials as they passed. Sade didn't miss the disgruntled looks from their fellow passengers who were lined up like cattle heading to the slaughterhouse.

Outside, the temperature was cool and the air laden with moisture. "I hope you have brought your umbrella, Sade. We are in for a few days of rain."

A uniformed gendarme leaned against the front fender of a Citroën Berlingo, which reminded Sade of the bastard child of a mom-mobile and a small crossover SUV. The rear hatch opened with a sharp *brpbrp* and the gendarme took their rolling cases and put them into the cargo space. Jean-Louis waved Caleb to the front passenger seat.

"There is more room for the legs," he explained. "And I have not been cramped up on a trans-Atlantic flight for eight hours." Then he opened the back door for Sade to climb in. She scooted across to sit directly behind the driver.

"So," Jean-Louis sighed after settling beside her. "About this dragon."

Chapter Six

Motives

"You know what I am." The vampire spoke softly and sounded surprised. He also made it a statement, not a question.

Sade shrugged and offered him a speculative look. "You're a vampire."

"And you have no problem with my..." He struggled for the right word. "For my being?"

"I've worked with vampires before. I'm just surprised that Interpol accepted a Magick within its august ranks."

That earned her a smile. Even his eyes crinkled in amusement. "I and my Human counterpart are something like you and Caleb. We work the magical crimes. I work nights, he works days. We sometimes compare notes." He gave a very Gallic shrug.

"My partner's a werewolf. So long as he's not left out in the rain, we get along fine too."

That got a growl from Caleb and a chuckle from the French vampire. "I am surprised that you recognized what I am. I am very good at being Human."

"And I'm very good at recognizing Magicks." Sade offered her own very Gallic shrug.

"I had heard this about you yet I did not quite believe. Can you recognize all Magicks for what we are?"

"Can a werewolf follow a magical trail?"

"Some, *oui*."

"Then you have your answer." Sade didn't know this dude and wasn't about to give away her trade secrets. The fact she had been marked by both a master vampire and the king of the Fae was strictly need-to-know and *Loo-te-no Zhan-Loo-ey Doo-ran* wasn't on that list. She switched subjects. "So, about this dragon?"

Jean-Louis laughed, the sound deep and rich and meant to entice. The sound washed over her with barely a ripple. This vampire didn't hold a candle to Sinjen.

"This dragon arrived a few days ago and things began to happen."

"Which dragon?"

"The Drakon of Clan Kholikikos, Sade, of course. Is he not the dragon with which you are most...familiar?"

She did not like the insinuation in Jean-Louis's voice. In her frostiest tone, she said, "What has he done now?"

"Nothing." Amusement glinted in his eyes.

Sade arranged her expression into an appropriate glower. "If he's done nothing, then why are we here?"

"Because, as I mentioned, things began to happen. We cannot link any of them directly to his actions, but we find it highly suspicious that these events began to occur upon his arrival."

"Would you care to enlighten us?" She pointedly included Caleb.

"Certain members of the Magick community here in Paris have gone missing since his appearance."

"And?"

Jean-Louis blinked at her. "What is it you mean *and*?"

"If you were on the wrong side of the Dragons and one popped into town, wouldn't you quietly disappear?" While the vampire pondered, Sade continued. "How do you know they hadn't already scheduled a..." She leaned toward Caleb. "What do Europeans call vacations?"

"Holiday."

"Yeah. That. For all you know, Durand, these disappearing Magicks are simply living their own lives on their own timetable. You have no direct correlation between his arrival and their disappearance."

"But this is Paris," the vampire argued.

"And?"

"Why is the dragon here?"

"I don't know. Why does anyone come to Paris? Maybe he wants to eat cheese and pastries and drink wine."

"I do not understand why you defend him." Jean-Louis looked sly now. "He just tried to kill you."

"Did he?"

"*Oui.*"

"And how do you know that?" Sade stared at him, leaning closer.

Jean-Louis leaned away from her, looking uncertain now. "But we were told that he tried to assassinate you."

"When? When were you told this? And when, exactly, did Nikos Constantine arrive in Paris?"

The vampire frowned in consternation. "He arrived a week ago, give or take a few hours."

"When were you told of the attack on Caleb and me?"

Offering that Gallic shrug again, Jean-Louis admitted he wasn't quite certain. "Maybe Monday. Or the day before. Perhaps the day after."

"Uh-huh. Do you show him leaving and reentering the country at any time since his arrival?"

His answer to that was a short, clipped, "No."

"So, you got word of this—" She made air quotes. "—assassination attempt before it actually happened. And your...I'm guessing the source was anonymous, *oui*?" At his nod, she flashed him a look that implied *seriously?* without saying a word. "Do ya think there might be a frame job going on here?"

Caleb cut his eyes to her and Sade realized her partner had some ideas about that but none he would discuss until they were alone and in a secure space. Not that she didn't trust Interpol. Or the vampire who represented them. Yeah, about as far as she could toss the Magick.

They rode through the mostly deserted streets of Paris, crossing the Seine into the area known as Saint-Cloud. Way back when, Interpol moved their HQ from Vienna to Paris and eventually, a new building was erected. Of course that was back in the Sixties and when it was bombed in the Eighties, the fancy new HQ was built in Lyon. Sade realized that she had no clue where the Paris satellite office was located. She caught Caleb's eyes and tilted her head. He answered her implied question with a very slight dip of his chin.

The driver turned onto the Rue Armengaud, slowing the car's speed to account for the narrow one-lane street. It slowed in front of a four-story glass and concrete building. Typical law enforcement building. An iron gate between two red-brick pillars opened and instead of parking at the modern building, the Peugeot slipped through the gate and metal clanked to a close behind them as the vehicle preceded down an asphalt drive.

Sade was tired and she wondered if her mind was playing tricks. The building they stopped in front of looked like... She blinked. It looked like a Hollywood set designer had been told to create a French chateau made of gingerbread with a heavy dose of Gothic just to be on the weird side. This soooo wasn't the original office building Interpol once occupied.

"Surprising, is it not?" Jean-Louis winked at her. "I should warn you now that almost all of the Interpol agents in Paris are of the Magick. After the bombing, the building was razed and when it was decided we needed an official presence here that was separate from the DCSI, this charming place was acquired. It is both home and office for us."

"Okay, then." Her response was lame but dammit, she'd had no idea. The majority of agents in Paris were Magicks? That was news to her *and* the FBI. They had their own equivalent to the MAGIC Unit so why was she and Caleb here?

"You have rooms booked at a hotel nearer to the center of Paris and closer to your American Embassy. This is good. Your arrival will have been noted, but there are those who will assume that you were met and brought here simply as a matter of courtesy. After daylight, the driver will take you to your hotel. Until then, we have work to do."

When Caleb and Sade walked outside into the morning sunlight, they looked like they'd been up all night. Which, technically, they had. Sade hated time changes and the jet lag that went with it. Caleb didn't seem to mind as much. As promised, the driver from the airport waited for them outside the front door. The ride back into Paris proper and to their hotel was made in silence. Caleb pretended to doze. Sade stared out the window, absorbing the sights she'd missed during the drive in the dark from the airport. Paris always fascinated her.

Their driver delivered them to the American Embassy. That was fine. They did need to check in. The hotel they'd booked was a short Metro ride away, while the hotel the Bureau booked for them was right across the street. Sade was pretty sure they'd be monitored. That was fine. She and Caleb had ways of avoiding detection.

Their credentials passed them through into the embassy. They played the diplomatic game with the on-duty officer and then headed across the street to the hotel. The manager greeted them at the door, then ushered them into the elevator, which ostensibly would deposit them on the floor where their rooms were located but took them instead down to the subbasement where they accessed the Concorde Metro Station.

Less than thirty minutes later, they were checked into their small hotel on the Rue de la Huchette. Since it was lunch time, they grabbed food from the small, hole-in-the-wall eatery a few doors down then returned to Sade's room to eat and discuss things.

Sade didn't beat around the bush. "Did you know Interpol was using Magicks?"

"Can't say I'm surprised. There were Magicks in key places long before the Rip."

"That's true. But to be so obvious? And what was the driver?"

"Not sure. Probably a wizard or witch. Human but...not."

"Yeah, that's the sense I got too." She bit into her gyros, chewed and swallowed. "So why are we really here?"

"My question is, who wants you specifically in Paris?"

"That's a good question. I'll make an appointment to see Crevan." *Le Vieil*, the leader of the Gargoyles occasionally had a soft spot for Sade. She'd be more likely to receive an audience than Caleb would.

"Just to check in?"

"Of course."

Caleb laughed. "No subterfuge."

"None at all."

They both yawned and agreed it was time to finish food and then nap. Caleb headed to his room but left the door between their rooms unlocked. Sade showered and changed into loose fleece pants and a long-sleeved T-shirt. She stretched out on her bed, ordered her brain to shut down and closed her eyes.

Sade didn't move. Each breath she took was a very careful inhalation—slow, easy, small. For a moment, she couldn't remember where she was. Paris. Hotel. Caleb in the adjoining room. What had tapped into her subconscious, waking her so precipitously?

She listened. Street noise. People talking. Footsteps. The narrow lane outside their hotel was closed to public vehicular traffic. There. Off in the distance. There was the clamor of traffic.

Eyes still closed, she mulled over her sudden wakefulness. Had she dreamed something? She wasn't prone to visions of prophecy but déjà vu reared its ugly head often in her day-to-day life. No memory of a dream. No unnatural sound. A faint, gray light teased her closed lids. Still daylight then, though likely coming on to evening. She needed to locate Caleb and get out on the streets. A light tap on the door between her room and Caleb's caused her to open her eyes and sit up.

"Yeah?" she called softly.

The door inched open and Caleb peered through. "You're awake."

"Sort of. What's up?"

"Roman's here."

Sade swung her feet off the bed and stood. "Here?"

"In Paris. Crevan ordered him to the Sanctuaire."

"Verity?" Verity was the witch who'd saved Roman's heart and become his mate during the battle for the souls of the Gargoyle race, the Garregyion, as they called themselves.

"She's with him."

"Okay." She drew out the word, thinking hard. "That could mean a couple of different things. Either things aren't bad here and this is just a normal trip and he doesn't want to be separated from her."

"Or things in New Orleans aren't safe to leave her there alone."

"Jean-Louis hinted at things happening here, that being one of the reasons our presence here was requested. I suspect Roman just wants to keep her close."

"We're supposed to meet him at the Irish pub."

Sade let out a short gigglesnort. "Sorry. What is it about us that we always find an Irish pub no matter where we go?"

Caleb laughed. "That's true. We do tend to gravitate to those particular establishments."

"I'm still trying to figure out why there's an Irish pub in Paris."

"Just be glad there is, especially one run by a leprechaun."

Chapter Seven

Double Double Toil and Trouble

The gargoyle, one foot planted, leaned a hip atop the wall along the Pont de la Tournelle Bridge, his back to the view of Notre Dame Cathedral that tourists lined up to see. Today, the walkway remained mostly empty. The cathedral, home to the Gargoyle Sanctuaire, had been partially demolished in the battle against the rogues. Seeing the magnificent architecture hidden by a spiderweb of scaffolding hurt in a way he couldn't explain.

"You are sure he is here?" Roman asked the werewolf standing next to him.

Caleb's hands were braced on the top of the wall and while he was paying attention to the gargoyle, his eyes were focused on a barge making slow headway along the Seine. "Pretty sure."

"Why would the dragon come to Paris? Athens is his demesne."

"Where's Sade?" Caleb glanced up in time to catch the change in the gargoyle's expression as understanding washed over the other Magick. "Yeah. That's why."

"Where is Sinjen?"

"That's a good question. Back in Washington, I guess."

"Washington and not Chicago?"

"Don't ask, Roman."

"Because you do not know or because you do not want to be in the middle?"

"Yes."

"Fine then. Moving on. According to the FBI's information, the dragon was here before you and Sade arrived."

"According to the information we received, yes."

"You do not trust the source." It wasn't a question.

"Interpol." Caleb's voice held no inflection.

"Ah. Yes. They do have their own agenda."

"Did you know they have vampires working for them?"

"Name me one major law enforcement agency who does not."

"Good point. But according to our liaison, most of the agents here in Paris are Magicks."

That got him a narrowed look from Roman. "What about the fae?"

"The Fae with a capital F or a particular fae?" Caleb let out a long-suffering sigh as Roman gave him The Look. "You know Ariel won't keep his nose out of this once he catches wind of it." He returned his focus to the barge, the action catching Roman's attention. "Of course he won't. We will bring him up to speed once he arrives." The gargoyle straightened and turned to stare at the river. "What do you find so fascinating down there?"

"There's a witch on that barge. Casting a spell."

Roman concentrated, eyes narrowed on the slow-moving canal boat as it approached their position. "There is, yes."

Caleb turned a sharp gaze on Roman. "Your witchling?"

"No. Verity is in the archives while waiting for Crevan to finish with Sade. There's some scroll or other he's promised to show her."

"Then who?"

"We should find out."

Huge, leathery wings unfolded as Roman shifted into one of his real forms. With one hard downbeat, he lifted into the air and sailed out over the water in pursuit of the craft that had just passed beneath them. Caleb raced across the bridge and scrambled down one of the abutments to the walkway lining the Seine. He loped past moored barges, his eye on the prize. Suddenly, Roman halted in the sky, hovering before turning around to double back in the opposite direction. The werewolf slowed.

"Stay with the barge!" Roman shouted as he passed. "Guard the witch."

Guard the witch? What had Roman discovered that he didn't know? Still, he trusted the gargoyle so he turned on the speed. Even in Human form, he could run with the wind. He reached the Pont de Sully bridge ahead of the barge. Using a moored canal boat as a springboard, he vaulted onto the suspect houseboat as it passed. The cloying odor of fresh magic invaded his nose and lungs but he ignored it, focusing instead on the scent of fear wafting up from below deck.

Two burly men emerged, mirror images of each other. "Talk about double trouble," Caleb muttered. The good news—they were Human. The bad—one had dragged the witch up on deck and currently held a gun to the girl's head. That's when he caught the hint of sparkling glitter behind the man with the weapon.

"Better late than never," he called out.

The two thugs exchanged glances and one growled in very bad English, "We are the late never, not you."

Caleb didn't bother to explain or understand the broken English. He charged the unarmed gorilla while the invisible fae wrestled with the goon holding the pistol. Of course, *unarmed* was a relative term when his opponent's biceps were as big as the werewolf's thighs. He partially shifted, shredding his clothes in the process, and went after the guy with teeth and claws.

The witch managed to jerk away and she crouched below the wheelhouse, out of the way. Ariel materialized so he could use his sword. The silver blade flashed beneath the sun, temporarily blinding his adversary.

"Do you want one alive for questions?"

Caleb glanced over at Ari's conversational tone and smirked. "No. The witch can tell us."

"As you wish." Ari made slashing motions that looked suspiciously like the letter Z and his guy sank to his knees before slowly toppling over to faceplant in his own blood.

A moment later, Caleb raked one hand across his punk's throat. He stepped back before blood spurted. His half of the double trouble landed in a heap beside his twin.

He and Ari turned to gaze at the witch. She stared up at them, her eyes huge, skin pasty white. Then color slowly crept back into her face. "Werewolf?" Caleb nodded. "Fae?" Ari nodded. She gazed skyward. "Was there a gargoyle too?"

"He'll be along shortly," Ari said. He gave her a courtly bow. "I am Ariel, in service to King Oberon. My friend here is Caleb Jones. He is with the American FBI."

Caleb gave her a quick nod, currently more interested in the man Ari had brought down. He used a foot to turn the thug over onto his back then stared at the fae. "Seriously?"

Ari gave him a haughty look. "What?"

"You've been watching those Zorro movies again."

"I have, yes. I admire that Catherine Zeta Jones." Ari's eyes lit up. "Is she perhaps a relation?"

Caleb, shifting back to Human, did a face palm and returned his focus to the witch. His shirt was in tatters but his trousers were mostly intact. "Are you up to explaining?"

She sank onto the gunnel, her eyes still wide as she gazed around the deck. "So much blood. I will have to sell my canal boat. There's not enough salt in all of France to scrub it clean." She looked up at Caleb when he cleared his throat. "No reflection on you, Mr. Jones. Thank you both for coming to my rescue." Her soft English accent was melodic.

"Our pleasure, miss." Ari continued his gallant act.

Caleb took a long look at the young woman. Mid-twenties. Even features with high cheek bones, upturned nose and full lips with slightly tilted eyes that gave her an elfin appeal. He wouldn't be surprised if there *was* some elfin blood mixed in there somewhere. It would help account for the magic. That she had some was obvious. She fairly reeked of the spell she'd been casting.

"Can we dock?"

The girl glanced around and looked surprised. "Oh dear. Yes. Of course. A moment!" She pushed off the gunnel and dashed up to the wheelhouse. She deftly maneuvered the barge to one of the few open places along the river walk. Caleb leaped off and caught the mooring rope Ari tossed him. He secured the boat's bow then headed toward the stern to tie it off.

Back on board, he waited for the girl to climb down. "I'm afraid we won't be allowed to stay here long. This isn't a public space and I have mooring back up the river."

"We can stay long enough to figure out what's going on," Caleb assured.

"Oh, of course. Well, where do I begin the tale?" She settled herself on the raised area built to give higher ceilings in the living space down below.

"The beginning is always a good start," Caleb suggested.

"*That* story would take more time than we have allotted. I shall begin with yesterday when those two...ruffians climbed on board and took me prisoner."

"Did they hurt you?"

Ariel's gruff interruption seemed to surprise her and she took a moment before answering. "Not really. Not physically. They needed me in one piece to work their spell, but they were quite horrible verbally in their insistence I work for them."

"What spell did they want you to cast?" Caleb held his impatience at bay.

"Oh, yes. Of course. You'd rather need that information, wouldn't you? A location spell."

Caleb waited a few moments but when she didn't continue, he nudged. "Who or what?"

"Beg pardon?"

"Who or what were they searching for?"

"Oh, silly me. They were looking for someone. A woman. I think. They didn't say but the strands of hair they gave me to use in the spell were long. I suppose they might belong to a man..." Her voice trailed off as she eyed Ariel's longer locks. "No, longer than yours. And almost black."

Caleb stiffened. "Why float down the Seine while working the spell?"

"That's simple. The closer I am to the original source, the easier it is to locate. They told me that whoever it was would be found near both the river and Notre Dame. They cast my boat off. The twins stayed with me while the third—"

"Third?" Caleb asked sharply. "There was no third person."

"In the wheelhouse. She was steering."

"She?"

"Yes. A woman. Older. Short gray hair. I can't tell you much more than that."

"Was she Human?"

"Ye—" She paused mid-word, considering. "Actually, I'm not sure. The gruesome twosome were very obviously Human. The person—and now you have me wondering if it was a female—up top felt..." She closed her eyes and crossed her arms over her chest. Her hands absently rubbed her biceps. "It didn't feel quite...right," she finally said. "A simulacrum? Is that even possible?" Her voice came out a whisper, speaking to herself rather than her audience.

Caleb and Ari exchanged a look. Before either of them could speak or the witch continue, the sound of leathery wings arrested their attention. Roman hovered over the boat for a moment then back-winged to a soft landing on top of the barge.

"Sade remains with Crevan and Verity is deep within the archives and protected," the gargoyle said.

Caleb nodded then asked, "Why did you take off like that?"

"I sensed something not...right."

The witch opened her eyes and they widened as she stared at the very large creature standing very close. "Simulacrum," she whispered.

Roman's eyes widened as he stared back. "Yes."

She shuddered. "It takes one very powerful to work such magic."

"Could you?" Caleb asked.

Shaking her head adamantly, the witch denied the ability. "No. One, dark magic. Two, I am strong but to have wrought that...abomination?" She shuddered. "I would have to work death magic to create such a thing and there are lines I refuse to cross." Gone was the slightly befuddled English miss. This witch knew her own mind and her powers.

Caleb glanced from Ari to Roman then back to the fae. "Could you?"

"No. Glamour myself to appear as someone else? Certainly. Any of us could. But a true simulacrum? The witch is correct. That takes magic far blacker than even the worst of us will stoop to."

"This is Human magic," Roman rumbled. "Wizard or Witch."

"Or Sorcerer," the witch murmured as she cast frightened eyes on the gargoyle.

Chapter Eight

Something Wicked This Way Comes

The witch had very little further to reveal. The three Magicks helped clean up the bodies then left her to right the rest of the boat and return to its original mooring. Caleb and Roman stood on the riverwalk watching her steer the craft around the end of L'île Saint-Louis to begin her trek back upriver.

In a shower of glitter, the fae appeared in front of them. Ariel dusted off his hands in an exaggerated manner. "Right then. I've dealt with the trash."

Caleb rolled his eyes up while maintaining an expression otherwise devoid of emotion. Roman let out a small snort.

Glancing around and noting the barge chugging away, Ari smiled. "This could almost be the lead-in to a joke. A fae, a werewolf, and a gargoyle meet on a barge in the middle of the Seine."

"Nothing to be laughing about," Caleb growled.

"Of course there is. My life has been far too boring and mundane lately. I drop by Sade's hoping to find some entertainment only to discover a very grumpy vampire and the note she left him stating she was—" The fae made air quotes. "—called into a case and flying off to gay Paree. Without him."

The werewolf and the gargoyle exchanged glances. "And I suppose you just had to rag on Sinjen about it?" Caleb ignored the headache forming behind his eyes.

"Of course I did!" Ari all but chortled. "It's almost as much fun to tweak his fangs as it is that damnable dragon's tail."

Now it was Roman's turn to roll his eyes skyward, and say with lack of expression, "You may be sorry you got involved."

"Why?"

"Because we're hunting the damnable dragon," Roman pronounced, his voice full or rocks and gravel.

Ari backed up a step. "Does he know?"

"He who?" Caleb asked.

"Either one of them."

"Yes and probably," the werewolf replied when Roman didn't. "You're an idiot, Ari."

The fae, for once in his mostly immortal life, wisely remained silent.

The three Magicks lined up in front of the two women. Sade glanced at Verity. The little witch shrugged while biting her lips to keep from smiling. Sade didn't manage to hide her smirk. Gargoyle. Fae. Werewolf. Roman. Ariel. Caleb. She didn't know whether to kiss them or kill them. She huffed out a disgusted breath.

"Roman is yours, Verity. You deal with him."

The gargoyle looked affronted. "My mate does not *deal* with me."

"Oh?" Verity stood a little straighter. "You smell of Witch magic that isn't mine."

"Yes." A slow smile cracked the stony facade of Roman's face. "Are you jealous?"

"Oh puh-lease. We'll discuss your *magical infidelity* later. Right now, we need to figure out—"

"No," Sade interrupted. "You two need to go back to New Orleans. Caleb and I will deal with this."

"What about me?" Ari piped up.

"There's absolutely no reason for you to be here." Sade was adamant.

"But there definitely is. I can help."

"Stir up trouble," Caleb muttered.

"I heard that, fuzzball."

"Boys!" Sade snarled.

"He's right." Roman's quiet rumble grated along Sade's last nerve. "We all need to be here. You will need our help before all is said and done, Sade. We don't know what the dragon is up to. Who tried to use the witch against us? Not Nikos. Dragons do not truck with Human magic."

"And he wouldn't hire Human thugs," Ari pointed out.

Sade sighed. "I have a bad feeling about this."

"What else is new?" Caleb asked no one in particular.

Giving her partner the side eye, Sade moved to the window and stared out at a barge moving slowly along the Seine. "Did the witch explain why they wanted her to cast a locater spell?"

"No. But they provided her with some of your hair." Caleb stared at Sade. "I want to know how they got hold of it."

"You and me both. It's not like I go to a hairdresser. Maybe they bribed a maid to clean my hairbrush or something."

Verity wrinkled her nose. "*Ick*. But that's like...dead hair. A witch would have to be very proficient to cast a location spell using it."

Sade rolled her eyes. "Well, I haven't been in any cat fights lately so no bitch has tried to snatch me bald." Movement down in the garden caught her attention. Speaking of cat fights... A sleek black shadow sauntered across a patch of sunshine. "Roman? Do the Sentinels keep black cats around?"

The gargoyle joined her at the window, his gaze immediately focusing on the furry critter. "Not that I'm aware of."

Verity slipped under his arm and stood on tiptoes to look out. "Oh, what a beauty. I wonder if he's bonded with anyone."

"You don't need a familiar," Roman grumbled.

She patted his chest with a dainty hand. "Of course not. I have you."

Ariel, having just taken a drink of wine, choked. Caleb pounded on his back, smirking as the fae sputtered.

The cat leaped up on a garden plinth, sat, and blinked large yellow eyes at Sade. She blinked back, at which point, the cat lifted a paw, licked it and began to groom himself.

"Sade?" Caleb appeared beside her, his cell phone in his hand.

"Hmmm?" The cat had her mesmerized.

"We have a problem."

"Yeah?"

"Dead body."

"Okay."

"Burned beyond recognition."

"So?"

He snapped his fingers in front of her face. "Sade!"

She turned her head and snapped, "What!"

"Burned body."

"I heard you the first time."

"Interpol says it was dragon fire."

"Well, shit."

"That would be my sentiment," Ari agreed.

She whirled and stabbed a finger at the fae. "You stay out of this."

"Too late, darling Sade. I'm here and involved." He flashed her an impish smile. "Need I remind you of the witch's rescue?"

"Need I remind you that the perps are dead and their boss escaped?"

The three Magicks exchanged glances that almost admitted their guilt.

"It's not as if they gave us any choice," Ari grumbled, not willing to throw Caleb under the bus.

"I was diverted by the simulacrum." Roman continued to stare at the cat in the garden. "I am...disturbed that I could not track it."

Sade released a frustrated breath. "Yeah, if a Gargoyle Sentinel couldn't track the gawddamned thing, I'm not sure what could." She turned from the window and squared her shoulders. "All righty then. Caleb, let's go check out this body. Roman, you stick with Verity and check out the Human connection. There's got to be some magical muckity-muck who'd know about the simulacrum." She stabbed a finger at Ari. "You go back to whatever rock you crawled out from and stay out of this."

The cheeky fae just grinned at her before turning to glitter and disappearing. Caleb sneezed violently. Verity grumbled something under her breath as she watched the dancing motes of faerie dust settle onto the antique carpet. Sade closed her eyes and gave a little shake of her head.

She walked out into the soft Paris sunshine, Caleb at her side. "Where is this body?"

"Tuileries Garden, about six blocks from the Arc de Triomphe."

"Cab, then." Sade gave an exaggerated shudder to indicate her dislike of Paris cab drivers.

They quickly paced through the grounds of the Notre Dame complex and hailed a cab on the Rue de la Cité. In French, Sade gave directions. In English, the driver said, "You want we go fast?" Then he pressed the gas pedal to the floor and zipped into traffic.

Dodging cars, buses, and pedestrians, the cabby kept up a stream of French curses punctuated by descriptions, in English, of the historic sites they passed. As an added bonus, he drove them past the Arc de Triomphe before bullying his way back to their destination. He pulled to the curb on Quai François Mitterrand, ignoring the plethora of police cars blocking the street.

Caleb offered cash to the cabby, who grinned at him. "You very fine Americans in Paris will need a ride back. I will wait. I am Francoise and I will be your driver, *oui*?"

Sade stepped out and already had her badge and ID ready for the gendarme charging their direction. He halted as she flashed her credentials.

"Yes. Please. This way. We have been waiting for you." He then aimed a barrage of French at the cabby who smirked in reply.

Sade pointed a thumb back in the cab's direction. "He's our driver. He stays."

The Paris cop led them to a set of stairs leading down to the riverwalk and left, probably to stand and exchange glowers with the cab driver. Sade and Caleb trudged down the stone steps and found a knot of gendarmes and plain clothes DGSI agents waiting for them.

"You are the American FBI Magick?" a uniformed man wearing officer brass asked as they approached.

Sade offered her hand. "Supervisory Agent Sade Marquis, MAGIC Unit. My colleague, Special Agent Caleb Jones."

The officer led the way to the body—what was left of it. It was tucked between the massive stone retaining wall and a short concrete bench that faced the river. The corpse appeared Human. Caleb crouched down near the body's head and inhaled deeply. His actions upset the police commander standing next to Sade.

"Werewolf," she explained, though doubted that would make the man feel any better. Movement caught her eye. A black cat perched on a stone sill about fifteen feet away. Two deep-set and grated windows were built into the wall. Another concrete bench sat between them. The cat, as still as a statue, watched with wide yellow eyes. Sade stared. There was no possible way that was the same cat from the gardens in Notre Dame. Yet there was a similar white patch on the cat's chest and the damn thing stared back at her with accusatory eyes.

"Human," Caleb announced, pushing to his feet. "Remains and magic."

The policeman sighed dramatically. "*Oui*. I was afraid of this." Then he blinked as Caleb's words sank in and he focused on the werewolf. "The magic is Human? Not Dragon?"

Sade went on alert. "What made you think it was a dragon?"

"We received a call from Interpol. They said there was a body, incinerated by dragon fire. That we needed to secure the scene until the American FBI could get there."

She gave Caleb a shifty-eyed glance before returning her gaze to the officer. "Who is your contact at Interpol?"

"Dietrich Berger."

Taken aback, Sade blurted, "Your Interpol contact is a German?"

The officer offered the typical shrug in response. "It is the way of Interpol."

"Uh huh." She wasn't convinced, and since it was still daylight, she needed to find out who'd contacted Caleb. Jean-Louis, being a vampire, would still be down for the count.

"You are positive it is not Dragon in origin?" The officer turned pleading eyes on Caleb.

"I'm sure. It's Human all around."

Sade interrupted the officer before he could whine again. "My partner has the best magical nose in the Bureau. Trust me. If he says the magic is Human based, it is." She looked at the body but directed her question to Caleb. "Can you tell gender?"

"Female."

"The magic hers or external?"

It was Caleb's turn to offer up the Werewolf version of the Gallic shrug. That meant he knew but didn't want to say in front of their audience. She was about to turn the scene back over to the French when the cat leaped to the ground and stalked over. All the Humans froze, fascinated by the animal. Tail stiff, it leaned in to sniff at the body's feet.

"Hey!" Sade shouted. "Scat!"

The cat relaxed back on its haunches and blinked up at her. She half expected it to open its mouth and speak. It didn't. "Caleb?" she whispered, not breaking eye contact with the cat.

"Magic," he agreed, his voice also low. "No clue which."

Every person there continued staring at the cat. Minutes passed but eventually, it stood, and with a flip of its tail, sauntered off.

"What was that?" a gendarme asked, his voice a bit shaky.

"No clue," Sade admitted. "But yeah, it freaked me out too."

She tilted her head back toward the steps leading to the street above, indicating it was time to move on. She held out a hand to the French officer in charge. "We've seen what we need to. It wasn't the dragon so this isn't our case." Ignoring Caleb's attempt to step on her foot, she continued. "If you need us for anything, Jean-Louis Durand is our Interpol liaison, or you can contact *Le Vieil*."

"The leader of the Sentinels?"

"Yes. Crevan will have Roman find us."

The man looked awestruck. "Mademoiselle Marquis, you keep very august company."

"Agent. I'm not a mademoiselle. And yeah, I guess I do."

She walked away, Caleb trailing after her. She could feel the French cops' stares zeroing in on the middle of her back until they hit the stone steps and started climbing. Out of sight, out of mind.

Chapter Nine

Making Sense

True to his word, Francoise's cab sat next to the curb, snuggled in between a police car and van. Sade and Caleb got into the back seat and the driver hurtled out into traffic before turning around to talk.

"You have solved the crime?" At Sade's grimace, he grinned and faced the windshield again. "*Oui, oui*. The real crimes is not like on the television and movies. See, I am the..." He paused, maybe searching for an English word but came up with a French word even the Americans would understand. "I am the connoisseur of American crime dramas."

"Awesome," Caleb muttered under his breath.

Sade watched the passing scenery. "Uhm, Francoise? Do you know where you're going?"

"Ah *oui*."

"Mmmkay. You wanna tell *us* where you're going, seeing as we're along for the ride?"

"Of course. You, Agent Sade, are going to the Interpol." He caught her gaze in the rear-view mirror. "And he," he jerked his thumb over his shoulder in Caleb's direction, "Is going back to Notre Dame to report to *Le Vieil* and the Legate. But first, you need the food so we go to find the food."

Sade exchanged a long look with Caleb then asked, "Just what are you, Francoise?"

"I am only Human." He slammed on the brakes and a stream of colorful French curses came out so fast, Sade couldn't translate them all. Moments later, Francoise goosed the gas pedal and he continued his mad dodge through traffic. He caught her eyes in the mirror again. "But I am also the connoisseur of *les magiques*." He tapped the side of his nose with his index finger—the universal sign for "I know this secret."

They ended up at a small cafe tucked back on a quiet street off the main tourist drags. The food was amazing, the atmosphere quiet and intimate enough for a low-voiced conversation. Their accommodating driver disappeared into the kitchen before they were even seated. Now, their plates cleared away and glasses of wine—at the insistence of the maitre'd—refilled, Caleb posited his idea.

"According to the witch, the third person was female. Roman veered off just as I caught up to the boat. I'm guessing he sensed whoever was piloting the simulacrum."

"So you're sure it was a simulacrum and not..." She searched for a word. "A replicant?"

"A what?"

"A thing that magic makes look Human when it's animated." She sighed. "Yes, I have no idea what I'm talking about but I like that idea better than some asshole burning up the life force of an innocent bystander to make and control his simulacrum." She took a sip of wine and wrinkled her nose. "Are you sure that body wasn't torched by dragon fire?"

"Yup. Human magic caused it to burn."

"Could you—"

"No." Caleb cut her off. "There was a bunch of stuff mixed in and I couldn't get an absolute fix on the actual spell." He hated to admit that and it wasn't just his ego over having one of the best noses in the Werewolf nation when it came to sniffing out magic.

"Will you recognize the user again?"

"Probably. There was something under the spell. Something..." He closed his eyes and his nose wrinkled and twitched as he searched through the lingering scents in his memory. He grabbed his glass and downed all the wine in it. "Foul."

The maitre'd let out a sharp hiss. Neither of them had noticed him coming up to their table.

"Not the wine," Sade hastily explained. "The wine is excellent. That's why he gulped it down."

Only slightly appeased, man stared down at them rather officiously. "You speak of burned bodies?"

Sade and Caleb exchanged a glance. "Why?" she asked.

"I know of several in the past few days. The police, they seem baffled. You say now that these deaths are caused by magic?"

"Maybe," Caleb offered cautiously.

"Ah *oui*." The pompous man pulled up a chair and sat with them. "I now understand the reason why Francoise brought you here."

"And here I thought it was because of the delicious food," Sade murmured just loud enough for the man to hear. That brought a fleeting smile to his lips.

"The first, it was a dog. A very large stray that hung around the neighborhood. We all fed him. Marcel, the florist, he found the poor animal behind his shop, stuffed into a delivery box."

"Did you report it?"

"*Non*. It looked like the thing died and someone tried to burn the body."

"Okay..." Sade pondered a moment. "Then what?"

"An old woman. She lived above the bookstore on the corner. The pompiers—" He paused to look at them.

Sade waved a hand for him to continue and explained to Caleb under her breath. "Firefighters."

"The pompiers, they came, and they put out the fire in the apartment. The old woman was there, on a rug in the parlor. Her body was completely burned."

"There's more?"

"*Oui*. A bargeman, tied up along the Seine not far from here. And a delivery driver. In his truck."

"All near here?" Caleb asked.

"*Oui*. All nearby in this quarter."

Francoise sauntered out of the kitchen, a pastry covered in powdered sugar in his hand. He took a big bite and chewed happily. "I can show you these places," he announced. "You," he pointed the pastry at Caleb, "can do the things with the nose."

"When did these other deaths occur?" Sade pressed.

"Within the week."

"And the bodies?"

"With the police."

"Even the dog?"

The maitre'd looked slightly guilty. "Non. He is buried in my garden."

Caleb caught her eye and nodded. "We'll do the flower shop and bookstore and then hit the garden. That should give me something solid to compare to the one this morning."

Three hours later, they were no closer to a suspect. Caleb had confirmed the use of Human magic and that there remained a trace of the conjurer, but no solid leads. Francoise's cab rolled to a stop at the gates to the Interpol office. Caleb promised to call if Roman had any news. She climbed out and waited on the sidewalk as the cab darted through traffic until it was out of sight.

She had some time to kill before Jean-Louis awoke from the day sleep and reported for duty. That was the problem with Vampires. They maintained odd hours. She glanced at her watch. Speaking of...was it too early—or too late to call Sinjen. She asked the gate guard. He told her to Google it. She did. She'd have to set an alarm and get up extra early to catch him.

As she cleared the gate, Sade caught a streak of black dashing beneath a bush. Just a glimpse from the corner of her eye. Was that...? *Naw*, she decided. Besides, it wasn't like black cats were rare. Not in Paris. Not anywhere.

While waiting for Jean-Louis to wake and arrive, she went through some of Interpol's files and got one of the computer geeks to call up the police files on the burning deaths. She wondered why no one reported the dog in light of the other deaths. She was engrossed in reading when the vampire leaned over her shoulder.

"You are interested in these..." His face scrunched into a frown. "What do your American firemen call them? Ah, *oui*." He snapped his fingers. "Ze crispy critters. But these were all from dragon fire."

Sade curled her lips between her teeth and closed her eyes, taking a moment to find some patience. "How do you know?"

He backed up as she pushed back from the desk. "Because that is what the report says, that the fire was so hot it had to be from the dragon."

"Did you have a werewolf on scene?"

The vampire blinked at her, his mouth slack but not quite hanging open. "No. Of course not."

"Uh huh. Well, trust me. None of these bodies were burned by a dragon."

Jean-Louis turned the tables on her, or so he thought. "How do you know?'

"I know because I have a Werewolf partner. And I know that dragon fire has a certain..." She snapped her fingers in mimicry of his earlier gesture. "*Je ne sais quoi.*"

Something a little feral glinted in the recesses of the vampire's eyes. Sade didn't blink. She stood and pushed deeper into his personal space. "I'm not stupid, Lieutenant Durand. And I'm not untrained. There's a reason I'm in charge of the FBI's MAGIC Unit."

Jean-Louis looked unimpressed. She dismissed him by turning around and gathering up the files spread across the desk she'd commandeered. She stacked them neatly and turned to the computer geek who was pretending to pay no attention. "Thanks for your assistance. I have what I need now." She glanced at Jean-Louis. "I'll be in touch if I need any assistance from you."

She walked out, leaving geek and vampire both speechless. Dark had fallen but she checked the lawn and shrubbery for eye shine. None. She strolled through the security gate and was not surprised when a cab rolled to a smooth stop in front of her. Settling into the backseat, she said, "My hotel, Francoise."

"Of course, Mademo—" He cleared his throat and finished a bit lamely. "Agent Sade."

He chattered in-between cursing other drivers. Though her thoughts were elsewhere, Sade listened with half an ear and watched his animated face and gestures via the rear-view mirror. When he stopped on Boulevard Saint-Michel at the head of Rue de la Huchette. Sade passed over money and cocked her head. "You got any relatives in the States, Francoise?"

Accepting the fare with a big smile, he shook his head. "*Non*."

"Huh." Sade climbed out, slammed the door, and stood watching as he zoomed back into traffic. "If I didn't know better, I'd say you do." Because whenever she looked at Francoise? Alice Cooper, the Director's admin came to mind. Alice had a way of *knowing* things. Shaking off the feeling of déjà vu, she turned and headed toward the hotel.

Caleb stood in the small lobby, his cell phone to his ear. She halted in front of him.

"Okay. Keep me posted." He ended the call focused on Sade. "Food. Then we'll talk."

Without further discussion, they stepped outside and walked a few doors down to the hole-in-wall Greek place. They ordered and Caleb grabbed a small table in the back while Sade waited for their food—gyros and Greek salad with extra orders of pita bread and tzatziki sauce. They ate in silence for a few minutes, then Caleb leaned forward.

"The dragon isn't even here."

Sade almost choked on the swallow of water she was taking. "What the fuck?"

"He was here for about twelve hours a week ago. Then someone caught a glimpse of him right before we arrived. No one's seen him in three days. Speculation is that he's back in the Dragon Realm."

"I repeat, what the fuck?"

"No answer to that."

"Obviously, since you aren't calling me on the language." She speared a strip of gyro meat from her salad, took a bite and chewed as she mulled things over. "I got my hands on both Interpol and DCSI police files. All of the deaths were contributed to dragon fire."

"For sure?" Caleb tapped his nose for emphasis. "Beg to differ."

"Yeah. They all surmised it was dragon fire and they didn't look any further." She dipped a corner of pita bread in the sauce, bit and chewed. "None of this makes sense." She sipped her water, lost in thought. After a moment, she added, "I think there's another player in town."

Caleb paused in the middle of taking a bite of his gyro. "Roman and I came to the same conclusion."

"Any ideas on who?"

"Maybe the more important question is what."

Caleb had a point. Sade shoveled some salad into her mouth. "There are traces of Human magic all over this."

"Yup."

"But we still need to track down Nikos and talk to him. I want to know who he's pissed off."

Caleb coughed, then swallowed. "You mean besides all of us?"

Sade ignored him. "I know jack about Dragon politics."

"I'll second that. They're even more insular than the Fae."

"And what human is stupid enough to fuck with a dragon?"

That got a snort from her partner. "You mean besides you?"

"I don't fuck with him."

"No, you just drive him crazy."

"That's on him, not me."

The order line was all the way out on the street so they finished up, bussed their table and headed out. "You want dessert?" Caleb nodded to the ice cream shop on the other side of their hotel.

"Naw. I'm good." One of the reasons she loved the Hotel du Mont Blanc—okay *many* reasons—had to do with the plethora of food available. A bakery perched on the corner, several restaurants—including one that served up burgers and fries, a pub, a crepe place, and a cheese shop all lined up along the narrow pedestrian street.

"My brain wants to explode from all the crap I've crammed into it today. I want some sleep. We'll start on the human element tomorrow after coffee and pastries."

"Sounds like a plan."

They parted at their doorways. Sade knew Caleb would be calling home to touch base with Adele. It didn't matter what time of day or where in the world he was, he always called her before going to bed. Of course, it helped that Adele was Human and wasn't down for the count during daylight hours. She glanced at her watch, did some calculations. Was DC six hours ahead or behind Paris time? She'd forgotten already. She gave up and checked the clock app on her phone. It was almost 10 pm here in Paris, which was not quite 4:00 pm in DC. Sinjen wouldn't be up for a few more hours.

She yawned, deciding on a shower, and setting her alarm for an early start. She'd call him then. Except she didn't sleep. Nope. She had a case to crack and she'd do whatever it took to solve it.

Sinjen prowled Sade's apartment. Why was he still here? He didn't like Washington. He didn't feel comfortable in Sade's space without her. It was barely full dark and a long night stretched in front of him. He should just call the airport and arrange to fly back to Chicago. He prowled, knowing he'd have to go out soon and feed, a chore that did not excite him.

He forced himself to settle on the couch and pick up the television remote. He was about to click on the TV when his cell rang. Sade.

"Good morning."

"How do you know what time it is here?"

"Sade..."

"Oh, whatever. Anyway..."

She was hedging. He heard it in her voice. "Will you discuss your case?"

"You know I can't."

She could and had and they both knew it. "Why did you call?"

He could hear her breathing on the other end and reminded himself that he was a patient man.

"I just wanted to touch base," she finally said. "I mean, I did sort of duck out on you while you were...you know...down for the count."

She had and it made him angry, something she was doing more and more of lately—this ducking out thing *and* causing him to lose his temper. Sinjen struggled to keep his voice even when he asked, "When are you coming back?"

"I just need another week."

She was lying. He squashed the anger welling up inside him. He'd known exactly who and what Sade was from the moment he'd first laid eyes on her. She'd stalked into his life, with those snapping green eyes, stubborn jut of her chin, wearing her badge like a suit of armor. Still, she had fascinated him then, and continued to do so. She should have been like all the other human women who'd enticed him

71

through the long centuries of his life. What was the modern phrase? One and done? Yes. He'd meant to seduce her, enjoy her, and be done with her. He almost laughed at his foolishness.

Sade was a siren whose song he couldn't resist. He'd gotten involved in her case back then and continued to remain at her beck and call. Still, he was egotistical enough to want her to focus on him. He blinked. No. Not him, but *them*. As a couple. Maybe he was the fool Mathias called him. A relationship between a vampire and a human? Especially when that human was the agent in charge of the FBI's MAGIC Unit? She had assignments. He understood her job was important—not only to her, but to the entire Magick community. But she'd taken off without a word. Then she put off calling him for a few days. And that damnable dragon was at the root of it.

Jealous? Damn straight he was. And she was asking for another week. Away from him.

"Sinjen?" His name sounded uncertain when she said it.

He'd been quiet for too long as he considered the complexity of their relationship. Her anxiety was almost palpable even across the distance that separated them.

"Come home, Sade." It wasn't an order, it was a plea.

Silence stretched. Seconds ticked off like, each one swooping in to perch along the edge of perception until time became a murder of crows anticipating the eminent battle so they could feast upon the fallen. When she finally spoke, it wasn't what he needed to hear.

"I can't. I have a job to do."

He pinched the bridge of his nose and swallowed the swell of dark disappointment attempting to engulf him. "As I am well aware."

"What's that supposed to mean?" Her voice whiplashed through the phone's speaker.

"Exactly what I said. Do your job, Sade. Whatever it takes." *As you always do,* he thought. Then, before she could reply, he added,

"Good night." He stabbed his cell, ending the call, then turned off his phone. "Coward," he acknowledged out loud, but better that than freeing his hurt and saying something that could not be taken back.

Light from the full moon filtered through the blinds as he stared out the window of Sade's DC apartment. Sinjen considered going to her, knowing it would be a mistake, perhaps one fatal to their relationship. Or was it already too late?

Chapter Ten

Up in the Air

Sinjen stared out the window of the private jet. He'd called the charter company immediately and was now winging his way toward Paris. He would arrive in time to disembark and make his way to his Paris accommodations before dawn. He fought the urge to tap into Sade's mind. He wanted to reach out, to touch her. Just for an instant. Just to reassure himself that everything was fine. Except it wasn't. He knew that. A wall had formed between them. He hadn't put it there yet he didn't believe Sade was aware of what she did to stack layer upon layer of stone and bricks and mortar in an attempt to keep him out. Or maybe she did.

He'd known going in that she had scars that were not visible to the naked eye. She scratched at them, they scabbed over, she scratched, they scabbed, until they built thick enough to hold her feelings in and kept the world out.

He cursed Mathias. His sire had used Sade, marking her as a child, moving her across a political chessboard, nothing more than a pawn. Mathias and Oberon had marked the child and the woman now lived with the scars. Her anguished words still tore at his heart. *I would see her dead before relinquishing her and, therefore, the battle to Oberon.* She'd quoted Mathias's words to him, along with her observation—and his own. She'd come right out and said that the man she adored, the man she thought of as a father and who should protect her and keep her safe from all harm would have killed her like an unwanted puppy to keep from losing what amounted to a game played by two spoiled children—the Seelie King and the powerful master vampire. That knowledge left deep scars that only appeared to have healed because more than once, he'd seen the open wounds left on her psyche.

He would stay low key on this trip. Wouldn't approach her. There were those who would keep an eye on her for him. The idea of being apart from her ripped deeply on a level he didn't want to explore. He uttered a dry bark of laughter. Apparently, he carried his own scars that hovered too close to the surface for comfort. Sade would never know he was in Paris. When her case closed and she and Caleb returned to the US, he'd be back before them, with Sade none the wiser. That was the plan. He did his best to ignore the warning uttered by the poet Robert Burns regarding the best laid plans of mice and men.

The time advantage of flying in a chartered jet landed him at Paris Airport-Le Bourget well before sunrise. He cleared customs easily and as if on cue, a cab rolled to a stop in front of him. He settled into the backseat. "Do you never sleep, Francoise?"

The little cabby grinned over his shoulder. "Life is too exciting to spend in sleep, Monsieur Sinjen."

With Sade in town? Yes, Francoise had the right of it. "I can imagine," Sinjen muttered before the cabby launched into a report of all that Sade had been up to.

Over the years, Sinjen had considered selling his Paris apartments. He didn't travel to the continent as much as he once did and never stayed for any extended period. Still, this place held fond memories for him. He owned the upper two floors of this 17th century mansion. The Seine flowed past right across the street and Notre Dame was a bridge away. The Ile Saint-Louis had once been an enclave for the Knights Templar, back before the dark days and the treachery of kings and popes alike.

The rooms hadn't changed much—wide-planked oak floors mingled with marble. He'd had the place renovated. Each room contained its own fireplace but there was also central heat and air. The kitchen and every bath had been gutted and updated. The baths he appreciated, luxuriating in soaking tubs or huge shower stalls as the mood hit. The kitchen, not so much. It was a cook's kitchen. Or a caterer's. He was neither, though he knew of one Michelin five-star chef who never lost his love of cooking, though he now required blood for sustenance. The thought of Sade in that kitchen doing more than gulping coffee made him smile. Caleb had once teased Sade that her idea of a grilled cheese sandwich was a slice of cheese between two pieces of bread slathered in mayo and heated in a microwave. Sade had not denied the accusation.

After strolling through the apartment and dropping his suitcase off in the master suite, he returned to the large salon. A row of mullioned windows filled one wall. The windows faced southwest and presented a magnificent view. He stopped at one and gazed out at the Seine with its historic backdrop of the City of Lights. Paris could be an enchanted place and he wanted to share it with Sade. He wondered now if he'd get the chance. Things were...what was the modern phrase? Up in the air? Yes. Things between them were unsettled and he didn't like the feeling.

Dawn crept across the landscape on silent feet. He'd lost track of time standing there, staring as Paris slowly came back to life. Day sleep would soon take him. When he awoke, he hoped to have a clearer plan. Sade, enigma that she presented, was his Achilles' heel. Common sense and all the wisdom he had gained in his long years of existence dictated he walk away from her, the sooner the better. He closed his eyes, picturing her. So many mental photographs to choose from. His favorite remained her entrance at the Cook

County Jail though watching her climax was a close second. So was the peace her face finally showed once she fell asleep in his arms.

Sinjen suspected Sade's sleep was troubled when they were apart. When they parted, her eyes were clear and she looked rested. When next he saw her, lines bracketed her mouth and the green of her eyes looked dull. *No*, he decided. She didn't sleep well when they were apart. She had seen and done much in her short Human lifetime, much of which also left scars. His Sade was a warrior, her badge a shield, her weapon always readily at hand for battle. He knew the signs. Once upon a time, he'd been a warrior and like recognized like. Perhaps that was why she drew him. He would make no trite comparisons. No bees to honey, moths to flames, ants to a picnic. No. What drew him to her was so much more—a soul-deep yearning of two hearts, each one recognizing the other.

Lights flickered on across the river and roof-top shadows fled before the searching fingers of dawn. He stripped as he hit the security panel in the bedroom. Steel shutters slid across windows. Doors locked. Lights flickered off. Naked, he crawled into the massive bed with cream-colored Egyptian cotton sheets so soft they felt like silk. He pulled the duvet over him and prepared to surrender. As always, his last thought was of her. Of Sade. Of the woman he would sacrifice everything to save. His last breath escaped with the whispered words, "My Sade."

Chapter Eleven
Leathered and Laced

She needed coffee. And food. Sade showered and dressed, banged on Caleb's door and got a growl for an answer.

"I'm headed out for a big breakfast. You comin'?"

The door opened and a bleary-eyed Caleb joined her. "Coffee," he muttered.

"My sentiments exactly."

"Bad news," he eventually added once they were out on the street.

"What?"

"Command performance at the Embassy this morning."

"Oh. Goody." Her dry tone mirrored her lack of enthusiasm.

They ate at a restaurant catering to American tourists. The place was outrageously overpriced but they could get a full American breakfast there—eggs, ham, bacon, sausage, potatoes, and various breads. And coffee, which was decent tasting. Finally full and fully caffeinated, they caught the Metro to the American Embassy. The Marine just inside the front pedestrian gate gave them a salute. Sade nodded in return.

They checked in and were told to go up to the DSS office. The Diplomatic Security Service dealt with all sorts of foreign investigations in addition to actual security involving the embassy building, grounds, and staff. Sade and Caleb were shown into the office of the head Foreign Service National Investigator.

The man, in his late forties and starting to bald, glanced up. "Feebees," he muttered like he had a bad taste in his mouth.

"Fizzny," Sade replied with a slight chin tuck.

"Marquis and Jones."

"Abrams."

"Long time no see."

"Coulda been longer."

"No shit." The FSNI leaned back in his desk chair. "Heard you two were in town." He grinned at Sade. "Something about a dragon?"

She ignored the dig. "Not your jurisdiction, Abrams. Why'd you request the command performance?"

The investigator sobered. "We've had some tourists go missing."

"Not *our* jurisdiction."

Abrams pushed a file across his desk. Caleb leaned closer to snag it. He opened it, read, glanced up at their DSS counterpart. He passed it to Sade without a word. She flipped through the reports, stopped. She looked up, one eyebrow raised. "Burned body?"

"Yes. The one you and Jones examined yesterday. She was American."

"So...this sorta is our jurisdiction."

Abrams nodded smugly. "That would be an affirmative."

She opened her mouth to respond but her phone rang. She glanced at the screen and grimaced. "The Director. I have to take this." She left the file on the desk and exited the office as she answered, "Sir?"

Ten minutes later, Caleb met her out in the hallway. He carried a shopping bag. "The Old Man?" he asked.

"Told us to cooperate with Abrams." She glanced at the bag. "There's some sort of Magick component to the other missing women?"

"Maybe."

"Fine. Let's get out of here and you can fill me in when there are no ears."

"Are you kidding me?" Eyes widened in horror, Sade stared at the skimpy dress made of sequin-encrusted latex.

Caleb just managed to keep his expression bland but had to look at his partner through half-lowered lids so she couldn't see the twinkling mirth he was sure danced in their depths.

"Orders straight from the Old Man, as you well know." He ducked his head and bit his lips, fighting for control until he could look at her and not give away what he held behind his back.

"What?" Her eyes narrowed in suspicion. "What aren't you telling me?"

A pair of shoes dangled from his index finger. Made of transparent plastic embedded with fake emeralds, the stilettos measured over four inches tall.

"Stripper heels? What the actual hell? No freaking way, Caleb."

"Hey, I'm not the one who volunteered us for undercover work. That's all on the Director."

"But not at Tricks-n-Dicks." Sade held up the dress. "*Un*covered is more like it."

"Four American women have gone missing in the last month. And according to Abrams, other foreign nationals disappeared too. Some came on a work visa, others just seemed to disappear off the street."

"What? Their work visas were for a strip club? I thought there was a prohibition on sex workers."

"Yeah...not exactly. And it's not just the Americans, though that's why we're involved. Some English, Spanish, and a couple of Greeks, all over the past three months. They told friends or family that they'd been invited to a club for a dance contest." Caleb glanced at the shoes and studied them intently before continuing. "There's something else. We traced one of the club's owners. It's...Nikos Constantine."

Blood drained from her face and she wanted to sink into a chair, head between her knees to keep from hyperventilating. "Oh, hell. Just shoot me now."

To say Sade was uncomfortable was an understatement. To say she'd kill her partner and tell the gods he died was not an exaggeration. She stared at her reflection in a grimy mirror surrounded by round light bulbs.

"Caleb?" She kept her voice so sweet a bee would OD listening to her.

His hesitant voice whispered through the earpiece. "Yeah?"

"You do realize I'm only wearing a leather bustier and lace thong."

"Uhm...."

"And here I thought the Spandex dress and the stripper heels were bad."

"Uhm..."

"Care to explain what the holyshitfaced motherfucking gawddamned hell is going on? I'm repeating myself here. You said Abrams said *under*cover, Caleb. Not all but naked."

"Uhm...yeah. About that, Sade. See, here's the thing..."

"You're—"

A man entered the dressing room without knocking, causing Sade to cut her sentence off.

"You will come with me."

Knees together, she reminded herself, swiveling on the stool. She gave the guy an appraising look. Cold eyes, blank face, tats staring at her from every piece of skin showing except his face. He could be a Russian hitman for all she knew.

"Yeah, I don't think so. You're not my type."

"You do not have a choice in this matter. Your number is up. Come." He snagged her arm and marched her from the room. They reached a stage, the curtain drawn. Another man grabbed her and the two shoved her into a gilded cage and locked the gate. They reached in, grabbed her hands and forced them into cuffs, then did the same to her ankles. The curtain parted as someone announced, "Lot number thirteen, a Human female."

Shit. She was in so much trouble. Once she got out of it, Caleb was dead meat. "Caleb?" she murmured and got only a squeal of feedback in her ear. Something in the cage had cut off all channels of communication.

"Where is she?" Sinjen's demand whipped through the phone line.

"Not your business, St. John." Caleb sounded bored. Or hoped he did. He'd lost contact with Sade but he wasn't about to tell her vampire lover. Who would likely go slightly berserk if he knew where she was. Good thing Sinjen was 4,000 miles away.

"Do not test me, Jones. You are her partner. Where is she?"

"Back off, dude. She's undercover."

"I am aware of that fact."

He was? How did he know? Caleb continued to bluff. "Then you know she can't contact you."

"I can't reach her."

"D'uh. That's what undercover and out of contact means."

"You do not understand, Wolf. I cannot *reach* her. Neither can Mathias."

Caleb actually backed up a couple of steps even though Sinjen wasn't in the room so there was no need to put space between them.

"Wait. You *marked* her?" He didn't know whether to be pissed or unsurprised. But if Mathias couldn't tap into Sade's location, something was terribly wrong. And why had Mathias tried to do the whole Vampire mind-meld thing to talk to Sade anyway?

"She's undercover, St. John. At a club called Nude Coolant." There was no sound from the vampire. Caleb swallowed hard. "That's French for something." He glanced at his notebook then spelled it out.

"The place is Noeud Coulant," Sinjen growled, pronouncing it *New COH-lawn*. "The English translation is Slip Knot."

Coughing softly over his awful accent, Caleb added, "It's a...Well, it's an underground club that caters to a very specific clientele."

"I know what the club is, Jones. What is Sade doing there?"

"I told you. She went undercover. Some humans invited there for some kind of dance contest went missing."

"Fool. Do you know what goes on in the back rooms of Slip Knot?"

The menace in Sinjen's voice sent shivers careening along Caleb's spine. "What do you mean?"

"It is a BDSM club, you idiot, and you sent Sade in there unprepared."

"Oh shit." He had to pull Sade out immediately. She was going to kick his ass nine ways from Sunday.

Sinjen uttered a quiet curse as he looked at his phone. "It is too late. There is an auction tonight."

Caleb didn't breathe for a moment, his entire body going cold. "What do you mean *auction*?"

"The owners take untried humans and auction them off to the highest bidder as slaves."

"Slaves..."

"Yes, Caleb. As BDSM slaves. Not all of them survive their Magick masters."

"Oh, crap." Caleb refused to hyperventilate. He heard movement on the other end of the line—silk brushing against leather. "I'll go get her."

"Do not bother. I am already here. I will deal with it."

The implication of what else the master vampire would deal with hung in the dead air as Sinjen ended the call. Caleb was fucked if something happened to Sade. If Sinjen didn't kill him, Mathias would.

Sade just thought the fucking stilettos were uncomfortable. She was trussed up like a damn Christmas goose. The bustier was laced so tight she had trouble breathing. The ball gag in her mouth didn't help things either. That had been strapped on her the moment she started cussing. Her tits weren't large but they spilled out over the top, just like her butt cheeks did at the bottom. The lace thong irritated her skin even more than the leather cuffs buckled around her wrists and ankles, holding her spread-eagled inside the cage. The damn thing spun around slowly giving every pervert in the joint a good look at her.

The auctioneer, in heavily accented French, began to speak. He described Sade as "inexperienced." "A fine physical specimen." "In need of a firm hand."

Whoa. Wait a minute. She stared at the auctioneer. What did he mean by that?

"We will start the bidding at—"

"One hundred thousand American," a deep, Eastern European voice shouted.

The bidding came so fast and furious Sade lost track. Until a very familiar voice called out, "One million."

Silence descended on the room. Sade managed to catch a glimpse of the tall shadow in the far corner. She would recognize that silhouette anywhere. Relief warred with humiliation. What was he doing here? More importantly, where would he come up with a million dollars?

The Eastern European yelled out, "One million—"

"Two million." Sinjen cut him off.

Sade gaped—inside at least. Hard to do so physically with the damn gag in her mouth. The curtain began to fall, cutting her off from the audience. Right before it hit the stage, a warbling voice called out, "Two million and one dollars."

The two Russian mafia types had her unbuckled and jerked out of the cage in mere seconds. Before she could react, they'd thrown a hood over her head, handcuffed her hands in front of her, and hustled her away. When she dragged her feet and stumbled every other step, one of them simply put his shoulder in her solar plexus and tossed her over it. She bounced with each trotting step.

Beyond the curtain, pandemonium erupted. She heard Sinjen yelling. And Caleb. Finally. It was about damn time her fucking partner showed up. A third familiar voice was raised in argument. Nikos. Fighting with Sinjen and Caleb. Oh shit.

Her guards tossed her onto something semi-soft. She heard them scurry out but didn't detect the sound of a lock. She jerked off the hood as she stood and headed for the door. She was two steps away when it flew open and she had to jump back to avoid being hit in the face by it.

Sade stared at the bantam-sized man standing in the doorway. He didn't appear dangerous. She stood a foot taller, despite the pointy hat covered in shiny stars perched atop his head. The dude looked like a cartoon wizard. She'd learned first-hand that Wizards shouldn't be trifled with, no matter what they looked like. Though, in her experience, none of them wore swirling robes covered in glitter.

He flicked his wrist then his fingers drew sigils in the air. His beady eyes bore into hers. "You will come with me."

She sucked in her cheeks, biting the insides to keep from laughing out loud. "Yeah...no."

The little caricature fumed and she expected to see smoke seeping from his ears. He traced more symbols in the space between them. "You must obey me."

"Yeah...not happenin'."

His puzzled expression morphed into a bitter beer face. "This cannot be. You *must* obey me."

"Yeah? How come?"

"Because I am your master."

"Seriously?"

"Yes. I paid good money for you."

"Ah. Well, about that. You are aware of the old adage, buyer beware?" At his glare, Sade added, "And the one about no refunds?"

A stream of gibberish erupted from his mouth and she could almost see the letters forming little skyrockets between them. Okay, little dude did have some magic. Good thing she was immune. Mostly. Too late, she saw the chasm open at her feet. She pitched forward into darkness. The wizard's cackling voice drifted down.

"You forgot the one about the last laugh."

Sinjen strode down the hall, shoulder-to-shoulder with Caleb. They paused at every door, smashing through them, surveying each room. At each empty space, the atmosphere turned more frigid. They'd been delayed from following Sade after the curtain came down. The thugs the club called security converged on them. Then that infernal dragon appeared. Sinjen could admit that Constantine looked flummoxed by Sade's presence on the stage, not to mention the auction event that had been underway.

He tried a door and when it didn't open, he kicked it. The door slammed against the wall. The room was empty. Sinjen's frustration bubbled over. "Where is she?"

Caleb stepped back as Sinjen's power surged. "I don't know." He hated to make that admission. He'd gotten Sade into this mess and he deserved the vampire's scorn. Sade's disappearance was all on him.

Magic swelled as a tall, impeccably dressed man appeared at the other end of the long corridor. Constantine and his games were partly responsible for this disaster. Sinjen acknowledged that had he not risen to the dragon's bait, Sade would now be safe in his arms instead of missing. He called to his rival. "The others are all empty?"

"Yes, gods be damned."

Nikos looked as perplexed—and angry—as Sinjen felt. He turned to the werewolf who was not only Sade's partner but her brother, in all ways that mattered but for shared blood. Caleb's ability to sniff out magic was legendary. "What does your nose tell you?"

Red feral lights flashed through Caleb's eyes. "Nothing." The word was barely recognizable beneath the growl.

"What do you mean *nothing*?" Nikos demanded.

"Just that. Nothing. No Sade. No magic. Just...nothingness."

Vampire and dragon exchanged looks. "Caleb, call Roman," Sinjen ordered. "The Sentinels need to be aware of this."

"What can the Gargoyles do that we cannot?" Smoke curled around the dragon's words.

"They can track her until I rescue her." And he would, Sinjen vowed, or die trying.

Chapter Twelve

Marco Polo

Sade blinked but nothing happened. Where was she? Her stomach clenched and a bout of nausea hit. She rolled to hands and knees, retching. At least her stomach was empty but the dry heaves sucked. Big time. What the fuck had happened? Her brain was as dark and blank as the space around her. She sat back and considered.

Paris. She and Caleb were in Paris. Had she been dumped in the catacombs? No. Even the catacombs had lights due to the tourists. A case. Bodies. Burned. Missing. Embassy. Her memory jumped forward. The nightclub. Slip Knot. Or something like that. Only in French. Holy shit! She patted her body. How was she not freezing? A fucking leather bustier and a lace thong. She'd been...she hit hands and knees again to retch. Auction. She'd been handcuffed spread-eagled in a gilded cage and put on auction. Untried. Untrained. Human female. Fuck her. Fuck them and them who brung 'em. As soon as she figured out where the hell she was and got out, she'd go hunting. Things blurred in her mind and then she remembered a cartoon character in a pointed hat that was covered in stars. And waking up here.

The gawddamned motherfucking Wizard dude had sent her through a fucking portal. Oh to the hell no! She pushed to her feet and froze as her head swam. There was no point of reference from which she could get her bearings. The darkness was absolute. Her stomach roiled again.

"Breathe," she reminded her lungs. She'd never been a good portal hopper. Travel through realms and other dimensions left her shaky and sick to her stomach. "Nice and slow." She breathed. "Caleb will be looking for me. And Roman."

She ignored the other two names that popped into her head. Nope. Not going there. With her luck, they'd killed each other while she was being dumped in whatever cesspool of a realm this was.

With caution, she reached out a hand. Nothing. Hand still extended, she turned a slow circle. Still nothing. All righty then. She hunkered down and felt along the floor. It felt like stone. Smooth, warm rather than cool. She plopped her butt down. If she blundered off into the pitch black, there was no telling what could happen. Her best bet was to sit right here on her ass and wait. It wouldn't be the first time Roman had come to rescue her from some unknown realm.

Caleb watched Verity, clamping down on his anxiety. "You're sure?"

"Yes. I have a lock." The witch glanced at her Gargoyle mate. "If we link, can you pinpoint her location and send Caleb?"

Roman shook his head. "I'll go." He was still upset that he'd been unable to locate her. Hiding her from his Sentinel abilities should have been impossible. They'd had to rely on Verity to produce a spell to find her.

"No!" Verity and Caleb denied him in unison.

"I need you here to anchor them, love," she told Roman.

"It doesn't—"

"The spell, Roman. I know you can hop in and out and transport but the spell...it's all cobbled together and so very wonky. I need you to anchor me. Send Caleb. I..." She inhaled deeply. "Caleb has to go. I don't know why but I feel it in my bones."

Roman cupped her cheek, looking deeply into her eyes. After a long perusal, he dipped his chin in one brief nod then kissed her forehead. "As you wish."

Caleb straightened. "What do I have to do?"

Verity pointed to a pentacle on the floor. Drawn in coarse sea salt, it shone snowy white against the dark granite of the floor. "Stand in the middle."

He did as she indicated. Standing tall, he held his breath as the incantation started.

"Focus on Sade," Roman reminded him.

And then he was tumbling through swirls of gray smoke. He sensed rather than saw that a solid surface was rushing toward him, or vice versa. Using every ability, he oriented his body and when his feet hit, he softened his knees so that he went to the floor and rolled.

"Who's there!" Not a question, a demand.

"Just me, Sade."

"Caleb?"

"Yeah?"

"How the hell...?"

"Later. Where are you?" He reached out a hand and then, with a laugh, called, "Marco."

"Polo," Sade answered immediately.

They repeated the children's game until he found her and grabbed hold. They both pretended she wasn't shaking. And that she wasn't mostly naked. Caleb stripped out of his jacket and draped it over her shoulders. She slipped her arms through the sleeves and zipped it up to her chin.

"Look on the bright side," Caleb quipped. "At least we found each other." He continued probing the darkness with every sense available to him.

Sade snorted, the sound both inelegant and pithy. "I'm getting damn tired of this whole Fox and Mulder routine." She shifted slightly but didn't lose contact with him. "Any clue about where we are?"

"Nope."

"Big help you are. Can you see anything?"

"Nope."

"I thought you could see in the dark."

"Hey, the last time you decided to fall through a portal, Roman fished you out. I'm a werewolf, Sade. I don't have magic like a gargoyle or a fae. Verity told me to stand in the middle of a pentacle she drew on the floor with salt and I did. Roman is supposed to get us out. If he can't, maybe Ariel can find us." He gave her a sidelong look when he realized the darkness seemed to be lightening. "Or Nikos. Dragons can shift realms too."

"Do *not* mention that gawddamned critter's name to me." She fumed, wanting to pace out her frustration, but in the pitch black of whatever hell they'd landed in, doing so would not only be foolish but could be dangerous.

"He tried to help," Caleb muttered, hating to admit it. "There at the club."

Sade stilled. She'd really hoped that she'd imagined his voice. "He was there?"

"Uh, yeah."

"He. Saw. Me?" She spaced out the words, horror filling her. "In this get-up?"

Caleb wisely did not mention the fact that Sinjen had been there as well, bidding on her. That might get him dead. By somebody's hand. It probably wouldn't matter whether Sade's or the vampire's. He'd still be dead.

"Well...sort of." He quickly changed the subject. "Somebody will find us eventually."

"Oh really? At least we aren't like...truly undercover and off the grid."

"True. We do have a gargoyle, a witch, and probably, by now anyway, a fae tracking us." He almost mentioned Sinjen but again snapped his mouth closed before betraying the vampire's presence in Paris. They'd parted at the club, Sinjen going off with Francoise.

Which kind of pissed Caleb off. "They'll come looking if Verity's spell failed and Roman couldn't hold the anchor."

"And they'll find us how?" Sade clenched her fists, growling. "Verity used a locater spell, right? Which was focused on me. Portal, remember? We don't even know which fuckin' realm we're in."

A soft chuckle echoed around them, the sound rich, dark, decadent—like dark chocolate wrapped around a caramel truffle. And Sade recognized it immediately. She punched Caleb's biceps and hissed, "I *told* you not to mention his gawddamned name!"

The air lit with dragon fire and a huge silver creature reared above them. Gold flecks glistened in coal-black walls hewn out of obsidian. They should have been burned crispy but Dragon magic was weird like that. And Nikolas Constantine, Drakon of Clan Kholikikos, had Dragon magic in spades. Not to mention he was a major pain in her ass. She inhaled deeply and pushed out a massive sigh.

"Oh, hi, Nikos," Sade called with forced nonchalance in her voice. "Don't mind us. We were just leaving."

"And how do you plan on doing that?" the dragon rumbled.

"Good question." She muttered under her breath, not that it mattered. The damn Magicks—especially the shifter types—had phenomenal hearing. Like being magic and mostly immortal didn't give them enough of an advantage.

"And do you have the answer, my darling Sade?"

The damn dragon was just toying with her now. "Asshole."

Caleb ducked his head where his forehead met the palm he'd raised. "He can hear you."

"D'uh."

"He's in dragon form."

"D'uh."

"Sade, you do remember the old saying, right?" When she only tucked her chin in order to glower down her nose at him, Caleb continued. "Be kind to dragons, for thou art crunchy when roasted and taste good with ketchup."

She snorted out a choked laugh. "Where the hell did you hear that?"

The tips of the werewolf's ears reddened. "I read it in a book," he mumbled.

Dragon fire flickered above their heads. "I like that quote," Nikos said. "What kind of book?"

Continuing to mumble, his face flushed now, Caleb added, "A romance novel. Del was reading it."

Sade managed to ignore the rolling laughter sheathed in fire and slow blinked at Caleb. "You read a romance novel." She spoke slowly, enunciating each word.

"No. I looked over Del's shoulder and read a paragraph."

Nikos lowered his head and his huge silvery-blue eyes glittered as he watched Sade. "When I eat you, Sade, it won't be with ketchup."

She punched him in the nose and the dragon jerked backwards, tripped over his tail and crashed to his rump. By the time he got his bearings, Sade stood feet apart, arms extended, Beretta resting in the firing position in both hands. "You have a dirty mind, Nikos. The last time I checked, guns worked in in the Dragon Realm. I might not be able to kill your sorry ass, but I can sure mess you up at this range. Now cut that sexy shit out and get Caleb and me out of here."

Caleb had no idea how Sade managed to hang onto her weapon, or where she'd hidden it. He'd seen her in that outfit too. He glanced over at the dragon.

Nikos resembled a contented cat—if that cat was from Cheshire. "As you wish, Lady Sade."

"Cut that shit out!"

Chapter Thirteen

Technically Speaking

Sinjen stewed all the way back to Notre Dame. As if sensing his need for silence, Francoise muttered his traffic imprecations under his breath. When they arrived at the cathedral, the little human parked his cab along the street and got out with Sinjen. The vampire wasn't in the mood the argue.

He strode down the hallway toward the rooms set aside for Roman and Verity. The cabby stayed hard on his heels. Sinjen fully intended to get to the bottom of things.

A cloud of gold glitter formed and Ariel appeared. He pressed back against the wall as Sinjen stormed passed, then fell in behind. Tabor popped his head out of a doorway, saw who was coming and ducked back inside. Good. The man might be a gargoyle but he was all about the formalities. Sinjen didn't have the time nor the inclination to deal with a paper pusher. Turning a corner, he came face-to-face with Varrick. Now *this* gargoyle was a force to be reckoned with.

"Ah, you are back. Good. Verity has news." Varrick peered around him and down at the human. "A new friend?"

"No. An old one," Sinjen replied, quickening his steps. By now, Francoise was huffing and puffing in his wake and muttering something about needing wine.

Just as Sinjen pushed open the door to Roman's quarters, his ears popped. In a puff of smoke, Caleb appeared. In a second puff, the damn dragon appeared, holding Sade—a Sade wearing very little beyond Caleb's jacket—in his arms.

She squirmed and struggled against his hold. "Cut that shit out, Nikos. I mean it. Put. Me. Down. Now. You motherfuckin'—"

"Sade!" Three male voices cut through her tirade, in unison. Only Ariel, who looked amused, and Francoise, who appeared stunned, remained silent.

Then the little Frenchman breathed, "*Sacre bleu.*"

"Yes, that! Exactly. Damn it, Nikos, put me the fuck down."

Laughing, the dragon dropped her legs so that she had to slide down his long, lean body. The jacket rode up, exposing her very delectable rear. Fae and human males looked far too interested. Gargoyles and werewolf studied their boots. As soon as her feet hit the floor, she shoved Nikos. Surprise skittered across his expression as she rocked him back.

"Sade..." Sinjen couldn't keep the warning growl out of his voice.

She froze and her back went stiff. Very slowly, she turned around to face him. She blinked, her jaw going slack and her mouth opening. She snapped it shut, blinked again and narrowed her eyes as they opened.

"What are you doing here?" Like she didn't know, but offense being the best defense and all that.

He stared. She stared back. He moved toward her as the dragon stepped in her direction. Nikos was intercepted by Roman. A second later, Nikos disappeared in a puff of smoke. The infernal lizard couldn't be trusted. For a fleeting moment, Sinjen wondered if Constantine had engineered this whole fiasco. He clamped down on that thought. He'd read the emotion on the dragon's face. His fury at seeing Sade trussed up in that cage was palpable. He also had not been pleased to discover that Humans had been auctioned off in his club.

Verity murmured under her breath. "Got him."

All eyes turned to her, which almost broke the stalemate between Sade and Sinjen.

"You tagged him?" Roman asked.

"Of course I did. Now I can track him." Eyes twinkling, the witch grinned up at her mate. Then she focused on Sade. "And if you don't behave, I'm going to tag you too."

"The hell you—"

"Sade!" Roman all but roared. "These are my quarters. On sacred property. You *will* watch your language."

"Jeez," she muttered to the floor. She raised her eyes to Sinjen. "What are you doing here?"

"You were missing."

"No I wasn't. Technically speaking, Caleb knew I was in the club."

"Did you have radio contact with Caleb?" Sinjen pressed. He'd gleaned that at least from the werewolf.

"Uhm..." Technically speaking, she hadn't."

"Even Mathias tried to reach you."

She did another slow blink. "Mathias?"

"Yes."

"But...why?"

"I do not know. I did not ask. I was a bit preoccupied trying to find you."

"What happened?" Varrick stepped into the conversation.

Sade explained about the undercover idea, only discovering too late that it wasn't a try-out for dancers but an actual human trafficking auction. "I will nail Nikos's hide to the wall for that."

"I think there will be others who are skinned before him," Caleb said. "He was one angry dragon."

Sade tilted her head. "You *were* there." She shook an accusatory finger at Sinjen. "And you! I didn't dream that." She looked abashed as she added, "And you bid on me. Two. Million. Dollars."

She rubbed her temples but the gesture did little to alleviate the headache. It did give her a moment to think. "Okay. If you, Caleb, and Nikos weren't a dream, that means the creepy wizard dude was real."

"Creepy wizard dude?"

Sade nodded in answer to Caleb's question. "About yay high." She held her hand, palm down and parallel to the floor just below her breasts. "Dark blue robe, with little glittery stars. And a wizard's hat. One of the pointy ones. With big stars. He said he owned me, that he'd bought me. And then...boom."

"Boom?" Ari arched a brow.

"Well, not literally. He drew sigils in the air and eventually, a portal opened and I dropped into nothing. It was dark and then Caleb showed up."

"It was pitch black," Caleb agreed. "I could smell her but could see nothing."

A giggle burbled out of Sade's mouth before she could stop it. "Marco," she said.

"Polo," Caleb replied with a smile. "Once we connected, it was only a matter of minutes before the dragon showed up."

"In dragon form," Sade added. Her eyes widened again. "Oh, fuck, were we in his lair? With his hoard? Shitdamnfuck. He may want to kill us now."

No one corrected her language. Knowing the location of a dragon's lair and hoard could be tantamount to suicide. Verity finally spoke up. "I have a general idea because I sent Caleb there but Nikos is the one who brought you two back. I don't think it will be a problem. Probably." She returned her attention to Sade. "As for you, you need to eat. To drink way more water. And get some sleep that's real sleep not some magic-induced coma thingy."

A little color returned to Sade's face. "Some magic-induced coma thingy. Is that a technical term?"

"Shut up." Verity rolled her eyes and pushed to stand up. "And just so y'all know, I don't think Nikos has anything to do with what's going on." She raised her chin as Roman and Caleb studied her. She squared off against them, holding up one finger. "First, this is all Human magic." She added a second finger. "Two, dragons don't truck with Human magic." Another finger went up. "Three, why would he bring Sade and Caleb right back here?" She turned her attention to Roman. "You were anchoring Caleb. Nikos followed that link and my spell directly here. He didn't have to. He's a dragon. He could have dropped them off anywhere. Heck, he could have killed them right there. No one would have been able to do a thing about that." She held out her whole hand, palm out in a halt-right-there gesture. "I didn't know *where* they were. I had locks on Nikos and Sade. Caleb dropped in between them. I didn't know it was the Dragon Realm. It could have been the North Pole for all I knew. If he's guilty, why would he expose himself?"

"Because he's a crafty wanker?" Ari asked unhelpfully. "Think about it. If one is in fact guilty, would it not make sense to act innocent to throw off suspicion?"

"It's not him," Sade said. She ignored Sinjen's growl of protest. "Verity is right. The bodies that were allegedly burned by dragon fire? Human magic only." She looked to Caleb, who nodded in agreement.

"I do want to ask him why he called you at that particular moment in DC, though." Caleb looked adamant.

"That makes two of us." Her stomach chose that moment to growl.

Francoise, whom everyone had forgotten, appeared beside Sinjen. "Come. I take you two to fine place to dine. *Allons-y.*"

"*Oui*," Sinjen said, taking Sade's hands and pulling her to her feet. "Let us go."

Chapter Fourteen

Think Twice

Sinjen left her long before dawn. Her rooms at the Hotel Mont Blanc filled with sunshine during the day and there was no way to sun-proof the space. He hadn't suggested she go with him to wherever he was staying. In fact, he hadn't awakened her at all, not even with a goodbye kiss. She'd pretended to be asleep. Francoise had managed to scare up fresh bread, wine, and cheese during the drive back to her hotel. Though there were plenty of late-night cafes, Sinjen insisted that they return to her rooms. The fact Sade wore only that bustier and Caleb's jacket might have had something to do with that demand. The little Frenchman left them to walk the half-block to the hotel, promising to be available should either need. Sade briefly wondered if the cabby had been parked out on the street, waiting for Sinjen to leave.

After he forced her to eat, Sinjen made love to her. Gently. Sweetly. Then he sipped from her, taking not much more than a taste of her blood. He'd held her afterward, murmuring in her ear until she'd dropped into sleep. Evidently, the brief time asleep had helped revive her flagging energy because the moment Sinjen left her bed, she'd awakened. And remembered that some of those whispers in the dark insinuated that he would leave her before dawn, that her rooms were not suitable for his day sleep. She understood his reticence but she'd also mumbled a question asking why he hadn't taken her to his place. She couldn't remember his answer after she fell asleep. Then he was up and gone. And he hadn't kissed her.

Unable to go back to sleep, she'd tossed and turned. Dawn was a bad dream away and she was restless. She always needed to replenish her energy after Sinjen drank from her, even if he was sparing in his thirst. She needed food and coffee but didn't want company. Feeling disgruntled and out of sorts, Sade slipped a note under Caleb's door. She didn't want to face her partner this morning. He'd take one look at her, recognize the sleepless night, and smell the lies she'd try to feed him to cover. To avoid that, she'd lied in her note, stating she was off for breakfast—which she was, and then she planned on meeting with the local police regarding the nightclub. Noeud Coulant. Slip Knot. Except she liked what Caleb called it better, especially given the outfit they'd forced her into. Nude Coolant. If she ever retired from the FBI, she'd open a cop bar and call it that.

Pushing through the hotel's door, the scents of Paris waking up assailed her nose. She hitched her backpack on one shoulder and followed the most prevalent—and delicious—fragrance to the bakery on the end of the block. Fresh bread. Fresh pastries. Fresh coffee. She grabbed a bag of hot croissants and a to-go cup of cafe au lait.

Strolling toward the Seine, she sipped her coffee and munched on a still-warm croissant. The sun was a couple of hours from fully showing its face so few people were out. As she crossed the bridge to the Île de la Cité, the sounds of feet pounding in rhythm reached her ears. A group in formation, wearing identical running suits passed her—probably the current class at the police academy, which was located just ahead of her. Pausing, she leaned against the bridge rampart, withdrew another croissant and ate while watching a cargo barge slowly drift down river, its lights casting a moon-like glow on the water.

She jerked at the sound of screeching tires and turned in time to see a sleek Peugeot sedan jerk to a stop in front of her. Jean-Louis's face appeared as the passenger-side window slithered down.

"Sade," he called. "I have found you. You must come."

"Come where?"

"Get in the car. We must hurry."

"Not going anywhere until you tell me what's going on."

"Sunrise is not far away and you have a train to catch."

"I do?"

"*Oui*. We have word of the dragon's whereabouts. If you want to catch him, you much catch the early train."

Ignoring both the irritation and the stab of intuition that cut through it, Sade got in the car. She didn't even have the door closed before the vampire zoomed away into traffic. "Where am I going?"

"At least to Lyon if not all the way to Geneva. He is one the train just before you. There is a ticket for you."

Sade pulled out her phone to text Caleb. The car swerved and her phone and coffee cup went flying. "What the hell?" She held onto her temper with scrabbling fingernails, figuratively speaking. She favored Jean-Louis with a glower. He offered his patented shrug in return.

"I think you will make it."

"You *think*? Color me not impressed—or encouraged." Sade didn't bother hiding the bite of sarcasm in her voice.

"It is not like we can control things like the train schedule."

"You're Interpol. You could have the train stopped and the Drakon removed."

"You are FBI. How much control can an agent assert over *les magiques*?"

"Okay. Good point."

The sleek car whipped around a corner. "Are you sure you want to pursue this particular Magick?"

Sade rolled her eyes. "Do I have a choice?"

The vampire considered his answer far longer that he should have. "I suppose not, given the circumstances." He slapped a fist to his heart, glanced at her, then focused back on the street and the traffic that was now getting congested as they neared the Gare De Lyon Paris train station. He finally glanced her way again. "What is your fascination with this dragon?"

She snorted. "It's not fascination on my part."

"Then what is it? You are quite dogged in your pursuit of him and this case."

"It's a matter of self-preservation." She studied the Interpol agent. "And it's a matter of truth and justice. Besides, your people are the ones who requested my assistance."

"You think he is guilty." Jean-Louis's flat voice insinuated he believed Sade had already made up her mind about guilt or innocence, because she was Human and the dragon was a powerful Magick.

"You think you know everything."

"I don't?"

"Dude, you don't have a fucking clue."

The car slammed to a stop in the loading zone in front of the station. Sade grabbed her backpack and scrambled around searching for her phone.

"You do not have time. You can buy a new one at the first stop or something. I will find your cell phone and keep it for your return." The passenger door was jerked open and a uniformed gendarme grabbed her arm.

Sade jumped out and found herself being hustled inside by the officer. As they dashed for the entrance, she yelled over her shoulder, "Tell Caleb I'll see him on the other side."

With an armed escort, she cleared whatever tape—red or otherwise—that was involved in getting her ticket, getting on the train with her weapon, and getting settled in her seat. The train pulled out and she watched the sun rise from the outskirts of Paris. When a food trolley came trundling down the aisle, she almost kissed the man pushing it. The scent of coffee hit her nose. After a bit of haggling, he left her the carafe and one cup. She might survive this trip after all.

Caleb paced the confines of the sitting room. Verity wisely stayed out of his way. And Roman's. The gargoyle's wings kept flaring out.

"Try her again," Roman ordered.

"I just did," Caleb snarled between gritted teeth. "It says the number is out of range."

Roman snatched Verity's phone from the table before she could grab it. He stabbed numbers onto the face, held it to his ear and got, "This number is not in service."

Six hours. Sade had been missing for six hours. All they had to go on was the note she'd left under Caleb's door. "Long night. Taking a walk to clear my head. Then going to Paris cops to check records on that club. See you at Notre Dame later."

How long was *later*? Caleb was furious with her. The walls were thick at the Mont Blanc but he was a werewolf. He'd heard her and Sinjen. And he'd heard Sinjen leave.

Sinjen.

The vampire would go off the rails when he found out she was missing again, so there'd be no telling him. And that meant Sade had to be back before sundown. The cops at DGSI insisted she had not arrived at any of their stations. And there is no way on God's green earth that Sade would just be wandering the streets of Paris in a snit for. Six. Hours!

A sharp tap on the door had all their heads turning as it opened and Tabor Sheva, the Second Sentinel and Crevan's left hand, walked in. "We have looked at all the pertinent CCTV feeds. She bought food and drink at Boulangerie Saint Michel—"

"That's the bakery just up the way from our hotel," Caleb interrupted."

"It is, yes. And then she strolled out to Place Saint Michel and walked to the bridge. She never made it to the other side."

Everyone exchanged uneasy glances but it was Roman who asked, "What about the camera on the bridge?"

"Yes. Well, about that." Tabor hemmed. Hawed. He wouldn't meet Roman's gaze as he added, "That particular camera went offline the moment Agent Marquis stepped on the bridge."

The door opened further and Varrick stuck his head in. He'd taken Roman's place as First Sentinel when Roman became the Legate of New Orleans. "Any of you know the human named Francoise?"

Caleb's gaze whipped to him. "Cab driver?"

"Yes, and one claiming that he has been hired by you and Sade for the duration."

"What about him?"

"He is downstairs and insists he knows what happened to her."

Before the room exploded, the tubby little Frenchman ducked around Varrick and made soothing motions with his hands.

"Did you take her somewhere?" Caleb demanded.

"*Non*, Monsieur Caleb. I was fast asleep in my bed."

"Then how—"

Francoise held up his hands to stave off Caleb's interrogation. "When I heard Mademoiselle Sade was—" He paused and leveled a look of pure disappointment at Caleb. "Missing—again—I began my own search for her. There are many people to contact and it has taken me all of these many hours to find the one who saw her this morning."

Verity was the one to urge him to continue. "What did you discover?"

"My friend, knowing I was her driver, thought to stop to offer his assistance but alas, he was not fast enough to reach her first. The traffic you see. Another car, it stopped. The driver and Mademoiselle, they spoke. Then she got into the car and they drove off."

"When was this?" Roman asked.

"Just a bit before sunrise, which is surprising given the driver who picked her up was a vampire."

"Sinjen?" Verity said the name softly.

"No." Francoise's denial came swiftly. "This vampire, he drove a very new and very expensive Peugeot. He is the same one who says he is with Interpol."

"Did your friend follow them?" Caleb had difficulty keeping his voice level, when he wanted so badly to snarl.

"*Oui*. He drove her to Gare de Lyon."

"The train station?" This time it was Varrick who interrupted.

"*Oui*. She was met there by a gendarme and they hurried into the station."

Verity asked what everyone was thinking. "Why would she go there?"

"To catch a train," Francoise replied. "To Lyon, or perhaps to Geneva."

"Why?" This from all the men.

"Because the rumor is that the dragon is there."

"Who is this guy?" Roman asked under his breath.

"Human but he knows a great deal about the Magick community in Paris." Caleb replied in the same *sotto voce* tone.

Varrick had a cell phone to his ear, giving orders to whoever was on the other end. When finished, he explained. "Two Sentinels will cover the train station in Lyon and more in Geneva."

"We're four hours too late," Roman muttered, figuring up the travel time. He turned to the woman he loved with all his heart—except for the portion that belonged to Sade. "Verity—"

"I can do another location spell. And if that doesn't work, I'll try a seeking spell." She offered a little smile that didn't reach her eyes.

"If I have to do that one, I'll be down for the count for probably twenty-four hours." She'd worked hard on learning her magic since discovering she was a witch. She was powerful but still inexperienced. Working deep or complicated magic sapped her strength.

"What do you need?" It was Tabor who asked.

"I'll get you a list." She sat at the table and drew a notebook from the canvas bag she used as a purse. She started jotting notes.

A very solemn group of men huddled in the far corner of the large work room, giving Verity space. Seven hours had passed. Her first spell had failed. Tabor then scurried around procuring more things for more spells. At one point, Francoise reappeared. He brought bread, cheese, coffees, and a leather satchel that he solemnly handed to Verity. She'd taken it and, for a brief moment, perked up after looking inside.

"We have to do something," Ariel said. "Can we call someone else in to do this?"

"No!" Verity snapped her head up and glowered at the men.

Undaunted, Ariel pushed. "It's been hours. Your location spells didn't work. Why not let another—"

"Because I'm the one casting it, that's why!"

Werewolf and gargoyle made soothing motions with their hands while backing away from Verity. Steam all but shot from the little witch's ears. The fae cast a baleful glare toward the gargoyle. "She's your mate, Roman. Can't you do something?"

Leathery wings exploded from Roman's back. "And you, Ariel Daoine, are sometimes too stupid to remain living. As you carry the title of the King's Seducer, I would have thought Oberon might

GHOSTS & THE ANCIENT STONES

choose a fae with more brains, though I suppose that is not the part of your anatomy important to your occupation."

A nimbus of glitter glistened around Ariel but Caleb stepped between the two Magicks. "You do remember that Sade is missing? And if we don't get her back before Sinjen gets here..." He deliberately trailed off the sentence, leaving the consequences up to Gargoyle and Fae imaginations.

Ari puffed up but stopped glowing. "I am not afraid of the vampire."

Werewolf and gargoyle exchanged a look that easily translated to "Fae arrogance."

Roman pointed a finger at Ari. "But you should take heed of the werewolf's words."

Caleb snarled, punctuating the gargoyle's advice.

"Why not just ask the infernal dragon?" Ari whined.

Making a slow survey of the room, Caleb growled, "Do you see the bloody dragon standing here?"

"Obviously not. Why not go find him?"

Roman closed his eyes, struggling for patience. "What do you think we are doing?"

Ari looked perplexed. "Verity is casting a seeking spell to find Sade."

"I am," she snapped. "Plus locate Nikos and then I have to conjure a returning spell to get Sade back." She didn't add that she was exhausted, and scared she wasn't skilled enough to do all that needed doing.

Ari saw the circles under her eyes, realized why, and surrendered. "Shutting up now."

"Where is Sade?"

The three-word question, asked in a calm, collected, and almost mild voice, all but exploded in the room, especially given the silence that followed.

All eyes turned to the dark, dangerous, and very pissed off vampire standing in the doorway.

Oh. Shit. Sinjen was in the building.

Chapter Fifteen

If Wishes Were Horses

Sinjen stared first at the gargoyle. He ignored the fae as his attention centered on Caleb. "I asked you a question. And it is becoming a question I tire of asking."

The werewolf met his gaze unblinking, though his guilty expression gave his true feelings away.

"We don't know." Verity stepped forward. "I'm in the middle of locating her..." She glowered at all the men standing around. "If I could have a little peace and quiet. With no interruptions." She bit out the words.

Every man there stared at his feet, working hard not to show their thoughts, though they all had the same one—she was like an angry kitten. All hiss and fluffed fur but with tiny claws that might hurt. Maybe.

Tabor and Varrick moved toward the door. Sinjen obligingly moved out of their way. The two gargoyles departed but the door remained open, Sinjen's obvious invitation for the others to step out into the hall to explain.

Ariel looked at Caleb and shrugged. "None of this is my fault. I'm not afraid of the great and powerful fanged one."

The werewolf grabbed the fae by the collar and frog-marched him out. Roman made a gesture indicating he would stay with Verity. Which didn't work.

"Out!" the little witch commanded. "*All* of you!"

Roman preceded Sinjen, who paused. In a very quiet and formal voice, he said, "I thank you, Mistress Montagne, for your assistance. Should I ever be in a position to reciprocate, please do not hesitate to ask." He offered a small bow in her direction.

Verity stared back at him, bemused. Then she blinked and nodded, realizing that Sinjen had just placed himself in her debt. That was a very heady place to be considering he was a master vampire. She almost waved his offer away but realized that would be an insult. Instead, she vowed, "We'll find her."

"Yes," he murmured. Then he stepped out and closed the heavy wooden door very softly behind him.

Tabor had disappeared but Varrick remained, standing shoulder to shoulder with Roman. The two gargoyles were flanked by Caleb and Ariel. Sinjen assumed a very casual pose, his back to the wall, shoulders braced against the stone, feet and arms crossed. "Which of you would care to explain this..." He paused as if searching for the right word. "To use one of Sade's favorite terms, this cluster fuck?"

There was some hemming and hawing and awkward clearing of throats. Ariel opened his mouth but snapped it shut with an audible whoosh of exhaled air when Roman elbowed him in the stomach.

"What did Sade tell you?" Caleb asked. "Ah, as expected," he added when Sinjen only raised one eyebrow.

"It's about a dragon," Ari piped up, his voice gleeful. He squeaked when Roman stomped on his foot.

"Constantine is involved deeper than just owning the nightclub."

The hair on the back of Caleb's neck raised at Sinjen's tone and the fact he'd made that a statement. "Maybe." He shrugged. "It's a long story."

"I have all night."

The five men stood in the hallway as Caleb explained the situation, their suppositions, and the current state of things. He didn't consider not sharing for a moment, and he also shared that Sade had come to the conclusion that Nikos Constantine was not involved, rather was being set up. He finished up with, "Can you reach her?"

"No. That is why I am here. I hoped the gargoyles had found her and a rescue was in progress."

Caleb was aware that Sinjen had marked Sade. He wasn't sure if the others knew. "Do you think Mathias can?" They all knew that Mathias had marked her as a baby. Sinjen gave him that death stare again.

The door to the room popped open and Verity stuck her head. "Still no Sade but I found her phone."

"How?"

"Where?"

The voices blended as the men crowded her. She held up one hand in a stop-right-there gesture. "I used the phone finder app. And it's at Interpol. I think. I looked up the address."

"Who is this Interpol vampire?" Sinjen asked.

"According to his ID, Lieutenant Jean-Louis Durand," Caleb said.

"I will deal with him." Sinjen turned to Verity. "Is there anything I can do to assist you?"

She shook her head. "Nope. I've got spells working on locating both her and Nikos, since no one has been able to contact him either."

Sinjen nodded and focused on Caleb. "You will keep me informed."

"I'm coming with—"

"No. I will handle the vampire. You will need to go to Sade as soon as she is found." With that, he turned on his heel and strode off. He picked up a human tail as he strode through the building.

"My cab is waiting. We will go to the Interpol."

Sinjen stopped abruptly and stared at the human. His voice slightly placating because he was done with Humans, he began, "Francoise—

"No." The little man interrupted. "She is gone because I decided to take a nap. I was not there and she got into the vampire's car instead of my cab. I have failed you." Francoise took off double-time, apparently unaware he'd surprised Sinjen.

Sinjen caught up to him almost immediately, his long stride twice the length of the cabby's. As promised, the cab awaited them on the street outside Notre Dame. The drive to Interpol was not made in silence, though Francoise directed no conversation his way. Sinjen almost smiled. The human's vocabulary was at least as...*colorful* as Sade's, except his was far more inventive. And in French.

The car screeched to a stop outside the gates and the Frenchman turned around. "I will await you here."

Sinjen inclined his head and exited. The guard at the gate took one look at him and started dialing numbers on the security phone. Sinjen passed the uniformed man without a glance. He pushed through the massive front doors and barely stopped at the main desk, only saying in passing, "Jean-Louis will see me."

No one attempted to stop him. He strode directly to Durand's office and was met at the door by the other vampire.

"Kristian St. John," Jean-Louis greeted. "To what do I owe the honor?" His unctuous voice all but oozed oily civility.

Sinjen didn't stop. He didn't slow down. He walked straight into the other man, grabbing him by the throat and forcing him backwards into the office. Sinjen kicked the door shut. No one in the outer area spoke or moved. Most of them were Human. They knew better than to get between two vampires.

With no inclination to be diplomatic, Sinjen lifted Jean-Louis off the floor by the hand still around the agent's neck.

"Where is she?"

Jean-Louis struggled to speak. "I...don't...know."

"You picked her up and put her on that train. Why?"

"Orders."

"Whose orders?"

"Don't know."

Sinjen stared into Jean-Louis's eyes. "Do you know who she is?"

"She is FBI."

"She is claimed by Mathias DeVrie."

Jean-Louis flailed but was unable to break Sinjen's hold. "No," he pleaded weakly.

"She was raised in his house. He marked her as an infant. And yet..." He perused the dangling and frantic vampire from head to toe and back. "You who are nothing set yourself up to see harm come to her?"

"No!" The protest was part cry of terror and part plea for mercy. "I had no choice."

"Who?" Sinjen asked again. "I will have a name or you will greet the sun this day."

Jean-Louis mumbled a name. It rang no bells in Sinjen's memory. He released his grip and stepped back. Jean-Louis crumpled on the floor. "Please," he begged. "Do not tell Mathias."

Unable to contain his contempt, Sinjen turned his back on the sniveling creature but paused when he glimpsed a cell phone in a familiar stainless-steel case. He snatched up Sade's phone, dropped it in his pocket, and strode out. None of the humans in the outer office had moved. Neither had the few Magicks. They remained statues as he exited. No one attempted to stop him from leaving. That was a good thing. There would be blood if they had.

His confrontation with Jean-Louis had been frustrating and mostly fruitless. Unable to lie to him, since he *was* a master vampire and Jean-Louis definitely wasn't, the Interpol lieutenant admitted that someone higher up had sent him to collect Sade and get her to the train station, but no reason for that order. Sinjen had that name now and would be doing his own investigation. Francoise said nothing as Sinjen slid into the backseat and took out his cell phone.

Sade hit something solid and had enough presence of mind to soften her knees, lean, and roll. She came up in a crouch, pistol in her hand. She had no clue where she'd landed but the place was pitch black. The darkness was suffocating, and both claustrophobia and vertigo hit. She closed her eyes, which didn't change a damn thing about her environment. But, she wasn't *supposed* to see light with her eyelids screwed shut so there was that. Was she back in Nikos's lair?

Heavy breathing filled the void and she held her breath. The sound stopped. *Oh,* she thought, and choked back a giggle, knowing it would spiral toward hysteria if she let it out. *She* was the one breathing hard. *D'uh.* She reached out a cautious hand, felt the space in front of her and then to each side. Nothing. She touched the surface beneath her. Hard but with a layer of...dust? Dirt? Hell, for all she knew, it could be fairy dust. That would be her luck. But at least this wasn't the same place as before.

It would help if she could remember how she got here, wherever the fuck *here* was. With utmost care, she twisted to feel behind her. More nothing. Common sense said sit still. Like getting lost in the woods, she should hug a tree and wait to get rescued. Except she wasn't in the damn woods and as queasy as her stomach felt, she'd likely gone through another fucking portal. Which totally sucked. She'd had enough of that growing up and during the Battle for the Realms while fighting the rogue gargoyles with Roman and his little witch, Verity.

The whole Scooby Gang had been there for that final clash, and it had taken them all to prevail. Had the battle occurred on the

Human plane, the devastation would have been monumental and she couldn't even comprehend what the death toll would have been. It was bad enough that parts of that war had spilled into Notre Dame and damaged the historic cathedral.

She hunkered down on her haunches and forced her brain to ignore the oppressive darkness. She needed to think but more importantly, she needed to remember. She closed her eyes, hoping her brain would realize they were in the dark because her eyes were closed.

Paris. She'd been in Paris. Caleb. With her partner. On a case. Early morning. Vampire. Not Sinjen. Though she'd been with him earlier. A different vampire. A car. A...train?

Yes! She'd gotten on a train to go find Nikos. Something happened on the train. Coffee. She'd gotten coffee from a trolley. Her phone. She patted her pockets. There was something about her...Jean-Louis. Interpol. She'd dropped her phone in his car and he'd told her to buy a new one at the station except there hadn't been time. Crap. Coffee. Her mouth filled with saliva and she tasted something...odd. Metallic. Poison? No. Magic? Oh hell yes.

She'd drunk her coffee and after swallowing the last drop, she'd been hurtled through a motherfucking portal. Her backpack. Where was her... She felt around. Her fingers brushed against leather. She scrabbled for the strap and hauled her pack to her. That was something at least.

Now, to figure out where in the vast hells of a hundred realms was she.

Something clicked. A light flickered over her head. The grating screech of grinding gears filled her ears. The floor started to move. What in the motherfucking hell? More lights flickered on. The floor sped up. Sade planted her butt and spread her legs in hopes that would help brace her. She wasn't moving in a straight line. Nope. She was going in a slow circle. Calliope music tinkled in the background.

More lights, flashing and dancing in time to the old-fashioned music. Figures emerged as they passed beneath the lights. A horse. White with a golden mane and tail, one front leg lifted and curled. A saddle and bridle, gaudy and gilded, adorned the animal. It rose and fell in time to the music. Carousel horse. The next figure was that of a dragon, glittering silver with wings outspread, also wearing a saddle painted red with a blue blanket embellished with symbols beneath it. A wolf flashed by, pitch black with glowing amber eyes, wearing a golden saddle. More horses followed. Up and down. Round and round.

She suddenly recognized the song and sang the words. "Here we go 'round the mulberry bush, the mulberry bush, the mulberry bush. Here we go 'round the mulberry bush, on a cold and frosty morning."

Sade clamped her mouth shut. *What the fuck?* Was she dreaming? Or had she truly been dumped through another portal. Bad enough she ended up in the Dragon Realm the first time. This place? She had no clue. It didn't feel Fae. Or Gargoyle. Not Dragon. Not...real. Was she caught in some weird dreamscape?

The carousel was completely illuminated now, lights sparkling and dancing. The music changed tempo. Sade groped for the nearest animal. A black charger, tall and muscled, and covered in fancy armor. She swung up into the saddle, ignoring the Cross of St. John on the horse's caparisons. She grabbed the reins and held on as the horse shifted beneath her. How did she know that the cloth draping the horse was called a caparison? And more importantly, how did she know the cross emblazoned across its hindquarters was a St. John's cross and not the Knights Templar cross?

"Dreaming," she muttered. "This can't be real."

So how did one go about waking up from a crazy-ass dream while basically caught in the Fae's Wild Hunt of a merry-go-round? She recognized the answer as it passed above her head.

"You catch the brass ring." *And make a wish.*

Sade's ears popped and she closed her eyes against the whirling kaleidoscope blinding her. She flexed her legs and waited to land. Colors and patterns gave way to thick fog. Figures moved through the gray haze. Her feet touched a solid surface but with little force this time. The shapes gained substance. Her gaze zeroed in on one face.

"Sinjen," she whispered.

"Where have you been for the past thirty-six hours?" Caleb demanded.

"I was on a—" She jerked back as his question hit home. "Thirty-six hours?" Sade looked around the room. Everyone nodded in turn as her gaze landed on each of them. "Thirty-six *hours*?" She stared around the room again then breathed out, "Oh, shit."

Sinjen, moving fast, caught her biceps as her knees gave out and she headed for a sit-down on the floor. Ariel was there almost as fast, dragging a chair with him. Sinjen maneuvered her onto the seat and he knelt in front of her.

Sade stared at him, green eyes wide. He studied her. Her skin was pale to the point it was almost translucent and the dark shadows beneath her eyes indicated lack of sleep. Her lips were dry, almost cracked. "You need food and drink," he declared. "And then sleep."

Verity appeared with a chilled bottle of water. She pressed it into Sade's hand. "Drink."

She did, which surprised Sinjen. And worried him.

"I was on the train," she murmured, glancing over at Caleb. "I had croissants and coffee before. But I wanted more coffee. There was a trolley. I bought coffee and a pastry. I..." She trailed off and her eyes refocused on Sinjen. "I opened my eyes to complete darkness.

And then there was a merry-go-round. I have no idea how long I was there."

"A what?"

"A carousel. Like an antique one. With horses. And a dragon. A wolf. And I had to grab the brass ring so my wish would come true."

"What did you wish, Sade?" Sinjen's voice was for her ears only.

"To come home to you."

Chapter Sixteen

A Losing Game

Francoise eased the cab to a stop in front of Sinjen's building and put it in park. Twisting in his seat he looked back. "Mademoiselle will be alright."

He might have meant it as reassurance but Sinjen took it as a question. "*Oui, mon ami*. She will sleep and be fine."

Opening the back door, Sinjen climbed out then reached back inside to gather Sade into his arms. He navigated through the front entrance and into the anciently elegant elevator. He got them inside his apartment without putting her down. She didn't rouse as he stripped her and put her into one of his shirts. Placing her in his bed, he pulled the covers over her shoulder after she turned onto her side and burrowed into the stack of pillows. He stood beside the bed, watching. Bewildered, Sinjen finally stirred and moved into the main salon of the apartment.

He didn't believe in soul mates. He'd been a servant of the Christian God a millennium ago. He'd worn the red cross of the Knights Templar, had fought to secure the Holy Land from the infidels. And then he'd lost his soul. In a single moment of sacrifice, he'd abandoned his humanity. He'd planned on dying. Had made his peace with the God he served. He awoke to face an endless life of debauchery, blood-sucking, and dishonor.

Until Sade Marquis walked into his prison and reminded him of the sunshine he could no longer enjoy. Sade would grow old and die. He would watch. And when she departed this world, he would follow her into the sun, praying the God he'd forsaken would be merciful and allow him to continue watching over her.

But he didn't believe in soul mates.

Unsure of how long he'd stood at the window staring across the river, he noticed the first glitters of light reflecting on the water. Dawn approached. He strode to the control panel and shut all the shutters that covered the myriad windows. He debated whether to join Sade in his bed, knew it was fruitless to even consider leaving her alone. She would sleep through the day. He'd ensured that. He would lie beside her. It was possible she would also sleep away the next night and day but he would deal with that if she didn't awake with him. Roman and Caleb were aware of what he'd done. Neither protested his action.

Stripping, he dumped his clothes into a hamper in his closet. The sight of women's clothing—all in Sade's style and tastes—hanging across from his own gave him a deep sense of contentment. And that worried him.

Let her go. His maker's words still echoed from the earlier conversation with Mathias. *I didn't sire a fool. Or did I?*

"I will not bargain her life." Sinjen repeated the words he lashed out at Mathias with, saying them out loud. Sade stirred. He fought to control his emotions, a hard battle all things considered. This woman in his bed created chaos in his life. She made him feel things. Desire things. She gave him hope.

Shoving all thoughts aside, he crawled into bed beside Sade and gathered her into his arms. They would sleep until the last rays of the sun drowned in the Seine.

Sade did not awake the following night. Sinjen needed to feed but he would not take from her. Instead, he showered and dressed. Opening the panels so the apartment was flooded with moonlight, he wrote her a note and left it on the pillow that still carried the imprint of his head. He penned the words in his bold script.

I have gone to fetch dinner.

He stepped out through the exterior door and was not surprised to find Francoise sitting in his cab waiting. Sinjen slipped into the backseat and the little cabby took off without a word. They crossed the Seine, turned right, and headed for the Eiffel Tower. The weather was nice. Tourists and Parisians alike would be flocking there like moths drawn to the lights of the famed landmark. Pickings would be easy.

Francoise rolled to a smooth stop and like many others, Sinjen alighted. When he was ready to leave, Francoise would be waiting. He strolled through the throng, cognizant of the glances—some covert, many far bolder—he garnered from both sexes. A sip here, a drink there. Nothing intimate. A simple al fresco dinner while he moved through the crowd like a silent ghost. It was better he sate himself here with strangers. She would still be weak when she awakened. And when she did, he would have a hearty meal delivered for her.

Gnawing hunger clawed at him. Hunger for her. For Sade. He stopped, head back, staring up at the magnificent steel lace and lights of the tower. He craved her. Not her blood, though that could sustain him for eternity. No. Her. The woman. The smile. The sleepy-eyed surrender as he brought her to climax. The snapping temper. The utter loyalty. Perhaps Mathias had the right of it. He should walk away. Sade represented redemption and he was one of the monsters. No one could redeem his soul.

Yes, it was hard to believe in mates of the soul when you had none. Turning, he retraced his steps to the street where Francoise had left him. As he knew would occur, the cabby pulled up within seconds. The earlier silence continued on the trip back to his apartment. Crossing the river on the Pont de la Tournelle, Sinjen noticed the large, winged creature perched atop his building. So did Francoise.

"Monsieur?"

"It is fine, Francoise. Just drop me at the door."

"But..."

"Do as I say."

"*Oui*, monsieur. As you wish."

The cab stopped. Sinjen stepped out but made no move to enter the building. Instead, he watched the car drive away. In moments, the sound of leather wings gliding through air reached his ears. The dark shadow briefly blotted out the moon before banking sharply and landing in front of Sinjen.

Vampire and ancient gargoyle stared each other down. Sinjen broke the silence. "*Le Vieil.*"

"You have been away from Paris for a very long time, Kristian St. John. You should go back to the new world you have made your home."

"Why?"

Crevan folded his wings and morphed into the hard-looking man that was his Human form. He'd led the Gargoyles for centuries and was far more warrior than diplomat. He turned and began to walk toward the Pont de Sully bridge.

Sinjen hesitated a moment, glancing up at his windows.

"She still sleeps. Come with me."

Sinjen fell into step with Crevan and they strolled the short block to the bridge. A few pedestrians passed them and he wondered what they saw? Crevan looked like a street tough with his close-cut hair, hard eyes, black T-shirt and jeans, motorcycle boots on his feet. Sinjen supposed he rather resembled what they used to call a dandy, though now he supposed the term was metrosexual. He was urbane in his clothing—charcoal gray slacks with a sharp crease, handmade leather boots, silver dress shirt partially cloaked by a leather jacket.

They turned onto the bridge's pedestrian walkway and stopped about midway. Notre Dame, encased in steel scaffolding, was visible beyond the next bridge up the river. Crevan braced his hands on the stone railing. "I do not believe I ever thanked you for your service to the Garregyion during the rebellion."

Sinjen looked down at the water before casting a sideways glance at the Gargoyle leader. He'd fought for Sade, though the part of him that remained in his Templar past had reveled in the battle. "I did what was necessary," he finally said.

"I know your reasons, Sinjen." The Old One sighed. "You must leave her."

"Mathias says the same."

"Yet you do not listen to your sire."

"This is none of your affair, Crevan."

"You are wrong. Mathias and Oberon knew not what they wrought those many years ago. She is now *L'nfant de L'homme.* Without her, there is imbalance."

"I have no plans to stop her from doing her job."

"It is not a job I am speaking of, Vampire. It is her very existence."

"I'm not following."

"If you stay with her, you both will die."

Sinjen's whole body jerked as if he'd touched an electric wire. He whipped his head around to stare at the gargoyle. "What are you saying? Sade is Human. She will eventually die no matter what." *And I will die with her*, he silently added.

"If you stay with her, it will be sooner than later."

"This is foretold?"

"This is known."

Numbing cold filled Sinjen as he stared at Crevan, gaze heated by both anger and fear.

"Speak plainly, Old One."

Crevan's wings unfolded and in the blink of an eye, he resumed his Gargoyle form. With one powerful downbeat, he rose into the night sky. His voice drifted down.

"If you stay with her, you have sealed your fates."

Chapter Seventeen

Drink Me

Once again, Sinjen found himself staring out at the Seine. A commercial barge floated past, churning up the barest of wakes. He had to decide what to do about Sade. He could ensure she slept one more day beside him and then they would awake—together—come evening. Mathias and Crevan were righteous in their condemnation of him. Sade was Human. He was not. For a brief moment, he wondered how Crevan knew that once Sade was gone from this earth, Sinjen would follow her. The Old One was one of the ancients. Perhaps he could read a man's intent by simply looking into his eyes. But...

Sinjen opened the window, closing his eyes to savor the breeze carrying the essence of Paris to his nose. Murky water. Ancient stones. The bright piquancy of centuries of human lives treading the streets. He opened his eyes and caught the brief flickers of light and shadow flitting along those avenues. He didn't believe in ghosts, but a man could be haunted all the same.

As he stood in the window, the sky lightened to a dove gray. Dawn would not be denied. He closed the window and turned away. As he had done every morning of his existence after Mathias changed him, Sinjen set about protecting himself from the ravages of day. *Not yet,* he thought. *One more day to hold her. One more night to make love to her. One more time to pretend she is mine.*

He stripped and slipped into bed beside the woman who held his existence in the palm of her hand. Drawing her close, he settled. Breathing in the scent of her hair, the fragrance that was uniquely Sade, he relaxed and waited. On a final exhale of breath, his life force fled before the grasping fingers of the sun.

Sade stood beside the bed. The room, shrouded in gloom, held just enough ambient light she could study the inert body lying there. She'd lost two nights, a day and part of another day. It was close to mid-afternoon. Her brain was a little foggy. That happened to Humans who went realm jumping. Sliding through portals was not for wimps. Her marks should give her some protection but yeah, no. Even when she traveled with Roman, she always arrived queasy and fuzzy headed. Her watch glowed slightly. Sunset was still hours away.

The piece of stationery on the antique chest beside the bed caught her attention. Sinjen's writing. The message made her grin, especially when her stomach grumbled. Caffeine. And food. In that order. Then she'd be right as rain. Leaving Sinjen with a gentle brush or her lips across his, she left the bedroom. A small lamp, activated by a motion detector, turned on. As she passed out of the hallway into the next room, a second light flicked on and the first one turned off.

She was impressed by the space. Of course, Sinjen had probably owned the apartment since before the dawn of time. Or at least from the time the place was built. Finding the kitchen, she discovered a coffee machine—one of those that brewed individual cups. It would do to get her by. She selected a little plastic cup of French roast and popped it into the machine. She smiled at the mug already in place. Her vampire knew her so well.

Wait. She froze, one finger hovering above the start button. *Her* vampire?

"Definitely need coffee," she muttered and stabbed the button. Then she rummaged in the refrigerator. She located a slab of cheese and hauled it out. In a nearby cabinet, she found a loaf of fresh bread. She'd survive until she could figure out where the hell she was, how the hell she'd get back to her hotel, and what the hell had been happening. Easy peasy.

And it was. She walked out the front door, saw the Seine, Notre Dame, and...a very familiar cab. Francoise rolled down the window and beamed at her. "I am here, mademo—*erm*—Agent Sade. Where do we go off to today?'

She realized she didn't have her cell phone and made a note to replace the one she'd lost in Jean-Louis's car. "Can I borrow your phone?" The cabby handed it over without a word and watched her over his shoulder as she climbed into the back seat.

"Food. Real food. Not bread and cheese. Meat."

"*Oui*. And then where?"

She held up a finger as Caleb picked up on the other end and said too brightly, "Good morning, sleepyhead."

"It's afternoon. My watch still works. Why didn't you come get me?"

"Because that portal trip zapped you. Sinjen had things handled."

"So where are we?"

"Not sure where you are but I'm with Roman, Verity, and the glitterby at Notre Dame."

"Why is Ariel still here?"

"No clue. We keep trying to make him go away. He's worse than that pesky cousin hanging around always wanting something to eat or drink and making trouble." There was noise in the background then he added, "Or like a stray cat that you didn't mean to feed."

Sade had no cousins but she'd take Caleb's word for it. And she knew about stray cats. "Tell him *I* told him to go home."

"No." Ari's voice came clearly through Caleb's phone. "The way you keep disappearing, I'm not going anywhere."

"Any luck on locating Mr. Wizard?" Silence. She'd been afraid of that. "Okay, fine. I'm headed to get food and then I'm going back to the hotel to shower and change clothes."

"Why?" That was Verity.

"Caleb, do you have me on speaker phone?" Silence. She let out a frustrated growl. "Fine. Why what Verity?"

"Weren't you staying at Sinjen's?"

"Yeah, why?"

"Uhm..." More silence, awkward this time.

"What the fuck, Verity?"

"Never mind."

"Dammit, Vee..."

"Okay, fine. I have it on pretty good authority that Sinjen has an entire wardrobe for you at his apartment."'

Sade glowered at Francoise, who suddenly seemed totally focused on driving as he maneuvered the car through traffic. "Vee..."

"Deliveries were made. From some of the really nice fashion boutiques."

"Probably for him."

"Uhm...no. These were all of the feminine variety."

Stunned, Sade sat back. She'd gotten up. Done her thing in the bathroom. Found her clothes in a hamper and she'd dressed. All but her underwear, the dirty pair shoved in the pocket of her slacks. That was one reason she wanted to hit her hotel room. Going commando wasn't all that comfortable.

"Wow," she finally said. "I never even looked."

Francoise *tsked*. She skewered the back of his head with a pointed stare, to no effect.

"Where is Sinjen?" Caleb was back.

"It's three in the afternoon. Where do you think he is?"

"Did you leave him a note?"

"No. Why would I—"

"Sade, think! How many times have you disappeared recently?"
She did a slow blink. "Uhm..."

"What is he going to think when he wakes up and there's no sign of you?"

"Uhm..." She thought fast. "I'll call him at sunset."

The red and white market umbrella offered her shade while she sipped coffee in between bites of the quiche. Francoise had dropped her off in front of the cafe and motored away. She wasn't far from Notre Dame and would walk there after she finished her...late lunch? Early supper? Lunper? Tension slowly drained away as she laughed at her pitiful attempt at humor. The air was warm, the street bustling, the food tasty. Sade just wanted a few minutes to not think. Not about the case. Not the pesky dragon. Not Sinjen.

Movement caught her attention. A sleek black shadow slunk along the curb across the street pacing a rather dapper man strolling along the sidewalk. He wore...were those spats? She choked back a laugh. The guy wore a bowler hat, a pince-nez in one eye and his suit and shoes—including the spats—looked like they came out of a costume shop and he was dressed for the turn of the 20th Century. He carried a cane, tapping it as he walked or occasionally twirling it to keep other pedestrians out of his space.

She ignored him to keep an eye on the cat, aware there was a certain amount of paranoia in her interest. The cat scooted across the street and tires squealed as brakes locked. Did the fucking cat get hit? She half rose from her chair peering at the spot where he should have been. Nothing.

Too late, she realized the dapper man was rushing her. She recognized him then, but before she could react, he'd pointed the cane at her and pulled some sort of trigger mechanism. She was suddenly drenched.

"What the motherfucking hell!" She pushed out of her chair and towered over the man. He tittered gleefully. "I knew you'd be mine again." Then he clapped his hands and Sade fell through a hole that suddenly opened up beneath her.

She was falling. Again. Only this time, light and dark formed a spiral pattern. Her stomach turned over and she choked down bile. This was like some Fifties horror movie where the mad scientist used a spinning spiral to hypnotize the heroine.

"I'm getting really fucking tired of all this shit, you misbegotten son of a slimy gawddamned toad."

Cackling laughter followed her. As did total darkness. And oblivion.

Sinjen awoke to silence. No Sade. No note. No message on his cell phone. He checked the closet. Nothing had been touched. He checked the hamper in the bathroom. Naturally, she would grab the dirty clothes rather than consider he might have provided for her. He automatically reached for her. Nothing.

He resorted to one of her favorite phrases. "Fuck me."

Not bothering to shower, he dressed and headed downstairs. He had Caleb on the phone before he got to the first floor.

"Where is she?"

"Well..."

"Caleb!"

"Is Francoise there?"

Sinjen stepped out into the twilight. The Frenchman leaned against his cab. "Yes."

"He'll explain."

Francoise did. About picking up Sade. The cafe. And her disappearance. "Agent Caleb, he is at the cafe sniffing her out as we speak. There were witnesses and the gendarmes they are also asking questions."

"Drive faster, Francoise."

"*Oui*, monsieur."

People took one look at him and scattered out of his way as he stalked from the corner where Francoise had to park to the cafe. A uniformed officer raised a hand to stop him, took one look and backed away awkwardly.

"What have you found?" he demanded when Caleb turned to him.

"As near as I can tell, we're still dealing with Human magic."

"He bespelled her?"

"Not exactly."

"Then *what* exactly?"

"Witnesses say he sprayed something on her. Like water. And then she just...poofed." He made an exploding motion with his hands.

"*Poofed*?"

"Yeah. Standing here one minute and then it was like the air was a curtain that ripped and she disappeared into it."

"Can we find her?"

"Verity's working on that. And a potion."

"A potion?" Sinjen felt as dangerous as he sounded.

"Her intuition says there's a spell and you'll need a potion to break it."

"Where is the dragon?'"

"In Switzerland as far as we know. Just like Interpol said."

"Can you discover anything else here?"

"Nope. I'm done. We need to get back to Notre Dame."

"We go."

Sade didn't remember landing. Laid out on a soft bed of what felt like moss, she gazed around the dreamscape, dazed and confused. Mostly immune to magic, this whole jumping through portals without her permission was unsettling. Each of the major non-Human Magick races had their own Realms, accessed through portals. Human-based Magicks, like Witches, Werewolves, and Vampires, couldn't access portals without some major magical mojo. In addition to, oh say the Dragon or Fae Realms, she'd heard of smaller "pocket" realms. This had to be one of those.

She was surrounded by an enchanted forest designed by a drunken cartoonist. And an apple, bright red and shiny, rested on her chest. She was no Snow White. Seriously, what the fuck? Trapped in her body, fully aware of what transpired around her, she couldn't move or speak. Even more disturbing, she expected the trees or some forest animals to burst into song and dance around her.

She heard what sounded like a champagne cork popping. Then a second one. Try as she might, she couldn't see anything but the stupid forest. Guttural voices—more growls than words—sounded somewhere behind her? Over her head? Someplace she couldn't see.

Someone picked her up but she got only an eyeful of dark material. He carried her, then set her gently down on something soft. Not tall enough to be Roman. Not weird enough to be Caleb. Totally not feely enough to be Ariel. That left Sinjen. Who else could it be? Yeah, the alternative answers were all bad. Like Dragon or Wizard bad. Hanging on for the duration of this crazy ride was her only way out. And until a body bent over her, she wouldn't be able to identify them.

"She's been drugged." Not Sinjen, she thought. Who then?

"Brilliant deduction, Dragon. Should I now begin to call you Sherlock?" *That* was Sinjen, at his arrogant, sarcastic best. But why was Nikos here? The dragon shifter and the vampire never got along—like duel-to-the-fucking-death not get along.

Sinjen, face bearing no emotion, regarded the dragon. "Why are you here, Nikolas Constantine?"

Nikos smirked. "Is it not obvious? You keep losing her."

"I do not *lose* her. She is snatched. Repeatedly." Sinjen cocked his head to one side. "You keep showing up where she is lost. A curious man might wonder if you find her so quickly because you stashed her away."

When Nikos spoke, smoke surrounded the words. "Are you impugning my honor?"

Sinjen barked out a derisive laugh. "You would only worry about honor if it was part of your hoard."

Before Nikos could retort, the air rippled. Sinjen glanced at the bistro table that had appeared from thin air. A small tumbler, illuminated by a beam of light, rested atop it. Following his gaze, Nikos reached over, grabbed the glass, and sniffed experimentally.

"Sparkling water."

The two men exchanged glances. Sinjen would do anything for the woman who lay inert on the elegantly-wrought brass bed with the feather mattress and linens. He would fight any Magick to keep her alive and with him, but could he trust the dragon who also coveted her? His emotions were in motion before his intellect engaged. "What magic does it contain?"

Nikos shrugged. "We would need the werewolf to say for sure. I would trust nothing this place provides. The elixir the witch gave us might work." A wicked grin appeared. "Or perhaps, as this looks like a scene from Snow White, I should kiss her. You know what they say about true love's kiss."

Sinjen's fangs appeared before he could control the quick flash of anger. "You do not love her, true or otherwise. You wish only to own her."

Nikos was amused. "Fine. Then you kiss her, since the rumor is rampant that a master vampire has been brought to his knees by a human."

Something fluttered on the table. A small square of paper with two words: DRINK ME.

"The witch's potion might kill her as easily as cure." Yet what choice did they have? He pulled the bottle out of his pocket and handed it to Nikos. "I'll hold her."

He scooped Sade into his arms and settled her back against his chest, her head tucked against his shoulder. Using one hand, he pried her mouth open. "Do it."

Nikos withdrew the stopper of the crystal bottle and upended it over Sade's open mouth. As soon as the last drop fell, Sinjen clamped her mouth shut.

She sputtered and coughed. Then her eyelids fluttered. She clawed at Sinjen's hand holding her mouth shut. He relaxed his grip. "Tastes like shit," she croaked.

Sinjen smiled. She'd live.

Chapter Eighteen

Love is a Battlefield

Sinjen insisted the debriefing be short once Nikos returned them to Notre Dame. Then he insisted Sade eat. Francoise drove them to a very classy restaurant. Sinjen looked elegant—as he always did. Sade felt grubby—as she often did around him. Well, he'd been prepared for portal hopping. She'd been in such a hurry to leave him earlier that she hadn't bothered to check out his place. Not that she'd wear any of the fancy clothes he'd bought her. Now they sat at a table with very attentive staff, a menu in French, and people studiously not looking at them. She'd ordered something with meat. Beef, to be precise. She needed the protein.

Her phone buzzed and vibrated across the table. She attempted to ignore it. When it stopped ringing, she slipped it into her pocket where it immediately buzzed and vibrated again. Sinjen stared at her, his expression stoic.

"Answer it."

She pulled it out and glanced at the screen. The Director's office. "I have to take this. I'm sorry," she said but wasn't sure she really meant it. From the expression on Sinjen's face, he didn't think she meant it either. Pushing back from the table, she stumbled as Sinjen stood with preternatural speed and pulled out her chair. He caught her arm and steadied her. His face still showed no emotion. "I'll take this outside. Just a few minutes, okay? It's work."

"It always is." Resignation tinged his voice. He had to let her go. To do otherwise would make her feel shackled and that would only make her pull away even more.

She turned and hurried toward the entrance, phone to her ear. Like the principal dancer in a chorus number, she waltzed and tangoed through the crowded restaurant. Subdued, Sinjen remained

135

standing, watching until she stepped outside. He had others watching there. She would be safe, would remain in the human plane. He could reach her at the first alarm, could keep her safe.

He retreated to his chair. To wait. Five minutes. Ten. Fifteen. The waiter appeared with Sade's order. Sinjen motioned for him to leave the plate with a negligent wave of his hand. The woman could eat it cold at this rate. At the thirty-minute mark, the heavy, cloying scent of gardenias enveloped him moments before two arms circled his neck and someone bit his earlobe.

"Hello, lover," a husky voice purred. "I've missed you."

Sade returned to the dining room just in time to see some bitch eating her food. She marched to the table, grabbed the woman by the hair and yanked her out of the chair so that she spilled onto the floor.

"Well, I never..." the woman sputtered. She looked to Sinjen for assistance. "Darling?"

"Get the fuck out of here," Sade ordered as she dropped into the chair she'd just helped the bitch vacate.

The woman stared first at Sade and then Sinjen. When he made no move to help, she managed to climb to her feet and with a show of bravado, lifted her nose into the air with a sniff and sauntered a short distance away. She paused long enough to look back at Sinjen.

"You never used to put up with...let me see, what *did* you call jealous fits?" The woman snapped her fingers. "Oh, right. Theatrics. She must have a cunt lined with gold for you to overlook this sort of drama now."

Sade was out of her chair and managed three steps toward the bitch before Sinjen's arm snaked around her waist and she was hauled back against his chest.

"She's not worth it, Sade. She got her scene. Don't indulge her further."

Pulling a self-defense move, one which she was well aware Sinjen allowed, she jerked out of his hold and whirled to face him. "Indulge her?" She sucked in air. "Indulge. *Her?*"

"Sit down, Sade." Those three words were saturated with infinite patience. They were also an order. Sinjen gestured with his hand for her to precede him back to their table. She stepped around him and returned to her chair. She made a production of shifting the chair the woman had occupied to the side and then maneuvering a second chair into its place. She also shoved her plate away. Sinjen sighed. When he noticed the waiter hovering nearby, he shook his head. Sade would be past eating now but he knew her. "*Un café s'il vous plaît.*"

Pleased he could be of service, the waiter darted away. Sade was sitting, back stiff, her lips pressed into a hard line when he took his own seat across from her.

"Who is she?"

"Does it matter?" It didn't. The woman was just an excuse for Sade to lose her temper. He and his former lover were easy targets.

"Yes."

"I knew her several years ago."

"*Knew* her? In the Biblical sense?"

"I repeat, does it matter?"

"I step out to take an important call and in moments, some bimbo is sitting in my chair eating my food? Yeah, Sinjen. It fucking matters."

The waiter chose that moment to appear. He slid a fresh china cup on a delicate saucer in front of Sade. The poor man couldn't help himself, he made a show of pouring the hot coffee from the silver pot into the cup. He bowed and speed-walked away, dignity mostly intact.

Sade wasn't ready to play nice. "You are avoiding the question."

"No. I see no point in indulging your snit."

"Oh. Now you won't *indulge* me." She made air quotes around the word.

Sinjen leaned back against the upholstered chair. "Her name is Margaret." He blinked. "Or Madeline. Frankly, I don't remember. She was a short fling several years ago. Before I met you."

"Did you fuck her in your bed in that fancy apartment?"

She *was* jealous, he mused. Or perhaps just spoiling for the inevitable fight that had been brewing between them for too long.

"No."

She was all set to lay into him but had to snap her mouth shut as she regrouped. "No?"

"No. As a rule, I do not take women to my living quarters. No matter which city I am in."

Sade blinked. *Touché,* he thought. Point to him.

"But..." She blinked again, apparently floundering for words.

Unusual and somewhat amusing. He waited for her expected profane outburst.

"It was work," she said instead, changing the subject.

"It always is." He kept his voice as soft as hers had suddenly become.

Sade stared into the cup of murky liquid she held. Not even coffee, elixir of the gods though it was, could help her mood—or get her out of this mess. She raised her gaze, which promptly collided with the vampire's piercing blue one. "I won't apologize."

"You never do." He looked so...resigned.

"It isn't my fault." She sounded defensive and hated herself for whining.

"It never is."

"That's not fair."

"What does fairness have to do with this, Sade?" Sinjen pushed his chair back from the table, his restless energy spilling out to electrify the atmosphere. Had they been somewhere private, he would have paced the entire room. Raking long fingers through his raven-black hair, he endeavored to control his emotions. "Have you finished your coffee?"

Glancing into the fragile cup she held, Sade raised it to her lips and gulped the hot liquid. She needed the fortification. She watched as the waiter bustled up with a leather case. He opened it with a flourish. Sinjen took the pen that was inside and signed his name. No money, no credit card involved. He lived in a totally different world and it wasn't that he was Vampire and she was Human. He was...royalty and she wasn't even Cinderella. She was the ugly stepchild. Margaret, Madeline, whatever-her-name, was beautiful. She shopped the fancy boutiques and wore clothes like the ones Sinjen very likely hung in his closet for her.

She wasn't that woman. She was an FBI agent. She wore slacks off the rack because blood, guts, and magical dirt didn't come out. She wore leather boots because they were sturdy. She dressed up if she had to but shopping? A shudder coursed through her—one she hoped Sinjen hadn't noticed. She was not his kind. Never had been. Never would be.

So why is he with me? she wondered. She knew for damn sure that her...down there was *not* lined with gold. "Lord," she muttered. If any of the Scooby Gang had been there to read her mind, they would have fallen over laughing. She could drop the f-bomb with ease. But words referring to *her* female parts? Yeah. Not so much.

Very gently, she replaced the cup in its saucer and stood before Sinjen could reach her chair. She turned and headed for the door. Of course, he caught up to her in a matter of steps. Neither of them spoke. Francoise zoomed up to the curb and stopped the moment they appeared. Sinjen held the door for her and she slid in and over.

He settled beside her. The cabby glanced at Sinjen in the mirror, got the message and pulled back into traffic.

A few minutes later, he stopped at the entrance to the Rue de la Huchette. The ride had not been made in a comfortable silence and Sade was slightly shocked that Sinjen opted to come to her hotel and not his apartment. He opened the car door and exited. He did not offer his hand, as he usually did, to help her from the car. Had he realized that she would have avoided contact just to make her point or did he truly not want to touch her?

She climbed out, rather clumsily. He shut the door and they turned to walk down the pedestrian lane to the hotel.

Sinjen stopped about halfway there. He waited until she realized he was no longer beside her and turned toward him.

"What?" *Ugh.* She sounded snippy. Well, she had the right. He'd let a woman sit in her place and eat her food. Her stomach chose that moment to remind her that portal hopping and no food was not smart. Her growling stomach should have gotten her a reprimand or a gloating smile. It brought neither. Sinjen almost looked sad.

He stared at the sidewalk for a long moment, then raised his eyes to meet her gaze. "About tonight—"

"*Pfft.*" She waved a hand to cut him off. She turned and kept walking to the hotel. She knew he didn't want to talk about the woman but about the fact she'd been snatched and transported to some weird pocket dimension. "Shit happens."

She waited at the door, expecting him to open it. He wasn't right behind her. In fact, it looked like he was dragging his feet to catch up. She pushed through the door and didn't wait for him.

When they were both in the lobby, she spoke. "Are you pissed because I caused that scene in the restaurant?"

She headed for the stairwell deciding the climb would be better than squeezing into the little elevator with the angry vampire. Of course, his magic mojo caused the elevator door to open just as she passed. They both stepped inside. "Look, I get to be mad."

Sinjen said nothing as the elevator chugged upward.

The door opened and they stepped out. She ignored the two men standing in the hall. "I can't believe you are so totally overreacting. I mean, seriously. You're the one who slept with her. I have every right to be upset. That bitch's lipstick is still on your ear. She *kissed* you. And then she fucking ate my gawddamned food." She opened her door, her angry gaze still fixed on Sinjen. "I am so ready to fuck this shit. You and me, buster. Right here. Right now." She whirled and stabbed a finger in the direction of Caleb and Ariel, who'd followed them into the sitting room. "Get the hell out, Hardy Boys."

She marched toward the bedroom and stood in that doorway until Sinjen passed into the darkness beyond. She hit the light switch and slammed the door all but simultaneously. "Fuck you!" she yelled. She wanted to hit something. Preferably Sinjen but that would do no good. So she cussed. And ranted. And waved her arms. Yes, she felt a little ridiculous but at the same time, it was cathartic. This fight had been building for a while.

"You knew what I did for a living the first night we met." She stopped in front of him and stabbed at his chest, not quite touching him. "You *knew*."

Sinjen watched her, his eyes hooded. She saw something flicker across his face and wondered what it was.

This is it, he decided. He ignored the empty loneliness flooding him. Without blinking, he said in a very quiet voice, "I'm not sure I can do this anymore."

She stopped breathing. There it was, the moment she'd been waiting for from the moment they met. Dread formed a block in her chest. "I can't help it if some asshole is dumping me around the Realms. It's my job."

A sound puffed out from between his lips—something between a snort and a chuckle. Sarcasm mixed with resignation coated his voice. "So you always say."

"This is who I am." She tried again. Didn't he understand? She *was* her job. If she was no longer an FBI agent, she had...nothing.

"You would have had me."

She glanced up, shocked that he'd read her mind.

"I don't have to. I know you. Far better than you know yourself. And I know I will never be enough. Everything comes full circle."

"What does that mean?"

"You once saved me. I'm returning the favor."

"What does that even mean?"

Sinjen opened the bedroom door and walked toward the exit.

"Don't you walk away from me!"

Sinjen didn't pause. As soon as his hand touched the doorknob, she yelled again.

"Fine. Run away. Don't bother coming back."

Sinjen opened the door and stepped out into the hall. Sade flew across the room. "Stay the gawddamned hell out of my life and leave me the fucking hell alone."

The door slammed hard enough the windows rattled. "Get out!" Sade yelled as she stomped to the bedroom.

"Well, that went well."

Ariel stared at Caleb like the werewolf had grown a second head. "Seriously?"

Caleb lifted one shoulder in a shrug the fae couldn't decide was negligent or arrogant. "You know what Sade is like when she's pissed."

"I fucking heard that!" The subject of their conversation stomped back into the sitting room. "Why the gawddamned fucking hell are the two of you still here? I told you to get the hell out when we got here."

Both men chided her simultaneously. "Language."

The werewolf caught the scent of her pain while the fae noticed the all but imperceptible wince. Sade glowered, her gaze so withering that had they been plants the two Magicks would have shriveled up, died, and blown away like dust in the wind.

"Would you like us to stake him in the heart?" Ari sounded a little too happy to comply.

"Oh fucking to the hell no," the furious woman yelled. "That doesn't even come close to what I'll do that that mother—"

"Sade," Caleb cut her off, his tone cajoling. "You know you don't mean that."

"He slept with her!" The heartbreak in Sade's voice rocked both Magicks back on their heels. Her eyes narrowed and her mouth formed a hard slash across her face. "I am so fucking done with that gawddamned asshole."

"He's a vampire." Ari stated the obvious, as if vampire and asshole were synonyms.

Caleb added in a dry voice, "And now a dead one." Except he knew sleeping with a woman before he'd met Sade was not the real reason for this dust up. Werewolf hearing and all that.

Sade flung a cushion at Caleb's head. "Vampires are already dead."

"Well, sort of. They are undead, not dead, technically speaking." Caleb barely managed to duck the thick, hardcover book she next hurled at him.

Ariel snagged the tome in mid-air. "Hey! That's a first edition."

Throwing up her hands, Sade marched to the far end of the room. "I should have seen this coming. He's a fucking vampire."

"And a master," Ari muttered.

"Centuries old. How many gawddamned women has he had? Why the holy fucking hell would he ever settle down with a total bitch like me?"

Werewolf and fae exchanged looks but remained stoically—and wisely—silent. Caleb would get the full story from her later. What he didn't understand was Sinjen's reaction to all of this. The man did not give in to Sade's tantrums. Or her insecurities. Sade spat a great deal of vitriol at Sinjen tonight. The vampire just stood there, taking it, until Sade said for the umpteenth time that he should leave her alone. With words far more profane. Then, without an ounce of emotion, Sinjen had said three words. Words no one else heard for the slamming door.

"As you wish."

Caleb had been watching him closely, all senses focused. He caught the look on his face before Sinjen exited. Things in Romancelandia had just gone south and there was a finality to Sinjen's statement that worried him. Sade's biggest fear was people abandoning her. And being alone. Her current rant was simply her way of covering up that oops moment, realizing she'd screwed up.

"I can't deal with this. Or the two of you right now. Go the fuck away!" She stormed into her bedroom, slamming the door behind her. They waited. A few minutes later, the door opened.

"Why the holy hell are you two still here?" she fumed.

Ari held up a bottle of wine. "Will this work or do I need to find something stronger?"

A soft tap at the door drew their attention. Caleb opened it cautiously. Francoise handed him a bottle of tequila and three shot glasses. "I find this to be a sacrilege. This is Paris. This is France. Tequila is a heathen drink." He passed off his bounty to the werewolf with a sniff, shut the door, and they heard him shuffling off down the hall.

Sade didn't bother with a glass. She grabbed the bottle, tore the seal off, and took a big swig. Ari settled into a mostly comfortable chair with the wine bottle and a glass, prepared to enjoy the show.

Caleb leaned against the door, resigned. This would be a long night, unlikely to be over until Sade ate the worm.

Chapter Nineteen

Until Dawn

Sinjen stared into the rich, citrine-colored liquid contained within the expensive Waterford crystal glass. He'd given up his mortal life long before this particularly fine Irish whiskey was first distilled but the scent of it, and the taste of it on his tongue reminded him of other times. Other places. He lifted the glass, inhaled. He was always a bit surprised that the aroma and the flavor were different. As he sniffed, fruity notes of ripe apple and pear were followed by a hint of hops and clove. He swirled the Jameson, watching light reflect through the cut glass to enhance the glints of whiskey gold inside. He sipped—just enough to settle on his tongue. Hops and almonds quickly followed by cocoa and the bite of oak. He swallowed. And savored the essence of butterscotch and chocolate left on his tongue.

Memory was an odd thing, especially when filtered through centuries rather than decades. Humans marked their existence by remembering the huge, life-altering events. Colleagues of his at the University of Chicago could relate in great detail where they were on that November day when John F. Kennedy was assassinated in Dallas. Or on April 19, 1995—the Oklahoma City bombing. And 9-11. The whole world remembered that date. He remembered Pearl Harbor. Hiroshima. The Hindenburg. Titanic, and events even further removed. He wondered how the true immortals kept track of all those history-shaping events. Or did they bother?

He took another sip, swirled the smooth whiskey around his mouth, settled a bit deeper into the chair. Dawn was still a few hours away but Chicago could almost rival New York with its skyscrapers and Paris with its lights. Almost. He shoved thoughts of Paris out of his head.

A song drifted up from the street below. He closed his eyes. Sade strutted from the shadows, all long legs eating up the space to the cell where the police held him. Yes, she had the look, the one Roxette sang about even now. Sinjen pushed out of the chair. He didn't want to remember.

Twenty minutes later, he occupied a table in the corner of a noisy bar. His waitress passed him her phone number as she served his drink. The slip of paper sat on the tabletop drinking up the ring of moisture left by a previous occupant's glass. Women checked him out with hungry eyes. Men reacted to his presence in two ways—some wanted to be him. Others wanted to prove their manhood by taking him down. He sipped whiskey, watched, winced as music, voices, and sports on the various TV screens all clashed.

He didn't want to be here but anyplace was better than his apartment. Too many memories there. Too many memories of her. Sade Marquis. The bane of his existence. The reason he opened his eyes every night. His phone buzzed in his pocket. Withdrawing it, he glanced at the screen. SADE CALLING. He thumbed the DECLINE button and laid the phone on the table.

Another song started to play. Another memory he didn't want to remember. Another reminder of what he wanted to forget. His phone beeped. Voice mail. He wanted to ignore it, wanted to delete it without listening.

Holding the phone to his ear, he listened to the recording. Her voice sounded husky, like they'd just made love. "What about now?" she said. "Is it too late?"

The walls closed in. Time to go. He left cash—and the soggy paper—on the table. Warm darkness folded around him as he walked back to his apartment building. Chuck, the night doorman, snapped to attention as he held the door. The normally garrulous man looked like he was about to swallow his tongue. Sinjen didn't give him an opening, not that it would stop the human under normal circumstances.

Chuck didn't follow him to the elevators, instead halting at the concierge desk. The leggy blonde manning the desk arched a brow at the doorman but her attention remained focused on Sinjen. The corners of her full mouth pulled up into a knowing smile but nothing about her drew more than a passing glance. He was only interested in one woman.

Even riding in the elevator brought back memories. He focused on the security camera hidden behind a fancy scroll-work panel. Sade had spotted it immediately. Until that ride up to his apartment, he'd never even considered the presence of security cameras. He was aware now. Always. No matter where he was. Because of her.

One of his neighbors was waiting for the elevator as the doors opened. He nodded to the woman while ignoring her interested gaze. He would need to feed sooner than later, but he'd find someone else, someone with no complications. He slipped into his apartment, ignoring the flashing light on his answering machine.

Still restless, Sinjen refilled the Irish crystal glass with Jameson and resumed his position out on his balcony. Feet up on the railing, lounging in the cushioned chair, he looked like a man who controlled his world, a man in charge, a man who could relax in the knowledge of that control. Anyone who knew him—few, indeed—would recognize that he was about to snap.

There were scant moments in his long exile from life since Mathias first turned him that Sinjen hadn't wished for a heart and the emotions that lodged there. As he stared at the cell phone, Sade's pleas echoing in his memory, he was glad that feelings no longer chained him. Did that make him a coward? Likely. Did he care? Not one whit. He'd wanted her the moment she strutted into his life. He'd been patient, had hunted, had seduced, had claimed. And he'd wanted to keep her. Until he couldn't.

Sade was Human. She would age. Die.

He was Vampire. He would not change, except to grow colder, more distant. Until an enemy managed to stake him or he walked into the sun to end his existence, he would not die. They'd argued over something of no consequence. And he'd allowed it as words from both Mathias and Crevan echoed in his head. He'd been a fool to ever consider keeping her. Sade didn't think when her blood was up. And even as a Knight Templar, he hadn't been a saint. She'd been feeling vulnerable and it was easy enough to play into her fears.

Sinjen hated himself for doing it. And he'd done the one thing guaranteed to cause her grievous hurt. He'd walked away. Left her. Supposedly over her jealous pique at an old lover—one he barely remembered. He hadn't thought of any other woman, not since meeting Sade. After Sade? Other women faded into the background, like so much white noise.

He swirled the whiskey, watching the lights sparkle through it. He hadn't wanted to end things quite so quickly but when events conspired to give him that out, he took it. The whole Paris fiasco left a bad taste in his mouth that not even excellent aged whiskey could mask. Who was targeting Sade? And why was the infernal lizard involved?

Sinjen savored another sip, despite the aftertaste of the lingering memories. After claiming her, Sinjen had not wanted to share Sade with the world. He was possessive and territorial. She'd been injured and he'd wanted nothing more than to wrap her in silk and keep her at his side for the rest of their days. Then duty called. As it always did with Sade. She'd refused to be caged and he discovered that he could deny her nothing. Until now.

The woman showing up at the restaurant had been...fortuitous. He mused—briefly—if her appearance had been a set up. He hadn't sent her away. Part of him wanted Sade's reaction. And she played into the situation, overreacting as she occasionally did. So often he found her antics entertaining but that night? He'd been out of sorts. Already dreading what must be done. Already missing her. He wanted one more night—taking her back to his apartments, making love to her, holding her in his arms as *l'morte d'aube* consumed him. He wanted to wake at sunset to find her still there with him. Something that seldom occurred.

But there was the woman, making herself at home, assuming he would take her for the evening. And Sade did what Sade did. Instead of getting his wish, he got the hard truth. This was it. The time had come. So, he'd turned off his emotions and did what he did. His fingers tunneled through his hair and he forced his hand to return to the arm of the chair. Closing his eyes, he leaned his head back.

The earth spun on its axis. He could feel the slip of time as sunrise edged ever closer. Maybe he would remain here on the balcony, looking out across the lake. He could watch the first rays of dawn without ill effect, then the lethargy of the day sleep would envelop his body. He could sit here, watch the day arrive performing her colorful dance. He would close his eyes, a last breath expelled from his lungs as his heart slowed and ceased beating altogether and finally find some semblance of peace.

What about now? Is it too late?

The words Sade recorded on that message jabbed into his heart. Yes, it was too late. He'd done what had to be done.

As much as the oblivion of true death beckoned, he wasn't that big of a coward. He rose from the chair, went inside and emptied the glass of the whiskey he could no longer enjoy into the sink. Courage, he realized, was saying goodbye to the one woman who filled his death with life, so she could live hers to the fullest. And strength was watching over her from afar to ensure that she lived it. Sade deserved her fairy tale ending. God knew he would never be a prince.

Chapter Twenty

Ready Player One

Sade listened to the ring tone. Over and over. Then voice mail clicked on. At least he hadn't blocked her, which she might have done in a momentary snit. Which is what their fight had been. A moment of jealous insanity on her part. And now he wouldn't take her calls. The computerized voice finished its instructions.

"Never mind," she said softly. At this point, it didn't matter. She'd left him numerous messages on his cell, the phone in his apartment in Chicago, and on his office phone at the University. Was he still here in Paris? She could pull rank and find out if he'd flown back to the States. But she wouldn't.

Three days. She'd been chasing her tail over the wizard—and trying to reconnect with Sinjen—for those same three days. There were no more leads to follow. No more dead bodies turning up. No villain to identify and catch. It wasn't Nikos. Even Interpol had dropped that line of investigation. Interestingly enough, Jean-Louis was noticeably absent. He was still in Paris as far as she could ascertain. She wondered if the visit Sinjen had paid him at the Paris offices had anything to do with Jean-Louis's disappearing act. At least Sinjen retrieved her phone and returned it her. She'd found it in her hotel room after he left.

She sat at one of the outdoor tables of the cafe next to their hotel and stared glumly at her cup of coffee. At this rate, she and Caleb should just head back to the States. The French police and Interpol were having no more luck than they were. A chair scraped and she looked up to find Caleb settling into it.

"Coffee that bad?"

She glanced at the cup curled in the palm of her hand. "It's okay. Order breakfast. We have time."

After his plate had been delivered, he ate slowly and watched her. "You look like something the cat dragged in." The look she trained on him didn't hold a candle to her normal scorching glower. "When's the last time you had a good night's sleep?"

"I'm sleeping."

She was on the defense. Which meant the dark circles under her eyes told the truth. Caleb wisely kept his opinions to himself. He finished up and reached for the bill. Sade didn't argue. Yes sirree. She'd definitely had a bad night. He pushed back from the table and dug in his pocket for cash, which he handed to the waitress who bustled up.

"Keep the change."

The young woman checked the tab, the bills he'd passed over and then flashed him a dazzling smile. "Merci, monsieur."

Sade was already headed up the street. He caught up to her and asked, "We walking or waiting for the ever-present Francoise?"

"Walking."

She turned the corner and headed for the bridge across the Seine. The cab was nowhere in sight. *Curious,* Caleb thought. They strolled north and waited for the lights to change. Traffic on Quai Saint-Michel was slow to stop but Sade paid no mind. A flash of black at sidewalk level caught his eye. Sade waded into traffic, fearless and with such a fierce look on her face that none of the motorists dared honk their horns at her. She stepped up onto curb on the far side. Caleb was a few seconds late in his warning. He saw what many would think was a shimmer of heat radiating from the pavement. He knew it was a spell.

"Sade!"

Two things happened—she disappeared and a small black cat went in after her.

Sade gazed across a mystical landscape painted in watercolors by a madman—a place both beautiful and savage. Instinct took over and her pistol was in her hand, except it wasn't a pistol. She stared at the lethal-looking sword gripped in her fist.

Muttering, "Somebody pinch me," she glanced over the prow of the boat, gazing at her reflection as it was captured in a mirror of ebony glass. Her very serviceable slacks and sweater had been replaced by—

"Seriously?" Shouting, she raised the sword and cursed the heavens, adding, "This is not fucking Gor and I'm not some fucking slave girl!"

Fingers teased her hair and she stiffened. Just the wind. Not a ghost. Or worse. The boat skated across the black expanse, no sign of ripples to mark its passage. The sail hung limp, and nobody manned the rudder. She was alone.

Meowrr.

Okay, maybe not alone. Totally. She glanced at the mast. A small black cat clung to the ropes wound about the pole, about eye level.

"You again?"

Mwwarr.

"Need help?"

Meeow.

"Fine." Sade sheathed the sword and stepped over to disentangle the cat's claws.

"What do you think of me now-ow-ow?" The disembodied voice echoed off the rocky cliffs lining the cursed stretch of water.

The cat hissed and darted up her arm to cling to the very narrow strip of leather covering her shoulder. "No claws," Sade ordered.

Then, in a loud voice that shaded toward a snarl, "Magic doesn't work on me." Then it occurred to her. Shit. Not magic, alchemy. Except...alchemy was a myth, right? Wracking her brain, Sade searched for the information she needed. Magic *didn't* work on her, hadn't since Mathias and Oberon had both marked her when she was a toddler. Shit. She was fucked so it was time to see the wizard—figuratively speaking because everyone knew wizards worked magic. Nope, she had a date with some Mad Hatter of a sorcerer. Two could play that game. "Let's stir the pot and see what surfaces."

Leaning over, she plunged the sword into the water. Glass shattered with a bright tinkling ring and a massive silver head reared up from the depths, maw open, teeth dripping black water and...Vikings? Seriously? The head lowered but before the dragon could eat her, she smacked him on the snout with the flat of her blade.

"Gawddammitalltohell, Nikos! We have to stop meeting like this!" If her presence in this realm was somehow his doing, she'd have new dragon-hide boots by morning.

Sade, cat, and dragon all survived the trip back to the Human plane. As soon as their feet touched the grass, the cat was off like a rocket. Not that she could blame the critter. She had a very deep desire to follow suit. Nikos, still in dragon form, had put down in the center of the Square de l'Île-de-France, a small memorial park at the end of the island across the street from the cathedral. It was the only open space large enough for an adult dragon to land.

A squadron of Gargoyles flocked above them. Varrick landed and tucked his wings tightly. "Are you all right?" The question was directed to Sade but his glower focused on Nikos.

"I'm fine." She glanced down to make sure she wore real clothes. The slave girl of Gor outfit had melted back into slacks and sweater, sword to her Beretta. Caleb ran up, barely panting. She turned to him. "Did you see what happened?"

"There was a shimmer, like a heat wave coming off hot asphalt. You stepped up on the curb and walked right into it. Disappeared." He glanced around. "Where's the cat?"

Sade jerked her thumb over her shoulder. "Poor thing got freaked out by ol' fire breath over there. Speaking of..." She turned back to Nikos. "You need to shift before the entire population of Paris turns out to stare." Silver scales began an iridescent dance. "And you better be wearing clothes, buster!"

The huge dragon blinked out of existence and the sardonic Human form he adopted stood in its place. He adjusted the cuffs of the expensive shirt beneath the tailored suit jacket. "I always wear clothes," he said in his intriguing Greek accent. "Except when I'm not."

A tic started in the corner of Sade's left eye. "How did you track me so fast?"

"I didn't. I was already there when you popped up in the boat."

She scrubbed at her forehead hoping that would help her brain wrap around things. "That was part of the Dragon Realm?"

"Yes."

"Were you actually eating those Vikings?"

His silvery blue eyes glistened with humor. "There have been no true Vikings in several centuries." A slow grin crooked one corner of his mouth. "And I must say your outfit was rather...fetching."

Caleb grabbed her around the waist before she could lunge for Nikos and growled, "Did you set up that portal?"

The dragon's demeanor immediately sobered. "No. And that is twice too many times that the Dragon Realm has been breached."

"Fucking wizard," Sade muttered. "I think someone is practicing alchemy. Take someone with a little magic and add in that shit? Anything can happen."

"Perhaps. There have long been rumors of an alchemical formula that would open portals for Humans." The dragon looked troubled. "I must look into this."

Before anyone could move, Nikos winked out of existence on the Human plane. Even Varrick was caught off guard. "Bloody dragon," he groused.

Sade commiserated with the First Sentinel. "My thoughts exactly."

They retreated to Roman's apartment where she had to relate her latest adventure. Caleb, Roman, and Varrick choked on their laughter. Verity did not. She laughed until tears leaked from her eyes.

"It wasn't funny," Sade groused.

Verity wiped a finger across her cheek. "I didn't even have to be there. I can't decide which is better—you dressed up or slapping the dragon across the nose."

That provoked a hint of a smile from Sade. "Okay. Yeah, that was pretty funny. The look on his face—"

The rest of her comment was cut off by Caleb's phone. His eyes flashed with a feral red gleam as he listened. "On our way," he said and cut the call. "That was Jean-Louis. Interpol has a lead on your Mr. Wizard."

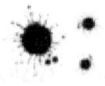

Frustration cut a deep swath through her. Sade gazed around the room, noting the chaos. Overturned furniture. Broken lamps. But no blood. And no wizard. Someone had gotten to her suspect first.

"He should have been alone." And he should have. Interpol had surveillance on the place.

Jean-Louis offered her a disdainful glance. "Why? Because you wish it so?"

"You know what they say about wishes and horses."

"Are you insinuating I am a beggar?" The vampire puffed up like the dandy he'd once been.

"No. I'm saying you're pretty much a horse's ass."

Jean-Louis bristled but a growl from Sade's Werewolf partner kept him silent.

"Caleb?"

"Humans. And a whiff of magic. I think your Mr. Wizard magicked himself away and whoever else was here tore the place apart."

"Frustration or looking for something?"

Caleb shrugged. "Your guess is as good as mine."

Jean-Louis cleared his throat. Sade and Caleb ignored him. He cleared it again.

"What?" Sade didn't look his way. She was too busy flipping through a large, leather-bound book.

"Agent Marquis."

That got Sade's attention. She and Caleb both whirled to face the man standing in the doorway. And the equally large weapon in his hands.

"I am pleased to finally meet you face to face." He shifted the barrel of the Desert Eagle slightly. "I am prepared for Werewolves, Agent Jones. Do not move."

Sade studied the intruder. She couldn't tell if he was a human but suspected he was something else. "Who are you?"

"The man who intends to kill you."

Chapter Twenty-one

No Regrets

Sade waited a dramatic beat. "You aren't the first who's threatened that. And I'm still standing." She gestured toward Jean-Louis. "You might be prepared for Werewolves but did you come loaded for Vampires?"

The man's lips twisted into a sick semblance of a smile. "Your assistance is appreciated, Durand. You may go now."

Cutting her eyes to him, Sade stared at the Interpol agent. "You're working for him?"

Jean-Louis gave her one of his damnable Gallic shrugs. "It is what it is, Agent Marquis. Interpol does not pay so well, you see."

She turned a beaming smile on him. "Dude, you are so gonna be a crispy critter when I get my hands on you."

Ignoring her, Jean-Louis checked something on his cell phone. "I see the money has been transferred. A pleasure doing business with you." He offered a mocking two-fingered salute to Sade and walked out.

The man gestured with his weapon. "Come here. We have places to be."

Sade tapped an index finger on her chin and stared up at the ceiling. "Let me think about that." She paused for a few beats then leveled her gaze on the man. "Uhm, no. My godfather told me never to go off with strange Magicks."

Something flashed in the man's eyes but Sade couldn't read the emotion. She glanced at Caleb. Her partner's nostrils flared. He casually uncurled three fingers, pointed downward, from the fist that had been clenched next to his thigh. Their assailant *was* some kind of Magick. Terrific. Caleb inhaled again and she watched him stiffen slightly. She inhaled. And caught it. The unmistakable odor that was

159

part cedar wood and part sulfur. Dragon. Oh. Shit. This guy was a dragon shifter?

The man focused on Caleb. "I have no quarrel with the Lycans but you should have picked your friends more wisely."

"What makes me so fucking special?" Sade sugar-coated her voice to draw his attention back to her.

The stranger studied her, a look of contemplation on his face. "This remains a mystery. You are crude. Human. There is nothing feminine about you. I do not understand why he desires you so much."

"He who?"

A few Greek words spilled out of his mouth and Sade made a mental note to check her Greek translator for curse words. Those sounded like dandies.

The dragon spat out a name and things started to finally make sense.

"What do you have against Nikos Constantine?"

"That is not your business. It only matters that he has plans to acquire you for his hoard. I will take you for mine or kill you. The choice is yours."

"The choice to live or die is yours, Balaskas."

The strange dragon whirled to face the hallway. In the blink of an eye, a black haze appeared right before the dragon vanished. Nikos stepped into view.

"What the fucking hell, Nikos?"

"This answers some of the questions." Nikos glanced around the room. "Come. There is nothing left here for us to discover. We will eat and talk." He glanced toward Caleb, who was growling deep in his chest. "All of us."

"Not hungry, Nikos, for anything but answers. So spill," Sade demanded.

Nikos looked disappointed but began. "I did not believe that Clan Nekyios would stoop so low."

Caleb leaned back against the kitchen cabinet. "Start at the beginning."

"Yeah. Who was that dude?"

"Timos Balaskas. He is of House Lemnos."

Her brow crinkled as she tried to remember Dragon 101.

"You will break something if you think any harder, Sade. House Lemnos is to Clan Nekyios what House Helios is to Clan Kholikikos. Kholikikos defeated Lemnos in the last dominion challenge so we rule now. As Drakon of the superior clan, I enforce not only my archon's laws, but the laws of the Realm."

"So...this dude is...what? Jealous? Pissed off at you?"

"Suicidal?" Caleb inserted his own two-cents worth.

"Perhaps all of the above. He has been playing his own game and I fear that he has involved the Humans in it."

"Mr. Wizard?"

"Perhaps. And Human thugs."

Sade exchanged a look with Caleb. "Frick and Frack on the witch's houseboat?"

"More than likely. As for your wizard, there is another problem."

"Really? Coulda fooled me."

"I do not appreciate your sarcasm. Apparently, an...artifact has gone missing."

Sade perked up. "What kind of artifact?"

"A very dangerous relic belonging to Dragonkin."

"Whose hoard got raided?"

"No one's. It belongs to all of Dragon kind and it is kept separate and safe."

Caleb pointed out the obvious. "Well, not so safe if it's missing."

Nikos favored Caleb with a glare, but Sade butted in before the two Magicks butted heads. "Do you think this Balaskas stole it?"

"This morning my answer would have been no. Now?" He moved slightly.

"If you do that whole French shrug thing, I'm going to punch you. Speaking of, did you happen to cross paths with that gawdammedmotherpissing Interpol vampire on your way in?"

Nikos blinked and backed up a step at both Sade's topic change and her vehemence. "No. Should I have?"

She continued muttering darkly under her breath. Caleb explained. "Durand set us up." He took another moment to gaze around the room. "How big is this *relic*?"

Holding up a fist, Nikos also looked around the room and realized it was in shambles. "What happened here?"

Sade stabbed a finger at Caleb. "You sniff again. I'll bring Nikos up to speed." It didn't take long to do either.

"Are you implying this human is in league with Balaskas?"

"I'm not implying anything. Here are the facts. One, the Dragons are missing a relic. Two, Caleb keeps finding traces of Human magic. Three, I keep getting dumped into the Dragon Realm. Four, there's a little pissant of a shit-faced weasel in Human Wizard guise who keeps popping up. You tell me how I should interpret that information."

"I admit it bears investigation. Balaskas is after me personally and my clan in principle. I admit that my relationship to you—"

"You slimy lizard!" Sade exploded. "We don't *have* a relationship."

"But we could have," Nikos challenged with a sly smile. "Where is your vampire lover? Why is he not here protecting you?"

"I don't need his protection."

"That is because he cannot take care of you."

"*Gah!*" She threw up her hands. "I don't need you or fucking anyone else to take care of me. And you just admitted that I wouldn't be in this gawdammed mess if it weren't for your obsession with me."

"I am *not* obsessed with you."

"You can't prove that by me, asshole."

A shrill whistle made them both wince. And shut up. "Children, please." Caleb waggled a finger. Sade glowered, the dragon hissed. "Should your relic smell like Dragon?"

Nikos opened his mouth to speak, then clamped it shut. A look of consternation crossed his face. "I don't actually know."

"Well, you might want to find out. The only trace of Dragon in this place is you and Balaskas. All the other magic? My nose says it's Human."

The dragon's eyes slitted and not because he squinted. His pupils changed shape and went silver and black. After a very long and very tense moment, he breathed one word. "No."

Sade ignored the smoke swirling around him and started to laugh. "Alchemy *is* involved. I'm right, aren't I?"

Two hours later, Sade sat on a bench beside the Seine. The top floor of the elegant building on the street behind her remained dark. Sinjen was no longer in residence. She had discovered that the code for the electronic locks was keyed to the time and place they'd first met.

She'd wandered through the apartment, touching the furniture, studying the artwork, staring out the windows. The place wore a mantle of age that bordered on repressive. She could almost feel the ghosts of the past treading through the various rooms. She definitely sensed Sinjen. His essence was embedded in every facet of the place. He'd spent a great deal of time in residence here.

Curiosity finally won out and she'd checked the closet. One side held clothes of a definitely feminine bent. She was surprised to find only two dresses—one a sleek black cocktail dress and the other an elegant formal in iridescent red silk. There were jeans. Slacks. Jackets. Blazers. A beautifully tailored suit in black with narrow red pinstripes. Shelves held boots—with various heel heights and from ankle to knee-highs. Tan. Black. Saddle brown.

There were blouses and shirts. In the built-in drawers, she found T-shirts and tanks. Sweaters. And underwear. The majority leaned toward very serviceable cotton panties and bras, but there were others—sexy scraps of silk, satin, and lace, matching in styles and colors.

She found one of his shirts in the hamper and pulled it out. Holding it to her nose, she inhaled deeply. It still smelled of him. Leather, ambergris, and raindrops hitting dust on a hot summer day. Closing her eyes, she sank onto the floor and cradled her cheek against the shirt.

After long moments, she raised her head, squared her shoulders and pushed off the floor. She considered leaving him a note but didn't. What could she say that she hadn't already said to voice mail and his answering machine? He'd have staff here, to look after the place and to clean and do laundry. She didn't want to leave a note where strangers could find and read it.

Now she sat on the bench. A few barges chugged slowly past. Traffic—auto and pedestrian—passed with a muted refrain above her head. The bench perched in the shadows and her dark clothing added to the illusion.

Alone. All alone. As she was meant to be. She'd taken a chance. Called Sinjen from *his* phone. He hadn't picked up. Not that she expected him to at this point. What had she been thinking? There was no way a man like Sinjen would ever stick with someone like her.

"Stupid, stupid, stupid," she muttered.

"Yes, yes you are."

Sade lunged to her feet and whirled. She'd been so sunk in her misery, she'd lost all situational awareness. As a result, this little twatwaffle managed to sneak up on her. She glared at the wizard. He still wore the ridiculous blue and night-glo stars robe and the pointed hat. She stood a foot taller than the guy but he definitely outweighed her. She was so done with this whole shit. "Dude, I just want you to know that I had my patience tested. I'm negative."

"But I own you. Bought and paid for."

"We already had that discussion. You wasted your money because if that club is owned by dragons? No refund, jackass."

"I do not care about the money. I'm claiming you."

"Listen you little toad, you do realize I'm the agent in charge of the FBI's MAGIC Unit, right?"

"You do realize that you are unique. That is why I want you. You are the *Enfant de L'homme*"

She huffed out a long-suffering sigh. "You're Human too."

The wizard turned shifty-eyed. "I am Magick."

"You're still Human. You shouldn't be able to open portals between Realms."

The little man puffed up like a bantam rooster. "I am a wizard. I have great powers." His expression turned sly. "If you join with me, that power would be yours too. Imagine what you could do with it."

Sade's answer was definitive. "No." She tapped the badge on her belt. "I have all the power I need right here. You are under arrest for magical crimes against humanity."

"You didn't even consider my proposition."

"Still no." She reached for her handcuffs.

Off in the distance, a creature roared. The wizard paled. "Was that a dragon?"

Grinning, Sade nodded. "Sounded like one to me."

A wolf howled. The wizard gulped. "Werewolf?"

"Yup." The cavalry had arrived.

The wizard blinked out of existence but his voice drifted back. "You will regret this."

Chapter Twenty-two

Pretty in Pink

Sade blinked. "How the holy fucking hell did he do that? He's a gawdamned Human!"

"Language, Lady Sade."

She looked up as Roman glided down to join her. She glanced around, feeling a bit guilty. "There aren't any nuns around," she mumbled.

A moment later, Nikos arrived, popping in from wherever with a small displacement of air. His nose twitched. "The wizard was here. I recognize his stench. Where did he go?"

Sade rolled her eyes. "You tell me, oh mighty and omnipresent Drakon. He keeps popping in and out of this plane of existence. Which, I will remind everyone, you and the Gargoyles say is not possible for a human to do without help. I'm telling you, he *poofed* out of here the minute he heard you roar. Way to go, by the way. Nice stealth mode there."

"The werewolf howled as well."

"Yeah, but unlike you, Caleb has to hoof it." She held up the set of handcuffs dangling from one finger. "I was thissss close to having him in custody." She held the thumb and forefinger of her other hand less than an inch apart.

Caleb vaulted over the railing from the street above and landed behind the bench. "What did I miss?"

"Mr. Wizard doing what everyone says is impossible."

Nose crinkled and red glints in his eyes, Caleb set immediately to work. He circled the spot where the wizard had stood. Four times. Then he stepped off in each of the cardinal directions, all but nose to the ground, figuratively speaking.

He finally returned. "I don't get it. It should be impossible for him."

Movement to her left drew her attention. Nikos was...fidgeting. What the ever-lovin' hell? "Nikos?" She drew out his name, a warning tone in her voice. "What do you know that we don't?"

His expression changed to one of resignation which matched the heavy sigh he exhaled. "I am not at liberty. I have to...check on some things."

"Get permission from the Archon, he means," Caleb muttered in Sade's ear.

Nikos focused an intense gaze on Sade. "Will you meet me in the cathedral gardens later?"

Something about his demeanor kept her from her usual waspish answer. "Yeah. I'll be around."

In a shimmer of silver, the dragon dissipated into thin air.

Sade shuddered. "That just freaks me the hell out every time."

To say Interpol had egg on their face was an understatement. Jean-Louis was nowhere to be found and his bosses were staying mum on the situation. Sade didn't want to bother the ancient vampire she'd grown up calling Aunt Polly. Dame Apolline was some high muckity-muck in the European branch of the Vampyre Conclave. Instead, she contacted Mathias. To say she wasn't worried about the former Interpol agent rearing his handsome head again after that call was an understatement. Too bad all her Vampire problems weren't so easily solved.

Nikos was back. He'd had no more luck tracking down the rogue dragon than she'd had finding Mr. Wizard. She wanted to go home.

Not that there was anything waiting for her in DC. Not anymore. But it was familiar. And routine. Too bad this case was still a priority.

After a night of tossing and turning, therefore little sleep, she'd dragged out of bed to find the cat, which had shown up on her walk back to the hotel, was now MIA, and a note under her door from Caleb saying he'd be at Interpol at least until noon. She'd showered, dressed, and stopped in for coffee and croissants at the bakery on the corner.

Currently, she stood on the Pont au Double, one of bridges over the Seine leading to the island where Notre Dame Cathedral stood still encased in a steel skeleton. She noticed, for the first time, that the iconic steeple was lying where it had crashed. The fire that followed the explosion, while devastating, hadn't been catastrophic—at least not to the Gargoyles. Roman stood on her right, Nikos on her left. One gave off the chill of carved granite, the other the heat of a volcano.

"Magic is a fragile thing," Roman said. "Like a human life."

"But Magicks aren't." Bitterness shaded Sade's voice.

Nikos glanced her way. "You are formed by the fires of your desires and longings, Sade."

"Bullshit."

"You aren't exactly Human."

She opened her mouth to scald him, but Roman's soft admonition stopped her, "He's right, Lady Sade. Because you were marked by Fae and Vampire both, you carry a touch of magic." She scowled at him but he continued unfazed. "As to the rest, you are driven by your viewpoint, by perceived injustices. You ingest it, push it deep, and then, when nothing makes sense and you are going under, drowning in the swirling brew of emotions, you explode."

"Do not," she muttered, knowing damn good and well that Roman was right.

Excited shouts and laughter and what sounded like cannon fire captured their attention. A mob tumbled up the Qual de Montebello headed toward the Square René Viviani. They were not the first group to dance by headed ultimately to the Eiffel Tower. This was some sort of jubilant celebration or a crazy marathon. Sade didn't know which. She hadn't exactly been keeping up with current events beyond her investigation. As the happy mob passed the green space of the square, a cannon fired again, the shell exploding above the crowd, raining pink powder down on them.

"Yes." Nikos pointed to the throng. "You look just like them when you detonate, all pretty in pink."

"You take that back!"

Nikos never saw her fist. Through a busted lip, he said, "I rest my case."

Roman pulled a handkerchief seemingly out of thin air. The dragon ignored the proffered item. He wiped his mouth with the back of his hand. In that blink of time, he'd healed. "You should be glad you *are* mostly Human, Sade." His voice held real menace. "There is not another in any of the Realms who would remain breathing after such an insult."

"You don't scare me, Nikos."

"Sade..." Roman's voice held caution.

"He doesn't." She whirled on Roman and stabbed a finger at his chest. "Nothing scares me anymore. And hasn't since I was three and Titania said she should kill me and Mathias said he would."

She walked away to stunned silence. Then Roman called her name. She didn't stop walking, just flipped him off with her middle finger without turning around. Death didn't scare her. In fact, it would be preferable to the misery she was currently experiencing.

"Fuck this shit," she said to the black cat who was suddenly sitting on the bridge railing.

Sade walked away. Nikos was angry and it was never wise to piss off a dragon. So far, she was batting five hundred when it came to pissing off powerful Magicks. Shit happened. She'd made a habit of doing just that in her career. Why not totally fuck up her private life while she was at it? The vibes she got from Roman were resigned rather than riled. That shit happened a lot too. Might was well bat a thousand while she was at it. Sinjen. Nikos. Roman. Ariel. She pondered what she could do to piss off Caleb.

The area teemed with people. Tourists and locals alike thronged the streets and sidewalks now that the runners had passed and the colored dust settled. The storm cloud on her face moved them quickly out of her way as she marched back to her hotel. She ignored the two gargoyles flying like silent shadows overhead. Varrick, the motherfucker, probably ordered them to ride guard duty. The one thing she couldn't ignore even now wound between her ankles as she waited for the light to change so she could cross the street.

"Go home," she muttered.

"*Mowrr.*"

"Seriously?"

A deep voice muttered something in French and Sade caught enough to turn just in time. A man had his foot locked and loaded to punt the black cat out into traffic. He wheezed out a breath as Sade jammed the barrel of her Beretta into the soft skin under his chin.

"Touch the fucking cat and die." She spoke English but the man translated and held his breath.

The light changed but no one in the knot of people moved. "Let's go, cat," Sade said as she pivoted and returned the pistol to its holster. The cat scampered up the back of her slacks, then sank claws into her jacket until it made it to her shoulder and perched there.

"Witch," the man spat.

"Nope," Sade said. "The word you're looking for is bitch."

She stepped off the curb and crossed the street alone. "Whatever," she said to the cat.

"*Meeworrar.*"

"My sentiments exactly."

The gargoyles circled overhead until she stepped into the hotel. The concierge said nothing about the cat. Smart man. Upstairs in her room, the cat leaped to the small table, posed dramatically for a moment so Sade could admire it, and then it raised a back leg and started to lick itself.

Shedding her jacket, weapons—the one holstered on her belt and the knife in her boot—and badge, she walked to the window and stared out. There wasn't much of a view but she'd never stayed at the Hotel Mount Blanc for the view. It was convenient. She pushed the panes open and breathed in. Aromas from every description of food wafted in. The hustle and bustle of busy people crowding the pedestrian way, the clamor of drinkers at a nearby bar did nothing to drown out the voices of the ghosts in her own head.

Everyone had warned her. Caleb. Roman. Ariel—though his advice was always suspect. Nikos, who had ulterior motives. Crevan. And Mathias. Mathias who made Sinjen. Who knew him best. They'd all told her to stay away from the former Knight Templar. Mathias had been the bluntest.

Do not ever give your heart to one of us, Sade. We of the Nysferanti do not have hearts or souls. We are destined to destroy Humans, not love them.

Words to live by, she decided belatedly. But she'd seen into Sinjen's soul, despite his disclaimer that he'd lost it centuries before. She'd felt his gentleness. Oh, he could be a ruthless bastard, no doubts there, but he had treated the secret heart of her with care. Until now.

She had to try one more time. Pulling out her cell phone, she stared at the number pad for a long moment.

"*Mrrrff?*"

She glanced at the cat. It had paused in its bath to stare at her with unblinking yellow eyes. "Yeah, yeah. I know. I'm a glutton for punishment."

Sade stabbed at the numbers and put the phone to her ear. It rang three times then rolled to a generic voice mail message. That was new. And discouraging.

"Okay then. I guess you really mean it this time. Fun while it lasted and all that bullshit. I know the drill. Promises, promises." She swallowed hard around the lump in her throat. She would not cry. "Hey, wasn't that a Broadway show or something? Not that either of us would go or anything." She had to swallow again and clear her throat to keep her voice from cracking. "Guess this is it then. I won't bother you again. Good—"

She clicked off the phone before she finished saying a final farewell.

Chapter Twenty-three

Rock, Paper, Scissors

Returning to Notre Dame late in the afternoon, Sade didn't go up to the rooms currently occupied by Roman and Verity. When the little witch wasn't tracking Sade's ass every time she went MIA, she was with Tabor down in the archives pouring over ancient tomes. Sade hated the catacombs. Those old books made her sneeze, which upset the scholars working down there. Instead, she found a bench back under one of the neat rows of trees dividing the garden into walkways.

Since the rebellion and the burning of the cathedral, this part of the grounds were off limits to tourists. They still flocked the sidewalks along the adjoining streets and the large square at the front of the building. The cat strolled up and flopped nearby, taking advantage of a small oval of sunshine. It lay there, baleful yellow eyes focused on Sade, tail whipping back and forth.

Human glowered at cat. Cat remained unperturbed. Typical. The dragon's words from that morning came back to haunt her. *"You aren't exactly Human."*

Chewing over that, she was lost in thought when Caleb dropped onto the bench beside her. "Penny for your thoughts."

She glanced at him. "They're not worth even that."

He bumped her shoulder with his. "He'll calm down, Sade. It'll be all right."

"No." She shook her head. "He's done with me."

Caleb snorted. "I don't believe that for a minute." He swiveled to face her. "I don't like him, Sade. He's a vampire. It's a species-deep mistrust. But I see him with you and by that, I mean that I *see* him. You mean something to him."

She continued shaking her head in the negative. "Not anymore. He left me." Her voice cracked and she looked away, realizing the cat was gone. She cleared her throat. "What'd you do, scare the cat off?"

"Cat wasn't here."

"Figures," she mumbled. "They all abandon me eventually."

Caleb bit his tongue. It was hard, watching her like this. Sade wasn't one to wallow. And she only whined about a lack of coffee and stupid people. He considered personally calling Sinjen or whether he should just fly to Chicago and use the guy as a chew toy. There was bad stuff happening and this whole deal was distracting her at a time when she needed to be focused. For the moment, he'd let things play out.

"Nikos has been cleared. Officially."

She lifted her shoulders. "I punched him in the mouth this morning so I figured that was the case."

Leaning around so he could see her face, Caleb carefully enunciated, "You punched the dragon in the mouth?"

"Yeah. It was a good punch too. Busted his lip. For about two point three nanoseconds. Then he healed."

"*Why* did you punch him in the mouth?"

"He pissed me off."

Caleb closed his eyes, seeking patience. "Sade. He pisses you off constantly."

"Well, he pissed me off more than usual. The word pink was involved."

He managed not to execute a facepalm. "Are you over your snit enough that we can go debrief him and Roman?"

She pushed off the bench and took two steps before turning back. "You could do that without me."

"Chicken."

So what if she didn't want to face Nikos right then. But Caleb was right. She trailed after him and without admitting she was doing

175

so, Sade kept an eye out for the cat. He was nowhere to be seen. Upstairs in Roman's rooms, two gargoyles, a dragon, and the newly-arrived werewolf sucked all the air out of the place. She pointed at Varrick. "Why are *you* here?"

"Orders from *Le Vieil*."

Since Notre Dame *was* Gargoyle territory, Sade couldn't say much and since Varrick called Crevan by his title, the Gargoyles weren't fucking around. Caleb told them what he'd learned at Interpol but was interrupted by Sade's phone. She glanced at the screen. *UNKNOWN CALLER*. She almost ignored it but the hair on the back of her neck prickled. She held up a finger to silence Caleb and answered with a brusque, "Marquis."

"I told you that you would be sorry. If I can't have you, neither can he."

Sade recognized the high-pitched whine immediately but he hung up before she could say anything. All eyes were on her. "My not-so-secret admirer, Mr. Wizard."

"What did he say?" Caleb looked concerned.

Surprised he hadn't been able to overhear the conversation, she rolled her eyes. "Some stupid and dramatic bullshit." She changed the timbre of her voice and whined out a pretty good imitation, even if she did say so herself. "I told you that you would be sorry. If I can't have you, neither can he."

"What does that mean?" Varrick glanced around at the others as if they'd have a clue.

Sade stared into space then focused on Caleb. Then Roman and Varrick before finally settling on Nikos. All there. All the men who were involved in this investigation. But one.

"Caleb, where's Ariel?"

After a slow blink, Caleb rubbed his chin, brows knitted as he thought back to the last time he'd seen the fae. "Truthfully? I have no clue."

Sade ran to the first set of windows and ripped the panes open. Leaning out, she raised her face to the sky. "Ariel! Ariel Daoine!"

Silence.

She exchanged a look with Caleb. He rolled his eyes. She slipped her phone out of her pocket and punched numbers.

Ariel picked up after the second ring. "*Bon jour*, my darling Sade, are you missing me?"

"Where are you?"

Something in the tone of her voice alerted Ari and he replied soberly, "I am at Versailles. Oberon is in residence. Why? What has happened?"

"Nothing."

Caleb barked out a laugh then in a voice that could be heard over the phone said, "Nothing but a couple more realm hops, a break-up with the vampire, a rogue dragon out to kill our least-favorite Drakon, and a crazy wizard who stole a magic relic."

"I will be there within the hour. I must finish something here first."

"No! I didn't call you to come running, Ari."

The fae's voice turned sly. "Then why did you call, darling Sade?"

She cut-off the call muttering, "gawddamned-glitter-fucking Fae."

Moments later, there was a knock on the door. Sustenance in the form of food and drink had arrived. While everyone's attention was focused elsewhere, Sade surreptitiously dialed another number.

"Sinjen," she whispered, listening to the ring. Her thoughts solidified. *Pick up the gawddamned phone, Sinjen. This is important. Where are you? Dammit, answer me.*

Click. "You have reached the number of Kristian St. John. Leave a message at the tone." *Beep.* She left her message demanding he call her back and she didn't care how pissed he was. She called his land line at home and office and left variations of the same message.

When she turned to face the others, they all recognized the flash of green fire in her eyes.

"I need some air."

The lights of Paris seemed dimmer here among the trees and plants of the formal gardens. She'd wandered around, unsure what she was seeking. Water burbled softly in the Fountain of the Virgin, the centerpiece of the gardens. She found a bench tucked up under the trees and sat. They'd worked all afternoon, and now it was dusk.

She caught a soft *mew* a moment before something brushed against her ankles.

"So, you decided to come out of hiding, huh?" She sat still. The cat was likely feral as it had a lean and hungry look and despite the fact he had a tendency to follow her around and climb her like a cat tree, he did his own thing. She reached into her backpack and pulled out what was left of the gyros Caleb dashed out to buy before heading back to their hotel. "Hungry?"

Tearing off a piece of the wrapper, she fished out a piece of gyro meat and tore it into small bites before leaning to place the wrapper on the bench just beyond arm's length. The cat studied her, yellow eyes unblinking. Sade ignored him. Her. It. The way her luck was running, the thing had to be male. She leaned her head back, eyes closed, and listened to the vertebrae pop in her neck.

"*Mwor?*"

"Yeah, long day. You?"

A black shadow slunk up onto the bench and sniffed the meat. "One hundred percent gyro, my friend. Lamb and beef. Hard to beat it."

The cat snagged a piece and ate daintily.

"I know. It's weird that I'm craving Greek food when I'm plagued by Greek dragons. Still, there's just something about the pita bread, meat, onions, and tzatziki sauce. Got introduced to them when I was in college and fell in love."

"Then there is hope for me yet."

The cat skittered away with a hiss and growl.

"That wasn't nice. Poor little guy is probably starving." Sade stood up and carefully added more meat to the wrapper. "Here ya go, cat. I'll keep you safe from the big, bad scaly lizard."

She turned to walk away, Nikos at her side. He all but purred, "But who is going to keep *you* safe, *mikró*?"

Patting her weapon, she smiled. "I came loaded for Dragon." She also didn't point out the squadron of Gargoyles silently winging through the night sky. Nikos would be as aware of them as she was.

They drifted out into the open walkway around the fountain. Stars, scattered by the hand of a careless god across indigo velvet, glittered above her. The sweep of endless sky filled her with a loneliness so intense, so deep, that her soul cried out.

No. She would not give into the dark demons devouring her heart. She stopped walking, staring at the fountain. "Did you find out anything more about the relic?"

"You are correct. It is alchemical in origin."

"So Human magic then."

"Yes."

"Makes sense."

"It does?"

"Yeah, up to a point. I don't have all the info I need. And I damn sure want to find out who that fucking pissant of a wizard is and how he manages to portal hop." And now that he'd used threats? The dude would be toast when she caught him.

"My people are working on that."

"Why should your people be involved? Don't you have enough to worry about with that bastard Balaskas on the loose?"

Nikos stilled and she glanced at him. His stony expression did not bode well for garnering any more information.

"Ah, Dragon business. Got it. Let's keep the puny human out of things even though the scaly bastard promised to kill her. Much easier to mount me in his lair that way."

"I will deal with Timon Balaskas. He will not trouble you again."

"Yeah, yeah. Promises, promises. I get a lot of those made and broken. You have a lot on your plate, Drakon. Best hop to, huh?"

Before she could walk away, warmth pressed against her back, alien, unfamiliar. An arm tightened around her ribs, just below her breasts.

"Beautiful Sade, *khriso mou.*" the dragon whispered in her ear. "My treasure." He rubbed his cheek against her hair. "Now that the vampire has abandoned you, I can make you mine."

"I'm not some perfect jewel to be coveted, Nikos. Definitely not something to be displayed on a pedestal in your hoard. That's what both you and Balaskas want."

"You *are* a jewel, Lady Sade—"

"Gawddammit. Do *not* call me that. Only one person gets to do that. Only Roman."

"Not even the vampire?"

Her heart twisted. "Especially not Sinjen."

"He never deserved you," Nikos hissed.

"And you do?"

"Perhaps not, but I desire you and *I* would not toss you away." Nikos stared into her eyes. "You are in danger yet he abandons you. Even when you call and beg, he ignores you. *I* do not treat my treasures with such cruelty, *mikró.*"

The words tore through her, hacking and slashing until her barriers were left in bloody shreds. She fought for control. She would not let Nikos see her wounds. She had only shared her fears with one man and look where that left her. That was the bottom line. She was broken. A pawn for much of her life, told by the man who held her existence in his hand that he would kill her in a heartbeat if it suited his purposes. She squeezed her eyes shut. Too many ghosts strolling through her memories tonight.

"No. You'd hide me away."

"You'd be protected."

"I keep telling you I can protect myself." She sucked in a breath. "And that's the difference. He knows I'm capable of taking care of myself."

"But why should you have to?"

"You want to claim me, to own me."

"I would treasure you."

"I don't want to be your treasure. I don't need anyone to take care of me. I don't need anyone at all."

"We *all* need someone, *mikró*."

She remembered that word, somewhere in the back of her mind. Little one. That's what it meant. Before she could deny the endearment, Nikos turned her, took her mouth in a breathless kiss. Her lips softened as she took him in, searched for some spark, found none.

"Sinjen."

Nikos pushed her away. "Do not brand his name on my lips."

She hadn't meant to speak that name aloud, but it was time she faced the truth. "There's just one. And it's not you."

Nikos walked away but stopped at a stone plinth and lounged against it. He wore his arrogance like a three-thousand-dollar suit. "The vampire is a fool. As are you, Sade. You should have never succumbed to his cold embrace." He gave her a slow smile that didn't reach his eyes. "You should have let me claim you, *khriso mou*. Your kiss—"

"Shut up!" Sade almost screamed the words. She stormed up to him, planted both palms against his chest and shoved. He actually backed up a step, then another as she charged him again. "I am so fucking done with the lies and the innuendos. I am gawddamned sick and tired of all the fucking games."

Caleb charged up but slid to a stop, standing slack jawed. Were those tears sparkling in Sade's eyes? Sade didn't cry. Not ever. He reached for her but missed. She had up a full head of steam that rivaled a bulldozer and she rammed all her anger into the dragon.

Nikos, always arrogant and audacious, was currently dumbfounded by her behavior. Oh, she'd punched him. A few times. But those had meant nothing, just a flare of her temper. This? This was beyond his experience with her. He did nothing to protect himself until she swung a closed fist at his face. He blocked that punch but didn't pay any attention to her other hand until it landed a blow to his midsection that literally knocked the fire out of him. He managed to turn his head and suck the flames back into his mouth before he singed Sade.

She glowered at him and damn him but he *did* covet the jeweled green of her eyes. Still bent over, he wheezed, "It is not my fault that he left you and now chooses to ignore you."

"I don't believe that for a gawddamned minute. You're the one who loves to fuck with him, to play your stupid mind games." She advanced on him again. "You said something to him. Or did something. Where the hell is he?"

"I don't know." He ground out the words.

She grabbed the front of his shirt and hauled him upright, then proceeded to shake him.

"Where in the gawddamned nine circles of hell is Sinjen?" She screamed the words.

"Sade, truly." Nikos moderated his voice, keeping it soft and calm. Her behavior was so far beyond the pale that he was truly worried now. He reached out and brushed one knuckle across her cheek. "You are crying."

She shoved at him and backed away. "No. I am not fucking crying." She pounded her right fist against her own chest, mimicking the rhythm of her heartbeat. "I'm a gawddamned thunderstorm and that's the rain falling."

Nikos tried again. He approached slowly, his hand still out. She backed away this time. "Sade. I don't want to hurt you. I never wanted to hurt you."

"I'm not fucking hurt, you gawddamned mother-fuckingasshole. I'm angry. And frustrated. And mad as fucking hell."

Werewolf and dragon exchanged baffled looks. Then they stared at Sade. Caleb saw it then. Saw the fear—no, saw the sheer terror that Sade had been holding inside since the night Sinjen walked out. As they watched, she dropped to a squat, her butt against her heels, her face buried between her knees. "I have to find him. So I can tell him."

The rustle of leather wings caught the attention of Caleb and Nikos. Roman, wings unfurled, settled beside them. A moment later, gold glitter sparkled and Ariel popped into existence.

The fae stalked toward the dragon. "What have you done?"

"Nothing. I kissed her." Nikos looked up at the sudden silence. "She said his name. Said I would never be the one."

Without a word, Roman moved to her, bent and lifted Sade into his arms.

"I'm not crying, Romo," she muttered her childhood name for him against his chest.

"No, Lady Sade. You never cry."

183

Two days later, her phone vibrated in her pocket. Grabbing it, she tried not to hope even as those hopes were dashed by the wrong vampire.

"Hello, Mathias."

"Where is Sinjen?"

"How should I know? He's pissed at me and not taking my calls."

"I can't reach him."

"Okay. So he's pissed at you too."

"No. Sade. I cannot *reach* him."

"Wait. What? Oh fuck me running. Where is he?'"

"This is what I am asking you."

"I don't know where the fuck he is. He left Paris and went back to Chicago for all I know. I've been calling him for days."

"Do you feel it?"

"Feel what?"

"Focus, Sade. He marked you. You should be able to feel the connection between you."

She shivered despite the warmth of the Paris sun. Icy fingers of dread clutched her. "You made him, Mathias. Why can't *you* feel him?"

Silence. She could almost hear Mathias planning his response. "Sinjen is a master in his own right," her godfather eventually answered. "He is capable of...suppressing our link."

That didn't make her feel better. She didn't want to ask but she had to know. "If he can cut you off, why wouldn't he do the same to me?"

"Sade." Reproach drenched her name.

"It's a fair question." This was a bone she couldn't stop gnawing.

"Despite everything, you are his. He would not leave you alone. Not willingly."

She might argue that, all things considered. "But he did, Mathias. Willingly."

"No, Child. He did not."

She jerked at the sound of that voice. Crevan stood three feet away and she'd had no clue he was there.

"*Le Vieil* is accurate, Sade. There were circumstances. He might have left you physically, but he will not deliberately sever your tie."

Silence stretched between them after that declaration. Sade couldn't help but mull over the possibilities. None of them were good.

Finally, Mathias offered a final order. "Find him."

"I will."

Chapter Twenty-four

Goin' Huntin'

Sade eyed Caleb. "There's no trace of him anywhere?"

"That's what I'm saying."

She sat down abruptly. Her brain might be in control but her knees refused to cooperate and buckled. She would not panic. They'd been searching for days. With the Dragon clans claiming sovereignty over the situation between Clan Kholikikos and Clan Nekyios and Interpol returning jurisdiction over the murders to the Paris police, the Director ordered her and Caleb home.

As soon as they touched down on American soil, Sade set to work looking for the wizard. And Sinjen. She needed to stay focused. And to stay focused, she needed to get pissed. She'd stay pissed because Sinjen still wasn't taking or returning her calls. He was pissed at her. That was all. He was off somewhere. Besides Chicago. She'd checked. Bless talkative doormen. Sinjen had been there. But then he...wasn't. There was no sign of a struggle in his apartment, according to the concierge who arranged for the cleaning service. He'd gone out one night, returned, and they hadn't seen him since.

"No sign of a struggle," she murmured. She had to hang onto that. Sinjen was a master vampire. At the height of his powers. He would not go down without a fight. And he would not... With a small gasp, she jerked her thoughts back from that precipice. A lump the size of a fist lodged in her throat. Nononono. No panicking. He would not just...NO!

"Don't go there," she ordered herself. Caleb gave her an odd look of concern mixed with confusion. Louder, she added, "Something's happened to him."

"He didn't—"

186

"I know that!" Sade sprang up and prowled around her office. "Sinjen would *not* walk into the sun." She stopped at her window, inhaled deeply and told the view outside, "I would know. If he did that. I'd know."

And she would. Sinjen was under her skin. She couldn't touch his mind as easily as he could hers, but she'd know if he ceased to exist. Still, whenever she thought about him there was only a void where his psyche should be. She headed for the door.

"Where are you going?"

Her Texas drawl snuck into her voice when she answered. "I'm goin' huntin.'"

"I'm coming with you."

Sade shook her head. "No. This is on me."

Because it was. She would find him. Or else.

Find the wizard, find Sinjen. Concentrate on finding the little turd. It shouldn't be this fucking hard. The wizard apparently sprang whole cloth into this world. No one knew who he was. Not Interpol. Not the FBI. CIA. DHS. ATF. US Marshals. The national police in every European country she'd contacted. Mathias had gone to the Concilium Magicae. None of the Human representatives knew him. They'd have turned his ass over in a heartbeat because Sade and the Vampires weren't the only ones looking. Not even the Dragons could find him.

She'd caught the train from Washington to New York. She had a slim lead that might point either to his identity or his location and she planned to spend the day in the Big Apple pursuing it. After hitting a couple of magic shops and talking to the leaders of NYC's most powerful coven of white witches, Sade was no closer to her prey.

Walking aimlessly, she stopped to grab a slice of pizza when the scents wafting from a tiny pizzeria almost brought her to her knees. New York style pizza. Tomato sauce, pepperoni, cheese. She folded the huge slice, grabbed napkins, and head toward her final destination. Considering how frustrating her day had been, she deserved a treat. She continued walking down 5th Street absorbed in eating.

Chewing and swallowing the last bite, Sade gazed up at St. Patrick's Cathedral from across the street. Gargoyles perched among the spires, soaking up the sun and watching her through unblinking eyes. She wondered how many of the pedestrians around her were aware they were under Magick surveillance. She dipped her chin in acknowledgment. The shadow of Atlas, struggling to hold up the heavens, fell across her. She knew how he felt and offered a two-fingered salute as she passed the iconic statue. At the corner, she turned right and a block later she was smack dab in the teeming crowd at Rockefeller Center. Sade had never felt so alone. She kept walking, though slowly as she massaged the crick in her neck she developed from constantly scanning her surroundings.

She had decisions to make. Too bad she had no one to talk to. Caleb was back in Washington being all Werewolfy with his mate, Adele. Roman and Verity returned to the States and he was busy with his duties as the Legate of New Orleans. Ariel was not the fae to discuss affairs of the heart with. Especially not *her* heart.

A shadow drifted across the sidewalk. She searched the skies but found nothing. With her luck, that damn dragon had cloaked himself invisible and was stalking her. Nikos was one of the decisions she had to make. Nikos and Sinjen.

Her heart hurt at the thought of the enigmatic vampire. "So I walk away," she murmured. "As soon as I find him."

"And then what?" the wind whispered.

Good question. Could she leave Sinjen behind? He'd left her and she didn't give a tinker's damn what Crevan and Mathias said about extenuating circumstances. He'd *left* her.

At the next corner, a busker strummed his guitar, watching her intently before launching into a Creedence Clearwater song. Sade listened to the whole thing then dropped a twenty into his guitar case. Good advice in the lyrics.

The musician gave her a chin lift. "Stay proud, Mary."

Mind made up, she strolled away, smiling. "The name's Sade but close enough."

He awoke to darkness though his body insisted the sun reigned supreme. After a millennium of nights, Sinjen knew. He shouldn't be awake. The day sleep was the only thing that gave his kind peace.

Fabric rustled. He focused on the wizened man in the corner of the basement. The old man's face split into a demented smile when he realized he had Sinjen's attention. "Welcome to your humble abode." He cackled and added, "It's hell, boy."

Then he disappeared, leaving Sinjen alone with his thoughts. Alone with his hunger. Alone with his need for the Human woman who was his life. He should never have left her. Should have ignored the old ones. What did they know?

He managed to stand by clawing his way up the wall. His head swam. His body insisted it was daylight and he should be sleeping like the dead man he was.

"Kristian St. John." The name tasted odd on his dry lips and he caught his tongue on his fangs. "I am Kristian St. John."

Sinjen.

There it was. The voice that haunted his dreams, a ghost of past, present, and future.

"Sade."

He said the name like a prayer. Dry laughter echoed around him and small cascades of dust rained down. His soul was damned. There were no prayers for one such as he. There was no salvation. No redemption. No peace.

Sinjen.

He roared, tormented by memories that were nothing more than vague ghosts swirling through mists and playing hide-and-seek among standing stones. He remembered riding across Salisbury Plain with his brothers-in-arms. Armor creaking, hoof beats thudding in the thick grasslands. And the specter of the ancient stones rearing up. Even then, bards sang of the legendary Merlin and the magic henge he created.

Knight Templar. He'd worn the white tabard emblazoned by the red cross. He'd fought in the Holy Lands. And he had sacrificed his life. No. Not his life. His soul. Mathias DeVrie. The man was not a man but an abomination. Yet only he could defeat *O Kim Bkze Bedoaru Gelmek.* Even now, even without understanding why, he was reluctant to use any but the ancient name for the witch. Sahirah. The name hovered there in his memory. He'd offered his blood and his life and had been repaid with centuries of torment.

Until...*her.* Bottle green eyes. Black hair. A beauty mark at the corner of her mouth. Long legs. A song played in his head. He'd been listening to it shortly before...

Before what?

Music danced just on the edge of his hearing. *She's got the look...*

He'd been thinking of her. Heard the song that reminded him of her. And then...nothing. *She's got the look.* Would she be looking for him?

No. She couldn't find him. She was Human. And he could not have her. To be with her meant her death. One way or another. The Old Ones. They'd been adamant. He could change her. Or she would change him. They would both die.

He'd walked away. Broken his promise. Was that not to be expected from one whose soul was as black as his?

Clawing at the walls of his prison, he roared again. Why could he not think? Why could he not remember? Escape. The sun. He could walk into the sun and end his torment.

He started digging.

Chapter Twenty-five

Making It Right

Sade had one stop to make before catching the late train back to DC. She cut back over to 5th Street and trudged the eight blocks to the New York Public Library. The lions rested on their pedestals and she swore one yawned while the other winked at her as she climbed the steps between them.

The woman she was looking for inhabited a tiny office on the ground floor. If she'd been thinking, she would have used the 42nd Street entrance. Instead, she clomped down the stairs from the first floor. She waited to get buzzed through into the office area. On this level, only the Children's Center and a forum room were accessible by the public.

Sade flashed her badge and ID several times before getting to the expert she needed. Agatha Bellwether, PhD was small and round and reminded Sade of Aunt Clara on "Bewitched." Her skin was smooth but crinkled at the corner of her eyes and mouth whenever she changed expressions. Frowzy hair the color of cooked carrots exploded around her face. Reading glasses leashed by a chain around her neck perched on the tip of her nose. And she was the foremost authority on Human Magicks genealogy in the United States.

After two hours with Agatha, Sade was bleary-eyed and dumbfounded by the amount of material housed in the various archives and basement storage areas of the library. She also had a name. Ichabod Trane. She was still rolling her eyes over that one. Turned out ol' Icky had a dragon in the woodpile about fifty Human generations back. That explained a lot of things. She still had no idea where to find him but at least she had a solid lead.

Her head still pretty much circling the drain, she exited the library the same way she'd entered—climbing the stairs to the first floor and heading out onto 5th Avenue. She stopped, right foot on one step, left foot on the step below. A sleek black cat sat perched on the stone lion's back. Sade could never remember which was Patience and which was Fortitude but there was the damn cat, sitting like a statue, tail curled over his front paws and staring at her with unblinking yellow eyes.

"What the fuck?" She muttered the expletive but a nanny with two youngsters in private school uniforms scowled while the kids grinned at her. Ignoring the cat, she continued down the steps and turned right. Penn Station was about a twenty-minute walk. She glanced at her watch. She was in good time to make it for the next train and if she missed it, she could definitely catch the last train, which ran at 8:13 pm.

She strode away, still ignoring the cat and wondering why trains couldn't run on an even schedule, say like, eight o'clock sharp. Pulling out her phone, she started making calls. Caleb got a voice mail. Nikos got a message left with Stavros, his second who happened to hate Sade's guts but considering what all was currently going down in the Dragon Realm, he deigned to take the message. She also checked in with the Director. Mathias would have to wait. It was an hour earlier in Dallas and the sun was still up there.

Navigating Penn Station was always fun—not—but she managed to get her ticket for the last train. She was in time to catch the 7:40, but she could hang out, get some coffee and food, take the 8:13 and still arrive in DC eight minutes faster because the late train was an express. Easy decision. Coffee and food. She found both and settled in for a short wait.

Boarding the train, she found a seat removed from other passengers in the car. In just under 3 hours, she'd be back in DC. Since her experience in Paris, train travel wasn't so relaxing. That was also another reason for not eating or drinking on a train. She didn't believe the wizard was here in the US, at least not at the moment.

And he might have nothing to do with Sinjen's disappearance but her gut, along with every cop and magical instinct she'd honed over the years screamed the two were connected.

She had a window seat and watched the city slide by as the journey began. The train ducked into a tunnel under the Hudson river and came back up in New Jersey. The scenery began to blur and she closed her eyes.

Sade, curled in a fetal ball, kept the covers pulled tight over her head. She'd made sure all the edges were tucked in before she shimmied between them. Everyone knew that the monsters couldn't get you if you were under the covers.

Bang. Clank.

What was that? She did her best to regulate her pounding heart, listening hard, sifting through all the possibilities in her mind as she scrambled to identify the sound.

Bang. Clank.

She soooo wanted to peek out, see what was making the noise. *No,* she reminded herself. *The monsters will get me.*

Bang. Clank.

Snuffle.

Pressing her hand against her mouth, she stifled the scream gathering deep all-the-way-to-her-toes down inside her.

Snuffle. Grrr.

Her mattress bounced as something heavy pounced.

Bang. Clank.

Claws scrabbled at the pillow where her head rested, pawing and digging. She clutched the sheets tighter in her fists. Her brain conjured all sorts of monsters—trolls with stinky garlic breath and rotting teeth that were still sharp, ghouls with their long, curved claws they used to dig up dead bodies in cemeteries—

Bang. Clank.

Whine.

Hot, fetid breath filtered through the sheet over her face followed by more digging.

"Wake up, Sade!"

The growling voice cut through her fear and she blinked against bright light as the sheet was ripped from her hands. Eyes flashing feral red stared down at her though the face remained in shadow. Lips moved and the white tip of a fang glinted as the figure turned away. Her instincts were to burrow back beneath the covers but she wasn't a coward. Nor was she a child.

Her legs cramped as she stretched them out and she winced. Lips dry, she didn't have enough saliva in her mouth to lick them. As her eyes adjusted, she took in her surroundings. Not her room—not the one she grew up in nor the one in her Washington townhouse. And it wasn't Sinjen's apartment. The shadow moved across the room, drawing her attention. That wasn't Sinjen either. Where the fucking hell was she? And what the fucking hell was she doing here?

"That language doesn't become a lady, Sade," the shadow said.

Wait. What? She had *not* voiced those thoughts aloud.

"You are in my realm, Sade, and my magic is much more...potent here."

He could read her fucking mind? Crap, crap, crap. She searched her memory for the most annoying earworm of a song she could remember the words to. She put her mind on a loop—Lady Gaga, Queen, The Monkees, and finished it off with "Macarena" and "It's a Small World."

The shadow winced and the light pressure in her head she'd only become aware of when it was withdrawn disappeared. Even kitten paws had claws. She needed to remember that while she figured out what the fuck was going on.

Now that she was awake and functional, as the last vestiges of her nightmare faded, she took stock of her situation. She was dressed. Sort of. Who the hell wore diaphanous nightgowns? Shit. Maybe this was still part of the nightmare. The bedroom was illuminated by candles—all shapes and sizes and probably hundreds of them. Flimsy curtains hung at an open window and danced with each breeze entering the room. Yeah, that wasn't dangerous.

Tucked back into a dark corner, the shadow watched her. She knew this because his eyes burned feral red continuously now. While singing "Small World" in her mind, she sorted through the monster drawer in her mental file cabinet. Not ghoul, goblin, or troll. Not a zombie. Nachthexens and bansidhes were female and if her jailer was female, she was gawdawful ugly. Not a wendigo. Werewolf? Maybe, if he was rogue. She was under the protection of Romulus Jones, the Texas pack alpha. Not Gargoyle. All those rogues had died in the Battle of New Orleans, not to mention that *Le Vieil*, Roman, and Varrick had the Sentinels on watch. Fae didn't have fangs or do that woo-woo red shit with their eyes. Vampire? Shit. That would totally suck.

Vamps were always on power trips. She knew this because Mathias DeVrie, the baddest of the bad-ass master vamps, was her godfather. And she'd been sleeping with Sinjen St. John for— She nipped that thought in the bud as her heart constricted. Then another thought hit her. Dragon. Oh to the fuck no! Granted, while the Drakon of Clan Kholikikos, Nikos Constantine, really wanted in her pants, there were those—like Stavros, whom she'd caused to be exiled for a time, who weren't too keen on their pairing. Shit.

Double shit. Nikos *was* a dreamwalker.

Darkness crashed as all the candles winked out. The strains of a song filtered in. "Total Eclipse of the Heart." Her worst nightmare and she was reliving it in her dreams.

Her alarm went off. Thank goodness the only monster under the bed was her radio, even if the words continued to play in her head. Even if every now and then, she got a little bit lonely. Even if the idea of life without Sinjen terrified her. She would find him. They'd be square. She didn't need him. He didn't want her. End of their story.

Pushing out of bed, she wandered into the bathroom. It had been after one before she got home and she'd pulled off her clothes and tumbled into bed. Now it was morning. Time to cast her nets wide and see if she could hook her fish. Brushing her teeth while the water in the shower heated, she ignored her reflection in the mirror. She knew what she looked like. She didn't need to see the dark circles under her eyes, the tight lines around her mouth.

She ducked under the water, washed her hair, scrubbed her body, and turned off the water. Snagging the towel she'd draped over the glass shower door, she wiped water from her face and wrapped it around her torso. Stepping out, she screamed.

Chapter Twenty-six

Don't Feed Them After Midnight

The cat sprawled in the middle of the bathroom floor, black fur a dark void against the white tile. He rolled and twisted in that way only cats can, all the while watching her with those big yellow eyes.

"What the hell!" Okay, so she felt a little stupid for screaming like a girly-girl but she didn't own a cat and this one should be in Paris. "What the fuck are you?"

The cat didn't blink.

"Not talking today? Fine. Maybe I should ask *who* the fuck you are."

That got her a slow blink. How the fuck did cats do a slow blink? Sade wrapped the towel tighter and headed for the closet. She needed coffee and clothes and as much as she needed the coffee first, she was so not going to wander around wearing only a towel—at least not until she figured who or what the fuck that cat was.

Ten minutes later, she had her first cup of caffeine and she felt almost Human. The cat perched on the kitchen counter scarfing down a can of tuna and seemed content enough. With her brain functioning on at least two cylinders now, Sade scrambled through her mental files for whatever the cat might be. Pooka came to mind. Harvey the Rabbit notwithstanding, pookas could shapeshift into almost anything. Caleb had encountered one in New Mexico that chose the form of a horse.

She finished off a second cup of coffee. "I'm going to my office. Good luck getting in there."

Grabbing her backpack, she headed for the front door. She was dressed for running. It was only a little over mile to the Hoover Building and she ran to work several times a week, then worked out in the basement gym, showered and dressed for business there.

She hadn't planned to do so today but the cat's appearance had her frazzled and there were times when a hard workout was just the ticket. She paused before shutting and locking the door.

"Don't make a mess."

Fifteen minutes to jog the mile between her townhouse and FBI HQ. Thirty minutes on a weight machine in the gym. Fifteen minutes in the locker room for shower, hair, minimal makeup, and clothes. One hour and five minutes after locking the cat in her house, she walked into her office to find the damn thing sitting on her desk. She rolled her eyes.

"Shoulda figured," she muttered, which she followed with an order, "Scat."

Unblinking, the cat stretched, long and lazily, before sauntering to the edge of the desk and leaping gracefully into one of her side chairs. He sat like some Egyptian statue, tail draped over his front feet.

An agent stuck his head in her open door and started to speak. Then he saw the cat. "Uh, Marquis, there's a cat in your office."

Sade arched one brow, ignoring the cat. "There is?"

The guy pointed to the chair. "Yeah. Sitting right there."

Angling her gaze, she stared at the cat. "Right...there. In my chair?"

He nodded vigorously. "Yes. Right there. A black cat." He blinked, added, "And they're bad luck."

The cat turned baleful yellow eyes on the agent. Who gulped.

"Did you want something, Huff?" she asked, breaking up the staring contest.

"Huh?" He blinked several more times, still eying the cat. "Oh. Yeah. Jones called in while you were working out. Said he's checking out a lead on your case and he'll touch base later."

"Okay."

Huff was still staring at the cat. "Are you telling me there *isn't* a cat sitting in that chair?"

The cat shifted his gaze to Sade. She ignored the attention, remaining focused on the agent standing nervously in her doorway. "Did you work graveyard?"

"No." Huff cut his eyes to her. "Why?"

"Just wondering about sleep deprivation."

Huff rubbed his eyes, blinked, and then one hand went to the back of his neck and rubbed there. "There isn't a cat in your office."

"How would I get a cat through security?" she asked, wondering how the cat actually *got* through security.

"Riiight." He backed out. "Anyway, that was Jones's message."

"Thanks, Huff. Maybe coffee will help." She held up her own mug. "Always works for me."

"Yeah, uh, thanks." Huff hurried off.

Sade eyed the cat. "How *did* you get through security?"

Wisely, the cat didn't answer.

Two days. No word on Sinjen. No new leads on Ichabod Trane. The cat was still with her. She still hadn't figured out how the cat got in. Or out. Of anywhere. Home. Office. Subway.

Caleb's lead turned out to be nothing. He was as frustrated as she. Roman and Verity remained in New Orleans. Ari was absent, which suited her just fine. And Nikos was nowhere to be found. That was also a plus. She wasn't sure, in her current state of mind, that she wouldn't stab the fae with cold iron and shoot the dragon with HE shells. She made a mental note to make sure she had a shotgun and high-explosive shells. You know, just in case.

After a morning filled with nothing but frustration, precipitated by a telephone call from Mathias before dawn, Sade wanted food. Like diner food. She clocked out and headed toward the side entrance. Exiting onto 10th Street, she headed up the block, crossed E Street without waiting for the light, and dodged tourists to cut into Lincoln's Waffle Shop. She could get a real breakfast—fried eggs, bacon, hash browns, pancakes or waffles or biscuits and gravy, along with copious amounts of coffee. Her stomach growled right before she heard a loud *MEOWRRRR*.

Glancing up the street toward Ford's Theater, she saw the cat doing his best Halloween Cat impression with arched back and fuzzed-out tail, teeth and claws all out. And she saw a short, round man wearing a bowler hat.

"Trane!"

He turned, kicked at the cat, and took off running.

Fuck her. The little weasel had been right here under her nose. The cat was fine and already charging up the sidewalk, Sade hot on his heels. They crossed F Street at a dead run, amid honks and squealing tires. That little fucker could run. He cut left around the corner on G Street and she vaguely noted St. Patrick's Catholic Church on her right.

Ichabod was still about a block ahead of her. She couldn't see the cat. The wizard had to dodge cars at 11th Street. She caught the light but dashed diagonally across the intersection when the little asshole jaywalked halfway down the block. She was gaining on him.

They hit the corner of G Street and 12th with her about ten feet behind. He didn't look back. He headed straight for the escalator leading down to the Metro Center subway station.

"Fuck me." She said it aloud this time and got a scowl from the older woman she dashed past.

Sade hit the top of the escalator and didn't slow down, leaping and running to catch up. She saw the tell-tale shimmer at the bottom too late to stop and hit the portal at a dead run.

This whole realm-hopping thing sucked. Sade surveyed the landscape. Barren. Drifting fog. Silence. She was alone, but not. The back of her neck prickled. Something was watching her. She was positive of it. A stone fortress loomed in the fog. Sighing, she trudged toward it.

Thick wooden doors hung like drunken sailors loitering around the entrance of a whore house. Stepping inside, every sense alert, she picked her way across the debris-strewn floor. A sweeping staircase beckoned. She climbed, unable to shake the sensation of being watched.

A mirror graced the landing. Sade ignored the face—not her own—staring back at her. She kept climbing. At the top, she stepped out onto a battlement and into a wall of sound. An army surged around the base of the tower and something sounding too much like a dragon for her peace of mind trumpeted. Leathery wings beat against the squalid air as an apparition dove from the sky.

"Holyfuckingfreakmethehellout—" Did Gargoyles have horses? The white creature's wings reminded Sade of Roman's when he was in Gargoyle form. The creature's tail was more dragon-like. The body and head were pure equine and fiery eyes glared at the puny hunters below.

The...whatever it was saw Sade and neighed. She caught the echo of booted feet rushing up the stairs to her position and she had just enough time to slam and block the door before the troops arrived. The flying horse swooped closer to her and Sade made a leap of faith, landing on the critter's back, clutching its mane. The flying horse-beast soared. Sade remembered to breathe. She wasn't terrified. Much. Nothing to it. Right?

"I got this."

And she did until two dragons popped into existence, one on each side of the horsey-dragon-thingy she was astride. They flew almost wingtip to wingtip until the battlefield was cleared and mountains loomed ahead. Her steed folded its wings and nose-dived to earth. Sade gripped with her legs, hands tangled in mane, and held on for dear life. She might have screamed.

At the very last instant, wings snapped out, there was a back-wing motion and her steed hit the ground with all four feet galloping. The thing slowed and turned to stare at the two dragons as they landed. It stamped a front foot and neighed a challenge. The large bluish dragon roared. Her steed pricked ears and then bowed, causing Sade to slide to the ground. She did not drop to her knees and kiss it.

The blue dragon transformed into a man she hadn't seen in a while. The bronze dragon shifted into one she knew all too well. Frick and Frack, otherwise known as Xan and Stavros.

"Shit," she muttered and held up a hand. "Don't tell me, I'm back in the fucking Dragon Realm." She didn't give them a chance to answer. "Did Nikos send you?"

They exchanged a glance.

"Great. Just...great. Why is Nikos all up in my business?"

Another glance exchanged, before Xan spoke. "What did you want him to do?"

"I don't know." To say she was not expecting the two men who faced her was a big, fat understatement. One looked noncommittal. The other glowered. That's because one had a good poker face and the other pretty much hated her guts. Sade paced away. She stopped, turned, and added, "Something. Anything."

The two dragons exchanged glances. "He sent us," Xan said. "Is that not something?"

"Don't you two have better things to do?"

Stavros did not change his bitter expression. "Yes. As the Drakon's Dankána, I have much better things to do than deal with your puny Human concerns."

She marched up to the dragon and went toe-to-toe. "You hate me, Stavros. I get that. I don't give a flying Philadelphia fuck. You obviously got back in Nikos's good graces since you are still his second. I'm guessing that Nikos is just a little miffed that a *puny* Human wizard stole a major Dragon relic and is now happily realm hopping ranks a little higher that my puny Human concerns. You should be—" She spread her arms wide. "Out there. Searching for the little fucker, not standing here all up in my business and acting like I need bodyguards."

"Agent Marquis," Xan said, tone carefully neutral. "You are the one who this little fucker has trapped in these same realms. The Drakon finds it prudent for us to be around to get you out. And," he added with a sly grin, "perhaps catch the little fucker."

He had a point. Dammit.

Chapter Twenty-seven

Friends in Low Places

Xan was the one who transported Sade back to DC. They popped into existence on the plaza in front of the FBI building. Stavros was nowhere to be seen. That was probably a good thing. The cat, however, was sitting in the middle of the petunias gracing one of the large, decorative concrete planters lining the area. He'd found a patch of sunshine and was basking in it.

"Seriously?" she grumbled then noticed Xan staring at the cat. The cat ignored the dragon by licking a paw and grooming an ear. "What?"

"The Drakon did not mention..." his voice trailed off and his expression turned contemplative. "I wonder if he knows?"

"Knows what?"

Xan returned his attention to her. "Nothing." He gave her a chin lift. "We will be available should you stumble through any other portals."

"I didn't stumble. I was chasing a suspect."

"A suspect with a powerful relic and enough magic to work it."

"Whatever." She turned her back to him and pushed through the revolving doors. The security guards took one look at her face and didn't say a word.

Caleb was waiting in her office. She filled him in, finishing with, "Do Gargoyles have horses and what sort of Magick critter would freak out a dragon?"

"Elephants freak over mice. Maybe dragons believe that whole superstition thing about black cats. As for Gargoyle horses, I have no clue. Want me to call Roman?"

"No, but we need to pull the subway feed and see where that little fucker got off or if he managed to poof from the station."

205

"I'll get on that, but Sade, we need to be real. I'm not sure we *can* track Trane."

"Then we have to figure out a way."

She ignored the look on Caleb's face. It hurt too much to see, knowing he saw right through her, knowing that she was walking a knife's edge of control.

"Yeah, Sade," he said softly. "We'll figure out a way."

Her landing wasn't soft. She'd fallen through so quickly she didn't have time for anything but hitting bottom. As soon as her feet connected, she flexed her knees but still collapsed onto her right hip.

"That's gonna leave a fucking bruise," she muttered.

"Naw," a gravelly voice growled in the dark. "Just tenderizes the meat."

Great. She wasn't alone in this hole. The last time this happened, she'd been in New Orleans and a crazy-assed sorcerer cold-cocked her outside Marie Laveau's crypt. She'd come to in a granite-lined prison with a hungry werewolf for a cellmate.

Ignoring the voice in the dark, she considered what had happened. She'd gotten home and had just enough time to strip off her blazer before there was a knock on the back door. That should have been her first clue. She had a tiny, fenced yard—which was a generous term for the space—and didn't share with any of the other houses in the row. Like an idiot, she answered. And promptly got tased. Okay. That pissed her off. And meant she was probably dealing with a human.

Regaining consciousness in a shed, she'd discovered a padlocked chain on the door. But, the place was built of wood, was old and flimsy, and she proceeded to kick her way out. When that proved too slow, she decided to run through the wall. Backing up all the way across the shed, she dug in and rushed the wall. And then nothing.

Because she'd gotten through the wall, gone about three steps and then the earth opened up and she fell through. As far as she could tell, she was still on the Human plane. That was a plus. The asshole wizard had some seriously weird earth magic though.

The other occupant inhaled, a long sniffling sound. "*Mmmm, sweet.*"

The smell hit her then. Oh, crap. Ghoul.

Caleb paced through Sade's townhouse. Adele wisely stayed out of his way. They'd made plans for dinner. He and Adele arrived to pick Sade up. Her lights were on, the door locked—he had a key and the alarm code. Coming in, he found her backpack and the blazer she'd worn that day at work were tossed on her couch. He'd called everyone, including the damn Drakon and wasn't that a kick in the ass.

Belatedly, since Sade hadn't decided to share, he learned that Nikos had permanently assigned Xan and Stavros to her. They swore she was still on the Human plane. Because she was, there was no help from that direction.

Mathias indicated that she was breathing but that's all he could say. There was some sort of block that kept him from reaching her and ascertaining her location. Did that mean she was unconscious?

Adele squealed and he whirled to face a very angry gargoyle who had just popped into the room.

"Jeez, Roman," Adele scolded, her voice still pitched a bit higher than normal. "Can't you land on the sidewalk and knock on the door like a normal person?"

She didn't back down as the gargoyle glowered at her. Then he ignored her and focused on Caleb, who jumped into the conversation with, "Where's Verity?"

"At home."

"But—"

"What did the Dragons say?"

"They can't find her."

"Mathias?"

"Same thing. You know this, Roman. I explained this over the phone. Does Verity still have a tracer on Sade?"

"She's working on it."

Caleb really wanted to punch something. The gargoyle, even in Human form, was out of the question. His phone rang. He answered without looking. "Jones."

"She is on the Human plane but I do not know where. The wizard bounced her through the Dragon Realm and back to the Human plane. Xan and Stavros are trying to track the relic, hoping to get a fix."

"Why can't you find this little turd, Constantine?" Caleb normally didn't curse. He was always very precise in his language because, in the magical hierarchy, werewolves ranked at the same level as hillbilly rednecks on the equivalent human social ladder. He'd come into Mathias's household as a pup, had grown up with Sade, gone to school and college and through the FBI Academy with her. He dressed up, not down. But at this moment, he was ready to rip the dragon, the gargoyle, and anyone else a new asshole.

"I am asking myself the same question, Jones. And when I catch up to Timos Balakas, I will rip the answer from his cursed hide."

Well, fuckin' A, as Sade would say. Caleb inhaled and attempted to get his temper under control. His voice sounded bleak to his own ears when he said, "She could be anywhere."

"We will find her." The assertion came in stereo—from the gargoyle in the room and the dragon on the phone.

Roman held up a finger. "Verity's calling." He was very calm when he answered, "Did you find her, love?"

"Sort of. Definitely Human plane but she's below ground. I have some coordinates." She rattled off longitude and latitude. Adele was busy punching them into a mapping app on her cell phone.

"I will see you there," Nikos growled and hung up.

Caleb turned to Roman. "Send me there. Now."

"Do you know what you're dealing with?"

"It doesn't matter."

"You could die."

"So be it." Caleb ignored Adele's sharp intake of breath. He'd forgotten his mate was in the room and he was ashamed but it didn't matter. This was Sade.

"You are as stubborn as she is."

"And that's why I'm going to bring her home. Just do it, Roman. Teleport me."

"No."

"You refuse?" Caleb whirled, tilted his head to stare up at a man he thought was his friend.

"We all have choices."

"Not this time."

"You don't have to do it alone."

"Yes, Roman, I do."

"We'll do this together. I love her too."

Chapter Twenty-eight

Remember Me

The sun beat down on him. Like a rabbit in a pot, he boiled inside his armor. He'd killed his horse, putting the poor beast out of its misery. The water skin he'd retrieved from his saddle was empty. And still the sun stabbed his eyes with bright knives. Ahead, walls made of mudbrick shimmered, a mirage drawing him to his death. He was ready. He'd come to this forsaken land to sacrifice his life for the cause.

Dropping to his knees, he swayed. Voices washed over him. Then he was on his back looking up into that blinding sky as water trickled across his parched lips. If he never saw the sun again, it would be too soon.

"It appears we have a hero," a deeply feminine voice said.

His body tensed in places it shouldn't. Not if he was half-dead. Not if he remained true to his vows as a Knight Templar.

"Yezzz, my queen," a voice hissed. Nominally male, it was higher pitched than the queen's.

"Prepare him."

When he next opened his eyes, the room was blessedly dark, lit only by flickering torches. He lay naked upon a flat stone. He closed his eyes once more, savoring the blessed darkness. He'd heard rumors of a witch, one who ruled her lands with magic and terror. She was despised and revered. No one spoke her name aloud for fear of being discovered. Sahira. She who comes.

"Get up, boy, lest you die right there. And trust me, we don't need another dead hero."

He startled, the muscles in his abdomen curling until he was almost sitting. The commanding voice, speaking English with a slight accent, drifted from the shadows.

"Who's there?"

"I am Mathias DeVrie." A man only slightly shorter than him stepped into the uncertain torchlight. "And you are Kristian St. John."

Sinjen. A woman's voice. Throaty and ending on a breathy sigh. A voice filled with need. With desire. A woman not yet sated. A woman only he could—

Sinjen roared, railing against the darkness of his prison and the hunger gnawing at his very being. He would not say her name. Not aloud, not where his captor could hear but in his heart, he shouted her name.

SADE!

She sat straight up in bed, her name still ringing in her ears. The cat sat silhouetted in front of the balcony doors. A moment of eye shine there and gone as he turned his head to stare out into the street. Dark shadows floated beyond her curtains. She fumbled for her phone on the nightstand. 3:00 am. Not exactly the witching hour but a medium once told her that this time of night-slash-morning was the ghosting hour. That those beyond the veil of time and space—as opposed to *the* Veil between the Realms—often communicated during this period.

Great. That's all she needed. A ghost. Except that had been Sinjen's voice. And he wasn't dead. Okay, he was. Except he was undead. Whatever. It had still been his voice ringing in her ears and bringing her into complete wakefulness a heartbeat later.

Climbing out of bed, Sade wandered to the window. The cat didn't move but didn't seem to mind she was there sharing the view.

Nothing moved out on the street. No cars. No pedestrians. A few lights shone in windows across the way.

"What's out there that's got you on alert?" she asked the cat.

He glanced up at her, blinked, then returned to perusing the quiet scene outside. Sade opened the French doors and stepped out onto the balcony. The cat followed. She sat in one of the chairs, he leaped up on the small table and perched.

A few clouds scuttled across the moon. Lights winked out, others flashed on. A dog barked in the distance. It should have been peaceful out here but it wasn't. Sade felt...unsettled. Something gnawed at the back of her memory. And she worried. Where *was* Sinjen? Was he safe? Not that he couldn't take care of himself but he was only a vampire. While they had their own brand of magic and strengths, other Magicks were more powerful in their own ways.

"I miss him," she whispered to the stars.

She and the cat sat until the sky turned a pale gray. Dawn approached. She had things to do. Places to be. Like avoiding any more sneak attacks. She'd gotten an earful from the three monsterteers when they'd dug her out of the ghoul's lair. Lucky for her, the thing had been content to wait for her die before eating her. Caleb, Roman, and Nikos read her the riot act. She'd just get an early start.

About an hour later and with one quick cup of coffee under her belt, she walked out her front door to find a black SUV parked next to the sidewalk. Stavros leaned against the front fender. Sade opened her mouth to argue then decided it wasn't worth the effort. The sooner she got to her office, the sooner she could ditch these two. She flashed the sulky dragon a cheeky grin and yelled, "Shotgun!"

Stavros scowled and opened the back door. The cat leaped in. Sade scowled back but climbed into the back seat and fastened her seatbelt.

"What? You don't trust my driving?" Xan asked from the driver's seat, flashing his own cheeky grin in the rear-view mirror.

"I don't trust the idiot DC drivers."

Once Stavros was installed in the front passenger seat, Xan pulled away from the curb. Traffic was light. And they weren't headed for the FBI building.

"Whoa, dude." Sade leaned forward between the seats.

"Nikos has news. We are meeting him as he wants to deliver it in person." Stavros didn't bother turning around as he explained.

Sade did not like the sound of that. She glanced at the cat, who had curled up in the other seat, perfectly content. She'd go along for the ride until she decided it was time to get off it.

What she didn't expect was to find Caleb and Roman standing with Nikos outside a derelict building somewhere in Bethesda, Maryland. She didn't wait for Stavros to open her door. The cat didn't follow. She'd think about that later.

"Somebody want to explain?"

Caleb and Roman stared at Nikos. Evidently, they were clueless as to the reason for this little tête-à-tête as well. The dragon didn't disappoint.

"My investigation has proven that Balaskas used Trane to find the relic."

"Yeah, and?"

"So impatient you are, Sade. There is now a death sentence hanging over Balaskas's head. The members of House Lemnos are being rounded up and arrested, though some have escaped. The entirety of Clan Nekyios is under suspicion of treason."

"Awesome blossom but that doesn't explain why I'm standing here."

"Trane double-crossed Balakas and those he serves. We tracked the relic to this building." His eyes fired with an unholy silver light. "I thought you would wish to be here."

"You thought right. Let's do this."

Sade watched the werewolf, the gargoyle, and the dragon duck through the narrow doorway—and tried not to make a bad joke. She followed them. They carefully searched the building from top to bottom. As she stepped off the last rickety step that led into the Stygian basement, she felt the far-too-familiar twisting of her brain and insides as she walked through the portal.

On the other side, she came up short as the others arranged themselves in a line. Beyond them, a wide plain stretched to the far horizon with a few gentle hills and rocky outcroppings to break the monotony. She pushed between Nikos and Roman but both men extended their arms, blocking her way.

"What the hell?" She ducked under the brawny barriers only to be hauled back by Roman's fist in her jacket. "Dammit—

"What do you hear?" Roman's voice sounded like granite grating against gravel.

Realizing all three Magicks were statue still, she froze. And listened hard. She glanced first to Caleb and then at Nikos. Wolf and Dragon hearing was far superior to her own. Caleb's head was up, nostrils flaring as he tested the air. A curl of smoke puffed from Nikos's mouth and his eyes no longer looked Human. When he turned to her, it was the dragon looking out. Roman transformed into his Gargoyle form in the blink of an eye.

"What do you hear, Sade?" Roman repeated.

Nothing. She heard nothing. No sound of any sort.

Then, in the distance, something roared. And something else screamed.

She checked behind her in case they needed to retreat. The doorway was gone leaving only a blank wall made of ancient stone.

"Well..." she muttered. "This won't end well."

"For us, or whatever's out there?" Caleb offered her a lopsided grin.

"Got the feeling this is a losing proposition for everyone."

"D'uh." Caleb rolled his eyes.

She pulled her weapon, checked the ammunition in its magazine. "Not funny, Caleb."

"Never is when it's life or death."

"Not gonna be us dying today," Sade vowed.

The creature heard the roar and the scream. His mouth watered, fangs fully extended. Thirsty. So very parched. There was not enough blood in the world to slake his appetite. Rusty chains rattled as he lifted his hands. Metal cuffs slithered up his arm. Spreading his hands, he studied the claw-tipped fingers.

Here there was only darkness and desperate need. Out there were living, beating hearts. He could hear them pounding in his head. Shuffling to the wall of his prison, he began the monotonous chore of scraping claws through plaster and wood and dirt and flinging it away. He would escape. He would feed. And he would exact his retribution.

"What the fuck?" Sade peeked out from under the bushes concealing them atop a low hill. The plain spread out before them. "Are those freaking dinosaurs?"

"*Shhh*," Caleb hissed.

One of the beasts turned to stare at the hill. No one moved.

Freaking Jurassic Park. That motherfucking little asshole had lured them into motherfucking Jurassic Park. She was loaded for

Magicks but fucking *dinosaurs*? No gawddamned way. All things considered, she wasn't sure even a full-grown dragon could take down that pack of velociraptors. Or whatever the hell they were. A thought niggled in her head that velociraptors had supposedly been about the size of a turkey and also had feathers. If that fucking turkey ate ham and roast beef for Thanksgiving maybe. These things were bigger. With teeth and claws.

Once the pack of carnivores finished tearing apart whatever they'd been eating, they moved off. Sade turned a glare on Nikos. "Do you have any fucking clue where we are?"

His silvery-blue eyes sparkled with humor. "I do, indeed, know where we are."

"And the relic?"

"Is not here." He held up a finger to cut off her tirade before she got up a good head of steam. "It was here and it has been moved. Your Mr. Wizard is becoming quite adept."

"He's not mine and that should worry the bejesus out of you."

Nikos sobered, all humor now gone from his expression. "It does."

"Do you know where he went?"

Something issued a trumpeting roar, a challenge to all. The few whatever-the-hell-they-were fled. Sade felt it then. All the way to her bones. The ground literally shook.

"What the flaming-lips-hell is that?"

Electricity skittered over her skin, leaving her hair floating in a nimbus around her head and every hair on her body standing at attention. Nikos shifted in a shimmering wave of energy. Then she was grabbed up in one of his clawed paws as he lifted into the sky, his powerful wings beating against the air. She looked back just in time to see Roman take off, Caleb riding piggyback.

As Nikos made a slow, gliding turn, Sade saw what the flaming-lips-hell it was. A massive herd of...mastodons? Mammoths?

Giant elephant-like critters stampeding like cattle or buffalo in some old Western movie. They charged across the plain then swept up and over the hill where the four of them had been hiding.

Sade gulped. They would have been so much toe jam if Nikos and Roman weren't so quick to recognize the danger. Then she saw the real danger—the four full-sized dragons in flight formation herding the mammoth mastodons.

"Oh, fuck me," Sade murmured. "Is this where I click my heels together three times and say there's no place like home?"

Nikos snorted bluish tinged flames from his nose. Damn, that had to burn.

All four dragons back-winged to a stop and in a synchronized pivot, headed directly toward them. More blue flame erupted from Nikos's nose. Was he laughing?

He trumpeted a draconic challenge. And dropped her. Sade had no chance to scream—not that she would have, she told herself—before Roman caught her. She scrabbled for her pistol but Roman squeezed her.

"No."

"But we have to help him!"

"No." Roman remained insistent. "He is the Drakon of the ruling clan. This is his fight."

Roman flew them to another hill, one that had an outcropping of rocks. He set down, lowering Sade to her feet as Caleb scrambled off his back. The three of them stood in mute and fascinated awe at the aerial battle taking place.

Realizing the other four dragons were all smaller than Nikos, she wondered if they were more maneuverable. They weren't. There were two with dull brown scales, one a sort of moss green color, and the fourth was the color of dried yellow mustard. Nikos was shining silver with just a shimmer of iridescent green to his scales. He was bigger. Faster. And far more deadly.

He raked his claws across a pair of brown wings while his mouth latched onto the throat of the second brown dragon. One plummeted in a death spiral and crashed to earth. Sade shuddered as those velo-whatevers rushed from seemingly nowhere and pounced on the downed dragon, ripping and tearing off scales to get to the meat below.

Nikos used the other brown's body to shield him from the sporadic rain of fire from the other two. He shook his giant head and flung the brown into the stream just let loose by the green. Brown and green crashed together, got wings tangled and they both fell toward ground.

Sade studiously avoided watching them hit. She focused on Nikos and the mustard dragon. The smaller dragon realized too late that he was outnumbered, outclassed, and far too close to the very lethal Drakon. Nikos opened his mouth and belched out a massive stream of blue-hot fire. It engulfed the other dragon who was desperately back-winging away. Sade blinked and as her eyes opened, there was no fourth dragon in the sky—just a fall of black ash.

Nikos had incinerated the beast.

"Holy fuck. Remind me to never really piss him off," she murmured.

Stavros and Xan popped into view. Stavros went dragon immediately. Xan remained in Human form. "I need to get the three of you back into the Human plane." His voice sounded calm but his eyes were starting to wheel with Dragon magic.

"I can—" Roman began before Xan cut him off.

"No, Gargoyle, you cannot. This is part of the Dragon Realm and it has been warded to let the three of you in but not out. Stavros and I would have been here sooner but we could not get through the ward at first. Stavros will deal with Nikos. I will get the three of you away.

Sade, her eyes wide, stared. "*Deal* with Nikos..." Her voice trailed off as she realized Nikos was now sweeping low over the plain scorching everything in sight.

"In this state, he will only recognize a dragon of his own clan. We must go."

He grabbed Sade while Caleb and Roman latched onto his arms with both hands. Sade had just enough time to gulp in a breath and close her eyes.

"You can open your eyes now, Agent Marquis." Xan sounded far too amused for her own good.

"Yeah, easy for you to say." She bent over, hands on knees to support her torso as she breathed through the nausea. "Have I mentioned that I fucking hate portals?"

Chapter Twenty-nine

Treading Water

The black SUV remained where Xan had parked it. Sade leaned against the front fender, still sucking in air. "How does that little twatwaffle do it?" It was only partially a rhetorical question. Before anyone attempted to answer, Sade's ears popped and both Nikos and Stravros materialized into being.

"That didn't take long," she muttered. While it seemed like they'd been gone hours, the sun in the Human plane had barely moved. Sade glanced at her watch. Only 8 am., though her body felt like it should be at least noon. Her stomach growled. The men stared at her.

"What?" she growled as menacingly as her stomach. "I didn't get a chance to eat and I've only had one cup of coffee."

Caleb curled his lips between his teeth, swallowed and cleared his throat. Speaking in a grave tone, he said, "I suggest we find a coffee shop ASAP and hope they have pastries." He glanced at Nikos. "Not sure you've met Coffee-deprived Sade." He choked off a laugh. "Of course, if you had, you wouldn't still be sniffing around."

Sade punched him in the arm. Hard. He pretended it hurt by rubbing his biceps and saying, "Ow?"

They all climbed into the SUV, Sade and Caleb sharing the third-row seat because a dragon and a gargoyle left little room for more passengers in the middle row. Xan unerringly found a coffee shop with a drive thru. He ordered, pulled around, flashed his cell phone for a scan, and then passed out coffees and bags of breakfast sandwiches, none of which would do more than barely dull the hunger of the alpha Magicks occupying the vehicle.

Sade drank and ate in silence. They were back in DC proper and fighting rush hour traffic when she leaned forward. "Answer me this..."

Both Roman and Nikos swiveled to face her, expressions expectant.

She stared at Roman. "I've been sent portal hopping since I was a toddler." The gargoyle nodded. "But I've never noticed until today."

"Noticed what?" Nikos asked.

"The time difference."

"What about it?" Again, it was the dragon who spoke.

"Does time pass differently? I mean, I know all the stories about Underhill and the Fae Realm but when Oberon and Mathias were jabbing at each other, time seemed the same. I mean, I didn't age any faster when I was with the Fae."

Dragon and gargoyle exchanged a look but neither spoke. Sade continued. "Today, what seemed like hours passed in the Jurassic Park realm. But here in the Human world? It wasn't all that long. At least according to my watch. How does that work? I mean, do I age faster when I'm in another realm because time is different? Or what?"

Nikos looked bemused. Roman did not. "You are Human," he said.

"D'uh, Roman. Well aware of that."

"Magicks age...differently."

Her eyes widened as her mouth tightened, then she gave them both a narrow-eyed stare. "So you're telling me that every time I go into another realm, I'm shortening my life span?"

"Not exactly." Roman hastened to reassure her. "It is magic but it is also...physics."

Sade threw out a hand. "Whoa. Stop right there. Don't. I barely got through physics in college. That whole space-time compendium bullshit? No. Just...no! It makes my head explode."

"I believe you mean the space-time continuum," Stavros interjected from the front seat, tone and expression both smirking.

"Whatever. Just answer me this. If I stay in one of those pockets with weird time, do I come out having only Human time pass? I mean, like if I'd been stuck in Jurassic Park for a year, would I come out a year older than I went in, or would I be only the weeks or months older based on whatever time passed here?"

"No."

"Yes."

She glowered at Nikos. "I don't like the yes word in this case."

"Sade," Roman said softly, calling her attention to him. "Technically, there isn't a yes or no answer. While you are in a pocket realm of uncertain time, you age there. When you return to the Human plane, you...revert."

"That is not strictly true," Nikos argued.

"No one has studied Human resistance and aging in the Magick Realms, Drakon." Roman dismissed the dragon and refocused on Sade. "We do not know if the human body simply snaps back to the moment one entered a realm or whether it actually retains a...biological memory of Human time and ages at the rate it would under normal Human conditions. Therefore, while a human might age a year while in a realm, that person would shed that age upon return to the Human world."

Sade rubbed her temples. "God but I hate science. *And* magic. Mixing them is like drinking boiler makers—good only for the bartender who gets big tips from the drunks."

As the big SUV was currently stopped in traffic at a red light, all five Magicks turned to stare at her. She stared back.

"What? It's true and y'all fucking know it."

"She has a point," Xan murmured.

"She does," Caleb agreed.

222

"Of course I do. But putting all that shit aside, let's get back to the point."

"And that would be?" Nikos asked dryly.

"Rip Van Winkle."

"Sade, that's just a story written by Washington Irving."

"I know that, Caleb. I actually made an A in my American Lit class. Riddle me this. Was Irving Human? Or was he one of the Magicks? I mean, think about the crap he came up with. The Headless Horseman. Good ol' Rip, and those little dudes bowling up in the mountains. How did he know about dwarves? 'Cause you can bet that's who those little people were. And why did he age Van Winkle?"

The car got very quiet. The light changed and traffic inched forward. Silence stretched. Sade fumed.

The SUV pulled up in front of the FBI building. Nikos exited and moved his seat so Sade and Caleb could exit. Roman exited on the street side and walked around to them.

"I have one more riddle for you," Sade said. "Ichabod Trane." She pivoted and marched toward the revolving doors.

Caleb offered a long look to both Roman and Nikos. "Somebody needs to find answers." Then he, too, strode to the entrance.

Roman and Nikos stood on the wide plaza watching the two disappear inside.

"How is he eluding us?"

"I don't know, Constantine. That he can hide from both the Dragons *and* the Sentinels is...disturbing."

"I have our best scholars on this and my entire guard is searching through every realm under Dragon control. We suspect the wizard can only use the stone to open Dragon-land portals."

"Tabor is scouring the archives and Crevan has ordered all squadrons to patrol and be on alert."

Nikos stared thoughtfully at the building. "I am not sure what else we can do."

"We can find the damned vampire so her heart doesn't continue to break." With those words, Roman disappeared.

"We are lucky," Nikos said to Stavros who joined him on the sidewalk. "We can teleport. We can shift. We hold magic in our very fingertips. And we have hearts that only lust after pretty baubles."

"She is not a bauble," Stavros growled.

Surprised, Nikos turned to his second. "Do not tell me you are also falling under her spell."

"No. She is Human. She has no magic. She will die much sooner than later. Yet..." He shrugged. "As much as I would be willing to dispatch her from this earth, I would be...unsettled after."

Sade stood at the window in her office and stared out. Darkness crept through the streets and lights flickered on. Traffic was now minimal and pedestrians appeared determined to reach their destinations. She didn't want to go home. And though her stomach grumbled, she wasn't hungry. Not for food anyway.

Caleb left an hour before, heading home to Adele. She was happy for her partner. She truly was. He'd been the redheaded stepchild, as they said in Texas, growing up. An orphan werewolf pup in a master vampire's household basically bonded to a human girl. Gods but she loved him and to see what he had with Adele? The deep, abiding love and acceptance? It both filled her heart and hurt it. Happy for him, devastated because she would never have that.

Except she had. Mostly. With Sinjen. And he'd tried to tell her but would she listen? Fuck no. Gods but she was a total bitch. He'd been patient. He'd waited. And then he was done. She couldn't blame him. But now he was in danger and she was determined to save him. Even if she had to let him go afterwards. The world without Sinjen in it? No. Just...no.

She was the reason he'd gone missing. She didn't know why Trane had fixated on her but she would find out. And she would find Trane. Then she would find Sinjen. And set him free. She refused to think about that stupid poster that had graced her bedroom wall as a preteen. She'd been such a fucking romantic back then. Then she'd grown up. Reality was no dream. And it never would be.

Stifling the urge to sigh, she cleared off her desk, locked up her files and turned out the lights. A few agents remained at their desks. Social pleasantries were exchanged and she hit the elevator. The security guards gave her a casual salute. Outside, she turned right and walked up Pennsylvania Avenue. She had no destination in mind so she strolled. And decided she didn't do enough of that. Not that she was into window shopping or sightseeing or any of that shit.

A block away, cheerful market umbrellas and lights drew her toward a sidewalk cafe. She asked for and got a table set back away from the sidewalk and street. She ordered a bacon cheeseburger, fries, and a bottle of Devil's Backbone, a Vienna lager beer brewed in Virginia.

She relaxed back into her seat and watched people. There was a couple on a first date—they were stiff and polite but smiling. There was another couple, stiff and formal and not polite at all. They both wore wedding rings and Sade wondered if they were married to the other or to...others. Either way, a breakup looked imminent. Three men drank beer and chowed on burgers, discussing work. They weren't subtle about occasionally checking out the four young women eating more dainty fare and discussing men.

Her food arrived, along with the cat. The waiter started to shoo it away but Sade flashed her ID. "He's with me," she explained. "Undercover."

The waiter's brows ducked under his bangs. "Cat shifter?" he whispered. There was no such thing but Sade let him think whatever he wanted. "Can I bring him something?"

The cat eyed her beer. She lifted the bottle and added, "And a bowl."

"You got it!" The kid hurried off.

She took a bite and chewed then broke off a piece of the bacon and a little of the beef. "Here. You look hungry."

The cat sniffed and then ate, delicate in his movements.

"Missed you in Jurassic Park today."

The cat stared unblinking.

"Glad you managed to catch a ride back." She tilted her head. "Or are you magic enough you can teleport?"

The cat blinked.

"Fine. I don't normally talk while I'm eating either." Because she normally ate alone and talking to yourself made other people nervous.

The waiter reappeared with a small bowl and the beer. He poured a bit into the bowl and waited like he was a sommelier in the process of doing the whole wine bottle ceremony. The cat sniffed the beer. Took a small lap with his tongue. Then the damn thing looked up at the waiter, *smiled,* and let out a satisfied *meow.*

Sade rolled her eyes but picked off a bit more meat and bacon and pushed it across the table. The cat nibbled. And lapped his beer. And Sade found herself oddly content.

Chapter Thirty

A Heartbeat Away

After another night of tossing and turning, Sade was in her office early. The cat had disappeared overnight and she tried not to care. The damn thing was some sort of Magick and therefore not to be trusted. She checked files from her agents that appeared on her desk overnight. Nothing major. That was good. She had enough to say grace over with Sinjen's disappearance, the stolen relic, and a rogue wizard thief with more power than he should have.

She marked the passage of time by glancing at her watch. Constantly. In addition to copious amounts of coffee, which entailed multiple trips to the break room for refills. She found Caleb in her office after one of these trips.

"What?"

"When's the last time you slept?"

"Last night." He gave her his patented big-brother *now Sade* look, which she ignored. "I'm waiting for the New York Public Library to open. I want to find out about Washington Irving."

"You aren't serious about him being a Magick are you?"

"Yes. If he wasn't, he knew a Magick. And there's this whole wizard thing. The names are too...coincidental. And when it comes to magic, there are no coincidences. Who *is* this guy? Why is he so fucking fixated on me?"

"All good questions."

She rolled her eyes. "Good of you to agree. You got anything?"

"Xan is keeping me in the loop. He and Stavros are still on standby to rescue you."

Snorting, Sade set her mug on the desk then plopped into her chair. "Rescue me?"

"Okay, transport you back to this realm. It's a good thing Verity tagged you with that spell."

She growled. "I feel like a fucking dog with a microchip."

"No comment. But, you have to admit, it has come in handy."

"I shoulda tagged that damn vampire," she muttered.

Caleb pretended not to hear.

Her desk phone buzzed and she grabbed it. "Marquis."

"Agent Marquis, this is Agatha Bellwether."

Caleb hummed the "Twilight Zone" theme.

"Interesting," Sade said, ignoring him. "I was just about to call you."

"I have some more information on that wizard."

"Ichabod Trane?"

"Yes. I've tracked down, with the help of a colleague, the genealogy on his dragon side."

"Clan Nekyios?"

"Sort of. The dragon involved was a minor member of House Andino, which owes its allegiance to House Lemnos. Apparently, the males of House Andino are known to interbreed with Human females."

"I don't *even* want to think about how that works." Sade rubbed her temple with two fingers. "So, basically, what you're saying is that there's a whole mess of Human Magicks running around out there carrying Dragon DNA?"

"I'm afraid so, yes."

"Well, fuck me running. I know a Drakon who is gonna get all pissy about this info."

"Well, yes, dear. I'm afraid you are correct there." When Sade said nothing, Agatha continued. "You mentioned you planned to contact me?"

"Oh. Right. Washington Irving."

"What about him, dear?"

"Was he a Magick?"

Now it was Agatha who said nothing for a long moment. Sade didn't push. She heard computer keys clicking and muttering. Finally, the woman said, "Not that we have a record of, though there's mention of a childhood friend in Tarrytown that he spent time with. The friend was from a Witch-bred family."

Sade searched her memory. "Tarrytown. Up the Hudson. Near Sleepy Hollow and the Catskills."

"That is correct, yes."

Caleb was walking across her office, his cell phone to his ear as Sade thanked the archivist. "You have been a huge help, Dr. Bellwether."

"You have my number, dear. Have a nice day."

She hung up and winced. Even her human ears could hear the screeching growl emanating from Caleb's phone. She recognized Stavros's voice. While Caleb dealt with the dragons, she snagged her phone and called the New York field office. She hung up after promises that agents were being dispatched to Tarrytown to track down information on Trane.

For the first time since Sinjen walked away, she could almost breathe easy—operative word being *almost*. Until she saw Sinjen alive and well, she would not relax. Her phone buzzed again, this time security at the front entrance.

"Agent Marquis, we gotta feller down here insisting he see you. Says he's just gonna pop...fucking hell. Merle, where'd that guy—"

Sade stopped listening as a shower of golden glitter sent Caleb into a sneezing fit. Moments later, Ariel materialized in her office, smiling and cocky and so damn full of himself Sade considered pulling out her weapon.

"Never mind," she said into the receiver. "He's Fae. And currently in my office."

The guard started to apologize but Sade cut him off, stating that Ari had been in her office and the building before so the normal safeguards might not work if he was determined to get to her. Which he had been. She also promised not to report the guards for dereliction. "Not your fault. He's a fucking Fae."

She hung up and glowered as Caleb continued to hack and sneeze. "Seriously, Ariel?"

"How was I to know the dog would be playing fetch, fair lady?"

Caleb growled and advanced on Ari. Sade stopped him with a look. "What the fuck, Ari? I might have shot you. Hell, I still might."

"I didn't want to wait for those dolts downstairs to clear me and in case you were in a foul mood and refused, I decided to pop on up."

"Answer my question, Ariel. Why are you here?"

"Posh. You take all the fun out of it." He quickly held up a finger as she advanced on him, murder in her eye, and a hand reaching for her weapon. "I have a lead."

"On what?"

"Why, your little wizard, of course."

Sade stopped. Caleb stifled another sneeze. "Talk," she ordered.

"It seems he can only pop into and out of realms controlled by the Dragons."

Caleb growled. "We know that, Ariel."

"Ah. Well, it so happens that I've discovered a pocket that hasn't been disturbed in ages. Literally. It's just a step beyond one of their realms where they—" He paused dramatically and leaned forward. "Have. Dinosaurs!"

Sade and Caleb exchanged a look. "Go on," she demanded.

"Given the circumstances, I tried to check it out. It's locked. I enticed a lady friend of mine who happens to be a dragon to try. She couldn't enter either."

Shrugging, Caleb dismissed the information. "Sounds like one of the Dragons is using it for hoard storage and has locked everyone else out."

Ariel stared at him. Caleb stared back. Ari finally rolled his eyes. "I suppose the Human Magicks are that uninformed."

Sade rubbed at her right eye, its lid suddenly twitching. "To the point, Ariel."

"Did you not land in an area of Nikos Constantine's lair? Just steps from his hoard, in fact? And did not Caleb follow you?" He paused dramatically. She snapped her fingers for him to hurry. He sighed. "Fine. The reason Dragons take such pains to keep the locations of their lairs and hordes secret is because Dragon Realms cannot be locked to keep out others. Booby trapped, yes. Hard to get to, definitely. But any other dragon or Magick with teleporting abilities and the location can enter.

"Well fuck me blind," Sade murmured then shot Ari a withering look as his eyes turned to molten silver.

He wisely continued with his explanation. "We—my friend and I—established that particular area was indeed part of the Dragon Realm. I did not bother to call Roman or Varrick as I figured if a dragon couldn't get through the ward, then neither could a gargoyle, despite their status as Sentinels."

"What does this have to do—"

"Think, Sade," Ariel chided in a soft voice. His expression was grave now. "This pocket shares a...wall, if you will, with the place you jokingly call Jurassic Park. It is warded against Magicks. What is so special that this would be so?"

Sade stared at her boots and blinked a few times. "A prison." Her head came up. "A prison to hold a Magick." She breathed one word. *Sinjen.*

"How do we find this place?" Caleb demanded.

231

Nikos stepped into her office. "I'll show you. I was just coming to get you because I have discovered the same information as the fae."

Days. Months. Years. He'd lost count, lost hope that time would slow. Once, when he was something other than a snarling beast, he'd thought of a lifetime of words to say to the woman who owned his soul. That was so long ago.

Was she even real?

Was he?

His hunger became a living need. He was no longer that man, no longer anything but a rabid animal starving for blood. But a voice whispered in his dark cell. She would come, the one with the bottle-green eyes.

And he then he would feast.

Her stubborn was as thick as the fog that surrounded this gods' forsaken place. The four Magicks watched her warily, like she was a bomb that might go off at any moment. Fitting, since that's exactly how she felt. Her last nerve was strung so tight she might explode.

"Think hard about this, Sade." Roman, steady as the granite from which his Gargoyle form was carved.

"We don't even know if he's in there." Ariel, ever the Fae version of devil's advocate—even though he was part of the reason they were gathered here..

"This is not the time to go off half-cocked." Caleb, doggedly determined to keep her safe. Ornery Werewolf.

She stared at Nikos, waiting for the dragon's response. When none came, she lifted her chin in challenge. "What are y'all afraid of?"

They all talked—arguments, logic, and emotions spilling together, their voices getting lost in the mist that was her need to get to Sinjen.

"You shouldn't go in alone," Nikos said. "And none of us carry enough humanity to get through that ward."

She could tell that pissed him off to no end. "So watch me from the entrance. I know y'all have my back. He's in there. I know he is. I won't leave him here to die."

"Do you love him so much then?" The dragon's face showed nothing.

Sade's answer was simple. And immediate. "Yes."

Nikos shoved a hand in his pocket and withdrew an object. He held it out to her on his palm. Sade stared at what looked like a blue marble. "What is it?"

"We call it the Dragon's Eye. It will allow me to *see*. We'll help if we can."

"I'll bring Sinjen home." It was a promise she would keep.

She stepped up to the hazy curtain shimmering along the face of the stone wall. Beyond it, she could barely make out stairs leading down into utter darkness. "Hope this sucker can see in the dark," she muttered before sucking in air.

With a quick glance over her shoulder, Sade placed her hand on the portal. A breath later, she landed in the basement of a derelict building. The blue marble gave off enough light she could make out her surroundings. She stood before a hole in the wall, a shadowed crypt in this long-dead place. A barred gate blocked the opening. She found a key hanging on a peg.

Snagging it, she tried it in the lock. The key turned, something clicked, and the gate swung open, its rusty hinges grating like a bansidhe's wail. She bit back her rising panic and ignored the icy fingers of fear racing up her spine. She stepped into the next room.

Something moved back in the deepest recesses and she peered closer. The creature's eyes flashed feral red beneath the flickering sodium lights filtering through broken windows, but Sade didn't react. Her right hand already rested on the butt of her Beretta, its clip filled with a combination of silver and lead bullets. She had intentionally omitted wooden ones. What she had loaded wouldn't kill a vampire but would slow him down enough she could get away. If that was a vampire. If it wasn't Sinjen.

Part of her brain tried to piece the setting together. They'd been in a field outside of Washington. There'd been a stone wall similar to the one inside Jurassic Park, the one that marked the passage between the old building in Bethesda that they'd entered to find the portal in the basement and the open grasslands on the other side. This one was the opposite. *Magic.* Her brain really might explode from trying to figure it out.

Easing closer, she contemplated the darker mass within the shadow. Those eyes remained fixed on her. She inhaled and almost gagged. Fetid air filled her lungs, choking her with the stench of blood and unwashed bodies, of damp earth, and dead things. It reeked of fear and despair. The creature watched her, a trapped animal prepared to defend his lair. Her heart broke just a little.

He stared at the intruder, the one who haunted him. "*In my sleep, you come.*" He said the words but not aloud. He watched, wary. His tongue teased the sharp points of his canines. They'd elongated as soon as he caught a whiff of her scent. Hungry. So hungry. He would lose all control if she stepped closer. *Oh, yes, please step closer*, he silently commanded.

Sade's eyes adjusted to the darkness and she stared in horror. Naked, his emaciated body was plain to see. "What has he done to you?"

Her voice ignited his rage and he lurched to his full height. "This place is mine," he declared. With lightning speed, he struck, knocking her to the ground. Looming over her as she groveled at his feet, his nostrils flared at the scent of her blood. She should fear him but nothing in her expression indicated she did.

She rose, a fluid movement so filled with grace he was distracted. She searched his face and for a brief moment, he wanted to hide from her gaze, suddenly ashamed of his monstrosity. He faded back into the shadows but she followed him. Her fault then, whatever happened next.

Grabbing her, he yanked her to him and threaded his fingers through her long hair—hair the color of the shadows in which he dwelled. He dragged her head back to expose her throat. His fangs gleamed in the uncertain light. "You are mine."

"Yes," she agreed. "Always." Her gaze sought his, collided. "What's happened to you, Sinjen?"

He didn't answer. His fangs were already jabbing into her soft skin. Her pulse throbbed sending waves of hot, fragrant blood against his tongue. He sucked. And licked. And bit deeper, tearing at the sweet flesh. He drank. And drank. She gripped his arm, not to stop him, but to hold him closer. What? As nourishment swelled his starved cells, his brain began to shed the animalistic desire to drain this Human dry, to use her until there was nothing left but a dry husk.

Who was she? He couldn't remember. Who was he? No memory there either. His only thought was filled with a blood-red haze of hunger. Feeding. Surviving. No matter what the cost. He was not supposed to care. He was Vampire. Master of his domain. Looking around, he shuddered as the memory of his incarceration bit at him.

Something touched his mind. *Sinjen.*

Sinjen. He knew that name, had been that man. Once. But no more and never again. He bit again. Drank again. Even deeper. He felt her heart stutter but still he thirsted. Her hand resting against his heart, her whispered words stopped him.

"I love you."

Memories flooded him. He knew this woman. Knew who and what she was. Sade. His. He stared in horror at the limp body in his arms. Her neck had been savaged and as he watched, the trickle of blood slowed as her heart stuttered. A tiny pulse of thick liquid oozed from the wound with each beat of that mortal organ.

There was no time to think. He tore at his wrist and forced her mouth open to take a few swallows of his blood. Not enough to change her. No. That she would never forgive. Just enough to speed the healing, to keep her alive until he could help repair the damage and get her to a hospital. He licked at her throat, the healing power of his saliva also working to repair the damage. Her pulse, though still slow, was steady now. No more blood. He licked her throat again but the ragged edges of her skin did not seal.

"Breathe!" he ordered, his voice as ragged as the torn skin of her throat.

She loved him enough to die that he might find his memory, his life. She humbled him, brought him to his knees. He sealed her ravaged throat with a kiss before ripping a sleeve from her shirt to bind the wound. He was naked but even had he been clothed, the rags would be filthy. "I don't deserve you."

Tough shit. You're stuck with me. Her voice echoed in his mind but he didn't know if it was Sade or wishful thinking.

"For your lifetime, love," he promised. *And my own.*

Her rich blood had revived him almost completely. Gathering her into his arms, he saw the blue marble that had fallen from her limp hand. He sensed the Dragon magic. He had to get her out. Get her to those who loved her, would keep her safe. From him.

He retrieved the stone and curled her hand around it. Maybe it was a talisman that allowed her into his prison. Maybe it would get them out. Picking her up, he retraced her steps. The gate remained open. He passed through it, climbed the steps. The shimmer at the top was visible. Shadows moved around on the other side.

On the landing, he shifted Sade to get a better grip. He would not lose her going through this door. He stepped into the shimmer. And bounced off. Fuck him. It must be warded against him—and probably Magicks, since none of those on the other side had accompanied her.

Something soft and furry brushed against his leg. He looked down. The black cat. And suddenly, the shadows were less distinct outside. Like a total eclipse of the sun had just arrived. He cared nothing for the sun. Let him burn to ash under its rays, just so long as Sade was safe.

The cat swatted at his calf, claws raking him lightly. The cat turned and passed through the shimmer. Then it returned. It sat and looked up at him. Sinjen nodded. "Lead. I'll follow."

The cat and Sinjen entered the shimmer at the same moment. He was free. And it was night. The infernal dragon, the gargoyle, the werewolf, and the fae all stood stone still, shocked beyond action. He dashed to Roman, pressed Sade into her guardian's arms.

"I almost killed her," he whispered. "There is no forgiveness."

Then he was gone.

Chapter Thirty-one

Fresh Start

Sade opened her eyes. She was in a bed. A hospital bed. Oh to the fuck no. She sat up and all sorts of monitors and alarms went off. A nurse charged in but before the woman could chastise her, Sade was on the offensive.

"Get this damn IV out of my arm or I will."

"Now, now—"

"Don't fucking now-now me. Get it out." Sade reached for the tape holding the needle in place.

The nurse, realizing she was serious, rushed over. "Don't. Leave it alone. I'll do it."

Sade glowered as the nurse closed clips and adjusted things, clucking all the while. "You need the rest of this transfusion."

"I'm fine."

The nurse peered down her nose, her expression imperious. Sade was immune. "Get me unhooked, get my clothes, and get a doctor in here to discharge me or I'm walking out."

The door swung open and Caleb peered in. She jabbed a finger in his direction. "Get me out of here."

"Sade..."

"Now, Caleb."

Her partner sighed. "At least finish off the blood bag."

"I. Am. Fine." She snarled the words out between gritted teeth. "Where is he?" Caleb paled a little and wouldn't meet her eyes. Her heart stopped beating. Literally. Which kicked off all sorts of alarms again before it stuttered to a start. "What did you do?"

"Nothing." And he hadn't. He'd been too shocked that daylight turned to night to even realize Sinjen was suddenly there, holding a limp Sade. The vampire thrust her into Roman's arms, admitted what he'd done and shifted into whatever the hell Vampires did when they flew away on the wind.

Roman had immediately looked at Caleb and demanded, "Where?"

His brain on auto-pilot, he'd answered, "George Washington. University Hospital. Level One trauma center." And then Roman was gone. Ari followed immediately and Nikos had grabbed Caleb and the two of them winked out.

Her throat injury was bad, but no longer life-threatening. Whatever Sinjen had done to speed her healing was working. Assured by the medical staff she would survive while also debating stitches versus super glue and transfusing her, Nikos and Ari returned to Sinjen's prison to ascertain what had happened.

The evidence was all there. Nikos confirmed that this particular pocket had a time warp that meant Sinjen had been there probably two years. There were signs of rat and mice carcasses. He'd been beyond feral.

Nikos made an admission to Caleb as he described the scene. "I do not know how he stopped himself from draining her dry. I do not know what she did to stop him. There was no sign of a struggle. It appears she went to him willingly."

Caleb had not been surprised. Sade loved the bastard. And he *had* saved her life more than once. That knowledge would weigh on her and she already carried the guilt that she was the root of Sinjen being trapped.

"He tried to dig his way out. Then he tried to dig the gate out. Everything had been warded. I could sense the shadows of it. He should not have been able to pass that outer ward to get her to us."

Caleb thought back. There'd been a dark shadow at Sinjen's feet at the very moment the vampire emerged with Sade cradled in his arms. And there was no mistaking the gentle if frantic hold he had on her.

"In fact," Nikos continued, "he should have been dead. Xan calculated the time differentiation. I have never heard of any vampire who could exist in such a way for that long."

"He was a Knight Templar." Caleb didn't know why he said that. Or what it had to do with the situation.

"Ah." Nikos seemed to accept that as sound reasoning.

"He should be insane."

"Yes."

"I've talked to Mathias."

"His sire?"

"Yes. Mathias says he is not. He knows that Sinjen has fed sparingly and caused no harm. Their link is there once more, but he has no knowledge of where Sinjen is."

Nikos sighed. "She'll want to know."

She would. And if he knew Sade at all, she'd go hunting. And there wasn't a damn thing any of them could do to stop her.

Sade wasted no time. She called Mathias. She called Roman. Caleb. Ariel. She even called the pesky dragon. He reluctantly explained what he, Xan, Stavros, and Ariel had discovered at the prison. No one knew where Sinjen had gone.

She berated Roman until she got Sinjen's exact words from the gargoyle.

I almost killed her. There is no forgiveness.

The words echoed around in her memory. And they made her heart hurt. She pressed a fist against her chest, the very thought of what he was going through killing her. She had to find him. She would see him safe and whole. And then she would hunt down that motherfucking wizard, string him up by his nuts and use him for a speed ball. And she wouldn't bother with boxing gloves to pummel him.

But first, she had to find Sinjen. She sipped at the lukewarm coffee in her mug and glanced at the cat sitting on the table beside her. Traffic was light on the other side of her balcony and she was enjoying the morning sun more than she should.

"You got any ideas?"

The cat lifted a back leg and started to groom his ass.

"Figures," Sade muttered. She took another sip and grimaced. She had one recourse. Crevan. *Le Vieil* was the keeper of magical knowledge. It was his duty to keep the balance between the Magick races and Humans. It was a suck-ass job and Sade didn't envy him. Her own job was similar.

She remembered the Rip. Pandemonium. Panic. Lynch mobs. Crevan and the Gargoyles stood between Magicks and Humans. They kept the Magicks from retaliating while Human leaders did everything in their powers to quell the suspicions. Things were still unsettled though a new normal had been achieved. Thank the gods that the US president was an elf and his FBI director a man who believed in justice. Thus, the MAGIC Unit was born and Sade recruited to serve. Now she was in charge.

"I guess I need to get on a plane to Paris."

The cat stopped licking, leg still extended, yellow eyes focused on her. Then he stood, stretched, hopped off the table and stalked inside the French doors leading to Sade's bedroom.

"Guess that means I need to pack."

Turned out she didn't need to pack. Varrick stood in her living room when she went down to refill her coffee cup.

His gaze swept her from top to bottom then returned to linger on the white bandage taped to the side of her throat. "Roman didn't lie."

"Roman doesn't lie," she countered.

"Considering, *Le Vieil* wasn't certain."

"Why are you here, Varrick?"

"*Le Vieil* wishes to see you."

"A command performance?"

"If you wish."

"Funny thing, I was just about to make a plane reservation and pack a bag."

"I will save you the expense."

"Handy."

He held his hands out in a placating gesture and his expression softened. "Sade, he wishes only to see for himself."

"Why?" But she knew. No one had actually explained the prophecy but the Gargoyles—and now many of the magical races—called her *L'enfant de L'homme*. The Child of Man. It had a special meaning to them and she always...felt the import of the words, like they were capitalized when referring to her like they were bestowing some kind of title upon her.

"Sade," Varrick repeated her name, his tone holding a gentle chide.

"Fine." She threw up her hands. "Whatever. I'll just grab my shit."

Sade stared at the ancient stone Sentinel. Crevan didn't blink, not that she expected the gargoyle to show the slightest sign of weakness.

"This is a path not to be traveled by Human feet, Child."

"I don't have a choice."

"There are always choices, Sade Marquis. Some you may make yourself. Others are made for you."

And that's why she was here. Someone else made choices she couldn't accept. "What do I have to do?"

"There is an incantation. And you would have to pay."

"I would have to pay *what*? Exactly." When dealing with Magicks, a smart person...didn't. A desperate one made sure everything was spelled out in black and white.

"You cannot do this, Child. Not and return whole."

She plastered on a cocky grin. "What? I have to pay an arm or a leg?"

Crevan's expression didn't change but she could feel the weight of his dismay pressing against her chest, as heavy as a ton of bricks. "No, Sade. More."

That didn't bode well. Smirk still in place—a mask of bravado to hide behind—she shrugged. "So, my life then?" Not that she hadn't already faced that dilemma.

"What would you give up?"

Sade stood stock still. For Caleb? Roman? Ariel? Yeah. An arm. A leg. Her life. But for Sinjen? For Sinjen she would give up everything, including her heart, her soul, her mortality. She'd already sacrificed most of those things. Crevan read her decision in her expression.

"You are a fool."

"No. I'm the woman who loves him."

"Then it is done."

Sade deep breathed through her nose and exhaled through her mouth. "A little warning next time?" she complained.

Crevan said nothing. He'd transported them before she had a chance to ready herself for the trip. It wasn't as bad as falling through a portal, but it took its toll on the Human body.

She glanced around. Everything was green and surrounded by rugged mountains. The place looked like a setting straight out of *Outlander*.

"You know what you must do."

"Are you sure?" Sade stared at a rudimentary labyrinth—stones laid out in a spiral. Yeah, she was definitely deep in the Scottish Highlands.

The Old One nodded. "Follow it into the crimson day."

His words meant nothing to her, but she did as directed as he began to chant. Around and around, until she was dizzy and falling through darkness. She landed, surrounded by crimson light, in a tumbled sprawl, but with senses sharp.

Snarls. And hunger beating at her like a living entity. She knew. She had found her heart. And would die bringing him back to life.

"Sinjen." His whispered name was a prayer.

Silence descended and the hunger withdrew. In the distance, a wolf howled. A sense of movement in the sky drew her attention. A dragon. No. *The* dragon.

Nikos landed several feet away, carefully avoiding her space.

"Seriously?"

The dragon grinned and smoke wreathed from his nostrils.

You tell me, khriso mou. This is your dream.

"I am *not* your treasure and you're a dreamwalker. Also, it pisses me off to have you in my head."

More smoke curled as the dragon laughed.

"Not funny. And I'm not sure this is a dream."

The Old One is a crafty devil.

She huffed out a disgusted sigh, pivoted and walked away from him.

Wrong direction.

She turned back, a brow raised. The dragon turned his head and looked toward a low hill.

"Whatever," she groused again, now headed that direction.

When you tire of the vampire, Sade...

She held up one hand, her middle finger on prominent display. Dragon laughter filled her head.

You know where to find me.

"Fuck off, Nikos." She yelled it but there was no heat in her tone.

She walked. And walked. And then walked some more. If the dragon purposely misguided her, she'd cut off his tail. She cut through woods and ignored the small pack of wild wolves that paralleled her. She very carefully crossed a sparkling stream by using the rocks set in a crooked path across it. Birds called in the trees and she caught a glimpse of a little humanoid face peeking out from under long green fronds. Brownie? She smiled at it but kept walking.

Finally, she hit the end of the trail. And it just had to be the ocean. Sade hated the sea. Okay, she didn't particularly like any body of water where she couldn't see the bottom and slimy things with spines and teeth swam beneath the surface. She glanced back. The dark shapes that shadowed her through the woods were still there, crowding her closer to the cliff-edge.

"Caught between the devil and the deep blue sea," she muttered.

Time was running out and her over-active imagination conjured up a pocket watch so she could see the seconds ticking away. For some inane reason, she had to get down to the water. She had no place to go but along the sheer drop looking for a way to get there. Picking up her pace, she kept moving, her furry escort staying even with her as they ran the ridge line above her.

Minutes or hours could have passed but when she arrived at the water's edge, it was no longer a crashing sea. Nope, still waters stretched before her, the surface unruffled by wave or wind. The wolves shifted out of the shadows and stood watching her boldly. Of course they did. She expected the Loch Ness Monster or at least the pesky dragon to rear its head out of the water. Or maybe a troop of Fae or an escadron of Gargoyles would surround her. Instead, lucky her faced a centuries-old warrior in chain mail and a white tabard emblazoned with a red Knights Templar cross.

Sinjen looked tired and her heart twisted. She blurted, "Why are you here?"

"You tell me, Sade. This is your dream."

"Dream?" Maybe it was, since Nikos had said the same. She'd done so much portal hopping that reality and dreams currently tended to overlap.

The vampire who'd once loved her looked distracted. Impatient. She half expected him to tap the toe of his scuffed leather boots. He tilted his head and raised an imperious eyebrow. Damn but he looked sexy when he did that. Sexy and infuriating. She really needed to remember the infuriating part.

"Sade." His voice snapped out her name, sharp as a whip, recalling her to the here and now. He was the only one who could make her lose focus like this. "Is there something you wanted?" Impatience again, like he had somewhere more pressing to be, or someone better to be with.

Her heart hurt as jealousy and insecurity warred within it. This man was everything to her. If she let him back in, he would just leave her again. Everyone did. The only thing she could count on, the only thing she would always have was her work. Sinjen had left her, despite promising not to. Caleb. Roman. Ariel. Even Nikos would leave her if she ever surrendered to him. He would conquer her and disappear. They all did. She trusted no one but herself.

Sinjen lifted his hand as if to cup her cheek then dropped it, his sapphire blue eyes icing over, shuttering any emotions that might be seen. "Time flies, Sade. You are mortal. Your days are finite."

She cursed under her breath not wanting his familiar chide grating over her skin, but therein lay the crux of the matter. He was all but immortal. And she was only Human. She would never be enough for him.

"Tell me what it is you want."

You not leaving me. You loving me again. The words stuck in her throat and she had to look down to keep him from seeing the tears swimming in her eyes. "A fresh start."

Her grief-stricken words whispered into the silence stretching between them—a silence like a gossamer thread that would break if anyone breathed.

His harsh laughter jabbed knives into her chest. His words twisted them. "A second chance, you mean. That takes work. Commitment."

"I know."

"Do you?" His fingers under her chin forced her to raise her head but she still refused to look at him. "Look at me, gods damn you."

Her gaze flew to his face. Sinjen *never* cursed. "Why do you run from me? Why do you deny what is between us? What will always be between us?"

"Because I'm going to get old," she screamed. "Because I'm going to die alone because you'll leave me long before then. You'll all leave me."

His face hardened. Had she expected him to soften toward her? Not really. This was the truth between them. Finally.

"I never figured you for a coward, Sade Marquis."

She rocked back, jerking out of his grip. "What the fuck?" Now her tears burned hot with anger. "Who in the gawddamned hell that is this universe gave you the right to say—

He didn't chide her for her language. No, he grabbed her and hauled her up against him, his mouth sealing on hers. He devoured her, his kiss ravenous and raw. Then it was over, as hard and quick as it had begun. He set her away from him.

"If you aren't willing to fight for us, then you are a coward, Sade."

Before she could deny or defend her actions, the hard leaked out of him and he looked as stricken as she felt.

"I am damned, Sade. There is no hope. No redemption. No forgiveness. You are mortal. Find the life you deserve. One with a man who deserves you."

She opened her mouth, then snapped it shut as he disappeared. That's when she realized the sun was shining. Sinjen had been standing in full sunlight.

Black dots swam in her vision as her knees gave out and she hit damp grass with her butt. Her fingers touched her lips, even as her tongue lingered over the taste of him in her mouth. Hesitantly, she squinted one eye open. No dizziness. Nor was she on that beach any longer. Instead of the labyrinth, she sat on green grass in the middle of a circle of standing stones. Their age weighed on her. Ancient stones. Ancient beings. Like the Gargoyles. The Dragons. The Fae.

In that moment, she knew. She knew what she wanted to do, knew what she had to do.

"Then wake up and do it," Sinjen's voice barked at her.

Easier said than done.

Chapter Thirty-two

The Standing Stones

Sade didn't dream. Well, she probably did—all Humans did. She just didn't remember hers. Except this time. Because she had to be dreaming. She lived a crazy, fucked-up life and it had been crazier and more fucked up lately, but this? This was beyond the pale. Everywhere she turned, giant sunflowers blotted out a sky so blue it dazzled her eyes.

"Toto, we aren't in Kansas anymore," she muttered. She glanced around looking for her version of Dorothy's intrepid canine companion. There was no sign of Caleb. She muttered some curses under her breath. This *was* a dream, right? Why in fucking hell would Caleb share her dreamscape?

"Think." There *had* been a dream. Sinjen, in the armor of a Knight Templar, standing on a beach bathed in sunshine. Then she woke up in the middle of an ancient stone circle. She'd walked...

She wriggled her toes, discovered she wore a favorite pair of serviceable leather boots. At least these boots were made for walking...

"Nope," she decreed. "I'm not letting that particular earworm invade my head. There's too much shit already in there that's fucking with me."

She'd hiked a mile or so through the Highlands and found a village with a train station. And now she was on a train. Wasn't she? Fuck her. She had *not* had the best of luck with trains recently. So this was either a freaky-crazy dream or she'd been punted through another portal. Hopefully, she'd figure out which sooner than later.

Turning in a circle, Sade picked a random direction and started walking. A playful breeze ruffled her hair and danced through the leaves and stalks of colorful flowers. She caught a glimpse of black fur slinking along the next row. The cat was back.

A voice accompanied the breeze, crooning a song. And was that music? She stopped, cocking her head to listen. Yes. Music. Faintly Celtic. A guitar, one that sounded...more. The notes enticed her as easily as the Pied Piper teased the rats and children in Hamlin. As the notes grew louder, the song became vaguely familiar but she couldn't pin it down in her memory. Stepping through the last row of flowers, she stood stock still. Bridges over a bay? Or a river. A long road of wet asphalt. In the distance, ancient stone buildings stood guard. Overcast skies turned everything to shades of gray. She kept walking until she hit the city. Asphalt changed to cobbled streets beneath her feet.

The music continued to lead her along a path—one she might have traveled once before. She couldn't remember. That should piss her off, that she couldn't remember.

"D'uh. Dream, remember?" Her voice echoed hollowly off the glass and stone of the store fronts surrounding her.

"Edinburgh," a voice called.

Her stop. She opened her eyes. Yes. A dream but as she glanced out the window, she stopped breathing. There were bridges over a bay. Or a river. Including the one the train now crossed. In the distance stood buildings made of ancient stones. Overcast skies turned everything to shades of gray.

The city rolled past until the train pulled into the station and stopped. She climbed out onto the platform. People rushed past and she turned in another circle to get her bearings. Announcements and chattering voices cluttered the air. She followed the crowd until she was on the sidewalk outside the building.

Yeah, this was real. She wasn't dreaming now. Was she? She'd never once been in a dream that affected all of her senses. She could feel the drizzle on her skin and she was chilled to the bone. Her feet slipped on slick cobblestones and that damn music whispered in her ear, tugging and teasing her to take another step. If she could wake up, if she could look deeper, she'd find a Magick's hand in all of this. As it was, she had no choice but to follow the dream—or her current reality—to its end.

Ahead, a sign swung from its metal bracket, making a soft creak each time it did. Which was weird because there was no wind. The music seemed to be coming from inside. She couldn't read the sign until she stood almost directly beneath it: *The Standing Stones*. Subdued light seeped through the pub's windows yet she couldn't see anything but shadows moving inside. Reaching out, Sade clasped the door handle, pushed it down, and leaned into the massive wooden door's weight. It opened on silent hinges. Huh. She'd figured it would creak with age and wear like the sign.

The quiet hum of conversation blanketed her shoulders as she stepped inside and shut the door behind her. The light was brighter than the windows had hinted, but shadows still cloaked the corners. Off to one side, a man sat alone. A notebook, open on the table where he sat, held his attention while a guitar balanced on his thighs and was cradled by one arm. A bottle of scotch and a half-full glass finished the still life. Other patrons sat scattered around the main room in groups of two or three or more. Off in the furthest corner, near the fire, a dark shape draped shadows around itself. Sade thought it was male, but she couldn't be sure.

A seat at the end of the bar opened up and Sade snagged it. She could watch the whole room from here, with a good, solid wall at her back. She ordered a pint of pale ale and settled in. Her instincts insisted there was a show coming. Sipping the beer, she waited.

The sleek car rattled and coughed as Sinjen drove along the road running parallel to an expanse of water. A bridge cut across the horizon, sleek and modern compared to the one he could see in the rear-view mirror. A sense of urgency beat at him as the car wheezed out a final chug and died.

Run.

Get away.

Escape.

Was he on the run? Odd. He didn't run from anything. Not anymore. He'd lived too many centuries, seen too much to turn tail. Climbing out of the car, he studied his surroundings through the gray haze. It wasn't sundown. In fact, there was at least an hour to go before that bane to his existence fled. Another oddity. His skin felt no prickle, no heat.

Sinjen recognized this place. Edinburgh. He'd spent time here during the wars—both the Great War and the World War that followed. He didn't hide the sardonic smile. Had Churchill guessed what he truly was? Probably. The old bulldog was nothing if not practical. A vampire volunteers to spy for England? Why, accept, of course. In the time he'd spent in Edinburgh, he'd come to know all the nooks and crannies, the basements and back alleys.

The urgency returned. Hurryhurryhurry. Places to be. Things to be done. No time to tarry, to remember. Despite the compulsion to run, he forced himself to wait, to assess. How had he arrived in Scotland? He had no memory of travel. As he searched his memory, that was not the only hole he found. Some...thing—some...*one* was out there. Waiting. For good or evil. A thought hovered right at the edges of his consciousness. Fleeting. Ephemeral. He couldn't grasp it, couldn't hang on to it long enough to examine it.

Go, the urgency demanded.

So he did. Drawn inexorably toward Edinburgh proper and Old Town, he settled into a ground-eating pace. Traffic remained light and the faint drizzle and clouds cloaked his unimpeded journey. As buildings almost as old as him crowded around, that nagging memory played hide and seek. In hopes of catching up to it, he dashed down alleys, jogged along dark streets. Old buildings turned to ancient ones, their age peopling the street with ghosts.

He continued his pilgrimage. Every corner he turned he expected to find...what? A face now hovered just behind his centuries of memories. Dark hair. Bottle green eyes. A beauty mark punctuating full lips. Up ahead, a pub beckoned.

Nikos, cloaked in shadow, warmed himself by the fire. Dragons hated damp and cold and Scotland was full of both. How had he come here? He was Drakon. His magic should repel any assault, yet here he was. He unerringly knew he was in Scotland. The accents, the scents, the sense of age and history in the ancient stones of this place. He suspected the pub was in Edinburgh but until he stirred himself to step outside, he wouldn't know for sure.

Apparently, he'd been snoozing here in this corner, insulated from the gazes of the curious, and he'd just surfaced to full awareness when the door opened and a woman with emeralds in her eyes stepped inside. The low murmur of voices cushioned noises from the street. Guitar music and a raspy voice stopped and started as the musician across the room was apparently writing a song. The man strummed, picked, sang, stopped to scribble in a notebook, only to begin again.

Not the night's entertainment then, Nikos decided. A simple songsmith working on both lyrics and tune. Delegating the distraction to the back of his mind, Nikos focused on why—and perhaps more importantly *how*—he'd arrived in this pub. His memory remained fuzzy, as if he'd drunk too much ouzo. Except he was a dragon and Dragons did not get drunk. Ever. Still, his brain was fogged and a slight ache throbbed behind his left eye. His body didn't respond as it ought to. It was sluggish and...

The songwriter added another line and Nikos was lost for a moment. He was warm, drowsy. A drink appeared at his elbow—speaking of ouzo. The fire snapped and crackled, flames dancing like a sensuous chorus line, lulling him into—

He snapped his eyelids open and bit back the curl of smoke threatening to shoot from his mouth. Magic. The place reeked of it. But for what reason? Why—and again *how*—had he been summoned to this place?

And then there was the damnable human woman at the bar. He watched her greedily. Emeralds were his weakness and that she wore a pair in her eyes made him covet her all the more. When she turned her head, the fire teased out russet highlights in the thick, black-silk fall of her hair. Tall and lithe, she could be a dancer. But she wasn't. No. Her grace was far more deadly in origin. His hunting instincts insisted she was hunter rather than prey.

Interesting. He shifted out of the shadows and watched her. She sipped at her ale and he wondered if she did more than wet her lips. And what luscious lips they were. Full. Red. And that captivating beauty mark. His gaze returned to her eyes. Forget the trimmings. Those glowing emeralds would have marked her as his no matter what. Still, he was intrigued. Would she be a worthy lover? He planned to take her and keep her no matter what, but if she came to his bed and satisfied him, all the better.

Then the vampire walked in.

Sade wouldn't make book on it, but she'd at least bet the pint in front of her that something Magick hid in that deep shadow beyond the fireplace. Was that why she'd been drawn here? Was this an assignment? She'd done enough realm jumping lately that as much as she thought this was Edinburgh, she couldn't be positive. For all she knew, either the Elves or the Fae had an alternate Edinburgh in their realms. Except there were cars. Not Fae then. They didn't like cold iron and technology often confounded them. Elves had better luck and they'd assimilated into the Human plane with less trouble and seemed to like it there.

What felt like a cold wind blew across the back of her neck though her hair, worn down and loose, didn't stir. Yeah. Definitely magic in the air. With casual indifference, she surveyed the room again. She was totally convinced a Magick hid in that far corner, but there was more power here. She watched the man with the guitar. He strummed a few notes, whispered some words, and wrote in his notebook. Then, after a sip of scotch, he played and sang. The room...stopped, like someone had hit the pause button on a remote control. No hum of conversation, clink of glasses, or any other sound. Just the guitar and the man's beguiling voice.

Her shoulders snapped back as her spine stiffened. Was he the sole source of magic in the room? Obviously powerful, but... Sade inhaled, then opened her mouth slightly and licked her lips, tasting the air. What a time for Caleb to be AWOL. She needed his nose for magic right then. Still, she always had a good sense of magic and what she discerned felt like...something she didn't recognize along with...gawddamned Dragon. Just her luck.

The songsmith glanced up at her as the room took a collective breath and normality seeped back in. He tilted his head, studying her as his fingers continued to strum, the action idle now as he focused on her.

"So you're the one," he said, his voice as clear as if he occupied the stool next to her and there wasn't another sound to be heard in the pub.

"I'm the one what?" She mouthed the words, just to see.

"The mortal Child who is immune from magic. Except you aren't quite, are you?"

She held her tongue, breathing through her first retort as the shadows beyond the singer parted and Nikos Constantine appeared. The dragon watched her but there was something in his eyes. She forgot about the minstrel as she tried to decipher what was going on with Nikos. His greed was apparent in his facial expression and the way his hand curled around the arm of his chair, as if he had to refrain from reaching for her. He'd always coveted her for reasons beyond any explanation she could get from him. He wanted her and that was enough of a reason for the Drakon. Except now, in addition to the avarice on his face, there was also...

Sade rocked back on her stool. He didn't recognize her. He still wanted her but the vaulted Nikos Constantine, Drakon of Clan Kholikikos, had no fucking clue who she was. What the holy fucking shades of hell was going on? He'd either tagged along or jumped portals on his own to hook up with her in several of those realms she'd been dragged to. How was it even possible, that here and now, he wouldn't know her from Eve? The fucking lizard hounded her whenever their paths crossed and had since they'd first met in New Orleans a couple of years ago.

Tearing her gaze from the dragon in human form, she stared at the singer again.

"What do you want?"

He tilted his head to the other side and lobbed her question back at her. "What do *you* want?"

"I want to know what the bloody hell is going on. And I want to know who you are and what you're up to."

The dude didn't quite smirk at her but it was damn close. "I'm a simple songsmith, writing a song to be sung when no one is listening."

"What good is a song if no one is around to listen?"

"Ah, but that is not what I said."

Sade replayed his words. *A song to be sung when no one is listening.* Not that nobody was around but that they weren't paying attention. Like now.

"And what will your song do?"

The smile he bestowed was indulgent, like she was a slow student who'd just surprised the teacher with a flash of intelligence. She pretended not to be irked.

The door opened and that cold wind that had teased her before arrived full force as a man dressed head to foot in black stepped inside. Her breath caught. Dark hair, tousled by the wind's loving fingers, blue eyes the color of sapphires, chiseled cheeks and jawline. Sinjen. Her heart thudded in her chest and she forgot to breathe. Gods but she'd missed him—missed him so much she forgot for just an instant that she was supposed to be pissed at him.

Movement in the corner of her eye jerked her attention away from the vampire she shouldn't love. Nikos was on his feet and threading through the tables, his eyes intent on her. She flicked her eyes toward Sinjen. Yeah, he was moving too. She slid off the stool and waded through the crowd to cut them off. While there was magic in this pub, it was also full of Humans. The last thing she needed was for innocents to be caught in a magical firefight, which could be literal since a dragon was involved.

The three of them converged in the center of the room, not far from the table inhabited by the minstrel. As the dragon and the vampire charged toward each other, she stepped between them, a hand braced and pushing against each muscled chest. "Whoa there, cowboys. We're in public. Let's take this outside where the nosy Humans aren't watching. Okie dokie?"

"I am Nikolas Con—"

"Yeah, yeah." Sade cut off the dragon's spiel. "You're Nikolas Constantine, Drakon of Clan Kholikikos, fearsome dragon and despoiler of innocent maidens." She almost laughed at the stunned expression on his face. She could have dumped a bucket of ice water over his head and gotten the same look.

"As for you..." She twisted her head to stare at Sinjen. "You're the big, bad master vampire. Kristian St. John, former Knight Templar and wielder of the all-powerful dick. Whoop-dee-do."

The men stared at each other then turned their bewildered gazes on her.

"Who are you?" they asked in unison.

"Seriously?"

"It matters not," Nikos declared. "You are mine." He grabbed her and tugged her toward him. Before she could get her balance and tug back, Sinjen fastened onto her other arm and reeled her back his direction.

"She is marked by my sire," Sinjen announced. "I claim her."

They each continued to hold one of Sade's arms, playing tug-of-war with her. "I am *not* a wishbone to be fought over by the two of you." She was angry, not afraid. Dragon and Vampire stilled, both staring at her. "Jeezpahleeze," she groused. "Y'all have fucking done this since the moment you met me. I'm getting gawddamned sick and fucking tired of—

"Language, Lady Sade," Sinjen chided softly. He kept his gaze focused on her, though his unease was growing by the second. How could he have not recognized her? And what the bloody hell was that dragon doing here pretending to be clueless as to her identity? Too many questions and not enough time to get answers. Sade's initial statement was correct. They needed to step outside to figure out what, to use a phrase from Sade, the bloody hell was going on. He did not release her arm until he'd snagged her hand and interlaced their fingers.

"Let her go, Constantine."

The dragon shook himself like a shaggy dog coming out of a cold stream. Understanding flooded into his eyes. He glanced around, tense and suspicious. "St. John," he acknowledged. "What are you doing here?"

"What are any of us fucking doing here?" Sade groused. She jerked her arm loose from a surprised Nikos, whirled and stabbed Sinjen in the chest with her index finger. "I'm done with this bullshit, Sinjen." He arched an infuriating brow at her right before his eyes turned to shards of blue ice as he looked beyond her.

"Back away, Dragon. If not for your arrogance—"

"My arrogance?" Sade was suddenly shoved aside by Nikos as the two men went head to head and then froze as time snapped to a halt once more.

Nothing moved. The songsmith watched from his table. Only he and Sade seemed immune. "Interesting," he allowed. "The magic is strong enough to hold a dragon and a master vampire but not you. You are not what you seem, Sade Marquis."

"Surprise, surprise. People have underestimated me my whole life."

"Aye, and still presumptuous, as all Humans tend to be."

"Who *are* you?" She eyed him closely. "Or should I be asking what you are?"

His fingers danced over the strings of the guitar. "No one of consequence. Just a humble songsmith as I said."

"Humble my ass. What the fuck is going on?"

The musician strummed his guitar, hummed, made a few notations in his notebook. Then he raised his head to look directly at her. In a voice so sweet her heart shed tears, he sang for her ears alone.

"Heroes sleep beneath the ancient stones,
Stirring to the piper's tune.
Ghosts from the past occupy the throne
And stare into your soul.
A voice through the mists of time

Whispers not a lullaby
But a battle cry.
I would see her dead,
See her dead.
See her dead."

Sade glanced around the pub. No one stirred. For all intents and purposes, she and the bard were the only ones alive. He set aside his guitar and stared deeply into her eyes. A shiver coursed through her. She wondered if he was one of the ghosts of which he sang and what he saw inside her soul. The chorus's words echoed in her heart.

"These are the words you must unlearn."

"Who are you?" she pleaded.

"No one important." He offered a slight shrug topped by a smile that was smug and sad in equal parts.

"Let me be the judge of that. Why are you here?"

That bought a glimpse of a dazzling grin. "I am neither here nor there. And my reasons for being either are my own."

Sade glowered. "Okay, fine. Then why am I here?"

"Why, to learn the lesson set before you."

"What lesson?"

"Did you not pay attention?"

She deflected his question. "If I didn't know better, I'd name you Puck."

A quick laugh from him at that, "Not that one. Guess again."

"Rumpelstiltskin."

A shadow moved. Sinjen. Was he there to see her dead? He'd tried, in his hunger, but had stopped. And fled, believing there was no absolution for what he'd done to her.

She pulled her attention back to the bard as he spoke again.

"There will be no more second chances," he said. "Not for any of you."

"And that's supposed to what? Make me afraid? Worried? Scared? Been there done that, dude. Got the gawddamned T-shirt and everything."

The minstrel *tsked* at her. "Life is what you make of it."

She rolled her eyes. "I don't need a fucking inspirational quote. I need answers." She reached over to grab the man.

The lights went out.

Sade froze, her breathing loud and rasping against the silence. A voice whispered through the darkness. "That's why it is what it is."

Chapter Thirty-three

Not Just Words

The lights came back on and sound filled the pub. Sade sat on the bar stool, her pint still in front of her. The musician was gone. And no one occupied the big armchair next to the fireplace. The back of her neck prickled and she turned her head to face the door. A blast of cold wind blew in as it opened and the man she'd been searching for stood silhouetted there.

"Sinjen." She breathed his name around the clutch in her chest.

His sapphire eyes fixed on her then he pivoted and walked away.

"No!" She jumped off the stool and pushed her way through a group just entering. The street outside was empty. "Sinjen!" She yelled his name. The silence of the ancient stones echoed back at her. Then she heard it. Footsteps. To her right. Heading away.

She ran.

Across the street, a stone wall topped with a spiked wrought-iron fence ran parallel with her. The street sloped down and she picked up speed. A metal gate in the wall loomed up, closed and locked for the night. Stone steps swept up behind the gate and a shadowy figure stood there.

Sade slowed, paying attention. And then she heard the pipes. Realized the shadow wore a kilt and played a lament. She squinted to read the sign. *Greyfriars Kirkyard.*

"Fuck me," she whispered. The kirkyard was supposedly haunted—by more than a little dog. The footsteps she'd been following had also slowed but now they sped up. So did she. Was she chasing a ghost?

"No," she insisted. Out loud. To make it more certain. She was chasing Sinjen and she *would* catch him. Mist swirled around and the drizzle made the pavers slick but she kept running. She was on

Grassmarket Road, not that the name meant anything to her. The sidewalk widened and she had plenty of space now. She ran faster but came to a screeching halt at the next cross street.

Edinburgh Castle loomed up on her right. The mist had parted and a foggy moon shone above the edifice. Something moved along the edge of the round tower. And the heart-rending notes of the lament played by the piper floated down to her.

"To hell with you, ghosts," she challenged. "This is a battle. Why aren't you playing fucking 'Scotland the Brave' or some such shit!"

Then she realized the footsteps had changed direction. With a final look at the castle, she sprinted up Castle Stables Road and took the cut-through to the street above, climbing the steps two at a time. At the top, on Johnston Terrace, she headed right again. There was traffic and that messed up her hearing.

Then she remembered. Sinjen had *marked* her. Seeking deep inside, Sade reached for him. A tiny spark flared. "Gotcha," she whispered. Like a homing beacon the gossamer thread that tied them together drew her forward. She crossed the street and found another pedestrian walkway. She jogged past The Witches Well monument and kept going.

She hit a park and sped up, her footfalls cushioned by dirt and grass. Settling in for a marathon, she crossed over the tangle of train tracks on what amounted to a land bridge, passing by the Scottish National Gallery.

Hell of a way to sightsee, she thought. And then she wondered where in the hell Sinjen was headed. She calculated she'd run a mile, maybe a mile and a half. At this pace, she was good for more. Another right on Princes Street, and more people. She dodged them and kept going, concentrating on that little radar ping in her head that was the key to Sinjen's location.

When the trail veered to the left, she knew where she was. Calton Hill. She slowed to a walk, though she wasn't winded. She followed the path higher and paused. There were several monuments and two very old buildings up here. Eeny meeny miny moe. The Horatio Nelson tower or the Stewart Greek thingy? She was more familiar with it because many of the photos she'd seen of this area included the Stewart Monument.

Standing still, she listened. Not with her ears, but with her soul. And she found him. She turned left and followed her heart.

She was close. He could feel her. Why he'd thought he could lose her was an exercise in futility. She was dogged in her pursuit. And were he honest with himself, he'd admit that he didn't want to lose her. He never had. He'd tried. Gods but he'd tried. He'd walked away. Stayed away. Tried to force *her* away. And here they were, standing on a dark hill in the middle of Edinburgh.

He still wasn't sure how he'd gotten here. Not Calton Hill specifically. But Scotland. And that car. The walk to The Standing Stones. And finding Sade there, but not recognizing her. And that bloody dragon. Resigned, he waited as her footsteps approached. She'd been angry with him in the pub. Perhaps she'd chased him down to end things. He could only be so lucky.

Except.

He knew. He would not walk away. Not again. And he would not allow Sade to walk away from him.

Except.

He'd almost killed her. He was dangerous. He shoved his hands in his pockets, threw back his head and wanted to howl. The pain swirling inside him had no outlet.

"Let her go." Mathias's voice.

"Let her go." Crevan's voice.

God help him, he would try. His black soul was damned but he'd once been a man of honor. Of duty.

She approached him from behind but he made no sign he was aware of her presence. Her fingertips grazed the small of his back and he could not control the shudder that racked his body.

"Sinjen." His name on her lips was like the answer to a prayer. "Please. Look at me."

He steeled himself. Found his backbone and his sense of duty. He turned. And lost the breath he didn't need to live. Her hair was a tousled mess, like she'd just opened her eyes the morning after a full night of lovemaking. A light sheen of sweat—or perhaps it was the drizzle that still misted the air—glistened on her face. Inhaling, he relished the rich, ripe scent of her. Cloves and gardenias. Moss and rain. The fragrances followed him into his daily death.

"Sinjen," she said again.

He had to get a handle on things, take control before he ended up on his knees in supplication before her.

"What is it you seek, Sade? What do you want from me?"

"Forgiveness."

He rocked back like she'd punched him and he looked stricken. "No," he murmured.

"You can't...or *won't*?" She didn't try to hide the pleading notes in her voice.

"Can't or won't what?" He was confused now.

"Forgive me."

"For what, Sade? What can there possibly be to forgive? "

"My being Human."

Sinjen staggered, both emotionally and physically. "No," he whispered. "There is nothing to forgive. It is I who am damned."

"That's not true." Her voice was as soft as his.

"It is." He half turned his body away but kept his eyes locked on her. "I almost killed you. I would have."

"No." It was her turn for denial. "You didn't. You wouldn't." She stepped toward him. He stepped back. "Sinjen, please." She stretched out her hand. "I love you."

And that was that. She undid him. He stepped into her. Sank to his knees. Wrapped his arms around her thighs and pressed his cheek against her belly. "There is no redemption. There is no forgiveness."

"There is none needed. You are my heart. My soul. My life." Her voice cracked and she ignored the tears. "Don't leave me. Not ever again."

"No." He still whispered but his arms tightened. "Not ever again."

And there it was. He could do nothing ever again to hurt Sade. He would walk into the sun first.

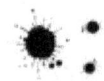

Unsure of just how much time had passed, Sinjen rose to his feet, took Sade's hand, and they walked down the hill. He led her to the nearby Parliament House Hotel, nestled near the base of Calton Hill. A few minutes later, they were in the hotel's finest suite.

Here in the light, even as soft as it was, Sinjen saw the dark smudges under Sade's eyes. She hadn't been sleeping. And he was the cause. One more black mark upon his soul.

"Stop that," she ordered, reading *his* mind for once.

"I'm sor—"

"No. Don't." She moved to him. "Check the windows to be sure." She followed her own decree and started checking them. He followed suit.

Sure now the rooms were secure, he turned to her. "A drink?"

She shook her head and sank into a leather armchair. She finally raised her chin—a good sign. "You aren't the only one fighting demons."

Sinjen cocked his head, taken aback by her bald assertion. Pulling a statement like that from her usually took guile and finesse. "I know," he answered in a quiet voice.

He sat on the edge of the bed and studied her. He'd toyed with an idea before this current situation. Now was probably not the time but...

"Do you trust me?" He wanted to retract those words immediately. That wasn't the way he'd intended to broach the subject.

"Yes." Her immediate answer stilled his doubts. "With my life."

He closed his eyes. When he opened them, *she* was kneeling in front of him.

She touched her throat where pink scars still peeked out of the collar of her shirt. "This wasn't you."

He opened his mouth but her finger on his lips stilled him.

"It wasn't *you*. What was a few weeks here was likely years in that place where Trane trapped you. You were feral. Starved. I've seen it happen to other vampires." She cupped his cheek in her palm. "I gave myself willingly, Sinjen. To you. To feed you. I would die for you. Do you understand that?"

Did he? Perhaps now, he was coming to that realization but he was not worthy of any sort of sacrifice.

"Stop," she whispered. "Don't. You are mine. I love you. And you stopped before you took my last drop. You stopped and you got me to safety. Whatever you did to help, it worked. I'm fine." She rubbed a fingertip over the worst of the scars. "See?"

He did see. And it was one more sin he'd committed. He'd fed her his blood. Again. Making her even less Human. Little by little he was stealing her humanity. *This* is what drove Crevan and Mathias.

This is what should be driving him away from her. But as he gazed into those eyes of liquid emeralds, he was a drowning man.

"Yes," he murmured. He bent his head and kissed her. It wasn't deep. It wasn't passionate. It was just perfect. "Do you trust me with your secrets?" he whispered against her mouth.

Her eyes narrowed.

"Demons, milady."

Okay. He had point.

Five minutes later, Sade sat in the chair. Blindfolded. She hated it but she'd be dammed if she let Sinjen know. She waited, tense, ears straining for the slightest sound, her nostrils flaring as she inhaled, searching for the elusive scent teasing her senses.

He hadn't bound her. She would have staked his ass if he'd even suggested it but he indicated this wasn't some sexy game. He'd elicited a promise from her—that she remain still. And blindfolded. Dammit.

"Do you still trust me?" Sinjen's faintly accented voice drifted through her.

She nodded, one quick jerk of her head. Material rustled and she pictured the smirk surely curving his full, sensuous lips. Fingers trailed over her cheek and then dropped to her chest, working free the top button of her shirt.

"Breathe easy, milady."

Oh, yeah. She remembered to do that. Breathe. She'd been holding her breath. Stupid, but there it was. She trusted the vampire standing behind her but...

"Listen to my voice, Sade. Focus on it. You have nothing to fear."

"But fear itself."

"Words, Sade. Are you afraid of them?"

Was she? Bits of remembered conversations haunted her memory. And her heart ached. No, she wasn't afraid but they hurt.

"No," she murmured. "But words can hurt."

GHOSTS & THE ANCIENT STONES

"Yes," he agreed. "They can and often do. What are the words that haunt you? That *hurt* you?"

Ghosts of the past reared their ugly heads. *See her dead. By my own hand.* More words. From Mathias. Her father. Titania. Oberon. Oh, Oberon's had cut deep when he told her that his order to seduce her was the only reason Ariel kept coming around. She was panting now. Had to get control back.

"What do the words in your head feel like, Sade?"

Sinjen's voice startled her into speaking without thinking. "Broken glass. Sandpaper. Sharp claws digging in my chest."

His hands cupped her cheek as he kissed her. "I love you."

She forgot to breathe again.

"What do my words feel like?"

"They feel like velvet, or silk. Say them again."

Sinjen removed the blindfold. "I love you."

She saw it there in his eyes. All of it. The depths of his feelings for her. The fear of hurting her. The need to protect. And the knowledge that he would lose her someday. Not that he would leave her...but that she would leave him.

Stunned by this revelation, she stared at him. She cupped his beloved face in her palms. "*Shhh,*" she murmured. "I'm here. I love you." She blinked moisture from her eyes and in a voice now strong, she assured him. "I would fight the very gods themselves for your soul. It is yours. You haven't lost it. You are not damned. You are mine. And I protect what is mine."

They both leaned in, foreheads touching, her hands on his cheeks, his on her thighs. They simply stayed like that as the earth turned and the sun edged inexorably toward the eastern horizon.

Sinjen finally spoke. "What do you want, love?"

She pressed her lips to his. "Just you. You make everything...right. You make me feel whole. Strong. But I also know I can let go. That if I fall, you'll catch me." She pushed her fingers into his thick hair, a slow smile easing onto her face.

He slipped his arms around her. "Always, milady. I will always be your shield." He sank back on his heels and laid his head in her lap, enjoying the feel of her fingers brushing through his hair. "You remind me of what I once was, what I still might be. It is good to remember. And to forget. I want to be with you."

"You always are. Even if we're apart." She moved one hand to cover her heart. "Here. I carry you here always."

Sinjen straightened and kissed her lips. He kissed her temples, her forehead, cheeks, and ended with a peck to the tip of her nose. "As I also hold you here in my own."

He stood and pulled her to her feet. Sade slid into him and they swayed slightly, as if the night's events left them a little bit drunk. He undressed her, then stripped his own clothes away. She looked shy now, the first time in a very long time that she had.

"Beautiful," he murmured. "And mine."

That brought a smile to her face, one that held a tiny hint of her cockiness. The tempest that so often raged between them had quieted, but he still felt bruised. He stilled. For centuries, he felt nothing and then this remarkable woman stalked into his life and emotions he'd long thought dead awoke. A sense of calm settled over him. A sense of rightness. He'd hurt her, thinking only to save her from himself. He would make it right.

Sade nuzzled the vee of his neck, her lips brushing the skin there. Her tongue flicked out to taste him. Satisfied, she sighed.

He understood her, probably better than she understood herself. Her needs, her desires. The intangible things she sought from him—the sense of security, the sense of belonging she craved but would never admit. And he understood that in her way, she wanted to return the favor, as it were. She *needed* him to see the man she saw. The man, not the monster.

Time was short but he would make slow, tender love to her. He would give them both the peace that came from not thinking, at least for a bit. The wounds that had opened inside him still ached, but Sade would soothe them. Her touch, her smile, her love always did. And he'd been a fool not to acknowledge that.

In bed now, he curled her into his arms. Skimming the line of her jaw, his lips found her beauty mark and then her mouth. He kissed her long and deep when her lips parted for him. She rolled to her back, spread her legs and he settled between them. He could feel her readiness as his cock nestled against her.

"Sinjen," she sighed. "Inside me. Please."

"Your wish is my command, milady." He lifted his hips and his cock found her entrance unerringly. He sank deep. And stilled. Something profound and quiet passed between them, an...acknowledgment or a pact. She melted against him, the gift of her giving herself to him would have brought him to his knees once again had he been standing.

This woman—the paradox of her—unraveled him. And fascinated him. She was hard. Strong. Loyal. Terrifyingly brave. Troubled. His. He moved with that thought. He would never own her but she was his, nonetheless. He entered and pulled out. Slow. Easy. Building her toward a climax with kisses and touches. Her pulse skittered beneath his lips as he kissed her throat. He would not taste her. Not tonight. Her scars were still too new, too huge a reminder of his loss of control, of how close he'd come to ending her. Ending them both.

He kept her on that edge, not by design nor desire but so his own body could catch up. She pressed her head back into the pillow so she could gaze up at him. And smiled. She knew what he was doing. Her hands caressed his chest, ruffling the light peppering of hair. Her legs wrapped around his back and she arched up into him, urging him to speed up. Her inner muscles clenched and released and he gritted his teeth.

Sade was so tough, yet so soft. Delicate skin stretched over hard muscles. He smiled as a hum of pleasure vibrated through her. He did as she silently commanded. In moments, they slid over the edge together. Mouth to mouth. Heart to heart. Soul to soul. He pushed any doubts away. They were here, together, connected.

She kissed her way up his throat and whispered in his ear. "Mine."

"Yes," he agreed readily, enjoying the note of possessive jealousy in her tone. He rolled to his back, taking her with him, but he stayed buried inside her warm, wet heat.

One of her hands rested on his chest. He lifted it and placed a kiss in the middle of her palm. They stared at each other, content, comfortable, floating in a bubble of calm that was unusual for them. He cherished this moment, didn't want it to end. But dawn was near and when the sun rose, he would lose her for the day's duration.

He claimed her back. "Mine." And smiled as her eyes lit up. "You will sleep, yes?"

She nodded. "Yes. And I'll be here when you wake up."

They didn't speak, just held each other, the peace of the moment soaking into their souls. He felt the coming dawn, kissed her breathless as the sun continued its climb up the ladder of the earth to reach the sky. As the first rays peeked over the horizon, he kissed her again and vowed, "I love you."

He closed his eyes and slipped away without a fight, knowing his soul was safe with her.

Sade remained cuddled to his side, head on his shoulder. She lifted one hand to his hair and her fingers stroked the incredible softness. He was a man of contradictions. He considered himself a monster yet he was one of the most honorable men she knew.

Beyond these walls, the world awoke. People embraced their lives. She was cocooned here. And for the first time in her memory, at peace. Her eyes drifted shut and she joined Sinjen in slumber. Whatever was out there could wait. For the moment, there was just Sinjen. Just Sade. Just...them. Together.

Chapter Thirty-four

One Last Time

Sade tumbled out of sleep. Fuzzy-brained, she peered around her. Well, crap. She wasn't in the hotel room. Nope. She was out the middle of...where? She had no clue. Something moved in the darkness. And she realized that a steady—if gentle—rain fell, soaking her clothes. And she *was* wearing clothes. Considering she'd fallen asleep on top of Sinjen naked, she was pretty fucking happy that she'd somehow gotten dressed.

It was dark out, and she had the sense that she might still be in Scotland. Was she sleepwalking? Had she stumbled into another damned portal?

Her sight sharpened and she realized the street beneath her booted feet consisted of well-worn cobblestones. Buildings loomed around her. Two and three stories, made of fitted granite or limestone. She wasn't a student of architecture but thought one or two might be medieval and the rest Georgian? Yeah, she was still in Scotland.

A figure shambled into view, walking up the street toward her. An old man huddled beneath an umbrella. His stumbling gait carried him inexorably toward the dilapidated structure at the end of the lane. He walked past with no acknowledgment of her presence. Was he ignoring her or did he just not see her? Was she even here?

Dream, part of her insisted but she wasn't so sure.

Memories flooded him and she felt them wash over and through her as he passed. A pretty woman, her face wreathed in a smile of welcome. Laughing children playing in the lane. The doors of the ancient building opened. Sade caught the scent of roasting venison and the sound of men, loud and boisterous as they tossed back mugs of ale. She glimpsed pretty wenches teasing and tossing their curls at

274

those men. The man still ignored her, though she had fallen into step beside him. His fate—his final rest—awaited him inside that ancient inn. It was time.

He stepped through the doorway and Sade made to follow but the doors slammed closed, shutting her out. She shouldn't have been surprised. This wasn't the first door slammed in her face. Always the outsider. Never quite good enough. Expendable.

I would see her dead...

She backed away from the inn, caught her heel on a cobblestone and almost wend down on her butt. She caught her balance. No. Those words did not matter. Not anymore. She had Sinjen. She did fit. With him. He wouldn't shut her out. Not again. He'd promised.

Thunder rumbled, heralding the passage of the storm as rain washed away tears she was only then aware of shedding. "I don't fucking cry!" She yelled it to the roiling clouds above her. With a furious gesture, she wiped the moisture from her cheeks. Where the fuck was she?

Dream.

No. It wasn't. She was wet. And cold. And alone. Her heart hurt. Hell, her fucking ankle hurt from twisting it on that cobblestone. Movement caught her eye and she focused on wisps of...smoke? Fog? Her instincts prickled. There was energy here and not just from the storm. These were not columns of mist rising from the ground. Nope. Wraiths. Those were wraiths passing by her as if she didn't exist.

Holy crappola. Was this like some sort of...way station? She searched her memory for the right word because growing up in the household of a master vampire hadn't been particularly conducive to a religious upbringing. *Purgatory*. The name hit her like a blow to her solar plexus. Purgatory, where you atoned for your sins. Where you got stuck when you weren't good enough to get into heaven but not so evil that you went straight to hell. The gods knew she wasn't good.

And since she was here, maybe she didn't have a one-way ticket the other direction.

Was it her time as well? Wait. She wasn't dead. Was she? Had Sinjen actually killed her and her soul just dreamed the hospital, and all the rest?

A tune teased her ears. Tilting her head, she both listened and tried to discern the direction it came from. It was faintly familiar but...wasn't. Intrigued, she ignored the rain to follow the music. To the graveyard. She pulled up short.

"Okay, if I'm dead, where's the white light? I never saw the white light!"

This was crazy. A dream, that's all it was. A crazy-ass dream and she would wake up any moment in Sinjen's arms. Except Sinjen was dead. Not dead *dead*. Just dead. No heartbeat, no breathing, not until the sun went down. She heard a plaintiff *meowrr*. That, too, was a familiar sound. She pushed the wrought-iron gate open. Rusty hinges yowled like a tom cat on the prowl.

"I'm not some dumb teenager in a horror flick," she muttered. "But I got a bad feeling about this." She walked into the cemetery despite her misgivings. The cat continued its caterwaul and she tracked the sound to the oldest section. Gravestones here were so ancient she could no longer read the names or dates.

She found the black cat sitting atop one of the limestone plinths, licking a paw while he watched her approach. She scowled at the animal. "Seriously? Is this your doing?"

He blinked at her. She blinked back. "By the way, you wanna play Stare or Dare, I'll win. Just sayin'."

Someone called her name and she whirled, took two steps and fell flat on her face. She stared at what was carved into the aged stone just beyond her nose. *Child of the Mortals.* And below it, the words, *Called by Destiny.* Well, fuck her. Was that why she was here? Because she had no choice? She pushed up to her hands and knees, the shred of stubbornness buried deep within forcing her out of the mud.

Dreams died so fucking hard and she'd stupidly held on to hers. She'd been called the Child of the Mortals her whole life—what she could remember of it, anyway. She should have known. Back when she was just a pawn tossed around by two powerful Magicks. What possessed her to think that she would ever find someone to love her? Someone who cherished her just because she existed. Memories punched her in the gut, refusing to fade away.

Boots appeared in her vision. She reared back, staring up at the hooded figure. "Come, Child."

He held out his hand. She took it.

"Walk with me."

She did, understanding she had no choice. They walked in silence as flickering lightning tantalized her with hints of the face hidden beneath the hood. After exiting the graveyard, they walked some distance before he asked, "What would you do, Child of the Mortals, one last time before you leave this world?"

One last time? Her heart was so wounded she couldn't think. Then the spark that was Sinjen surged inside her and she knew. "Tell him goodbye."

"Do you love him so much then?"

Did she? She considered the question. They brought out the best and the worst in each other. He was her light and her dark, all mixed up in her head. And her heart. She'd been willing to die to save him.

She was about to answer when he stopped, turning her to face him. She still couldn't see the face hidden by the hood. "I could give you what he can't."

She studied the shadows that obscured his face. Hard determination emanated from him, along with an incongruous gentleness. And an overwhelming sense of age. She felt the promise in his words but they didn't matter. Her heart held room for only one. "No, you can't."

Thunder and lightning crashed, rendering her both deaf and blind, a cacophony that could herald the end of her world. From inside that chaos, words reached for her.

"I can't what?" *His* voice. Warmth suffused her. *His* arms holding *her*.

She choked on the words, but finally got them out. "Leave me."

Silence filled the void between them, then his promise whispered in her ear. "Never."

"Sade." Frantic hands griped her arms and shook her roughly. "Come back to me, Sade. From wherever you are, you come back to me right bloody now."

He and the cat watched from the shadows. "I owe you a can of tuna." The cat smirked. "Will you stay with her then?'

The cat stared at the couple on the bed. The vampire had gathered the human into his lap, hugging her, caressing her, kissing her. Murmuring to her. Making vows and promises he had every intention of keeping but the cat knew. They'd both been marked by Destiny. And like her twin sisters Karma and Fate, she could be a real bitch. Tilting his head, the cat stared up at the figure standing next to him.

"Aye. As I thought you might."

Manannán mac Lir bent to stroke the cat before he faded back into the shadows. He would keep watch over the Child of the Mortals and her vampire. Destiny was far from done with them.

Chapter Thirty-five

A Little Help From My Friends

The vampire and the dragon followed Alice Cooper into the impressive office. They exchanged a knowing look as the little woman left them and closed the door behind her. They turned their gazes to the human sitting behind the large desk, a vista of Washington DC at night visible behind his bulk. George Bailey, FBI Director and Sade's boss, waved a meaty hand in the general direction of two armchairs planted in front of the desk.

"Sit." He waited until the two men situated themselves then he stared at them. They stared back. After a tense few minutes, Bailey broke the stalemate. He jabbed a finger in the dragon's direction. "You are Nikolas Constantine, Drakon of the reigning Dragon clan."

Nikos offered a toothy smile. "That would be Clan Kholikikos."

Bailey ignored him, focusing on the vampire. "Can't say I'm pleased to see you again, St. John, given the circumstances, but the Concilium Magicae has offered you both up. Do I need to explain why you are here?"

Nikos, cocky as ever, adjusted his cuff-linked sleeves. "Dragonkin is always pleased to assist the Human authorities."

Sinjen fixed Nikos with a withering glare while remaining silent. Bailey was not one to trifle with.

"How is she handling things? What's in her head?" Bailey didn't need to explain who he was talking about.

"Nothing but serenity and bliss." Sinjen managed to say this with a completely straight face, his voice laced with sincerity.

Bailey snorted, his disbelief evident. "And your assessment, Constantine?

Nikos didn't blink, clear his throat, or give any evidence of the turmoil sloshing inside him. "Agent Marquis remains the epitome of professionalism."

The big man leaned back until his leather chair creaked, the sound punctuated by thuds as his feet landed on this desk. Fingers steepled on his chest, Bailey regarded them with gimlet eyes. "Do you gentlemen truly expect me to believe the shit you're shoveling? This *is* Sade Marquis we're talking about. I'm not wearin' hip boots."

He had a point.

"She's coping," Sinjen admitted. "And she is...angry."

"Pissed, you mean." Bailey almost smiled.

"Yes. She is frustrated..." Sinjen glanced at Nikos. "This wizard keeps eluding her."

"The Dragons are dealing with this." Nikos's arrogance flashed.

"Really? You can't even locate the artifact Trane is using. In fact, without Sade you would not even know the man's identity."

Nikos half rose out of his chair and turned on Sinjen. "Now you listen—"

"Boys!" Bailey's voice cut through the tension as his feet hit the floor. The two Magicks turned angry eyes on him. "Sit and settle."

Only George Bailey would dare call two age-old Magicks *boys*. Or order them around. Sinjen decided to find his manner amusing. He glanced at Nikos and understood the dragon chose to do the same.

A short rap on the door interrupted the face-off. Alice didn't wait for an invitation. She sailed in carrying a tray. Sinjen and Nikos did settle back in their chairs as she bustled about. She set a steaming mug of black coffee on the desk next to the Director's elbow. She moved around behind the chairs. She set two tall and narrow glasses on a small table next to Nikos's chair. One held a milky liquid, the other clear.

"I wasn't sure of your preference though I suspect you'll need it straight before all is said and done."

The dragon's lips twitched. The efficient Ms. Cooper had added a touch of water to the ouzo, turning it milky. Like the director's assistant, he suspected he'd need the straight shot as well.

The cup she set on the table next to Sinjen's chair was made of pewter. The liquid inside was thick but not quite viscous and a deep carnelian red in color. He didn't need to taste it to know it was a blood supplement and likely served just under Human body temperature.

Curious that Director Bailey would go all out on the hospitality. Sinjen reached for the glass, keeping his face bland and his thoughts to himself. He tasted the blood in his cup. O positive. Sade's blood type. He cut his eyes to the little woman who was far more than she seemed. She ignored him and bustled out the door.

Bailey sipped his coffee and stared between the Magicks. He knew the score, was well aware of the situation and the rivalry. But he sensed a difference now. Things had happened in Paris and Edinburgh. His agent had changed. He could only hope it was for the better.

"Here's the deal. Your council has given me the two of you for the duration. You have one mission. Keep Sade safe."

Nikos snorted a laugh and managed to look embarrassed as twin swirls of smoke wreathed his face.

Ignoring him, Bailey continued. "That will entail the two of you working together. Due to the vampire's restrictions, all physical or on-scene investigations will be conducted after sundown."

Nikos leaned forward to protest but Bailey cut him off. "Use your days for your own hunt, Drakon. I want St. John on this." Bailey stared long and hard at each man before continuing. "And I want you two to cooperate and work together."

Sinjen leaned back in his chair and took another swallow from his cup. Drinking the supplement wasn't near as fulfilling as drinking from the source but it would keep him alive.

Nikos throttled his anger by reaching for the milky ouzo. He tossed the entire contents down and swallowed. It didn't help so he snagged the glass of pure ouzo and did the same. The licorice flavor coated his tongue. He was Drakon. He did not take orders from anyone but his Archon. This was especially true about a human or a vampire. His phone pinged. He ignored it. It pinged again. And he ignored it.

Alice's voice ghosted through the intercom on the desk phone. "Director, please inform the Drakon that he should answer his phone. Mr. Panos, the royal magistrate, is calling."

Nikos retrieved his phone from his coat pocket. This time he answered.

"Yes?"

"Please hold for the Archon, Drakon Constantine."

He didn't have to hold long. His king's voice reverberated from the speaker and while Valantis spoke in Greek, Nikos was fairly certain at least the vampire understood what was being said. He ended the call the only way he could, with a "Yes, your majesty." And dropped the phone back into his jacket pocket.

Bailey echoed—in English—what King Valantis had said. "Are we clear?"

"Perfectly." Nikos showed no sign of the displeasure he felt.

"Yes, sir." Sinjen's voice held a hint of laughter.

"Good. You'll find Sade in her office."

They headed out shoulder to shoulder but they did not find Sade in her office. She was standing in the hallway when the elevator doors opened. Before anyone could react, her phone rang. She held up a finger, glanced at the caller ID and answered the call.

"Hey, Del."

"Sade?" Adele's whisper put her on instant alert.

"What's wrong?" She caught the sounds of snarls in the background. "Where are you, Adele?"

"Home. In the bathroom."

"Why are you in the bathroom? Is that Caleb I hear?"

"Yes. Sort of."

"Adele!"

"Something's happened."

"You have to talk to me. I can't fix it if I don't know what's broken."

"Well...this weird little dude walked up to us. We were outside. In the park. Taking a walk."

"Get to the point, hon."

"Yes, right. This guy walked up and said some mumbo-jumbo and when Caleb went to grab him, the guy blew glitter all over Caleb and..."

"And he shifted and can't shift back."

"Something like that. And he's really...*really* angry. Like...he tried to bite me. Which is why I'm locked in the bathroom."

"Just kill me now. We're on our way. Fill up the tub. If he gets through that door, jump in and scrunch up."

"What will that do?"

"Caleb hates wet fur but it might help wash away the spell and the faerie dust if he comes in after you. Werewolves are allergic."

"Oh. Oh! Yes. I remember that now. Derp."

Sade heard water running as she stepped into the elevator. Sinjen let go of the door and Nikos hit the button for the first floor. Nikos could not teleport from inside the building. Out on the plaza? He'd get them to Caleb's house in a hurry. She didn't stop to wonder why these two were together—and wandering around FBI headquarters unescorted. Time for that later.

"Describe the weird dude, Adele." Sade was certain of the little fucker's identity but she needed to keep Adele talking. The woman was a damn fine forensics geek and very logical, so long as she was calm and in control. The fact her husband was currently a drooling, raging wolf did not check those boxes.

"Shorter than me. White beard. Sort of a nappy dresser. Tweeds. Like he was from England or something."

"Or something," Sade muttered. "Did any of the spell spill over on you?"

"No. At least I don't think so. He did his thing and then just sort of...*poofed*. Caleb started to change. There were people in the park. Families. One man was dialing 911 and I was afraid the police would shoot Caleb."

There might have been a good possibility of that. Angry Werewolves didn't go rampaging around DC uncontrolled. Or ever. Adele gasped and Sade heard wood getting shredded.

"How long, Sade?"

The elevator opened and the three of them ran full tilt across the lobby and out onto the plaza. "Seconds, Del. Hang on."

Nikos grabbed Sade with one arm and Sinjen with the other and then, just like Ichabod Trane, they *poofed* into thin air. She had just long enough to inhale and then they were on the sidewalk in front of Caleb's house.

"Thanks for the lift and all but—"

"But nothing, Sade." Sinjen blocked her way up the front walk.

"No offense, Sinjen, but you aren't Caleb's favorite person." She jabbed a thumb over her shoulder to indicate the dragon at her back. "And he *definitely* isn't. If Caleb is stuck in wolf form or worse, his half-form, you two need to stay out here."

"He was trying to get to his mate," Nikos said dryly. "And I suspect there is Dragon magic involved here."

"All the more reason for you to stay—"

Adele's scream ended the argument. The three of them charged the front door. Nikos got there first and hit it with a shoulder. It bounced open. Sinjen was right behind him, Sade bringing up the rear and cussing a blue streak.

They pelted up the stairs and skidded to a halt in the master bedroom. A very wet and bedraggled wolf cowered at the foot of the king-size bed. A very angry human had him by his jowls.

"Look at this mess," Adele yelled. "I just stripped and refinished that door. It took *days*. And what do you do? You claw and bite and eat your way through it. Now I have to find another door to fit. Do you have any idea how hard it is to find period correct doors? Of course you don't!"

Caleb tried to duck his head, his ears laid flat against his skull, his tail tucked beneath him. He whimpered.

"And then! What do you do then? You jump in the freaking bathtub. In. The. Freaking. Bathtub. And now thirty gallons of water is at this very moment soaking into the floor and dripping its way onto the ceiling of the dining room and onto my antique dining table. That seats twelve. With upholstered chairs!"

She released Caleb and threw up her hands. "How *could* you!"

That was definitely not a question. Sade noticed that Sinjen and Nikos were slowly backing out of the room, both having obviously decided that they weren't needed to rescue a damsel in distress. Sade wondered if she should rescue Caleb. It wasn't his fault, exactly.

"Uhm...Adele?"

Angry eyes focused on her. "It's about time you got here. Do something!" Adele jabbed an index finger at Caleb. "Make him change back so he can mop the damn floor before there's any more damage."

The woman stomped from the room. Werewolf and Human stared at each other. "Did the water wash off the faerie dust?" Caleb sneezed. "Yeah, guess not."

Nikos stuck his head around the door jamb. "Your vampire is soothing the woman and checking for leaks in the ceiling. I will deal with the water on the floor up here."

Sade eyed him narrowly. "Oh, hell no! You'll burn the fucking house down."

Nikos appeared both affronted and amused. It was an interesting look on him. "I intended to use towels. However, I now suggest you deal with the water and I will deal with the werewolf." Caleb growled. "I am a dragon. There is both Fae and Dragon magic surrounding you."

Considering, Sade looked from Wolf to Dragon. "How did Trane get his hands on Fae magic?"

"That is a very good question."

Lifting her eyes to the ceiling, Sade mumbled, "I know I'm going to regret this but..." She inhaled, thinking hard about a certain fae and then she called his name out loud. "Ariel?"

Caleb growled but subsided when she glowered at him. "Do you have any better suggestions?"

She headed to the bathroom and dragged all the towels from the linen closet. Dropping them on the floor she returned. No Fae. "Ariel!"

Nothing. Dammit. He was always around when she didn't want him but when she needed him? The glittery asshole was nowhere to be found. She schlepped into the bathroom and started grabbing towels and wringing them out in the tub. She felt the pressure change in the room and turned to find Ariel sitting on the vanity's marble countertop.

"Where have you been?"

He eyed the mess, gave her a look, and then leaned over to peer through the doorway. "You've been busy."

"Not me. A little asswipe named Ichabod Trane."

Ari blinked at her. "He's Human."

"D'uh."

"How did he get Fae magic?"

"You tell me. Right after you and the dragon figure out how to change Caleb back."

He blinked again. "Fae *and* Dragon magic? That isn't possible."

"Go argue with the resident dragon. He says that Caleb is caught by both."

Ari did not hop off the counter. *Nooo*, Sade thought. He wouldn't get *his* feet wet. Nope, he just teleported from one room to the next. She continued wringing out towels and mopping up water while she listened to Fae and Dragon argue while a very perturbed werewolf growled.

"Owww!" Ariel yipped.

Sade looked out. The fae cradled one hand to his chest. "What?"

"Tell the mangy mutt I was simply looking for a talisman. The bastard bit me."

Caleb looked appropriately chastised beneath her scowl. She gathered up all the towels into a large bundle, walked out and thrust them into Nikos's arms. "Take those to the laundry room."

She ignored the curl of smoke emanating from the dragon's nostrils, turning to the fae. "Ari, go wash that bite. You don't want Werewolf cooties."

When Caleb snarled she swatted his nose. "I've had about enough of you, buster. Now hold still." She ran her fingers through his ruff, over his chest, then down his sides and back. She found a small burr at the base of his tail.

"This it?" She held it up between forefinger and thumb. Ariel squinted from the bathroom doorway. "Probably. Ask the dragon when he gets back."

Nikos walked in, followed by Sinjen and a much calmer Adele. Ari smothered a laugh as he joined them. "Someone's in the doghouse." He *oofed* when Sade nailed him in the solar plexus with her elbow.

She held up the object she'd pulled from Caleb's fur. "What the fuck is this thing?"

Nikos studied it. He exchanged a look with Ariel. "Is that a drifter?"

"What the hell is a drifter?" She huffed a breath when the Magicks all stared at her. "Indulge the Human, boys."

"It's an Irish word," Sinjen said. He spelled the word *draíochta* for her and said it slowly. "Dree-if-ta."

Ariel looked impressed as he explained. "It's basically a magical charm. A way to contain a spell."

"So how do we reverse it?" Adele crossed her arms over her chest. "I need my husband in Human form because he has about ten loads of laundry to do before he goes to bed tonight."

Ariel rubbed the back of his neck and looked sheepish. "There's the rub, love. The container and the delivery system might be Fae, but the magic?" He cut his eyes to Nikos. "That's all draconic."

Adele was not appeased. "I don't care whose magic it is, somebody better fix this or else."

Caleb groaned. Sade took one look and started shooing people. "Out. Naked wolf alert. Del, get him some pants. Everyone else, outta here. Now!"

At the word *naked*, the men all backpedaled for the door. Sade kept her back to Caleb and once everyone was out in the hallway, she firmly shut the door behind her.

"We'll wait downstairs," she instructed.

"What did you do?" Ariel watched Nikos.

"Nothing. I thought it was something you did."

"No."

They looked at Sinjen, who shrugged. All three Magicks stared at Sade as they hit the first floor.

"What? Don't look at me. I'm the non-magical Human, remember?"

"Where is the *draíochta*?" Nikos asked.

She opened her palm to reveal the thing. Dragon and Fae exchanged another long look. She narrowed her eyes as she watched them. "What?"

"Nothing." Their denial came in stereo.

The bedroom door opened upstairs and a haggard Caleb, barefoot in old jeans and a T-shirt, descended the stairs, Del close on his heels. "I want this little fucker."

Sade went wide-eyes and her mouth dropped open. Caleb *never* cussed. Trane had stomped on the werewolf's very last thread of patience.

"I might be able to help with that."

All eyes turned to the fae.

Chapter Thirty-six

Magic Beans

Ariel held up his hands, palms out to stave off questions. "I don't have actual information. Had I, I would have passed it along before now. However, it just occurred to me that there is a minor member of the Seelie Court living in the area. He runs some sort of gallery. Art, I believe. He is an idiot but I heard a rumor that he came into a great deal of funds recently."

"Let me guess, his great aunt Hyacinth Peasbottom died and left him her estate?"

He favored her with a long-suffering look. "Your sarcasm is duly noted as we are all well aware that there are no inheritances in the Court. I simply bring up his existence because he's been known to be a braggart who is more talk than action."

"Duly noted," Sade said. "And appreciated." She glanced at her watch. "Any chance he's open all night?"

"I would not know..." Ariel's eyes unfocused, like he was listening to something only he could hear. In a few moments, he blinked. "I must go."

Sade grabbed his arm. "Whoa, whoa, whoa, dude. We need to talk."

"While speaking with you is always a pleasure, lovely Sade, alas, I do not have the time."

She squeezed his arm and tugged. "You need to make time, Ariel."

"Not now." His pale celadon eyes snapped with a flash of green fire and Sade released him immediately.

"Ari..."

The fae cupped her cheek. "Not now, sweets. Duty." And then he was gone.

She turned around and looked at the others. "Do any of you have any idea of what the fucking hell is going on with him?" Her question received only negative responses. "Fine. Whatever. We need to find a Fae-owned gallery thingamajig because our primary source, jerk that he is, boogied without giving us a name."

Sade put some FBI drones on the search for Fae-owned establishments in and around DC. They were far better equipped to set up the parameters for a computer search. Dawn was still a few hours away but she wanted coffee. Her phone pinged—a text from the head computer squint. He'd found a cluster of Magick businesses not far from Georgetown. A list followed, and one of them was a 24/7 coffee shop.

"Thank the coffee gods," she muttered. After requisitioning an official vehicle, she led Sinjen and Nikos to the basement parking garage.

"Where are we going?"

She eyed the dragon. "Coffee."

"Coffee?"

"Yes." And she said no more, slipping behind the steering wheel as Sinjen slid into the front passenger seat. Caleb and Nikos exchanged scowls but got into the back. At least she'd had the sense to request an SUV rather than a sedan.

She found a parking space down the block from the coffee shop. Caleb froze as he climbed out. Sade stopped and watched him. Head back, nostrils flaring, eyes a little glazed, Caleb was onto something.

"Magic," he growled.

"Good." Sade smiled. "We're in the right place."

Caleb's eyes had gone wolf. "I'll scout around."

"Go for it." She flashed a big smile at her other escorts and strode down the street toward the neon sign with a cup giving off steam.

"Coffee," Nikos muttered.

"I suggest the two of you stay out here. I hope to get some answers about our Fae gallery owner and maybe the little shit wizard."

Sinjen opened the door for her and she passed through. He didn't follow and put up an arm to block Nikos. "She can handle this. And we are close enough if she can't."

Sade got her order and found a table where her back wasn't too exposed. She'd taken one sip of the most excellent coffee when a shadow fell over the table. All righty, then. This was going to be easier than she'd thought. She didn't look up as she said, "The only magic that works on me is right here in this cup of coffee. Disturbing me while I'm drinking it is very risky business."

Two chairs scraped on the floor and two bodies settled into them. The goblin eyed her warily. The Magick seated beside him snorted his disdain. The door opened and her escorts sauntered in.

Sinjen leaned against hostess stand and wondered what Sade would do next. The dragon sidled up to him.

"Aren't you going to do something?'

The rivals stared at each other, then a slow smile crept across Sinjen's face—one that even reached his eyes. "You'll learn."

At that seeming taunt, Nikos headed for Sade's table. He loomed up beside her, radiating menace. The two Magicks sneered, wrongly believing the weak Human needed rescuing.

With a graceful wave of her hand, Sade jammed her Beretta into the dragon's balls. "I'm not a damsel in distress."

Nikos didn't move, though he did gulp once, soundlessly.

Sinjen remained impassive. He'd learned long ago that Sade was always good for a show.

Sade leveled her gaze on the Magicks sitting at her table. "It's early," she explained. "Or late, depending on which side of midnight you woke up. I came in for a cup of coffee. That's all. And then you pea brains decide to get all up in my face. As a trained investigator, this makes me wonder what you've been up to."

The first gulped in imitation of the dragon. The second leaned against the back of his chair with a superior air. *Fucking Fae*, Sade thought.

"Do you even know who I am?"

The fae continued to sneer. "A human too stupid to live?"

The goblin tugged on his boss's sleeve. "Lord Enmoore?"

The fae shrugged him off. "The operative words in that sentence are stupid, human, and live."

The dragon moved, then flinched as Sade snapped off her pistol's safety. She settled a sunny smile on the pompous creature. "Let me introduce myself. My name is Sade Marquis."

Her statement dropped into absolute silence. Then chairs scraped on the floor and people stood, heading for the exit. Lots of Magicks frequented this place and apparently, her reputation preceded her.

"Lord Enmoore!" the goblin hissed, his voice filled with urgency and panic.

"Am I to quake in my boots at your name?"

Enmoore wasn't the brightest Magick she'd ever encountered. She set down her cup and in a conversational tone, said, "All I wanted was a cup of coffee. No conversation. No hassle. No magical idiots to ruin my morning. Yet here you are. Just so you know, I had my patience tested and the test came back negative." She'd seen that meme and it always made her laugh. It was so apropos she used the phrase whenever appropriate. Like now. She leaned forward. "Let me explain the facts of life...Enmoore, is it?"

The fae sputtered when she said his name like he was a commoner. "Now you listen—"

Before his next word, she'd reached across the table, gripped his throat in a choke hold and placed the barrel of her Beretta against the soft skin under his chin. "No," she said softly. "You listen. I'll reintroduce myself. Supervisory Agent in Charge Sade Marquis, FBI MAGIC unit."

The little goblin flinched. The fae remained frozen. Iron was poison and not even High King Oberon himself could withstand a bullet to the brain. Sade could see the wheels turning in Enmoore's head and knew the moment he connected the dots.

"The Child of Mortals," he whispered. His eyes sparked with fear and magic swirled around him.

Yeah, this guy was so far from Fae royalty that his magic barely registered. He was trying to teleport but having trouble collecting enough energy to get the job done. The fact that his only minion was a goblin had been Sade's first clue. Still, she hoped he'd point her in the right direction. She eased her weapon away and settled back into her own chair. She opened her mouth to ask her first question when a small red dot appeared on Enmoore's forehead.

Nikos reacted first and took Sade to the floor, covering her with his body. While tumbling out of her chair, she just managed to catch the look of surprise on the fae's face as a large hole appeared where the dot had been before Enmoore disappeared from her sight. She shoved at the heavy body pinning her down.

"Gawdammitalltohell, you fucking Dragon. Get off me! You have now royally fucked up my case. Again!"

The dragon's weight disappeared and Sade scrambled up before Sinjen could extend a hand. She glanced at the fae lying dead under the table. Piggish eyes blinked at her from behind a chair.

The goblin looked terrified so Sade kept her voice level. "What's your name?"

"Uzzu?"

"You're asking me?"

"Uzzu," he said, more definitively this time.

"Can you help me out here?"

The goblin blinked at her. "You wish me to eat his body?"

She shot a glare up at Sinjen and Nikos, both of whom were trying to stifle laughter. "You know, one and or both of you could have gone outside in an attempt to catch the shooter."

Sinjen shrugged. "Caleb is better at tracking."

She returned her attention to Uzzu. "Your former boss is evidence now so no eating. I have questions. I hope you have answers."

He blinked again but nodded, still uncertain.

"Ichabod Trane."

Face screwed up in concentration, Uzzu finally shook his head. "This is someone?"

"A Human Wizard."

"Oh." The little creature blinked several more times and then understanding washed over him. "Oh! Yes. Cartoon man."

Sade snorted out a laugh, unable to control it. It was pretty damn sad when a *goblin* considered you to be a caricature. In the distance, sirens wailed. That would be the local DC cops coming. She glanced up at Sinjen. "We aren't far from dawn. You should head back to my place before sunrise."

He knew she was right but he was loath to leave her alone with only the dragon. Caleb would be hot on the trail of the sniper and Sade would not abandon her duties. This incident was strictly her jurisdiction. He pulled out his phone and placed a call, walking away as it was answered. Time to call in the reserves.

By the time he finished his call, the local police had arrived, along with the two Dragon lieutenants belonging to Nikos. Sade would be guarded but the idea of leaving her with Dragons still rankled. He walked back to her.

"Uzzu here is a material witness. He's coming to FBI headquarters with me. My partner is tracking the shooter. If you see a Werewolf, do me a favor and do *not* shoot his ass."

Both cops nodded, eyes wide. Sinjen couldn't decide who terrified them more—the dead fae, the goblin, the dragon, or the human woman who commanded the room like she owned it. He smiled and thought again about how magnificent she was.

Sade's phone pinged and she held up a finger. "That's the Fae embassy. Hold on, guys." She paused in her conversation when she overheard one of the cops calling for the ME's office. "Nix that. Victim is Fae. Death is a bullet to the brain. No need for the ME. The Embassy will send someone and I'll get the bullet for chain of custody. Um-kay?" She refocused on the phone call.

"Name? His minion called him Lord Enmoore." Sade had to move the phone away from her ear because the fae on the other end was laughing uproariously.

The call ended with the promise the Embassy would send someone to collect the body. Sade's ears popped as the air pressure in the room changed and she stepped closer to the Human cops to keep them from freaking. It wasn't every day a Gargoyle Sentinel and a Fae courtier popped into existence at the same time.

Sade tossed a sour glance in Sinjen's direction then addressed the fae. "Sade Marquis."

"Maytee Feeah, assistant to the second assistant protocol officer. Do I need to spell it for your report?" The fae did not offer her hand.

Sade shook her head. And spelled out the name Maiti Fiadh based on what she knew of Gaelic. "Am I close?"

The woman smiled, a genuine one. "Spot on. Now, what's to do about this poor sod?" She toed Enmoore's body.

"Good question. He and his goblin buddy came and sat at my table. I think he was just up to some typical Magick bullshit. Silly Human walks into a Magick business and he came to hassle me. Thing is, I suspect he's part of my investigation in another case. I plan to question the goblin to find out."

"So you shot him?" Maiti raised an inquiring eyebrow.

"What?"

"Well, you are a bit notorious for being quick on the draw, Agent Marquis."

Sade held up one finger so it could be plainly seen by Roman, Sinjen, and Nikos. She heard material rustle and figured Nikos was surreptitiously checking his package. She answered through clenched teeth. "I don't normally shoot people who are just annoying. I damn sure don't shoot anyone I want to interrogate."

"Ah. Well, I won't say anything. Never hurts to keep the commoners in awe of one."

Sade started to refute that then closed her mouth. It wasn't worth the effort. "I need verification on identity and I need to retrieve the bullet."

"Of course." Maiti bent over from the waist and peered at Enmoore's face. She waved a hand along the length of his body and then rolled him. "I'll let you retrieve the bullet as I've no gloves. And he is definitely Enmoore."

And that confirmed what Sade thought. Most Fae only had one name. Only those higher up the food chain carried two. That explained the laughter when she'd first identified him as a lord. That made things simpler. A low-level Fae would be nothing off Oberon's nose. He'd keep his people out of things. She collected the bullet, having pulled a set of Nitrile gloves from her pocket and putting them on.

"Can you tell me what he was doing here?"

Something tugged on her pants leg. She looked down to find Uzzu crouched beside her. He pointed to Enmoore's coat pocket. "His keys?"

"Thanks, Uzzu." Sade went through all the fae's pockets. She bagged up some US cash, a few Fae items, a business card holder, and a set of keys."

When she'd finished, she looked around. The DC cops were staring starry-eyed at Maiti, who drank a cappuccino with whipped cream while sitting across the table. Vampire, Gargoyle and Dragon were now huddled with Caleb. She motioned her partner over.

"Give him a sniff."

Caleb grimaced but did so. His eyes flashed to wolf and he growled. The cops automatically reached for their weapons. "Those pistols clear holsters, boys, there's going to be so much paperwork you may never see the light of day again." She glanced at Sinjen. "Speaking of..."

He walked up to her, pulled her to her feet. And kissed her. Hard. With tongue. In front of everyone. Then he turned her loose as Roman touched him and they disappeared.

"Fucking Vampire. I swear to the gods I am going to stake his ass one of these fine days."

Maite laughed, the sound like tinkling bells and a spring rain on a tin roof, all at the same time. The cops were back to being bewitched. "Aye, and tis a fine ass indeed. I'd say you're a lucky woman, Agent Marquis, but he *is* Vampire."

Sade's lip curled into a snarl that could match Caleb's but he called her attention back to Enmoore's body. "His magic is fading but it's consistent with what was in the *draíochta*. Plus, I can smell Trane. They've been in close proximately within the last few hours."

"Good to know. You need anything else from the body?" Caleb shook his head. Sade lifted her chin in Maiti's direction. "Tell your boy toys bye. The body is all yours."

Maiti stood and wiggled fingers at the two cops. "Bye, lads. Come by the Embassy when you get off duty." She turned and winked at Sade. "Two for one. A bargain." Then she touched the body and *poofed* out of existence.

"What do you need for your report?" she asked the still-beguiled cops. They stared at her. She snapped her fingers until the dazzled look in their eyes faded. "Fucking Fae," she muttered.

Chapter Thirty-seven

Boys Will Be Boys

Sade unlocked the door and pushed it open. Pistol in hand, she went high and Caleb went low. This was probably overkill, considering she was with the four monsterteers. Sinjen, Roman, and Nikos stood back, watching. And probably smirking. She didn't care. She was in charge and they were doing this by the book. So, by the book, their entry had been postponed until a federal judge signed the search warrant.

A few lights set at odd angles gave a ghostly glow to the space. She checked nooks and crannies, following Caleb's lead. "Anything?" she whispered.

He shook his head. "Nothing. No one is here."

Lights flickered on overhead. She glanced back. Nikos stood by a light switch. She'd been told this was an art gallery. What spread around them was a jumble of...stuff. Statues? Twisted metal...sculptures? She had no clue what to call half this shit. There were paintings though. Other things perched on shelves, pedestals, easels, the floor.

One painting caught her attention. She approached and stood about four feet away from it. Head tilting this way and that, Sade studied the painting—a surrealistic mishmash of...tulips? She glanced at the title card: *Across the Atlantic*. Well, that made sense. Not. What did tulips have to do with the Atlantic? What was most of this junk? *Avant garde*, she reminded herself. She wasn't supposed to understand this crap.

Roman's voice drifted over her. "She's feeling guilty," Roman said.

"There's no reason." Caleb was quick to refute the gargoyle.

"Were you not attacked? While you were with your mate. Who is Human and therefore vulnerable?"

"It's not her fault."

The voice of the werewolf, who was both her partner and her brother of the heart, pulled her back to reality. They were rehashing a conversation they'd had on the drive over. Family. Damn straight she was pissed at Trane for going after her family.

"But you are not related to her," Nikos said.

"Family isn't blood. Not always. Sometimes, family is what we make it," Caleb said.

"When did you get so fu...uh...reaking sentimental?" Sade amended her curse before Roman or Sinjen could express disapproval. Jeez. Gargoyles could be so fucking judgmental and she was convinced Sinjen did it just to aggravate her.

A song played in her head. Gypsies, tramps, and thieves made for interesting family values. She'd learned that families came in all shapes and sizes. Her gaze hit this motley crew—Vampire, Gargoyle, Werewolf, and that damned infernal Dragon. The only one missing was the Fae who drove her crazy. Why the hell did Nikos keep showing up? Beyond his desire to get into her pants. Sade snorted. Yeah, that would happen when a popsicle stayed frozen in hell.

Speaking of, where *was* Ariel? He was always around when she didn't want him underfoot. Except for now. She glanced at Sinjen, who stood aloof from the discussion. She caught her hand mid-gesture as it rose to rub the ache in her chest. Forcing the now-fisted hand into her pocket, she worked hard to shove the damn doubts and uncertainty from her mind. He'd left her but he came back, she reminded her heart.

None of this mattered. She had a job to do. Crimes to solve. Villains to catch and put in jail. People to protect—Magick and Mundane alike.

Family isn't blood. Except it was. Blood. Sweat. Tears. And she would shed every drop of hers to keep her family safe. She knew what she had to do. The only obstacle to her plan involved the four

Magicks who'd come to stand beside her, also staring at the painting until it began to resemble a stained-glass window. *Glamour.*

"Do you see it?" she whispered.

A chorus of "yes" answered. Sade, standing the closest, stepped forward with her hand outstretched. Sinjen grabbed her with an arm around her waist and hauled her back against him.

"No."

"Let go."

"No."

"He's right, Sade. We have no idea where that leads, who set it up—"

She cut Caleb off in mid-sentence. "Enmoore, obviously."

"Enmoore who is currently lying on a slab at the Seelie Court Embassy."

She didn't really need her partner's reminder but she conceded. "Okay, fine. You have a point. What do you suggest?"

Caleb just gave her a look before glancing around their gathered company. "You have four Magicks here who can investigate this."

She almost laughed. "A werewolf, a gargoyle, a vampire and a dragon walk through a portal. Sounds like a really bad joke to me."

"This portal contains some Dragon magic. I will go through to see what is on the other side," Nikos said.

"Wait." Sade pushed at Sinjen's arm in a futile attempt to get him to release her. "You can sense Dragon magic?" She held up a hand. "Yes, you can sense Dragon magic, I meant can you sense Dragon magic in *this* portal?"

"No. I sense Dragon magic on the other side."

"Trane." Sade spat out the name but also realized she might have no choice. Trane had somehow bastardized his magic. Nikos might be the only one who could transfer through the portal and survive whatever realm was linked to it. "Okay. You check it out but come right back. Is that understood?"

"Yes, your highness. Whatever you desire, your highness."

"Shut up."

Nikos approached the now shimmering gate and disappeared through it. Sade didn't realize she was counting off the minutes until he reappeared, none the worse for the wear, but then again...Dragon.

"Well?"

"Is she always this impatient?" Nikos directed his question to the other three Magicks.

"Taking the fifth," Caleb muttered.

"Wise choice," Roman agreed.

Sinjen wasn't in the mood to be diplomatic. "Actually, there are times when she's worse."

"Thanks a lot. All of you. Now tell me what the fuck is on the other side."

"It is a realm I am unfamiliar with. Rather swampy, much like the bayous around New Orleans so all of you might be acquainted with the environs. There is only a slight distortion entering and I detect no shift in time."

Sadie glanced up and around at Sinjen, who still held her plastered against him. "Does that mean it's nighttime there?"

"Yes. It is dark, with a full moon. None of us will have trouble seeing."

"Easy for you to say," she groused.

"Stand by," Caleb said. He headed outside, returning a few minutes later carrying a backpack. He rummaged in it and pulled out an LED flashlight, which he handed to Sade.

"You are such a Boy Scout."

"Always prepared." He snapped off a three-fingered salute.

"I will enter first," Nikos said.

"I have the rear guard," Roman added.

"Me," Caleb said, hoisting the pack then pointing at Sade. "You, and Sinjen behind you. That way we have two and two with you sandwiched in the middle."

"I'll remind you that I'm the one in charge and I can take care of myself." She might as well have been talking to thin air. Nikos, followed closely by Caleb, disappeared.

Sinjen urged her forward and she fought the dizzy nausea that always hit when she had to go through one of these motherfucking torture-chamber doors. Sinjen's hand remained on her shoulder. For a moment, there was nothing but silence, like everything in the swamp was holding its breath waiting for what came next.

The portal closed behind Roman but a faint shimmer of stained-glass colors marked its location. That was a good thing. Caleb's head came up and she watched him test the air. His eyes went wolf. He'd found a trail. Pushing past Nikos, he took the lead. The rest of them followed.

The trail wound through cypress trees dripping Spanish moss. Occasional splashes were heard from nearby water.

"The first person to crack a joke about the creature from the Black Lagoon is gonna get smacked." Sade's instruction was met by a muffled chuckle from the front of their little pack.

Up ahead, a faint luminescent glow showed through the thick foliage. Something large plopped into the unseen water. Sade touched Nikos's shoulder and whispered, "Any clue who's realm we're in?"

He shook his head, attention obviously focused on their surroundings. "There is the stench of Dragon."

She started to point out that *he* was a dragon and therefore, she wondered about his own scent but Sinjen squeezed her shoulder. He knew her too well. Instead, she stayed on point. "Any idea of which dragon?"

"No." And didn't he sound pissy about that. She suddenly pictured Nikos at the next big gala celebration where all the Dragons had to pass down the receiving line and there was the Drakon sniffing each one that went by. She curled her lips between her teeth but a snort escaped through her nose.

Caleb stopped and like dominoes, everyone stopped behind him. He motioned Nikos forward and Sade followed despite Sinjen's mutter. Another gateway shimmered at the base of a massive cypress tree. It looked like something out of "Lord of the Rings"—a round door made of wooden slats and metal brackets set into the tree trunk.

"I don't know if I'm in Middle Earth or Narnia," Sade whispered.

"It sure isn't Kansas," Caleb added.

Caleb approached the portal and sniffed. He examined it, then walked around the tree, still sniffing. Sade resisted the temptation to remind him that he shouldn't mark a territory in the middle of Dragon stomping grounds. He came back around the tree. And shrugged. "Smells of Trane and Dragon."

"Great." Sade studied the door then glanced over at Nikos. "Any ideas?"

"Open it and find out." The dragon did not sound particularly enthused. She was discovering that when Dragons encountered a situation, they either wanted to eat it or burn it down. If neither of those were options, then good luck.

"Fine. Let's go."

She touched the doorlatch before anyone could stop her. Air whooshed around her and it felt like she'd been sucked into a huge vacuum cleaner hose. Her body was wrenched along the tube by the suction. Ears popped, stomach churned, and stars flashed before her eyes. Then the portal spit her out.

"Fuck me!"

Sinjen touched the door a nanosecond before Nikos. He, too, was sucked into the darkness. Pulling on his vampiric powers, he turned to mist and let the air current draw him along. He opened his mind and touched Sade's. If he'd been solid, he would have smiled. She was cursing a blue streak—always a good sign. He was still mist when he was spit out at the end. He returned to human form almost immediately.

"You are okay?" He reached out to cup her cheek, noticing a slight bruise beginning to form.

"Slid into home plate when I landed."

He kissed her in relief.

Nikos did not have enough Greek or Dragon curses as the portal captured him. He was angry at being trapped. He was angry that a mere Human with barely a drop of Dragon blood could do so. He was angry that he'd been dumped into this situation because that Human *had* that minuscule amount of DNA that made him a problem for the ruling Dragon clan.

He landed in a roll and glanced up to see the damnable vampire kissing Sade. Just one more aggravation he had to endure.

Caleb growled and pounded on the door. Roman attempted to teleport beyond it. Neither had any success. Despite wanting to howl, Caleb finally stopped his frantic efforts, his hands scraped and bleeding. "Well, that didn't go as expected."

"I also have concerns," Roman agreed. "I suspect the door was set as a trap."

"If that's the case, whoever set it is in for a big surprise. Sade's loaded for bear. Figuratively speaking. And when a master vampire and a pissed-off dragon pop out behind her?" Caleb didn't even attempt to hide his grin. "As my Alpha used to say, 'Katie, bar the door, we're gonna be havin' a come to Jesus meetin.'"

Roman was worried but he returned Caleb's grin. "Sometimes we forget that she can take care of herself. Mostly."

"Mostly we forget or mostly she can take care of herself?"

"Yes."

"So what's our Plan B? Wait for them here or head back to the gallery?"

"They are with the dragon. If what's behind door number one is another pocket of the Dragon Realm, he is capable of getting all of them back to the Human plane."

"In that case—" He slapped the side of his neck and looked at the large black smear on his palm. "I hate mosquitoes so I vote we go back to the gallery."

"I second that."

Sade waited. No Caleb. No Roman. She would not fret. Much. "Where are they?"

"I suspect they were blocked." Sinjen put his arm around her and drew her away from the swirling eye of the portal.

"Agreed." Nikos rubbed the back of his neck. "This is not part of the Dragon Realm but I suspect I was able to follow because the other *was* draconic."

"You suspect a trap?" Sinjen glanced around.

"I do, yes. This Trane character, he is after Sade. She has been his goal from the start, yes?"

Sade had to agree but she didn't speak, letting Sinjen continue his own thought process. "Yes. And he trapped me to draw Sade into his web."

She was not going back through that discussion. That part of their relationship was still too fragile. She had a different idea though. "I think he thought I would kill you to protect myself and then he would put my guilt-ridden and broken heart back together." She glanced around and realized that her eyes were adjusting to the dark because objects and the scenery were starting to come into focus. She stopped breathing. It wasn't her eyes. It was the light. It was getting brighter.

"Shitdamnfuck." She whirled to Sinjen and grabbed his arm, tugging him...somewhere. She didn't know where. There were rocks around. Hills. There had to be a cave or something where she could get him out of the sun.

"Sade?" Sinjen eyed her with concern.

"The sun! It's coming up. We have to get you in a cave. Or something."

"Breathe, Sade. It is not the sun."

"Yes, it is." She was close to full panic mode. "I could barely see when I landed and now I can see almost everything."

Sinjen snagged a waving hand and used it to reel her into his body. "Easy, milady. It is not the sun. I would feel it coming. Whatever this light is, it is not inimical to my kind."

"No," Nikos agreed. "It is not sunlight. Not the sun of the Human plane." He tilted his head, considering. "So it is the solar energy that is your nemesis. Interesting." As he glanced around, his Dragon peered out. And picked up a faint trail of magic. "This way." He started off, expecting Sade and Sinjen to automatically follow.

Sade studied Sinjen. "Are you positive?"

"Yes, love. I am positive. Even at its brightest, this light will not harm me. Truthfully, I had not considered that there might be realms where sunlight was not part of their architecture."

"Architecture?"

"These pocket realms are...constructed, Sade. It takes a great deal of magic to create one."

"Are you coming?" Nikos sounded imperiously annoyed.

Sade rolled her eyes and answered, "Yes, Dad."

She stared at the...*suggestive* rock formations before cutting her eyes to the handsome vampire on her left. The dragon, wearing his Human form, standing on her right, cleared his throat. Yeah, Nikos had gone there in his head, just like she had. Sinjen remained stoic, but she caught the slight twitch at the corner of his mouth.

"Does this place have a name?"

Both men choked. Sinjen studied his boot tips, cheeks sucked in like he was biting them. Nikos stared at the sky as if contemplating taking wing.

"Gynts plgrm." One of them mumbled through a cough.

"Come again?"

Both men turned away, laughter erupting.

Fine. Everyone's mind was in the gutter and she'd just made a double entendre, but seriously? It didn't matter if a male was 30 or 3,000, they reacted like little boys reading "Playboy." Someone had to be the adult here. "Hey, assholes, I don't go realm hopping every day. Where the fuck are we?"

Before Sinjen could censure her language, Nikos sputtered, "Giants Playground."

Sinjen added, "Some call it the Hard Rock—"

Sade cut him off. "*Gah*! Please tell me it's almost over."

"What?" the two Magicks asked in stereo, both doing their best to look innocent.

"Your juvenile antics. Jeez, why are y'all so hard—"

The men's rowdy laughter drowned out her voice and left them short of breath.

"Okay, fine. If y'all can't grow up, then just let me die now."

"That can be arranged." The voice came from nowhere. And everywhere.

They froze. Fun and games were over.

Chapter Thirty-eight

No Place to Run

Sinjen and Nikos converged on Sade. She ignored their protective reflexes, turning in a slow circle, eyes searching for the source of that voice. She caught a shimmer—like a skinny heat wave. It wasn't a portal. Nope. This was an attempt to hide. And Ichabod Trane had just enough magic to pull it off.

She stared at the shimmer. "C'mon out you little pudfucking pissant. You too big a damn coward to face me in your real form, Icky?" She stepped toward the shimmer and had to shake off both Vampire and Dragon as they grabbed her arms. "Don't," she ordered in a low command. "I need to get to my weapons. Back off."

Nikos growled deep in his throat. "This one is mine."

She whirled and jabbed a finger in his chest. "No, no, bad Dragon. Don't make me get a newspaper to swat your nose."

He looked positively affronted. Then he promptly ignored her. "Where is it?" he roared.

Sinjen jerked Sade back just in time to avoid the stream of flame that erupted from the dragon's mouth.

"What the ever-lovin' fuck, Nikos!" She turned to look for the shimmer that marked Trane's glamour. It had disappeared. She inhaled. Nope. No crispy critter. Nikos had missed.

"Trane, you can't get away," Sade called. "You're under arrest."

"You can't catch me."

"Sure I can." She waved her hand behind her back, giving signs to Sinjen and Nikos. She knew Sinjen would follow her lead. Nikos? He was a wild card and one she didn't have time to trump at the moment. First, she had to locate the little shit. Then she had to get him into magic-proof handcuffs. Once that was done and he was in an interrogation room, they'd find out all the rest.

That was the plan.

"Yo, Trane, you ever read any L. Frank Baum?"

"What are you talking about?"

She had to keep on talking. And keep him focused on her. That would give Sinjen and Nikos time to find and look behind the curtain. "L. Frank Baum. He wrote the Oz books."

"Oz? He's Australian?"

Lord but this dude was a cretin. How the hell had he managed to create all this magical mayhem? "No, dickwad. He's an American. Wrote *The Wonderful Wizard of Oz*. You know...like the movie, with Judy Garland?"

"Wasn't she an old actress?" Before Sade could reply, Trane added. "Wait. There was a dog. A witch was in that movie."

Sade put on her best Wicked Witch of the East face and voice, "You and your little dog, too, Dorothy."

There was such a long pause, Sade worried she'd lost Trane. He finally spoke, but his voice came from a different place. Dammit.

"I find this conversation irrelevant."

"Just makin' small talk, dude. Because you know what happened in the end right?" When he didn't respond, she continued. "They looked behind the curtain and discovered that the all-powerful Wizard of Oz was just a bumbling con man."

Sinjen and Nikos continued stalking the elusive voice.

When Trane didn't respond, she decided to get down to things. "Fine, let's cut to the chase. Where's the artifact?"

"What artifact?"

"The one you stole from the Dragons. They're awfully pissed at you, Ichabod And you know what they say, right?" She didn't wait for a reply. "Piss off a dragon and you end up as the marshmallow in a s'more."

"As long as I hold the Pétra Pýlis, they cannot touch me."

"Wouldn't bet on that," she muttered. Did she press him on the stone or did she switch subjects to keep him off balance? She so wanted to be on her turf to question this little twatwaffle. There was one question she genuinely wanted the answer to, so she asked. "Why me, Icky?"

"Do not call me that!"

Ooh, she'd touched a nerve. "Not a big fan, Icky. From my perspective, the shoe fits."

"I own you."

"Wrong. No one owns me. So tell my why you want to."

"You are the Child of the Mortals." He sounded so incredulous that she could almost hear the "d'uh" he didn't say.

"Yeah, yeah. What's that mean to you?" She never had figured out why the Gargoyles were so big on calling her that.

"You are destined."

"For what?"

Silence.

"Answer her." That was Sinjen, at his coldest.

"You! You should be dead. You were supposed to die before she found you, but then you were supposed to kill her in your hunger. And then go mad."

"Yeah, that didn't happen, dickwad. You're batting a thousand—you've pissed off a dragon *and* a master vampire. You are such a moron."

The air shimmered off to Sade's left and she swiveled to face the spot. Trane wavered into view. Red-faced, he was all but spitting as he yelled, "No! It is you who are the cretins." He swept his arm out. "All of you. You do not know what you've wrought." He pointed a finger at Sade. "Do you not understand? You are the Child of the Mortals. You were sent here on a mission."

Sade remembered to close her mouth and realized that Sinjen and Nikos were both standing frozen in place. "What the hell?"

"You are destined, Sade Marquis. You are the only Human immune to the magic of the monsters. You are destined to be their downfall."

"What the ever-loving fuck?" She cut her eyes to Sinjen and realized that he *couldn't* move. "Fuck me," she muttered. This puddfucking imbecile had managed to ensorcel both Sinjen and the dragon. And the fact she was still standing might lend credence to the asshole's argument. She was immune to magic. Mostly. Not all. But a lot. Capturing Ichabod Trane was all on her.

"So what's the plan?"

Trane blinked at her, a look of surprise adding to his comical appearance, because the dude was back in his star robe and hat. "T-the plan?"

"Yeah, Icky. Your plan. You wanted me. Here I am. What is it you expect of me? What is it you intend to do to vanquish the Magicks?"

"N-not all Magicks," he stammered again. "Just the monsters."

Sade thought back over her career. Yeah, she'd encountered some awful monsters but the majority of them? They'd all been of the Human variety. She kept that observation to herself. "And?"

"And what?"

"How am I supposed to vanquish them? Do I sneak into their nurseries at night and kill their children?" Fuck her but the little dickwad was thinking that over. She hurried to move his thoughts to something else. "Do I call them out one by one in a gladiator-style challenge? I mean, fuck, Icky. You're the alleged brains here. Evidently, I'm just your murder weapon."

"No, no." He stepped closer and his earnestness positively radiated like a white-hot aura. "You are my consort. We will breed the ones who will fight the final battle. It will be Armageddon."

"Nope, sorry. You already missed that opportunity. The rogue Gargoyles beat you to it. And they're all dead now. So...there ya go."

She'd also been creeping closer to him and was almost near enough to grab him and slap cuffs on him. She slowly raised her hand to snatch Trane's wrist but fell back as a stream of blue fire all but singed her cheek. "Gawddammitalltohell, Nikos!" She rolled, coming up with her weapon in hand only to find Nikos still frozen in place. A dark shadow flew across the ground and Sade looked up. Well, shit on a shingle but they were toast. A reddish-brown dragon banked to make a return flight.

There was a patch of scorched earth where Trane had been standing. She didn't have time to worry if the pain-in-her-ass Wizard was alive or dead. She, Sinjen, and Nikos were all sitting ducks. She dropped the magazine in her pistol and yanked a different one out of her hip pocket. She slammed it in and waited. She heard her name yelled at the same moment she dropped and rolled as flames swept the spot where she'd been. Flat on her back, she tracked the dragon and pulled the trigger, putting the first seven bullets in the magazine in the vicinity of the dragon's mouth and nostrils. She followed that up with two tight patterns of four shots under each wing.

"Hope to holy hell those bullets actually work," she muttered as Sinjen jerked her up and into his arms. They watched Nikos shift and lift into the sky, following the other dragon.

"Bullets won't—"

"These are special." Sinjen raised a brow and she grinned. "They're hollow-points packed with ichneumon musk."

Sinjen burst out laughing and was still doing it when Nikos landed beside them and shifted back into Human form.

"Delighted you find this so amusing," the dragon snipped.

"I take it the asshole got away. Who was it?"

"A minor member of House Nekyios. And yes, he teleported into another pocket. I did not want to take the time to follow. I will find him when the time comes. He is wounded."

Sade punched Sinjen's arm. "See? It does work."

Now Nikos gave her an arched look. "What worked?"

"Never mind." Sade was not about to reveal that she might have stumbled onto something that—if it hit the right spot—might kill or disable a dragon in Dragon form. Not to mention that Nikos got his pride stung. He was the mighty Drakon of the ruling clan and that a *minor* member of his rival's clan got the best of him? Yeah, he was tweaked.

"Where is Trane?"

She pointed at the burned spot. "Hopefully, that's not what's left of him."

Nikos wrinkled his nose. "No. Balaskas's minion missed. The wizard also teleported."

"So where do we go from here?" Sade looked from Sinjen to Nikos. They both shrugged.

At that moment, two things occurred. The damn black cat strolled out from under a bush and twined himself through Sade's legs and Ichabod Trane shimmered into existence right beside her. The wizard was reaching for her when the cat did that whole Halloween cat thing—arched back, tail straight up, and hissing. At Nikos.

The dragon shifted and headed into the sky. What the ever-loving fuck? Sade slapped Trane's hand away and then caught the shadow. A second dragon. This one more red than brown and almost as big as Nikos. She was out of anti-Dragon ammo. She couldn't save Trane and Sinjen both. Could a vampire survive dragon fire? She didn't want to find out. Her heart won out over duty. She took three running steps and buried her shoulder in Sinjen's middle. They hit the ground and rolled, ending up behind a small outcropping of rock. She couldn't worry about Trane now. Besides, he'd teleported himself out of danger not ten minutes ago.

Sade realized that Sinjen was frantically beating at her back. That's when she smelled burnt leather. Realizing her jacket was on fire, she did the ol' stop-drop-and-roll exercise from grade school. That effectively put out the dragon flames burning their way through the expensive leather.

"Gawddammitalltohell. This was my favorite. That fucking twatwaffle—both of them—are gonna pay."

She rose to a crouch and realized the dragons were engaged in aerial combat and she had no shot to take—not that her bullets would make a difference. There was no sign of the wizard. "Where'd that little pussfucker go?"

That's when the odor hit her. Scorched meat. There was a small burning pile of...Wizard where Trane had been standing.

Sade scrubbed at her face and breathed through her mouth. Too bad the taste of BBQ Wizard was almost as bad as the stench. She glanced up. "Nikos is gonna be sooo pissed if Balaskas doesn't know where that artifact is hidden."

The air exploded around them. Sade felt the change in air pressure first and once again took Sinjen to the ground. Rocks and dirt shifted down over them. When the fallout stopped, Sade blinked open her eyes and stared down at Sinjen.

"What the hell just happened?"

"You absolutely terrify me."

"Huh?"

"You do realize that as a Vampire I am much harder to kill or injure than you, who is merely Human?"

She blinked a couple of times. "Yeah, so?

"You have now, in the space of minutes, attempted to save my life twice."

"And?"

He shook his head and kissed her hard. "What am I to do with you?"

"Uh...love me?"

He folded her into his arms. "I do, Sade, more than you will ever know."

The cat meowed and Sade looked around. Their position behind the outcropping had kept them out of the worst of the blast zone. Peering down at them, the cat blinked his yellow eyes as if to say, "Stop lollygagging. We have places to be."

Sade gave the animal the side-eye. "Were you a crow in a previous lifetime?"

The thing arched and hissed at her, a look of disgust firmly entrenched on his face. She almost laughed. But she had a history with crows showing up when weird shit happened and this cat seemed to have taken a page from their play book.

The rustle of giant wings got her moving, the pistol still in her hand. She scrambled to her feet. Sinjen reclaimed his in one smooth move.

"Fucking Vampires," she muttered.

"I heard that." Sinjen was amused.

The huge silver dragon landed. Looking a little worse for the wear, Nikos folded his wings and shifted. His impeccable shirt had one sleeve singed off. There was a smear of blood on his opposite shoulder and a black smudge on his cheek.

"You okay?" Sade asked the question automatically.

Nikos snarled at her. "No."

"Where are you—"

A stream of angry Greek words cut her off. She figured he'd live. Probably. She glanced around. There was no second dragon body anywhere to be seen. Several of the rock formations had toppled and more than a few trees were still burning.

"What the hell happened?"

Another stream of Greek. She glanced at Sinjen.

"Balaskas got away but he detonated a device in order to do so."

"A device?"

"A sonic firebomb," Nikos snarled. "They have been outlawed since the last war." He glanced around. "Where is the wizard?"

Sade pointed to the now-scattered pile of ash. "He didn't teleport this time."

And that brought on a third string of infuriated Greek.

She glanced at Sinjen. "I really need to learn to speak Greek. I bet those are some prime cuss words."

Sinjen shook his head and gathered her to his side. "Only you, Sade. Only you."

Chapter Thirty-nine

Lightning Strikes Twice

Sinjen wondered if a vampire was stronger than a dragon in Human form, then decided he didn't care. He and Nikos faced each other on the plaza outside of FBI headquarters. Sade was upstairs giving her report to the Director. They'd detoured by a hospital to get her back looked at. She had mostly first-degree burns but there were a few patches with second-degree and one spot that sustained a deep third-degree burn. He'd planned on being in Bailey's office with her so he could insist she have time off for rest and rehabilitation.

Instead, he was standing out here staring down this infernal dragon. Without conscious command, his hand shot out and grabbed the dragon by the throat. "You have sniffed around her for the last time, Constantine." He didn't like the blaze of inner fire lighting the dragon's eyes.

A curl of smoke surrounded the words Nikos spoke. "She is her own woman, not yours to claim."

"Nor is she yours."

The fire died as abruptly as it had appeared. "As I am well aware."

Considering why Constantine put up no fight, Sinjen inhaled, the action forcing his temper to cool. Only Sade could make his blood run so hot. Only Sade could drive him so crazy he would provoke a Drakon—especially when he might owe Nikos his life—and Sade's. He loosened his grip on the dragon's throat, then he dropped his hand and stepped back.

"You should not have taken her there." Sinjen's complaint sounded as tired as he felt, still not fully recovered, either physically or emotionally, from his ordeal. Though, he had managed to convince Sade otherwise.

"If I had held my tongue..." Constantine's voice trailed away. He breathed deeply, shook his head, his expression proclaiming him to be the world's biggest fool, then he continued. "She was the only one with any hope of bringing you back, St. John. And she was determined." There was warmth, familiarity...even affection in his voice.

The implication was there. If there was any chance to save him and Nikos kept silent, condemning him to a life of insanity and monstrous hungers, Sade would never forgive the dragon—or herself. "I know."

"She loves you."

"I know this too."

"Do not break her heart." With that admonition—and the implied *again*, the dragon was gone.

"I won't," the vampire promised.

Sade perched on the edge of the seat in front of the Director's desk. The ER doc had smeared a bunch of pain-killing ointment on her back but it was already starting to wear off. Sleeping was going to be a bitch for the foreseeable future.

"So Ichabod Trane is dead."

"Crispy critter, sir. He managed to teleport during the first dragon attack but not the second. I don't know if he was just out of magic mojo or if Balaskas, as a Drakon, was faster than his minion."

"And you received those burns during the attack."

She'd sort of left out the part about throwing herself at Sinjen to save him and taking a glancing blow of dragon fire in the process. "Yes, sir."

"What about this artifact?"

Yeah, about that. She had to tread carefully here. "I believe that is now out of our jurisdiction, Director. Drakon Constantine informed me officially that situation with the missing artifact—the Dragons call it the Pétra Pýlis—is strictly a draconic matter now."

Bailey leaned back in his chair and steepled his fingers over his stomach. "And how do you feel about that?"

She winced as the third-degree burn on her back throbbed. "Frankly, sir, I say leave them to it. There's a feud brewing between Clans Kholikikos and Nekyios. So long as that stays in the Dragon Realm, it's not really our jurisdiction."

"And the wizard? His death was caused by a dragon."

"True. But technically speaking, that could be considered Dragon-on-Dragon crime." Yeah, right. If she stretched the genealogy and DNA to the outer limits. "Dr. Bellwether, who is an expert in the field, is sending me official documentation that Ichabod Trane was part Human and part Dragon."

Bailey snorted. "That's reaching, Marquis."

"Yessir, but still technically true. The ruling Dragon clan is currently satisfied—mostly—with the outcome. Human or not, Trane stole from them. They consider his blood tie to the Dragon race of sufficient quantity to claim him, making it a Dragon-on-Dragon crime. A rival dragon, who was also involved in the theft of the artifact, killed Trane so it is up to them to deal out whatever justice they require."

"You talk a good story, Marquis, and it keeps the Bureau out of magical politics. I'm okay with that. Now. About you."

She stiffened. "What about me?"

He ignored her question, instead reaching for his intercom button. A tap at the door beat him to it. "Come."

The door swung open and Alice walked in holding a few papers. Sinjen followed her. She handed the papers to the Director and turned to Sinjen. "You look a little peaked, dear. May I bring you a cup of supplement?"

He shook his head. "No, I'm fine, but thank you for the concern."

"Of course, dear." And then she was gone, shutting the door softly behind her.

"Geez. She could have offered me some coffee. I'm a little peaked too."

"No more caffeine for you," Sinjen ordered. "You are going home to bed."

Bailey looked up from the papers. "Indeed she is. And she's on sick leave for at least two weeks or until I get an updated medical report."

"Director Bailey!" Sade began her argument but stopped when she registered the look on both his face and Sinjen's. "Okay, fine. I'll take two weeks off."

"Don't sound so enthusiastic," Bailey said, without smiling. "Get her out of here and keep her out until she's medically cleared. Got me?"

"I do, sir, yes," Sinjen replied, only he *was* smiling.

"Where do you want to go?"

Sade opened one eye and tilted her head a little so she could see Sinjen. She was currently in her own bed, on her stomach, and Sinjen was rubbing some of that miracle ointment on her back. "What?"

"You have two weeks off. Where would you like to go?"

She knew immediately. "New Orleans."

"We'll fly down tomorrow night."

The cat, perched on the pillow beside Sade's head, stopped washing a paw and stared at them. Sade rolled her eyes. "You'll like it there if you haven't been yet." She stared back at the critter. "I still want to know who you are." The cat didn't blink. "Fine. I can't keep calling you the damn cat so..." A slow grin curled her lips. "Loki. I'll call you Loki."

The cat stared a moment longer then went back to washing.

"Damn cat."

Sinjen stifled a laugh. "Indeed."

Epilogue

Hell in a Handbasket

A dragon, a gargoyle, and a werewolf walked into a bar. That they were in Human glamour didn't matter a whit to the human and the vampire sitting in the back booth.

"Welcome to Déjà Vu!" the bartender yelled. "Just sit anywhere."

The three didn't need his invitation. Their gazes had already locked on Sade and Sinjen.

"Fuck me, when did my life turn into a bad joke?" Sade muttered.

"Language," the vampire chided in his modulated English accent.

"Fuck you."

"Later. First, we need to ascertain what...what do you call them? The Scooby Gang? Yes. I wonder what they want."

Sade rolled her eyes and scowled at the approaching Magicks. Caleb, her Werewolf partner, slid onto the opposite bench, followed by Roman, the Legate of New Orleans and the Gargoyle Sentinel who'd protected her since childhood. Nikos, Drakon of Clan Kholikikos, opted to lean a shoulder against the wall at their backs.

"Problem?" Sade didn't try to keep the growl out of her voice. She was on R&R while recovering from injuries received in the line of duty as supervisory agent of the FBI's MAGICAL unit.

The three Magicks exchanged glances before staring at Sinjen. The vampire stared back. The stalemate lasted until the waiter bustled up, drinks on a tray. They'd been in before and Jon Martine was good at his job.

"Do you know where Ariel is?" Roman didn't waste time.

"Ari?" Sade glanced at Sinjen as if he held the answer. He shrugged and focused on Roman. "Why?" she asked.

"When was the last time you saw him?" This from Caleb.

She thought hard. "Paris?" She blinked. "No. Here. When...?" Her voice trailed off in a question and she glanced at Sinjen again.

"Yes," Sinjen affirmed. "He was present when I carried you out."

"Well, then, I guess that's the last time?" She snapped her fingers. "No. He popped in while you—" She glanced at Caleb. "You were having that...Werewolf moment."

Caleb growled something then looked between Roman and Nikos. "That's not good news."

"Duty calls," Roman said.

Nikos added, "Sadly. I suspect we're all going to—"

"Hell in a handbasket," Caleb finished.

"What does that even mean?" Sade groused, pushing at Sinjen to get out of her way. "Wait. Do you mean that figuratively? Or literally?"

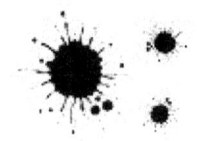

Please go to the next page to discover the music that helped inspire this book, info about the author, and a list of all her books!

Playlist

Author's Note: Music is a large part of my creative process and this is especially true with the books in The Penumbra Papers series. If you are curious about my playlist, here is the soundtrack by chapter. I've listed the songs here for informational purposes only. If you're interested, I set up a mix list on YouTube of the "soundtrack." You know, in case you want to listen while you're reading. Since this is print, you'll just have to type in the web address. Sorry about that. Technology isn't quite ready for interactive print yet. Head to:

https://www.youtube.com/c/SilverJames

In the Beginning
    Roxette - She's Got the Look (Sade's Theme)
    Chapter 1: Perfectly Confused
    AJR - Bang
    Chapter 2: In Control
    U2 - The Troubles
    Chapter 3: Patience is a Virtue
    Chris Cornell - Patience
    Chapter 4: Heartbeats
    Hozier - Better Love (Legend of Tarzan)
    Chapter 5: About a Dragon
    Lord Huron - The Night We Met
    Chapter 6: Motives
    Kenzie - Motives
    Chapter 7: Double Double Toil and Trouble
    Lauren Daigle - Rescue
    Chapter 8: Something Wicked This Way Comes
    Coldplay - Magic

Chapter 9: Making Sense
Imagine Dragons - Whatever It Takes
Chapter 10: Up in the Air
Godsmack - Under Your Scars
Chapter 11: Leathered and Laced
Chris Isaacs – Wicked Game
Chapter 12: Marco Polo
Naughty Boy - No One's Here to Sleep (from How to Get Away with Murder movie)
Chapter 13: Technically Speaking
Alan Silvestri - No Trust (Avengers Endgame soundtrack)
Chapter 14: Think Twice
Beatles - Ticket to Ride
Chapter 15: If Wishes Were Horse
Flo Rida - Right Round
Chapter 16: A Losing Game
Duncan Laurence - Arcade
Chapter 17: Drink Me
Shawn Mendes - In My Blood
Chapter 18: Love is a Battlefield
John Legend and Lindsey Stirling - All of Me
Lady Gaga - Million Reasons
Chapter 19: Until Dawn
Daughtry- What About Now (Acoustic version)
Chapter 20: Ready Player One
Ruelle - Game of Survival
Chapter 21: No Regrets
Billie Eilish - Bury a Friend
Chapter 22: Pretty in Pink
Green Day - Boulevard of Broken Dreams (I Walk Alone)
Chapter 23: Rock, Paper, Scissors
Demi Lovato - Skyscraper

Lady Gaga & Elton John - Sine From Above
Epilogue: Hell in a Handbasket
TobyMac - Help Is On The Way (Maybe Midnight)

Thank you for reading this book!

Reviews and word-of-mouth recommendations help other readers find books to enjoy. I appreciate every review. Please consider leaving one on the site where you purchased this book and/or on the book review site of your choice. If this is your first Penumbra Papers book, please check out my other stories in this series as well as the books and series in my Moonstruck world of Wolf shifters, or my sexy contemporary series from Harlequin, Red Dirt Royalty. Keep reading for the list of all my titles.

About the Author

Silver James likes to take walks on the wild side and coffee. Okay. She loves coffee. LOTS of coffee. Warning: Her Muse, Iffy, runs with scissors and can be quite dangerous. She's the author of four award-winning series: Moonstruck, Nightriders MC, The Penumbra Papers, and Red Dirt Royalty. She's a former military officer's wife, mother and grandmother, and had careers in the legal field, fire service, and law enforcement. Now retired from the "real world,"

she lives in Oklahoma and spends her days at the computer with her Newfoundland/Pyrenees dog, the two cat who rule them all, and the myriad characters living in her imagination. She writes dark paranormal romantic thrillers, urban fantasy, and sexy contemporary romance for Harlequin Desire.

If you're ready to walk on the wild side or want to find out more about Silver and her books, you can connect with her on social media.

WEBSITE: www.silverjames.com

FACEBOOK: AuthorSilverJames

X: @SilverJames_

Be sure to sign up for Silver's newsletter (instructions on her website) to get first looks at upcoming projects, fan-only contests, and other sooper sekrit stuffs.

BOOKS BY SILVER JAMES

Urban Fantasy

Penumbra Papers:

That Ol' Black Magic

Season of the Witch

The Devil's Cut

The Sound of Silence

Ghosts & the Ancient Stones

Paranormal Romance

Moonstruck Genesis:

Moonstruck: Secrets

(Contains the books Blood Moon and Bad Moon plus additional chapters and cut scenes)

Moonstruck: Lies

SILVER JAMES

(Contains the books Hunter's Moon and Wolf Moon
plus additional chapters and cut scenes)
Moonstruck: Betrayal
(Contains the books Bride's Moon and Rogue Moon,
plus additional chapters and cut scenes
along with the brand-new novella, Moon Crossed)
Moonstruck: Retribution
(Contains the books Christmas Moon, Blue Moon, and
Moon Shot, plus additional chapters and cuts scene)
Moonstruck:
*Blood Moon – Book 1
*Bad Moon – Book 2
*Hunter's Moon – Book 3
*Wolf Moon – Book 4
*Bride's Moon – Book 5
*Rogue Moon – Book 6
*Christmas Moon – A Moonstruck Novella #7
*Blue Moon – Book 8
*Moon Shot – Book 9
(A Moonstruck/Hard Target Crossover Novel)

Series set in the Moonstruck World:
Hard Target
Double Cross – Book 1
**Double Trouble – Book 1.5
(A Hard Target companion novella set in
Roxanne St. Claire's Barefoot Bay World)
Crossfire – Book 2
Nightriders MC
Night Shift – Book 1
*Remember the Night – #1.5

Night Moves – Book 2
Night Fire – Book 3
Night Fall – Book 4
Night Wish – Book 5
Moonstruck Mafia
Boston
New York
Chicago
**Other Books set in the
Moonstruck World:
Moonstruck Wolf**
(standalone novels that contain
some crossover characters)
**Blood & Fire (revised)
**Crash & Burn (revised)
**Montana Moon (revised)
**Rescue Moon (revised)
**SEAL Moon (revised)
**Assassin's Moon (revised)
Under the Assassin's Moon (revised)
Susan Stoker's World
Fighting for Elena: Tarpley VFD
(Fighting for Elena is also available in audio)
Fighting for Justice: Tarpley VFD
**Supernatural Noir
Standalone Titles**
*Café Midnight
(Paranormal Noir Mystery)
*Midnight Clear
(SciFi Christmas Romance)

Contemporary Romance
From Harlequin Desire
Red Dirt Royalty

Cowgirls Don't Cry
The Cowgirl's Little Secret
The Boss and His Cowgirl
Convenient Cowgirl Bride
Redeemed by the Cowgirl
Claiming the Cowgirl's Baby
The Cowboy's Christmas Proposition
Billionaire Country
Twice the Temptation

From Wild Rose Press:
Time Travel/Reincarnation Paranormal
Faerie Reign

Faerie Fate
Faerie Fire
Faerie Fool
*Faerie Reign
(Digital 3-book boxed set at a special price)
*Faerie Faith (Twelve Brides of Christmas)

Contemporary Romance
Class of '85 Reunion Series:

*Fairy Tales Can Come True
*Promises, Promises

Dearly Beloved Series:

*Best Laid Plans
*Available in digital format only

GHOSTS & THE ANCIENT STONES

**Books previously published in a shared world created by another author that have been updated, with all elements copyrighted by that author removed, and republished under a revision or reassignment of rights.

Don't miss out!

Visit the website below and you can sign up to receive emails whenever Silver James publishes a new book. There's no charge and no obligation.

https://books2read.com/r/B-A-QAOC-FHGPB

Connecting independent readers to independent writers.